Dear Reader,

I'm delighted to welco⬚⬚⬚⬚⬚⬚⬚⬚⬚⬚⬚⬚
Bestselling Author Coll⬚⬚⬚⬚⬚⬚⬚⬚⬚⬚⬚
celebration of Harlequin⬚⬚⬚⬚⬚⬚⬚⬚⬚⬚⬚⬚⬚
this collection features fa⬚⬚⬚⬚⬚⬚⬚⬚⬚⬚⬚ from some
of our readers' most cheri⬚⬚⬚⬚⬚⬚⬚⬚ors. Each book
also includes a free full-length story by an exciting
writer from one of our current programs.

Our company has grown and changed since its
inception 75 years ago. Today, Harlequin publishes
more than 100 titles a month in 30 countries and
15 languages, with stories for a diverse readership
across a range of genres and formats, including
hardcover, trade paperback, mass market paperback,
ebook and audiobook.

But our commitment to you, our romance reader,
remains the same: in every Harlequin romance, a
guaranteed happily-ever-after!

Thank you for coming on this journey with us. And
happy reading as we embark on the next 75 years of
bringing joy to readers around the world!

Dianne Moggy

Vice-President, Editorial

Harlequin

Maisey Yates is a *New York Times* bestselling author of over one hundred romance novels. Whether she's writing strong, hardworking cowboys, dissolute princes or multigenerational family stories, she loves getting lost in fictional worlds. An avid knitter with a dangerous yarn addiction and an aversion to housework, Maisey lives with her husband and three kids in rural Oregon. Check out her website, maiseyyates.com, or find her on Facebook.

A 2021 Vivian Award finalist and DEIA activist in the romance industry, **LaQuette** writes sexy, stylish and sensational romance. She crafts dramatic, emotionally epic tales that are deeply pigmented by reality's paintbrush. This Brooklyn native writes unapologetically bold, character-driven stories. Her novels feature diverse ensemble casts who are confident in their right to appear on the page.

New York Times Bestselling Author

MAISEY YATES

CLAIM ME, COWBOY

**HARLEQUIN
BESTSELLING
AUTHOR
COLLECTION**

**HARLEQUIN®
BESTSELLING
AUTHOR
COLLECTION**

PLEASE RECYCLE
THIS PRODUCT IS RECYCLABLE

Recycling programs
for this product may
not exist in your area.

ISBN-13: 978-1-335-00876-3

Claim Me, Cowboy
First published in 2018. This edition published in 2024.
Copyright © 2018 by Maisey Yates

A Very Intimate Takeover
First published in 2021. This edition published in 2024.
Copyright © 2021 by Laquette R. Holmes

Harlequin Enterprises ULC
22 Adelaide St. West, 41st Floor
Toronto, Ontario M5H 4E3, Canada
www.Harlequin.com

Printed in U.S.A.

CONTENTS

CLAIM ME, COWBOY

Maisey Yates

For Jackie Ashenden,
my conflict guru and dear friend. Without you,
my books would take a heck of a lot longer to write,
and my life would be a heck of a lot more boring.
Thank you for everything. Always.

November 1, 2017
LOOKING FOR A WIFE—

Wealthy bachelor, 34, looking for a wife. Never married, no children. Needs a partner who can attend business and social events around the world. Must be willing to move to Copper Ridge, Oregon. Perks include: travel, an allowance, residence in several multimillion-dollar homes.

November 5, 2017
LOOKING FOR AN UNSUITABLE WIFE—

Wealthy bachelor, 34, irritated, looking for a woman to pretend to be my fiancée in order to teach my meddling father a lesson. Need a partner who is rough around the edges. Must be willing to come to Copper Ridge, Oregon, for at least thirty days. Generous compensation provided.

Chapter 1

"No. You do not need to *send pics*."

Joshua Grayson looked out the window of his office and did not feel the kind of calm he ought to feel.

He'd moved back to Copper Ridge six months ago from Seattle, happily trading in a man-made, rectangular skyline for the natural curve of the mountains.

Not the best thing for a man who worked at an architecture company to feel, perhaps. But he spent his working hours dealing in design, in business. Numbers. Black, white and the bottom line. There was something about looking out at the mountains that restarted him.

That, and getting on the back of a horse. Riding from one end of the property to the other. The wind blocking out every other sound except hoofbeats on the earth.

Right now, he doubted anything would decrease the tension he was feeling from dealing with the fallout of his father's ridiculous ad. Another attempt by the old man to make Joshua live the life his father wanted him to.

The only kind of life his father considered successful: a wife, children.

He couldn't understand why Joshua didn't want the same.

No. That kind of life was for another man, one with another past and another future. It was not for Joshua. And that was why he was going to teach his father a lesson.

But not with Brindy, who wanted to send him selfies with "no filter."

The sound she made in response to his refusal was so petulant he almost laughed.

"But your ad said…"

"That," he said, "was not my ad. Goodbye."

He wasn't responsible for the ad in a national paper asking for a wife, till death do them part. But an unsuitable, temporary wife? Yes. That had been his ad.

He was done with his father's machinations. No matter how well-meaning they were. He was tired of tripping over daughters of "old friends" at family gatherings. Tired of dodging women who had been set on him like hounds at a fox hunt.

He was going to win the game. Once and for all. And the woman he hoped would be his trump card was on her way.

His first respondent to his counter ad—Danielle Kelly— was twenty-two, which suited his purposes nicely. His dad would think she was too young, and frankly, Joshua also thought she was too young. He didn't get off on that kind of thing.

He understood why some men did. A tight body was hot. But in his experience, the younger the woman, the less in touch with her sensuality she was and he didn't have the patience for that.

He didn't have the patience for this either, but here he was. The sooner he got this farce over with, the sooner he could go back to his real life.

The doorbell rang and he stood up behind his desk. She was here. And she was—he checked his watch—late.

A half smile curved his lips.

Perfect.

He took the stairs two at a time. He was impatient to meet his temporary bride. Impatient to get this plan started so it could end.

He strode across the entryway and jerked the door open. And froze.

The woman standing on his porch was small. And young, just as he'd expected, but... She wore no makeup, which made her look like a damned teenager. Her features were fine and pointed; her dark brown hair hung lank beneath a ragged beanie that looked like it was in the process of unraveling while it sat on her head.

He didn't bother to linger over the rest of the details—her threadbare sweater with too-long sleeves, her tragic skinny jeans—because he was stopped, immobilized really, by the tiny bundle in her arms.

A baby.

His prospective bride had come with a baby.

Well, hell.

She really hoped he wasn't a serial killer. Well, *hoped* was an anemic word for what she was feeling. Particularly considering the possibility was a valid concern.

What idiot put an ad in the paper looking for a temporary wife?

Though, she supposed the bigger question was: What idiot responded to an ad in the paper looking for a temporary wife?

This idiot, apparently.

It took Danielle a moment to realize she was staring directly at the center of a broad, muscular male chest. She had to raise her head slightly to see his face. He was just so…tall. And handsome.

And she was confused.

She hadn't imagined that a man who put an ad in the paper for a fake fiancée might be attractive. Another anemic word. *Attractive.* This man wasn't simply *attractive*…

He was… Well, he was unreal.

Broad shouldered, muscular, with stubble on his square jaw adding a roughness to features that might have otherwise been considered pretty.

"Please don't tell me you're Danielle Kelly," he said, crossing his arms over that previously noted broad chest.

"I am. Were you expecting someone else? Of course, I suppose you could be. I bet I'm not the only person who responded to your ad, strange though it was. The mention of compensation was pretty tempting. Although, I might point out that in the future maybe you should space your appointments further apart."

"You have a baby," he said, stating the obvious.

Danielle looked down at the bundle in her arms. "Yes."

"You didn't mention that in our email correspondence."

"Of course not. I thought it would make it too easy for you to turn me away."

He laughed, somewhat reluctantly, a muscle in his jaw twitching. "Well, you're right about that."

"But now I'm here. And I don't have the gas money to get back home. Also, you said you wanted unsuitable." She spread one arm wide, keeping Riley clutched firmly in her other arm. "I would say that I'm pretty unsuitable."

She could imagine the picture she made. Her hideous, patchwork car parked in the background. Maroon with lighter patches of red and a door that was green, since it had been replaced after some accident that had happened before the car had come into her possession. Then there was her. In all her faded glory. She was hungry, and she knew she'd lost a lot of weight over the past few weeks, which had taken her frame from slim to downright pointy. The circles under her eyes were so dark she almost looked like she'd been punched.

She considered the baby a perfect accessory. She had that new baby tiredness they never told you about when they talked about the miracle of life.

She curled her toes inside her boots, one of them going through a hole at the end of her sock. She frowned. "Anyway, I figured I presented a pretty poor picture of a fiancée for a businessman such as yourself. Don't you agree?"

The corners of his lips tightened further. "The baby."

"Yes?"

"You expect it to live here?"

She made an exasperated noise. "No. I expect him to live in the car while I party it up in your fancy-pants house."

"A baby wasn't part of the deal."

"What do you care? Your email said it's only through Christmas. Can you imagine telling your father that you've elected to marry Portland hipster trash and she comes with a baby? I mean, it's going to be incredibly awkward, but ultimately kind of funny."

"Come in," he said, his expression no less taciturn as he stood to the side and allowed her entry into his magnificent home.

She clutched Riley even more tightly to her chest as she wandered inside, looking up at the high ceiling, the incredible floor-to-ceiling windows that offered an unparalleled mountain view. As cities went, Portland was all right. The air was pretty clean, and once you got away from the high-rise buildings, you could see past the iron and steel to the nature beyond.

But this view… This was something else entirely.

She looked down at the floor, taking a surprised step to the side when she realized she was standing on glass. And that underneath the glass was a small, slow-moving stream. Startlingly clear, rocks visible beneath the surface of the water. Also, fish.

She looked up to see him staring at her. "My sister's work," he said. "She's the hottest new architect on the scene. Incredible, considering she's only in her early twenties. And a woman, breaking serious barriers in the industry."

"That sounds like an excerpt from a magazine article."

He laughed. "It might be. Since I write the press releases about Faith. That's what I do. PR for our firm, which has expanded recently. Not just design, but construction. And as you can see, Faith's work is highly specialized, and it's extremely coveted."

A small prickle of…something worked its way under her skin. She couldn't imagine being so successful at such a young age. Of course, Joshua and his sister must have come from money. You couldn't build something like this if you hadn't.

Danielle was in her early twenties and didn't even have a checking account, much less a successful business.

All of that had to change. It had to change for Riley.

He was why she was here, after all.

Truly, nothing else could have spurred her to answer the ad. She had lived in poverty all of her life. But Riley deserved better. He deserved stability. And he certainly didn't deserve to wind up in foster care just because she couldn't get herself together.

"So," she said, cautiously stepping off the glass tile. "Tell me more about this situation. And exactly what you expect."

She wanted him to lay it all out. Wanted to hear the terms and conditions he hadn't shared over email. She was prepared to walk away if it was something she couldn't handle. And if he wasn't willing to take no for an answer? Well, she had a knife in her boot.

"My father placed an ad in a national paper saying I was looking for a wife. You can imagine my surprise when I began getting responses before I had ever seen the ad. My father is well-meaning, Ms. Kelly, and he's willing to do anything to make his children's lives better. However, what he perceives as perfection can only come one way. He doesn't think all of this can possibly make me happy." Joshua looked up, seeming to indicate the beautiful house and view around them. "He's wrong. However, he won't take no for an answer, and I want to teach him a lesson."

"By making him think he won?"

"Kind of. That's where you come in. As I said, he

can only see things from his perspective. From his point of view, a wife will stay at home and massage my feet while I work to bring in income. He wants someone traditional. Someone soft and biddable." He looked her over. "I imagine you are none of those things."

"Yeah. Not so much." The life she had lived didn't leave room for that kind of softness.

"And you are right. He isn't going to love that you come with a baby. In fact, he'll probably think you're a gold digger."

"I am a gold digger," she said. "If you weren't offering money, I wouldn't be here. I need money, Mr. Grayson, not a fiancé."

"Call me Joshua," he said. "Come with me."

She followed him as he walked through the entryway, through the living area—which looked like something out of a magazine that she had flipped through at the doctor's office once—and into the kitchen.

The kitchen made her jaw drop. Everything was so shiny. Stainless steel surrounded by touches of wood. A strange clash of modern and rustic that seemed to work.

Danielle had never been in a place where so much work had gone into the details. Before Riley, when she had still been living with her mother, the home decor had included plastic flowers shoved into some kind of strange green Styrofoam and a rug in the kitchen that was actually a towel laid across a spot in the linoleum that had been worn through.

"You will live here for the duration of our arrangement. You will attend family gatherings and work events with me."

"Aren't you worried about me being unsuitable for your work arrangements too?"

"Not really. People who do business with us are fascinated by the nontraditional. As I mentioned earlier, my sister, Faith, is something of a pioneer in her field."

"Great," Danielle said, giving him a thumbs-up. "I'm glad to be a nontraditional asset to you."

"Whether or not you're happy with it isn't really my concern. I mean, I'm paying you, so you don't need to be happy."

She frowned. "Well, I don't want to be unhappy. That's the other thing. We have to discuss…terms and stuff. I don't know what all you think you're going to get out of me, but I'm not here to have sex with you. I'm just here to pose as your fiancée. Like the ad said."

The expression on his face was so disdainful it was almost funny. Almost. It didn't quite ascend to funny because it punched her in the ego. "I think I can control myself, Ms. Kelly."

"If I can call you Joshua, then you can call me Danielle," she said.

"Noted."

The way he said it made her think he wasn't necessarily going to comply with her wishes just because she had made them known. He was difficult. No wonder he didn't have an actual woman hanging around willing to marry him. She should have known there was something wrong with him. Because he was rich and kind of disgustingly handsome. His father shouldn't have had to put an ad in the paper to find Joshua a woman.

He should be able to snap his fingers and have them come running.

That sent another shiver of disquiet over her. Yeah, maybe she should listen to those shivers… But the compensation. She needed the compensation.

"What am I going to do...with the rest of my time?"

"Stay here," he said, as though that were the most obvious thing in the world. As though the idea of her rotting away up here in his mansion wasn't weird at all. "And you have that baby. I assume it takes up a lot of your time?"

"He. Riley. And yes, he does take up a lot of time. He's a baby. That's kind of their thing." He didn't respond to that. "You know. Helpless, requiring every single one of their physical and emotional needs to be met by another person. Clearly you don't know."

Something in his face hardened. "No."

"Well, this place is big enough you shouldn't have to ever find out."

"I keep strange hours," he said. "I have to work with offices overseas, and I need to be available to speak to them on the phone, which means I only sleep for a couple of hours at a time. I also spend a lot of time outdoors."

Looking at him, that last statement actually made sense. Yes, he had the bearing of an uptight businessman, but he was wearing a T-shirt and jeans. He was also the kind of physically fit that didn't look like it had come from a gym, not that she was an expert on men or their physiques.

"What's the catch?" she asked.

Nothing in life came this easy—she knew that for certain. She was waiting for the other shoe to drop. Waiting for him to lead her down to the dungeon and show her where he kept his torture pit.

"There is no catch. This is what happens when a man with a perverse sense of humor and too much money decides to teach his father a lesson."

"So basically I live in this beautiful house, I wear your

ring, I meet your family, I behave abominably and then I get paid?"

"That is the agreement, Ms. Kelly."

"What if I steal your silverware?"

He chuckled. "Then I still win. If you take off in the dead of night, you don't get your money, and I have the benefit of saying to my father that because of his ad I ended up with a con woman and then got my heart broken."

He really had thought of everything. She supposed there was a reason he was successful.

"So do we… Is this happening?"

"There will be papers for you to sign, but yes. It is." Any uncertainty he'd seemed to feel because of Riley was gone now.

He reached into the pocket of his jeans and pulled out a small, velvet box. He opened it, revealing a diamond ring so beautiful, so big, it bordered on obscene.

This was the moment. This was the moment when he would say he actually needed her to spend the day wandering around dressed as a teddy bear or something.

But that moment didn't come either. Instead, he took the ring out of the box and held it out to her. "Give me your hand."

She complied. She complied before she gave her body permission to. She didn't know what she expected. For him to get down on one knee? For him to slide the ring onto her fourth finger? He did neither. Instead, he dropped the gem into her palm.

She curled her fingers around it, an electric shock moving through her system as she realized she was probably holding more money in her hand right now than she could ever hope to earn over the course of her lifetime.

Well, no, that wasn't true. Because she was about to earn enough money over the next month to take care of herself and Riley forever. To make sure she got permanent custody of him.

Her life had been so hard, a constant series of moves and increasingly unsavory *uncles* her mother brought in and out of their lives. Hunger, cold, fear, uncertainty...

She wasn't going to let Riley suffer the same fate. No, she was going to make sure her half brother was protected. This agreement, even if Joshua did ultimately want her to walk around dressed like a sexy teddy bear, was a small price to pay for Riley's future.

"Yes," she said, testing the weight of the ring. "It is."

Chapter 2

As Joshua followed Danielle down the hall, he regretted not having a live-in housekeeper. An elderly British woman would come in handy at a time like this. She would probably find Danielle and her baby to be absolutely delightful. He, on the other hand, did not.

No, on the contrary, he felt invaded. Which was stupid. Because he had signed on for this. Though, he had signed on for it only after he had seen his father's ad. After he had decided the old man needed to be taught a lesson once and for all about meddling in Joshua's life.

It didn't matter that his father had a soft heart or that he was coming from a good place. No, what mattered was the fact that Joshua was tired of being hounded every holiday, every time he went to dinner with his parents, about the possibility of him starting a family.

It wasn't going to happen.

At one time, he'd thought that would be his future.

Had been looking forward to it. But the people who said it was better to have loved and lost than never to have loved at all clearly hadn't *caused* the loss.

He was happy enough now to be alone. And when he didn't want to be alone, he called a woman, had her come spend a few hours in his bed—or in the back of his truck, he wasn't particular. Love was not on his agenda.

"This is a big house," she said.

Danielle sounded vaguely judgmental, which seemed wrong, all things considered. Sure, he was the guy who had paid a woman to pose as his temporary fiancée. And sure, he was the man who lived in a house that had more square footage than he generally walked through in a day, but she was the one who had responded to an ad placed by a complete stranger looking for a temporary fiancée. So, all things considered, he didn't feel like she had a lot of room to judge.

"Yes, it is."

"Why? I mean, you live here alone, right?"

"Because size matters," he said, ignoring the shifting, whimpering sound of the baby in her arms.

"Right," she said, her tone dry. "I've lived in apartment buildings that were smaller than this."

He stopped walking, then he turned to face her. "Am I supposed to feel something about that? Feel sorry for you? Feel bad about the fact that I live in a big house? Because trust me, I started humbly enough. I choose to live differently than my parents. Because I can. Because I earned it."

"Oh, I see. In that case, I suppose I earned my dire straits."

"I don't know your life, Danielle. More important,

I don't want to know it." He realized that was the first time he had used her first name. He didn't much care.

"Great. Same goes. Except I'm going to be living in your house, so I'm going to definitely…infer some things about your life. And that might give rise to conversations like this one. And if you're going to be assuming things about me, then you should be prepared for me to respond in kind."

"I don't have to do any such thing. As far as I'm concerned, I'm the employer, you're the employee. That means if I want to talk to you about the emotional scars of my childhood, you had better lie back on my couch and listen. Conversely, if I do not want to hear about any of the scars of yours, I don't have to. All I have to do is throw money at you until you stop talking."

"Wow. It's seriously the job offer I've been waiting for my entire life. Talking I'm pretty good at. And I don't do a great job of shutting up. That means I would be getting money thrown at me for a long, long time."

"Don't test me, Ms. Kelly," he said, reverting back to her last name, because he really didn't want to know about her childhood or what brought her here. Didn't want to wonder about her past. Didn't want to wonder about her adulthood either. Who the father of her baby was. What kind of situation she was in. It wasn't his business, and he didn't care.

"Don't test me, Ms. Kelly," she said, in what he assumed was supposed to be a facsimile of his voice.

"Really?" he asked.

"What? You can't honestly expect to operate at this level of extreme douchiness and not get called to the carpet on it."

"I expect that I can do whatever I want, since I'm paying you to be here."

"You don't want me to dress up as a teddy bear and vacuum, do you?"

"What?"

She shifted her weight, moving the baby over to one hip and spreading the other arm wide. "Hey, man, some people are into that. They like stuffed animals. Or rather, they like people dressed as stuffed animals."

"I don't."

"That's a relief."

"I like women," he said. "Dressed as women. Or rather, undressed, generally."

"I'm not judging. Your dad put an ad in the paper for some reason. Clearly he really wants you to be married."

"Yes. Well, he doesn't understand that not everybody needs to live the life that he does. He was happy with a family and a farmhouse. But none of the rest of us feel that way, and there's nothing wrong with that."

"So none of you are married?"

"One of us is. The only brother that actually wanted a farmhouse too." He paused in front of the door at the end of the hall. He was glad he had decided to set this room aside for the woman who answered the ad. He hadn't known she would come with a baby in tow, but the fact that she had meant he really, really wanted her out of earshot.

"Is this it?" she asked.

"Yes," he said, pushing the door open.

When she looked inside the bedroom, her jaw dropped, and Joshua couldn't deny that he took a small amount of satisfaction in her reaction. She looked... Well, she looked amazed. Like somebody standing in front of a great work of art. Except it was just a bedroom. Rather a grand one, he had to admit, down to the details.

There was a large bed fashioned out of natural, twisted pieces of wood with polished support beams that ran from floor to ceiling and retained the natural shape they'd had in the woods but glowed from the stain that had been applied to them. The bed made the whole room look like a magical forest. A little bit fanciful for him. His own bedroom had been left more Spartan. But, clearly, Danielle was enchanted.

And he shouldn't care.

"I've definitely lived in apartments that were smaller than this room," she said, wrapping both arms around the baby and turning in a circle. "This is… Is that a loft? Like a reading loft?" She was gazing up at the mezzanine designed to look as though it was nestled in the tree branches.

"I don't know." He figured it was probably more of a sex loft. But then, if he slept in a room with a loft, obviously he would have sex in it. That was what creative surfaces were for, in his opinion.

"It reminds me of something we had when I was in first grade." A crease appeared between her eyebrows. "I mean, not me as in at our house, but in my first-grade classroom at school. The teacher really loved books. And she liked for us all to read. So we were able to lie around the classroom anywhere we wanted with a book and—" She abruptly stopped talking, as though she realized exactly what she was doing. "Never mind. You think it's boring. Anyway, I'm going to use it for a reading loft."

"Dress like a teddy bear in it, for all I care," he responded.

"That's your thing, not mine."

"Do you have any bags in the car that I can get for you?"

She looked genuinely stunned. "You don't have to get anything for me."

It struck him that she thought he was being nice. He didn't consider the offer particularly nice. It was just what his father had drilled into him from the time he was a boy. If there was a woman and she had a heavy thing to transport, you were no kind of man if you didn't offer to do the transporting.

"I don't mind."

"It's just one bag," she said.

That shocked him. She was a woman. A woman with a baby. He was pretty sure most mothers traveled with enough luggage to fill a caravan. "Just one bag." He had to confirm that.

"Yes," she returned. "Baggage is another thing entirely. But in terms of bags, yeah, we travel light."

"Let me get it." He turned and walked out of the room, frustrated when he heard her footsteps behind him. "I said I would get it."

"You don't need to," she said, following him persistently down the stairs and out toward the front door.

"My car is locked," she added, and he ignored her as he continued to walk across the driveway to the maroon monstrosity parked there.

He shot her a sideways glance, then looked down at the car door. It hung a little bit crooked, and he lifted up on it hard enough to push it straight, then he jerked it open. "Not well."

"You're the worst," she said, scowling.

He reached into the back seat and saw one threadbare duffel bag, which had to be the bag she was talking about. The fabric strap was dingy, and he had a feeling it used to be powder blue. The zipper was broken and there were four safety pins holding the end of the bulging bag together. All in all, it looked completely impractical.

"Empty all the contents out of this tonight. In the morning, I'm going to use it to fuel a bonfire."

"It's the only bag I have."

"I'll buy you a new one."

"It better be in addition to the fee that I'm getting," she said, her expression stubborn. "I mean it. If I incur a loss because of you, you better cover it."

"You have my word that if anything needs to be purchased in order for you to fit in with your surroundings, or in order for me to avoid contracting scabies, it will be bankrolled by me."

"I don't have scabies," she said, looking fierce.

"I didn't say you did. I implied that your gym bag might."

"Well," she said, her cheeks turning red, "it doesn't. It's clean. I'm clean."

He heaved the bag over his shoulder and led the way back to the house, Danielle trailing behind him like an angry wood nymph. That was what she reminded him of, he decided. All pointed angles and spiky intensity. And a supernaturally wicked glare that he could feel boring into the center of his back. Right between his shoulder blades.

This was not a woman who intimidated easily, if at all.

He supposed that was signal enough that he should make an attempt to handle her with care. Not because she needed it, but because clearly nobody had ever made the attempt before. But he didn't know how. And he was paying her an awful lot to put up with him as he was.

And she had brought a baby into his house.

"You're going to need some supplies," he said, frowning. Because he abruptly realized what it meant that she had brought a baby into his house. The bedroom he had installed her in was only meant for one. And there was no way—barring the unlikely reality that she was related to Mary Poppins in some way—that her ratty old bag contained the supplies required to keep both a baby and herself in the kind of comfort that normal human beings expected.

"What kind of supplies?"

He moved quickly through the house, and she scurried behind him, attempting to match his steps. They walked back into the bedroom and he flung the bag on the ground.

"A bed for the baby. Beyond that, I don't know what they require."

She shot him a deadly glare, then bent down and unzipped the bag, pulling out a bottle and a can of formula. She tossed both onto the bed, then reached back into the bag and grabbed a blanket. She spread it out on the floor, then set the baby in the center of it.

Then she straightened, spreading her arms wide and slapping her hands back down on her thighs. "Well, this is more than we've had for a long time. And yeah, I guess it would be nice to have nursery stuff. But I've never had it. Riley and I have been doing just fine on our own." She looked down, picking at some dirt beneath her fingernail. "Or I guess we haven't been *fine*. If we had, I wouldn't have responded to your ad. But I don't need more than what I have. Not now. Once you pay me? Well, I'm going to buy a house. I'm going to change things for us. But until then, it doesn't matter."

He frowned. "What about Riley's father? Surely he should be paying you some kind of support."

"Right. Like I have any idea who he is." He must have made some kind of facial expression that seemed judgmental, because her face colored and her eyebrows lowered. "I mean, I don't know how to get in touch with him. It's not like he left contact details. And I sincerely doubt he left his real name."

"I'll call our office assistant, Poppy. She'll probably know what you need." Technically, Poppy was his brother Isaiah's assistant, but she often handled whatever Joshua or Faith needed, as well. Poppy would arrange it so that various supplies were overnighted to the house.

"Seriously. Don't do anything… You don't need to do anything."

"I'm supposed to convince my parents that I'm marrying you," he said, his tone hard. "I don't think they're going to believe I'm allowing my fiancée to live out of one duffel bag. No. Everything will have to be outfitted so that it looks legitimate. Consider it a bonus to your salary."

She tilted her chin upward, her eyes glittering. "Okay, I will."

He had halfway expected her to argue, but he wasn't sure why. She was here for her own material gain. Why would she reduce it? "Good." He nodded once. "You probably won't see much of me. I'll be working a lot. We are going to have dinner with my parents in a couple of days. Until then, the house and the property are yours to explore. This is your house too. For the time being."

He wasn't being particularly generous. It was just that he didn't want to answer questions, or deal with her being tentative about where she might and might not be allowed to go. He just wanted to install her and the baby in this room and forget about them until he needed them as convenient props.

"Really?" Her natural suspicion was shining through again.

"I'm a very busy man, Ms. Kelly," he said. "I'm not going to be babysitting. Either the child or you."

And with that, he turned and left her alone.

Chapter 3

Danielle had slept fitfully last night. And, of course, she hadn't actually left her room once she had been put there. But early the next morning there had been a delivery. And the signature they had asked for was hers. And then the packages had started to come in, like a Christmas parade without the wrapping.

Teams of men carried the boxes up the stairs. They had assembled a crib, a chair, and then unpacked various baby accoutrements that Danielle hadn't even known existed. How could she? She certainly hadn't expected to end up caring for a baby.

When her mother had breezed back into her life alone and pregnant—after Danielle had experienced just two carefree years where she had her own space and wasn't caring for anyone—Danielle had put all of her focus into caring for the other woman. Into arranging state health insurance so the prenatal care and hospital bill for the delivery wouldn't deter her mother from actually taking care of herself and the baby.

And then, when her mother had abandoned Danielle and Riley…that was when Danielle had realized her brother was likely going to be her responsibility. She had involved Child Services not long after that.

There had been two choices. Either Riley could go into foster care or Danielle could take some appropriate parenting classes and become a temporary guardian.

So she had.

But she had been struggling to keep their heads above water, and it was too close to the way she had grown up. She wanted more than that for Riley. Wanted more than that for both of them. Now it wasn't just her. It was him. And a part-time job as a cashier had never been all that lucrative. But with Riley to take care of, and her mother completely out of the picture, staying afloat on a cashier's pay was impossible.

She had done her best trading babysitting time with a woman in her building who also had a baby and nobody else to depend on. But inevitably there were schedule clashes, and after missing a few too many shifts, Danielle had lost her job.

Which was when she had gotten her first warning from Child Services.

Well, she had a job now.

And, apparently, a full nursery.

Joshua was refreshingly nowhere to be seen, which made dealing with her new circumstances much easier. Without him looming over her, being in his house felt a lot like being in the world's fanciest vacation rental. At least, the fanciest vacation rental she could imagine.

She had a baby monitor in her pocket, one that would

allow her to hear when Riley woke up. A baby monitor that provided her with more freedom than she'd had since Riley had been born. But, she supposed, in her old apartment a monitor would have been a moot point considering there wasn't anywhere she could go and not hear the baby cry.

But in this massive house, having Riley take his nap in the bedroom—in the new crib, his first crib—would have meant she couldn't have also run down to the kitchen to grab snacks. But she had the baby monitor. A baby monitor that vibrated. Which meant she could also listen to music.

She had the same ancient MP3 player her mother had given her for her sixteenth birthday years ago, but Danielle had learned early to hold on to everything she had, because she didn't know when something else would come along. And in the case of frills like her MP3 player, nothing else had ever come along.

Of course, that meant her music was as old as her technology. But really, music hadn't been as good since she was sixteen anyway.

She shook her hips slightly, walking through the kitchen, singing about how what didn't kill her would only make her stronger. Digging through cabinets, she came up with a package of Pop-Tarts. *Pop-Tarts!*

Her mother had never bought those. They were too expensive. And while Danielle had definitely indulged herself when she had moved out, that hadn't lasted. Because they were too expensive.

Joshua had strawberry. And some kind of mixed berry with bright blue frosting. She decided she would eat one of each to ascertain which was best.

Then she decided to eat one more of each. She hadn't realized how hungry she was. She had a feeling the hunger wasn't a new development. She had a feeling she had been hungry for days. Weeks even.

Suddenly, sitting on the plush couch in his living area, shoving toaster pastries into her mouth, she felt a whole lot like crying in relief. Because she and Riley were warm; they were safe. And there was hope. Finally, an end point in sight to the long, slow grind of poverty she had existed in for her entire life.

It seemed too good to be true, really. That she had managed to jump ahead in her life like this. That she was really managing to get herself out of that hole without prostituting herself.

Okay, so some people might argue this agreement with Joshua *was* prostituting herself, a little bit. But it wasn't like she was going to have sex with him.

She nearly choked on her Pop-Tart at the thought. And she lingered a little too long on what it might be like to get close to a man like Joshua. To any man, really. The way her mother had behaved all of her life had put Danielle off men. Or, more specifically, she supposed it was the way men had behaved toward Danielle's mother that had put her off.

As far as Danielle could tell, relationships were a whole lot of exposing yourself to pain, deciding you were going to depend on somebody and then having that person leave you high and dry.

No, thank you.

But she supposed she could see how somebody might lose their mind enough to take that risk. Especially when the person responsible for the mind loss had eyes that were blue like Joshua's. She leaned back against the couch, her hand falling slack, the Pop-Tart dangling from her fingertips.

Yesterday there had been the faint shadow of golden stubble across that strong face and jaw, his eyes glittering with irritation. Which she supposed shouldn't be a bonus, shouldn't be appealing. Except his irritation made her want to rise to the unspoken challenge. To try to turn that spark into something else. Turn that irritation into something more...

"Are you eating my Pop-Tarts?"

The voice cut through the music and she jumped, flinging the toaster pastry into the air. She ripped her headphones out of her ears and turned around to see Joshua, his arms crossed over his broad chest, his eyebrows flat on his forehead, his expression unreadable.

"You said whatever was in your house was mine to use," she squeaked. "And a warning would've been good. You just about made me jump out of my skin. Which was maybe your plan all along. If you wanted to make me into a skin suit."

"That's ridiculous. I would not fit into your skin."

She swallowed hard, her throat dry. "Well, it's a figure of speech, isn't it?"

"Is it?" he asked.

"Yes. Everybody knows what that means. It means that I think you might be a serial killer."

"You don't really think I'm a serial killer, or you wouldn't be here."

"I am pretty desperate." She lifted her hand and licked off a remnant of jam. "I mean, obviously."

"There are no Pop-Tarts left," he said, his tone filled with annoyance.

"You said I could have whatever I wanted. I wanted Pop-Tarts."

"You ate all of them."

"Why do you even have Pop-Tarts?" She stood up, crossing her arms, mimicking his stance. "You don't look like a man who eats Pop-Tarts."

"I like them. I like to eat them after I work outside."

"You work outside?"

"Yes," he said. "I have horses."

Suddenly, all of her annoyance fell away. Like it had been melted by magic. *Equine* magic. "You have horses?" She tried to keep the awe out of her voice, but it was nearly impossible.

"Yes," he said.

"Can I… Can I see them?"

"If you want to."

She had checked the range on the baby monitor, so depending on how far away from the house the horses were, she could go while Riley was napping.

"Could we see the house from the barn? Or wherever you keep them?"

"Yeah," he said, "it's just right across the driveway."

"Can I see them *now*?"

"I don't know. You ate my Pop-Tarts. Actually, more egregious than eating my Pop-Tarts, you threw the last half of one on the ground."

"Sorry about your Pop-Tarts. But I'm sure that a man who can have an entire nursery outfitted in less than twenty-four hours can certainly acquire Pop-Tarts at a moment's notice."

"Or I could just go to the store."

She had a hard time picturing a man like Joshua Grayson walking through the grocery store. In fact, the image almost made her laugh. He was way too commanding to do something as mundane as pick up a head of lettuce and try to figure out how fresh it was. Far too…masculine to go around squeezing avocados.

"What?" he asked, his eyebrows drawing together.

"I just can't imagine you going to the grocery store. That's all."

"Well, I do. Because I like food. Food like Pop-Tarts."

"My mom would never buy those for me," she said. "They were too expensive."

He huffed out a laugh. "My mom would never buy them for me."

"This is why being an adult is cool, even when it sucks."

"Pop-Tarts whenever you want?"

She nodded. "Yep."

"That seems like a low bar."

She lifted a shoulder. "Maybe it is, but it's a tasty one."

He nodded. "Fair enough. Now, why don't we go look at the horses."

Joshua didn't know what to expect by taking Danielle outside to see the horses. He had been irritated that she had eaten his preferred afternoon snack, and then, perversely, even more irritated that she had questioned the fact that it was his preferred afternoon snack. Irritated that he was put in the position of explaining to someone what he did with his time and what he put into his body.

He didn't like explaining himself.

But then she saw the horses. And all his irritation faded as he took in the look on her face. She was filled with...wonder. Absolute wonder over this thing he took for granted.

The fact that he owned horses at all, that he had felt compelled to acquire some once he had moved into this place, was a source of consternation. He had hated doing farm chores when he was a kid. Hadn't been able to get away from home and to the city fast enough. But in recent years, those feelings had started to change. And he'd found himself seeking out roots. Seeking out home.

For better or worse, this was home. Not just the misty Oregon coast, not just the town of Copper Ridge. But a ranch. Horses. A morning spent riding until the sun rose over the mountains, washing everything in a pale gold.

Yeah, that was home.

He could tell this ranch he loved was something beyond a temporary home for Danielle, who was looking at the horses and the barn like they were magical things.

She wasn't wearing her beanie today. Her dark brown hair hung limply around her face. She was pale, her chin pointed, her nose slightly pointed, as well. She was elfin, and he wasn't tempted to call her beautiful, but there was something captivating about her. Something fascinating. Watching her with the large animals was somehow just as entertaining as watching football and he couldn't quite figure out why.

"You didn't grow up around horses?"

"No," she said, taking a timid step toward the paddock. "I grew up in Portland."

He nodded. "Right."

"Always in apartments," she said. Then she frowned. "I think one time we had a house. I can't really remember it. We moved a lot. But sometimes when we lived with my mom's boyfriends, we had nicer places. It had its perks."

"What did?"

"My mom being a codependent hussy," she said, her voice toneless so it was impossible to say whether or not she was teasing.

"Right." He had grown up in one house. His family had never moved. His parents were still in that same farmhouse, the one his family had owned for a couple of generations. He had moved away to go to college and then to start the business, but that was different. He had always known he could come back here. He'd always had roots.

"Will you go back to Portland when you're finished here?" he asked.

"I don't know," she said, blinking rapidly. "I've never really had a choice before. Of where I wanted to live."

It struck him then that she was awfully young. And that he didn't know quite *how* young. "You're twenty-two?"

"Yes," she said, sounding almost defensive. "So I haven't really had a chance to think about what all I want to do and, like, be. When I grow up and stuff."

"Right," he said.

He'd been aimless for a while, but before he'd graduated high school, he'd decided he couldn't deal with a life of ranching in Copper Ridge. He had decided to get out of town. He had wanted more. He had wanted bigger. He'd gone to school for marketing because he was good at selling ideas. Products. He wasn't necessarily the one who created them, or the one who dreamed them up, but he was the one who made sure a consumer would see them and realize that product was what their life had been missing up until that point.

He was the one who took the straw and made it into gold.

He had always enjoyed his job, but it would have been especially satisfying if he'd been able to start his career by building a business with his brother and sister. To be able to market Faith's extraordinary talent to the world, as he did now. But he wasn't sure that he'd started out with a passion for what he did so much as a passion for wealth and success, and that had meant leaving behind his sister and brother too, at first. But his career had certainly grown into a passion. And he'd learned that he was the practical piece. The part that everybody needed.

A lot of people had ideas, but less than half of them had the follow-through to complete what they started. And less than half of *those* people knew how to get to the consumer. That was where he came in.

He'd had his first corporate internship at the age of twenty. He couldn't imagine being aimless at twenty-two.

But then, Danielle had a baby and he couldn't imagine having a baby at that age either.

A hollow pang struck him in the chest.

He didn't like thinking of babies at all.

"You're judging me," she said, taking a step back from the paddock.

"No, I'm not. Also, you can get closer. You can pet them."

Her head whipped around to look at the horses, then back to him, her eyes round and almost comically hopeful. "I can?"

"Of course you can. They don't bite. Well, they *might* bite, just don't stick your fingers in their mouths."

"I don't know," she said, stuffing her hands in her pockets. Except he could tell she really wanted to. She was just afraid.

"Danielle," he said, earning himself a shocked look when he used her name. "Pet the horses."

She tugged her hand out of her pocket again, then took a tentative step forward, reaching out, then drawing her hand back just as quickly.

He couldn't stand it. Between her not knowing what she wanted to be when she grew up and watching her struggle with touching a horse, he just couldn't deal with it. He stepped forward, wrapped his fingers around her wrist and drew her closer to the paddock. "It's fine," he said.

A moment after he said the words, his body registered what he had done. More than that, it registered the fact that she was very warm. That her skin was smooth.

And that she was way, way too thin.

A strange combination of feelings tightened his whole body. Compassion tightened his heart; lust tightened his groin.

He gritted his teeth. "Come on," he said.

He noticed the color rise in her face, and he wondered if she was angry, or if she was feeling the same flash of awareness rocking through him. He supposed it didn't matter either way. "Come on," he said, drawing her hand closer to the opening of the paddock. "There you go, hold your hand flat like that."

She complied, and he released his hold on her, taking a step back. He did his best to ignore the fact that he could still feel the impression of her skin against his palm.

One of his horses—a gray mare named Blue—walked up to the bars and pressed her nose against Danielle's outstretched hand. Danielle made a sharp, shocked sound, drew her hand back, then giggled. "Her whiskers are soft."

"Yeah," he said, a smile tugging at his lips. "And she is about as gentle as they come, so you don't have to be afraid of her."

"I'm not afraid of anything," Danielle said, sticking her hand back in, letting the horse sniff her.

He didn't believe that she wasn't afraid of anything. She was definitely tough. But she was brittle. Like one of those people who might withstand a beating, but if something ever hit a fragile spot, she would shatter entirely.

"Would you like to go riding sometime?" he asked.

She drew her hand back again, her expression... Well, he couldn't quite read it. There was a softness to it, but also an edge of fear and suspicion.

"I don't know. Why?"

"You seem to like the horses."

"I do. But I don't know how to ride."

"I can teach you."

"I don't know. I have to watch Riley." She began to withdraw, both from him and from the paddock.

"I'm going to hire somebody to help watch Riley," he said, making that decision right as the words exited his mouth.

There was that look again. Suspicion. "Why?"

"In case I need you for something that isn't baby friendly. Which will probably happen. We have over a month ahead of us with you living with me, and one never knows what kinds of situations we might run into. I wasn't expecting you to come with a baby, and while I agree that it will definitely help make the case that you're not suitable for me, I also think we'll need to be able to go out without him."

She looked very hesitant about that idea. And he could understand why. She clung to that baby like he was a life preserver. Like if she let go of him, she might sink and be in over her head completely.

"And I would get to ride the horses?" she asked, her eyes narrowed, full of suspicion still.

"I said so."

"Sure. But that doesn't mean a lot to me, Mr. Grayson," she said. "I don't accept people at their word. I like legal documents."

"Well, I'm not going to draw up a legal document about giving you horse-riding lessons. So you're going to have to trust me."

"You want me to trust the sketchy rich dude who put an ad in the paper looking for a fake wife?"

"He's the devil you made the deal with, Ms. Kelly. I would say it's in your best interest to trust him."

"We shake on it at least."

She stuck her hand out, and he could see she was completely sincere. So he stuck his out in kind, wrapping his fingers around hers, marveling at her delicate bone structure. Feeling guilty now about getting angry over her eating his Pop-Tarts. The woman needed him to hire a gourmet chef too. Needed him to make sure she was getting three meals a day. He wondered how long it had been since she'd eaten regularly. She certainly didn't have the look of a woman who had recently given birth. There was no extra weight on her to speak of. He wondered how she had survived something so taxing as labor and delivery. But those were questions he was not going to ask. They weren't his business.

And he shouldn't even be curious about them.

"All right," she said. "You can hire somebody. And I'll learn to ride horses."

"You're a tough negotiator," he said, releasing his hold on her hand.

"Maybe I should go into business."

He tried to imagine this fragile, spiky creature in a boardroom, and it nearly made him laugh. "If you want to," he said, instead of laughing. Because he had a feeling she might attack him if he made fun of her. And another feeling that if Danielle attacked, she would likely go straight for the eyes. Or the balls.

He was attached to both of those things, and he liked them attached to him.

"I should go back to the house. Riley might wake up soon. Plus, I'm not entirely sure if I trust the new baby monitor. I mean, it's probably fine. But I'm going to have to get used to it before I really depend on it."

"I understand," he said, even though he didn't.

He turned and walked with her back toward the house. He kept his eyes on her small, determined frame. On the way, she stuffed her hands in her pockets and hunched her shoulders forward. As though she were trying to look intimidating. Trying to keep from looking at her surroundings in case her surroundings looked back.

And then he reminded himself that none of this mattered. She was just a means to an end, even if she was a slightly more multifaceted means than he had thought she might be.

It didn't matter how many facets she had. Danielle Kelly needed to fulfill only one objective. She had to be introduced to his parents and be found completely wanting.

He looked back at her, at her determined walk and her posture that seemed to radiate with *I'll cut you.*

Yeah. He had a feeling she would fulfill that objective just fine.

Chapter 4

Danielle was still feeling wobbly after her interaction with Joshua down at the barn. She had touched a horse. And she had touched *him*. She hadn't counted on doing either of those things today. And he had told her they were going to have dinner together tonight and he was going to give her a crash course on the Grayson family. She wasn't entirely sure she felt ready for that either.

She had gone through all her clothes, looking for something suitable for having dinner with a billionaire. She didn't have anything. Obviously.

She snorted, feeling like an idiot for thinking she could find something relatively appropriate in that bag of hers. A bag he thought had scabies.

She turned her snort into a growl.

Then, rebelliously, she pulled out the same pair of faded pants she had been wearing yesterday.

He had probably never dealt with a woman who wore

the same thing twice. Let alone the same thing two days in a row. Perversely, she kind of enjoyed that. Hey, she was here to be unsuitable. Might as well start now.

She looked in the mirror, grabbed one stringy end of her hair and blew out a disgusted breath. She shouldn't care how her hair looked.

But he was just so good-looking. It made her feel like a small, brown mouse standing next to him. It wasn't fair, really. That he had the resources to buy himself nice clothes and that he just naturally looked great.

She sighed, picking Riley up from his crib and sticking him in the little carrier she would put him in for dinner. He was awake and looking around, so she wanted to be in his vicinity, rather than leaving him upstairs alone. He wasn't a fussy baby. Really, he hardly ever cried.

But considering how often his mother had left him alone in those early days of his life, before Danielle had realized she couldn't count on her mother to take good care of him, she was reluctant to leave him by himself unless he was sleeping.

Then she paused, going back over to her bag to get the little red, dog-eared dictionary inside. She bent down, still holding on to Riley, and retrieved it. Then she quickly looked up scabies.

"I knew it," she said derisively, throwing the dictionary back into her bag.

She walked down the stairs and into the dining room, setting Riley in his seat on the chair next to hers. Joshua was already sitting at the table, looking as though he had been waiting for them. Which, she had a feeling, he was doing just to be annoying and superior.

"My bag can't have scabies," she said by way of greeting.

"Oh really?"

"Yes. I looked it up. Scabies are mites that burrow into your skin. Not into a duffel bag."

"They have to come from somewhere."

"Well, they're not coming from my bag. They're more likely to come from your horses, or something."

"You like my horses," he said, his tone dry. "Anyway, we're about to have dinner. So maybe we shouldn't be discussing skin mites?"

"You're the one who brought up scabies. The first time."

"I had pretty much dropped the subject."

"Easy enough for you to do, since it wasn't your hygiene being maligned."

"Sure." He stood up from his position at the table. "I'm just going to go get dinner, since you're here. I had it warming."

"Did you cook?"

He left the room without answering and returned a moment later holding two plates full of hot food. Her stomach growled intensely. She didn't even care what was on the plates. As far as she was concerned, it was gourmet. It was warm and obviously not from a can or a frozen pizza box. Plus, she was sitting at a real dining table and not on a patio set that had been shoved into her tiny living room.

The meal looked surprisingly healthy, considering she had discovered his affinity for Pop-Tarts earlier. And it was accompanied by a particularly nice-looking rice. "What is this?"

"Chicken and risotto," he said.

"What's risotto?"

"Creamy rice," he said. "At least, that's the simple explanation."

Thankfully, he wasn't looking at her like she was an alien for not knowing about risotto. But then she remembered he had spoken of having simple roots. So maybe he was used to dealing with people who didn't have as sophisticated a palate as he had.

She wrinkled her nose, then picked up her fork and took a tentative bite. It was good. So good. And before she knew it, she had cleared out her portion. Her cheeks heated when she realized he had barely taken two bites.

"There's plenty more in the kitchen," he said. Then he took her plate from in front of her and went back into the kitchen. She was stunned, and all she could do was sit there and wait until he returned a moment later with the entire pot of risotto, another portion already on her plate.

"Eat as much as you want," he said, setting everything in front of her.

Well, she wasn't going to argue with that suggestion. She polished off the chicken, then went back for thirds of the risotto. Eventually, she got around to eating the salad.

"I thought we were going to talk about my responsibilities for being your fiancée and stuff," she said after she realized he had been sitting there staring at her for the past ten minutes.

"I thought you should have a chance to eat a meal first."

"Well," she said, taking another bite, "that's unexpectedly kind of you."

"You seem…hungry."

That was the most loaded statement of the century. She was so hungry. For so many things. Food was kind of the least of it. "It's just been a really crazy few months."

"How old is the baby? Riley. How old is Riley?"

For the first time, because of that correction, she became aware of the fact that he seemed reluctant to call Riley by name. Actually, Joshua seemed pretty reluctant to deal with Riley in general.

Riley was unperturbed. Sitting in that reclined seat, his muddy blue eyes staring up at the ceiling. He lifted his fist, putting it in his mouth and gumming it idly.

That was one good thing she could say about their whole situation. Riley was so young that he was largely unperturbed by all of it. He had gone along more or less unaffected by their mother's mistakes. At least, Danielle hoped so. She really did.

"He's almost four months old," she said. She felt a soft smile touch her lips. Yes, taking care of her half brother was hard. None of it was easy. But he had given her a new kind of purpose. Had given her a kind of the drive she'd been missing before.

Before Riley, she had been somewhat content to just enjoy living life on her own terms. To enjoy not cleaning up her mother's messes. Instead, working at the grocery store, going out with friends after work for coffee or burritos at the twenty-four-hour Mexican restaurant.

Her life had been simple, and it had been carefree. Something she hadn't been afforded all the years she'd lived with her mother, dealing with her mother's various heartbreaks, schemes to try to better their circumstances and intense emotional lows.

So many years when Danielle should have been a child but instead was expected to be the parent. If her mother passed out in the bathroom after having too much to drink, it was up to Danielle to take care of her. To put a pillow underneath her mother's head, then make herself a piece of toast for dinner and get her homework done.

In contrast, taking care of only herself had seemed

simple. And in truth, she had resented Riley at first, resented the idea that she would have to take care of another person again. But taking care of a baby was different. He wasn't a victim of his own bad choices. No, he was a victim of circumstances. He hadn't had a chance to make a single choice for himself yet.

To Danielle, Riley was the child she'd once been.

Except she hadn't had anyone to step in and take care of her when her mother failed. But Riley did. That realization had filled Danielle with passion. Drive.

And along with that dedication came a fierce, unexpected love like she had never felt before toward another human being. She would do anything for him. Give anything for him.

"And you've been alone with him all this time?"

She didn't know why she was so reluctant to let Joshua know that Riley wasn't her son. She supposed it was partly because, for all intents and purposes, he was her son. She intended to adopt him officially as soon as she had the means to do so. As soon as everything in her life was in order enough that Child Services would respond to her favorably.

The other part was that as long as people thought Riley was hers, they would be less likely to suggest she make a different decision about his welfare. Joshua Grayson had a coldness to him. He seemed to have a family who loved and supported him, but instead of finding it endearing, he got angry about it. He was using her to get back at his dad for doing something that, in her opinion, seemed mostly innocuous. And yes, she was benefiting from his pettiness, so she couldn't exactly judge.

Still, she had a feeling that if he knew Riley wasn't her son, he would suggest she do the "responsible" thing and allow him to be raised by a two-parent family, or whatever. She just didn't even want to have that discussion with him. Or with anybody. She had too many things against her already.

She didn't want to fight about this too.

"Mostly," she said carefully, treading the line between the truth and a lie. "Since he was about three weeks old. And I thought… I thought I could do it. I'd been self-sufficient for a long time. But then I realized there are a lot of logistical problems when you can't just leave your apartment whenever you want. It's harder to get to work. And I couldn't afford childcare. There wasn't any space at the places that had subsidized rates. So I was trading childcare with a neighbor, but sometimes our schedules conflicted. Anyway, it was just difficult. You can imagine why responding to your ad seemed like the best possible solution."

"I already told you, I'm not judging you for taking me up on an offer I made."

"I guess I'm just explaining that under other circumstances I probably wouldn't have sought you out. But things have been hard. I lost my job because I wasn't flexible enough and I had missed too many shifts because babysitting for Riley fell through."

"Well," he said, a strange expression crossing his face, "your problems should be minimized soon. You should be independently wealthy enough to at least afford childcare."

Not only that, she would actually be able to make decisions about her life. About what she wanted. When Joshua had asked her earlier today about whether or not she would go back to Portland, it had been the first time she had truly realized she could make decisions about where she wanted to live, rather than just parking herself somewhere because she happened to be there already.

It would be the first time in her life she could make proactive decisions rather than just reacting to her situation.

"Right. So I guess we should talk about your family," she said, determined to move the conversation back in the right direction. She didn't need to talk about herself. They didn't need to get to know each other. She just needed to do this thing, to trick his family, lie…whatever he needed her to do. So she and Riley could start their new life.

"I already told you my younger sister is an architectural genius. My older brother Isaiah is the financial brain. And I do the public relations and marketing. We have another brother named Devlin, and he runs a small ranching operation in town. He's married, no kids. Then there are my parents."

"The reason we find ourselves in this situation," she said, folding her hands and leaning forward. Then she cast a glance at the pot of risotto and decided to grab the spoon and serve herself another helping while they were talking.

"Yes. Well, not my mother so much. Sure, she wrings her hands and looks at me sadly and says she wishes I would get married. My father is the one who…actively meddles."

"That surprises me. I mean, given what I know about fathers. Which is entirely based on TV. I don't have one."

He lifted a brow.

"Well," she continued, "sure, I guess I do. But I never met him. I mean, I don't even know his name."

She realized that her history was shockingly close to

the story she had given about Riley. Which was a true one. It just wasn't about Danielle. It was about her mother. And the fact that her mother repeated the same cycle over and over again. The fact that she never seemed to change. And never would.

"That must've been hard," he said. "I'm sorry."

"Don't apologize. I bet he was a jerk. I mean, circumstances would lead you to believe that he must be, right?"

"Yeah, it's probably a pretty safe assumption."

"Well, anyway, this isn't about my lack of a paternal figure. This is about the overbearing presence of yours."

He laughed. "My mother is old-fashioned—so is my father. My brother Devlin is a little bit too, but he's also something of a rebel. He has tattoos and things. He's a likely ally for you, especially since he got married a few months ago and is feeling soft about love and all of that. My brother Isaiah isn't going to like you. My sister, Faith, will try. Basically, if you cuss, chew with your mouth open, put your elbows on the table and in general act like a feral cat, my family will likely find you unsuitable. Also, if you could maybe repeatedly bring up the fact that you're really looking forward to spending my money, and that you had another man's baby four months ago, that would be great."

She squinted. "I think the fact that I have a four-month-old baby in tow will be reminder enough."

The idea of going into his family's farmhouse and behaving like a nightmare didn't sit as well with her as it had when the plan had been fully abstract. But now he had given names to the family members. Now she had been here for a while. And now it was all starting to feel a little bit real.

"It won't hurt. Though, he's pretty quiet. It might help if he screamed."

She laughed. "Oh, I don't know about that. I have a feeling your mom and sister might just want to hold him. That will be the real problem. Not having everyone hate me. That'll be easy enough. It'll be keeping everyone from loving him."

That comment struck her square in the chest, made her realize just what they were playing at here. She was going to be lying to these people. And yes, the idea was to alienate them, but they were going to think she might be their daughter-in-law, sister-in-law...that Riley would be their grandson or nephew.

But it would be a lie.

That's the point, you moron. And who cares? They're strangers. Riley is your life. He's your responsibility. And you'll never see these people again.

"We won't let them hold the baby," he said, his expression hard, as if he'd suddenly realized she wasn't completely wrong about his mother and sister and it bothered him.

She wished she could understand why he felt so strongly about putting a stop to his father playing matchmaker. As someone whose parents were ambivalent about her existence, his disregard for his family's well wishes was hard to comprehend.

"Okay," she said. "Fine by me. And you just want me to...be my charming self?"

"Obviously we'll have to come up with a story about our relationship. We don't have to make up how we met. We can say we met through the ad."

"The ad your father placed, not the ad you placed."

"Naturally."

She looked at Joshua then, at the broad expanse of table between them. Two people who looked less like a couple probably didn't exist on the face of the planet. Honestly, two strangers standing across the street from each other probably looked more like a happily engaged unit than they did.

She frowned. "This is very unconvincing."

"What is? Be specific."

She rolled her eyes at his impatience. "Us."

She stood up and walked toward him, sitting down in the chair right next to him. She looked at him for a moment, at the sharp curve of his jaw, the enticing shape of his lips. He was an attractive man. That was an understatement. He was also so uptight she was pretty sure he had a stick up his behind.

"Look, you want your family to think you've lost your mind, to think you have hooked up with a totally unsuitable woman, right?"

"That is the game."

"Then you have to look like you've lost your mind over me. Unfortunately, Joshua, you look very much in your right mind. In fact, a man of sounder mind may not exist. You are…responsible. You literally look like The Man."

"Which man?"

"Like, The Man. Like, fight the power. *You're* the power. Nobody's going to believe you're with me. At least, not if you don't seem a little bit…looser."

A slight smile tipped up those lips she had been thinking about only a moment before. His blue eyes warmed, and she felt an answering warmth spread low in her belly. "So what you're saying is we need to look like we have more of a connection?"

Her throat went dry. "It's just a suggestion."

He leaned forward, his gaze intent on hers. "An essential one, I think." Then he reached up and she jerked backward, nearly toppling off the side of her chair. "It looks like I'm not the only one who's wound a bit tight."

"I'm not," she said, taking a deep breath, trying to get her jittery body to calm itself down.

She wasn't used to men. She wasn't used to men touching her. Yes, intermittently she and her mother had lived with some of her mother's boyfriends, but none of them had ever been inappropriate with her. And she had never been close enough to even give any of them hugs.

And she really, really wasn't used to men who were so beautiful it was almost physically painful to look directly at them.

"You're right. We have to do a better job of looking like a couple. And that would include you not scampering under the furniture when I get close to you."

She sat up straight and folded her hands in her lap. "I did not scamper," she muttered.

"You were perilously close to a scamper."

"Was not," she grumbled, and then her breath caught in her throat as his warm palm made contact with her cheek.

He slid his thumb down the curve of her face to that dent just beneath her lips, his eyes never leaving hers. She felt…stunned and warm. No, hot. So very hot. Like there was a furnace inside that had been turned up the moment his hand touched her bare skin.

She supposed she was meant to be flirtatious. To play the part of the moneygrubbing tart with loose morals he needed her to be, that his family would expect her to be. But right now, she was shocked into immobility.

She took a deep breath, fighting for composure. But his thumb migrated from the somewhat reasonable point just below her mouth to her lip and her composure dissolved completely. His touch felt…shockingly intimate and filthy somehow. Not in a bad way, just in a way she'd never experienced before.

For some reason she would never be able to articulate—not even to herself—she darted her tongue out and touched the tip to his thumb. She tasted salt, skin and a promise that arrowed downward to the most private part of her body, leaving her feeling breathless. Leaving her feeling new somehow.

As if a wholly unexpected and previously unknown part of herself had been uncovered, awoken. She wanted to do exactly what he had accused her of doing earlier. She wanted to turn away. Wanted to scurry beneath the furniture or off into the night. Somewhere safe. Somewhere less confrontational.

But he was still looking at her. And those blue eyes were like chains, lashing her to the seat, holding her in place. And his thumb, pressed against her lip, felt heavy. Much too heavy for her to push against. For her to fight.

And when it came right down to it, she didn't even want to.

Something expanded in her chest, spreading low, opening up a yawning chasm in her stomach. Deepening her need, her want. Her desire for things she hadn't known she could desire until now.

Until he had made a promise with his touch that she hadn't known she wanted fulfilled.

She was just about to come back to herself, to pull away. And then he closed the distance between them.

His lips were warm and firm. The kiss was nothing like she had imagined it might be. She had always thought a kiss must reach inside and steal your brain. Transform you. She had always imagined a kiss to be powerful, considering the way her mother acted.

When her mother was under the influence of love—at least, that was what her mother had called it; Danielle had always known it was lust—she acted like someone entirely apart from herself.

Yes, Danielle had always known a kiss could be powerful. But what she hadn't counted on was that she might feel wholly like *herself* when a man fused his lips to hers. That she would be so perfectly aware of where she was, of what she was doing.

Of the pressure of his lips against hers, the warmth of his hand as he cradled her face, the hard, tightening knot of desire in her stomach that told her how insufficient the kiss was.

The desire that told her just how much more she wanted. Just how much more there could be.

He was kissing her well, this near stranger, and she never wanted it to end.

Instinctively, she angled her head slightly, parting her lips, allowing him to slide his tongue against hers. It was unexpectedly slick, unexpectedly arousing. Unexpectedly everything she wanted.

That was the other thing that surprised her. Because not only had she imagined a woman might lose herself entirely when a man kissed her, she had also imagined she would be immune. Because she knew better. She knew the cost. But she was sitting here, allowing him to kiss her and kiss her and kiss her. She was Danielle Kelly, and she was submitting herself to this sensual assault with almost shocking abandon.

Her hands were still folded in her lap, almost primly, but her mouth was parted wide, gratefully receiving every stroke of his tongue, slow and languorous against her own. Sexy. Deliciously affecting.

He moved his hands then, sliding them around the back of her neck, down between her shoulder blades, along the line of her spine until his hands spanned her waist. She arched, wishing she could press her body against his. Wishing she could do something to close the distance between them. Because he was still sitting in his chair and she in hers.

He pulled away, and she followed him, leaning into him with an almost humiliating desperation, wanting to taste him again. To be kissed again. By Joshua Grayson, the man she was committing an insane kind of fraud with. The man who had hired her to play the part of his pretend fiancée.

"That will do," he said, lifting his hand and squeezing her chin gently, those blue eyes glinting with a sharpness that cut straight to her soul. "Yes, Ms. Kelly, that will do quite nicely."

Then he released his hold on her completely, settling back in his seat, his attention returning to his dinner plate.

A slash of heat bled across Danielle's cheekbones. He hadn't felt anything at all. He had been proving a point. Just practicing the ruse they would be performing for his family tomorrow night. The kiss hadn't changed anything for him at all. Hadn't been more than the simple meeting of mouths.

It had been her first kiss. It had been everything.

And right then she got her first taste of just how badly a man could make a woman feel. Of how—when wounded—feminine pride could be a treacherous and testy thing.

She rose from her seat and rounded to stand behind his. Then, without fully pausing to think about what she might be doing, she placed her hands on his shoulders, leaned forward and slid her hands beneath the collar of his shirt and down his chest.

Her palms made contact with his hot skin, with hard muscle, and she had to bite her lip to keep from groaning out loud. She had to plant her feet firmly on the wood floor to keep herself from running away, from jerking her hands back like a child burned on a hot oven.

She'd never touched a man like this before. It was shocking just how arousing she found it, this little form of revenge, this little rebellion against his blasé response to the earthquake he had caused in her body.

She leaned her head forward, nearly pressing her lips against his ear. Then her teeth scraped his earlobe.

"Yes," she whispered. "I think it's quite convincing."

She straightened again, slowly running her fingernails over his skin as she did. She didn't know where this confidence had come from. Where the know-how and seemingly deep, feminine instinct had come from that allowed her to toy with him. But there it was.

She was officially playing the part of a saucy minx. Considering that was what he had hired her for, her flirtation was a good thing. But her heart thundered harder than a drum as she walked back to Riley, picked up his carrier and flipped her hair as she turned to face Joshua.

"I think I'm going to bed. I had best prepare myself to meet your family."

"You'll be wearing something different tomorrow," he said, his tone firm.

"Why?" She looked down at her ragged sweatshirt and skinny jeans. "That doesn't make any sense. You wanted me to look unsuitable. I might as well go in this."

"No, you brought up a very good point. You have to look unsuitable, but this situation also has to be believable. Plus, I think a gold digger would demand a new wardrobe, don't you?" One corner of his lips quirked upward, and she had a feeling he was punishing her for her little display a moment ago.

If only she could work out quite where the trap was.

"I don't know," she said, her voice stiff.

"But, Ms. Kelly, you told me yourself that you *are* a gold digger. That's why you're here, after all. For my gold."

"I suppose so," she said, keeping her words deliberately hard. "But I want actual gold, not clothes. So this is another thing that's going to be on you."

Those blue eyes glinted, and right then she got an idea of just how dangerous he was to her. "Consider it done."

And if there was one thing she had learned so far about Joshua Grayson, it was that if he said something would be done, it would be.

Chapter 5

Joshua wasn't going to try to turn Danielle into a sophisticate overnight. He was also avoiding thinking about the way it had felt to kiss her soft lips. Was avoiding remembering the way her hands had felt sliding down his chest.

He needed to make sure the two of them looked like a couple, that much was true. But he wouldn't allow himself to be distracted by her. There were a million reasons not to touch Danielle Kelly—unless they were playing a couple. Yes, there would have to be some touching, but he was not going to take advantage of her.

First of all, she was at his financial mercy. Second of all, she was the kind of woman who came with entanglements. And he didn't want any entanglements.

He wasn't the type to have trouble with self-control. If it wasn't a good time to seek out a physical relationship, he didn't. It wasn't a good time now, which meant he would defer any kind of sexual gratification until the end of his association with Danielle.

That should be fine.

He should be able to consider any number of women who he had on-again, off-again associations with, choose one and get in touch with her after Danielle left. His mind and body should be set on that.

Sadly, all he could think of was last night's kiss and the shocking heat that had come with it.

And then Danielle came down the stairs wearing the simple black dress he'd had delivered for her.

His thoughts about not transforming her into a sophisticated woman overnight held true. Her long, straight brown hair still hung limp down to her waist, and she had no makeup on to speak of except pale pink gloss on her lips.

But the simple cut of the dress suited her slender figure and displayed small, perky breasts that had been hidden beneath her baggy, threadbare sweaters.

She was holding on to the handle of the baby's car seat with both hands, lugging it down the stairs. For one moment, he was afraid she might topple over. He moved forward quickly, grabbing the handle and taking the seat from her.

When he looked down at the sleeping child, a strange tightness invaded his chest. "It wouldn't be good for you or for Riley if you fell and broke your neck trying to carry something that's too heavy for you," he said, his tone harder than he'd intended it to be.

Danielle scowled. "Well, offer assistance earlier next time. I had to get down the stairs somehow. Anyway, I've been navigating stairs like this with the baby since he was born. I lived in an apartment. On the third floor."

"I imagine he's heavier now than he used to be."

"An expert on child development?" She arched one dark brow as she posed the question.

He gritted his teeth. "Hardly."

She stepped away from the stairs, and the two of them walked toward the door. Just because he wanted to make it clear that he was in charge of the evening, he placed his hand low on her back, right at the dip where her spine curved, right above what the dress revealed to be a magnificent backside.

He had touched her there to get to her, but he had not anticipated the touch getting to him.

He ushered her out quickly, then handed the car seat to her, allowing her to snap it into the base—the one he'd had installed in his car when all of the nursery accoutrements had been delivered—then sat waiting for her to get in.

As they started to pull out of the driveway, she wrapped her arms around herself, rubbing her hands over her bare skin. "Do you think you could turn the heater on?"

He frowned. "Why didn't you bring a jacket?"

"I don't have one? All I have are my sweaters. And I don't think either of them would go with the dress. Would kind of ruin the effect."

He put the brakes on, slipped out of his own jacket and handed it to her. She just looked at him like he was offering her a live gopher. "Take it," he said.

She frowned but reached out, taking the jacket and slipping it on. "Thank you," she said, her voice sounding hollow.

They drove to his parents' house in silence, the only sounds coming from the baby sitting in the back seat. A sobering reminder of the evening that was about to unfold.

He was going to present a surprise fiancée and a surprise baby to his parents, and suddenly, he didn't look at this plan in quite the same way as he had before.

He was throwing Danielle into the deep end. Throwing Riley into the deep end.

Joshua gritted his teeth, tightening his hold on the steering wheel. Finally, the interminable drive through town was over. He turned left off a winding road and onto a dirt drive that led back to the familiar, humble farmhouse his parents still called home.

That some part of his heart still called home too.

He looked over at Danielle, who had gone pale. "It's fine," he said.

Danielle looked down at the ring on her finger, then back up at him. "I guess it's showtime."

Danielle felt warm all over, no longer in need of Joshua's jacket, and conflicted down to the brand-new shoes Joshua had ordered for her.

But it wasn't the dress, or the shoes, that had her feeling warm. It was the jacket. Well, obviously a jacket was supposed to make her warm, but this was different. Joshua had realized she was cold. And it had mattered to him.

He had given her his own jacket so she could keep warm.

It was too big, the sleeves went well past the edges of her fingertips, and it smelled like him. From the moment she had slipped it on, she had been fighting the urge to bury her nose in the fabric and lose herself in the sharp, masculine smell that reminded her of his skin. Skin she had tasted last night.

Standing on the front step of this modest farmhouse that she could hardly believe Joshua had ever lived in, wearing his coat, with him holding Riley's car seat, it was too easy to believe this actually was some kind of "meet the parents" date.

In effect, she supposed it was. She was even wearing his jacket. His jacket that was still warm from his body and smelled—

Danielle was still ruminating about the scent of Joshua's jacket when the door opened. A blonde woman with graying hair and blue eyes that looked remarkably like her son's gave them a warm smile.

"Joshua," she said, glancing sideways at Danielle and clearly doing her best not to look completely shocked, "I didn't expect you so early. And I didn't know you were bringing a guest." Her eyes fell to the carrier in Joshua's hand. "Two guests."

"I thought it would be a good surprise."

"What would be?"

A man who could only be Joshua's father came to the door behind the woman. He was tall, with dark hair and eyes. He looked nice too. They both did. There was a warmth to them, a kindness, that didn't seem to be present in their son.

But then Danielle felt the warmth of the jacket again, and she had to revise that thought. Joshua might not exude kindness, but it was definitely there, buried. And for the life of her, she couldn't figure out why he hid it.

She was prickly and difficult, but at least she had an excuse. Her family was the worst. As far as she could tell, his family was guilty of caring too much. And she just couldn't feel that sorry for a rich dude whose parents loved him and were involved in his life more than he wanted them to be.

"Who is this?" Joshua's father asked.

"Danielle, this is my mom and dad, Todd and Nancy Grayson. Mom, Dad, this is Danielle Kelly," Joshua said smoothly. "And I have you to thank for meeting her, Dad."

His father's eyebrows shot upward. "Do you?"

"Yes," Joshua said. "She responded to your ad. Mom, Dad, Danielle is my fiancée."

They were ushered into the house quickly after that announcement, and there were a lot of exclamations. The house was already full. A young woman sat in the corner holding hands with a large, tattooed man who was built like a brick house and was clearly related to Joshua somehow. There was another man, as tall as Joshua, with slightly darker hair and the same blue eyes but who didn't carry himself quite as stiffly. His build was somewhere in between Joshua and the tattooed man, muscular but not a beast.

"My brother Devlin," Joshua said, indicating the tattooed man before putting his arm around Danielle's waist as they moved deeper into the room, "and his wife, Mia. And this is my brother Isaiah. I'm surprised his capable assistant, Poppy, isn't somewhere nearby."

"Isaiah, did you want a beer or whiskey?" A petite woman appeared from the kitchen area, her curly, dark hair swept back into a bun, a few stray pieces bouncing around her pretty face. She was impeccable. From that elegant updo down to the soles of her tiny, high-heeled feet. She was wearing a high-waisted skirt that flared out at the hips and fell down past her knees, along with a plain, fitted top.

"Is that his…girlfriend?" Danielle asked.

Poppy laughed. "Absolutely not," she said, her tone clipped. "I'm his assistant."

Danielle thought it strange that an assistant would be at a family gathering but didn't say anything.

"She's more than an assistant," Nancy Grayson said. "She's part of the family. She's been with them since they started the business."

Danielle had not been filled in on the details of his family's relationships because she only needed to know how to alienate them, not how to endear herself to them.

The front door opened again and this time it was a younger blonde woman whose eyes also matched Joshua's who walked in. "Sorry I'm late," she said, "I got caught up working on a project."

This had to be his sister, Faith. The architect he talked about with such pride and fondness. A woman who was Danielle's age and yet so much more successful they might be completely different species.

"This is Joshua's fiancée," Todd Grayson said. "He's engaged."

"Shut the front door," Faith said. "Are you really?"

"Yes," Joshua said, the lie rolling easily off his tongue.

Danielle bit back a comment about his PR skills. She was supposed to be hard to deal with, but they weren't supposed to call attention to the fact this was a ruse.

"That's great?" Faith took a step forward and hugged her brother, then leaned in to grab hold of Danielle, as well.

"Is nobody going to ask about the baby?" Isaiah asked.

"Obviously *you* are," Devlin said.

"Well, it's kind of the eight-hundred-pound gorilla in the room. Or the ten-pound infant."

"It's my baby," Danielle said, feeling color mount in her cheeks.

She noticed a slight shift in Joshua's father's expression. Which was the general idea. To make him suspicious of her. To make him think he had gone and caught his son a gold digger.

"Well, that's…" She could see Joshua's mother searching for words. "It's definitely unexpected." She looked apologetically at Danielle the moment the words left her mouth. "It's just that Joshua hasn't shown much interest in marriage or family."

Danielle had a feeling that was an understatement. If Joshua was willing to go to such lengths to get his father out of his business, then he must be about as anti-marriage as you could get.

"Well," Joshua said, "Danielle and I met because of Dad."

His mother's blue gaze sharpened. "How?"

His father looked guilty. "Well, I thought he could use a little help," he said finally.

"What kind of help?"

"It's not good for a man to be alone, especially not our boys," he said insistently.

"Some of us like to be alone," Isaiah pointed out.

"You wouldn't feel that way if you didn't have a woman who cooked for you and ran your errands," his father responded, looking pointedly at Poppy.

"She's an employee," Isaiah said.

Poppy looked more irritated and distressed by Isaiah's comment than she did by the Grayson family patriarch's statement. But she didn't say anything.

"You were right," Joshua said. "I just needed to find the right woman. You placed that ad, listing all of my assets, and the right woman responded."

This was so ridiculous. Danielle felt her face heating. The assets Joshua's father had listed were his bank account, and there was no way in the world that wasn't exactly what everyone in his family was thinking.

She knew this was her chance to confirm her gold-digging motives. But right then, Riley started to cry.

"Oh," she said, feeling flustered. "Just let me… I need to…"

She fumbled around with the new diaper bag, digging around for a bottle, and then went over to the car seat, taking the baby out of it.

"Let me help," Joshua's mother said.

She was being so kind. Danielle felt terrible.

But before Danielle could protest, the other woman was taking Riley from her arms. Riley wiggled and fussed, but then she efficiently plucked the bottle from Danielle's hand and stuck it right in his mouth. He quieted immediately.

"What a good baby," she said. "Does he usually go to strangers?"

Danielle honestly didn't know. "Other than a neighbor whose known him since he was born, I'm the only one who takes care of him," she said.

"Don't you have any family?"

Danielle shook her head, feeling every inch the curiosity she undoubtedly was. Every single eye in the room was trained on her, and she knew they were all waiting for her to make a mistake. She was *supposed* to make a mistake, dammit. That was what Joshua was paying her to do.

"I don't have any family," she said decisively. "It's just been me and Riley from the beginning."

"It must be nice to have some help now," Faith said, not unkindly, but definitely probing.

"It is," Danielle said. "I mean, it's really hard taking

care of a baby by yourself. And I didn't make enough money to…well, anything. So meeting Joshua has been great. Because he's so…helpful."

A timer went off in the other room and Joshua's mother blinked. "Oh, I have to get dinner." She turned to her son. "Since you're so helpful, Joshua." And before Danielle could protest, before Joshua could protest, Nancy dumped Riley right into his arms.

He looked like he'd been handed a bomb. And frankly, Danielle felt a little bit like a bomb might detonate at any moment. It had not escaped her notice that Joshua had never touched Riley. Yes, he had carried his car seat, but he had never voluntarily touched the baby. Which, now that she thought about it, must have been purposeful. But then, not everybody liked babies. She had never been particularly drawn to them before Riley. Maybe Joshua felt the same way.

She could tell by his awkward posture, and the way Riley's small frame was engulfed by Joshua's large, muscular one, that any contact with babies was not something he was used to.

She imagined Joshua's reaction would go a long way in proving how unsuitable she was. Maybe not in the way he had hoped, but it definitely made his point.

He took a seat on the couch, still holding on to Riley, still clearly committed to the farce.

"So you met through an ad," Isaiah said, his voice full of disbelief. "An ad that Dad put in the paper."

Everyone's head swiveled, and they looked at Todd. "I did what any concerned father would do for his son."

Devlin snorted. "Thank God I found a wife on my own."

"You found a wife by pilfering from my friendship

pool," Faith said, her tone disapproving. "Isaiah and Joshua have too much class to go picking out women that young."

"Actually," Danielle said, deciding this was the perfect opportunity to highlight another of the many ways in which she was unsuitable, "I'm only twenty-two."

Joshua's father looked at him, his gaze sharp. "Really?"

"Really," Danielle said.

"That's unexpected," Todd said to his son.

"That's what's so great about how we met," Joshua said. "Had I looked for a life partner on my own, I probably would have chosen somebody with a completely different set of circumstances. Had you asked me only a few short weeks ago, I would have said I didn't want children. And now look at me."

Everybody *was* looking at him, and it was clear he was extremely uncomfortable. Danielle wasn't entirely sure he was making the point he hoped to make, but he did make a pretty amusing picture. "I also would have chosen somebody closer to my age. But the great thing about Danielle is that she is so mature. I think it's because she's a mother. And yes, it happened for her in non-ideal circumstances, but her ability to rise above her situation and solve her problems—namely by responding to the ad—is one of the many things I find attractive about her."

She wanted to kick him in the shin. He was being a complete jerk, and he was making her sound like a total flake... But that was the whole idea. And, honestly, given the information Joshua had about her life...he undoubtedly thought she *was* a flake. It was stupid, and it wasn't fair. One of the many things she had learned about people since becoming the sole caregiver for Riley was that even though everyone had sex, a woman was an immediate pariah the minute she bore the evidence of that sex.

All that mattered to the hypocrites was that Danielle appeared to be a scarlet woman, therefore she was one.

Never mind that in reality she was a virgin.

Which was not a word she needed to be thinking while sitting in the Grayson family living room.

Her cheeks felt hot, like they were being stung by bees.

"Fate is a funny thing," Danielle said, edging closer to Joshua. She took Riley out of his arms, and from the way Joshua surrendered the baby, she could tell he was more than ready to hand him over.

The rest of the evening passed in a blur of awkward moments and stilted conversation. It was clear to her that his family was wonderful and warm, but that they were also seriously questioning Joshua's decision making. Todd Grayson looked as if he was going to be physically assaulted by his wife.

Basically, everything was going according to Joshua's plan.

But Danielle couldn't feel happy about it. She couldn't feel triumphant. It just felt awful.

Finally, it was time to go, and Danielle was ready to scurry out the door and keep on scurrying away from the entire Grayson family—Joshua included.

She was gathering her things, and Joshua was talking to one of his brothers, when Faith approached.

"We haven't gotten a chance to talk yet," she said.

"I guess not," Danielle said, feeling instantly wary. She had a feeling that being approached by Joshua's younger sister like this wouldn't end well.

"I'm sure he's told you all about me," Faith said, and Danielle had a feeling that statement was a test.

"Of course he has." She sounded defensive, even though there was no reason for her to feel defensive, except that she kind of did anyway.

"Great. So here's the thing. I don't know exactly what's going on here, but my brother is not a 'marriage and babies' kind of guy. My brother dates a seemingly endless stream of models, all of whom are about half a foot taller than you without their ridiculous high heels on. Also, he likes blondes."

Danielle felt her face heating again as the other woman appraised her and found her lacking. "Right. Well. Maybe I'm a really great conversationalist. Although, it could be the fact that I don't have a gag reflex."

She watched the other woman's cheeks turn bright pink and felt somewhat satisfied. Unsophisticated, virginal Danielle had made the clearly much more sophisticated Faith Grayson blush.

"Right. Well, if you're leading him around by his… *you know*…so you can get into his wallet, I'm not going to allow that. There's a reason he's avoided commitment all this time. And I'm not going to let you hurt him. He's been hurt enough," she said.

Danielle could only wonder what that meant, because Joshua seemed bulletproof.

"I'm not going to break up with him," Danielle said. "Why would I do that? I'd rather stay in his house than in a homeless shelter."

She wanted to punch her own face. And she was warring with the fact that Faith had rightly guessed that she was using Joshua for his money—though not in the way his sister assumed. And Danielle needed Faith to think the worst. But it also hurt to have her assume something so negative based on Danielle's circumstances. Based on her appearance.

People had been looking at Danielle and judging her as low-class white trash for so long—not exactly incorrectly—that it was a sore spot.

"We're a close family," Faith said. "And we look out for each other. Just remember that."

"Well, your brother loves me."

"If that's true," Faith said, "then I hope you're very happy together. I actually do hope it's true. But the problem is, I'm not sure I believe it."

"Why?" Danielle was bristling, and there was no reason on earth why she should be. She shouldn't be upset about this. She shouldn't be taking it personally. But she was.

Faith Grayson had taken one look at Danielle and judged her. Pegged her for exactly the kind of person she was, really—a low-class nobody who needed the kind of money and security a man like Joshua could provide. Danielle had burned her pride to the ground to take part in this charade. Poking at the embers of that pride was stupid. But she felt compelled to do it anyway.

"Is it because I'm some kind of skank he would never normally sully himself with?"

"Mostly, it's because I know my brother. And I know he never intended to be in any kind of serious relationship again."

Again.

That word rattled around inside of Danielle. It implied he had been in a serious relationship before. He hadn't mentioned that. He'd just said he didn't want his father meddling. Didn't want marriage. He hadn't said it was because he'd tried before.

She blinked.

Faith took that momentary hesitation and ran with it. "So you don't know that much about him. You don't actually know anything about him, do you? You just know he's rich."

"And he's hot," Danielle said.

She wasn't going to back down. Not now. But she would have a few very grumpy words with Joshua once they left.

He hadn't prepared her for this. She looked like an idiot. As she gathered her things, she realized looking like an idiot was his objective. She could look bad in a great many ways, after all. The fact that they might be an unsuitable couple because she didn't know anything about him would be one way to accomplish that.

When she and Joshua finally stepped outside, heading back to the car amid a thunderous farewell from the family, Danielle felt like she could breathe for the first time in at least two hours. She hadn't realized it, but being inside that house—all warm and cozy and filled with the kind of love she had only ever seen in movies—had made her throat and lungs and chest, and even her fingers, feel tight.

They got into the car, and Danielle folded her arms tightly, leaning her head against the cold passenger-side window, her breath fanning out across the glass, leaving mist behind. She didn't bother fighting the urge to trace a heart in it.

"Feeling that in character?" Joshua asked, his tone dry, as he put the car in Reverse and began to pull out of the driveway.

She stuck her tongue out and scribbled over the heart. "Not particularly. I don't understand. Now that I've met them, I understand even less. Your sister grilled me the minute she got a chance to talk to me alone. Your father is worried about the situation. Your mother is trying to be supportive in spite of the fact that we are clearly the worst couple of all time. And you're doing this why, Joshua? I don't understand."

She hadn't meant to call him out in quite that way. After all, what did she care about his motivations? He was paying her. The fact that he was a rich, eccentric idiot kind of worked in her favor. But tonight had felt wrong. And while she was more into survival than into the nuances of right and wrong, the ruse was getting to her.

"I explained to you already," he said, his tone so hard it elicited a small, plaintive cry from Riley in the back.

"Don't wake up the baby," she snapped.

"We really are a convincing couple," he responded.

"Not to your sister. Who told me we didn't make any sense together because you had never shown any interest in falling in love *again.*"

It was dark in the car, so she felt rather than saw the tension creep up his spine. It was in the way he shifted in his seat, how his fists rolled forward as he twisted his hands on the steering wheel.

"Well," he said, "that's the thing. They all know. Because family like mine doesn't leave well enough alone. They want to know about all your injuries, all your scars, and then they obsess over the idea that they might be able to heal them. And they don't listen when you tell them healing is not necessary."

"Right," she said, blowing out an exasperated breath.

"Here's the thing. I'm just a dumb bimbo you picked up through a newspaper ad who needed your money. So I don't understand all this coded nonsense. Just tell me what's going on. Especially if I'm going to spend more nights trying to alienate your family—who are basically a childhood sitcom fantasy of what a family should be."

"I've done it before, Danielle. Love. It's not worth it. Not considering how badly it hurts when it ends. But even more, it's not worth it when you consider how badly you can hurt the other person."

His words fell flat in the car, and she didn't know how to respond to them. "I don't…"

"Details aren't important. You've been hurt before, haven't you?"

He turned the car off the main road and headed up the long drive to his house. She took a deep breath. "Yes."

"By Riley's father?"

She shifted uncomfortably. "Not exactly."

"You didn't love him?"

"No," she said. "I didn't love him. But my mother kind of did a number on me. I do understand that love hurts. I also understand that a supportive family is not necessarily guaranteed."

"Yeah," Joshua said, "supportive family is great." He put the car in Park and killed the engine before getting out and stalking toward the house.

Danielle frowned, then unbuckled quickly, getting out of the car and pushing the sleeves of Joshua's jacket back so she could get Riley's car seat out of the base. Then she headed up the stairs and into the house after him.

"And yet you are trying to hurt yours. So excuse me if I'm not making all the connections."

"I'm not trying to hurt my family," he said, turning

around, pushing his hand through his blond hair. His blue eyes glittered, his jaw suddenly looking sharper, his cheekbones more hollow. "What I want is for them to leave well enough alone. My father doesn't understand. He thinks all I need is to find somebody to love again and I'm going to be fixed. But there is no fixing this. There's no fixing me. I don't want it. And yeah, maybe this scheme is over the top, but don't you think putting an ad in the paper looking for a wife for your son is over the top too? I'm not giving him back anything he didn't dish out."

"Maybe you could talk to him."

"You think I haven't talked to him? You think this was my first resort? You're wrong about that. I tried reasonable discourse, but you can't reason with an unreasonable man."

"Yeah," Danielle said, picking at the edge of her thumbnail. "He seemed like a real monster. What with the clear devotion to your mother, the fact that he raised all of you, that he supported you well enough that you could live in that house all your life and then go off to become more successful than he was."

She set the car seat down on the couch and unbuckled it, lifting Riley into her arms and heading toward the stairs.

"We didn't have anything when I was growing up," he said, his tone flat and strange.

Danielle swallowed hard, lifting her hand to cradle Riley's soft head. "I'm sorry. But unless you were homeless or were left alone while one of your parents went to work all day—and I mean *alone*, not with siblings—then we might have different definitions of nothing."

"Fine," he said. "We weren't that poor. But we didn't

have anything extra, and there was definitely nothing to do around here but get into trouble when you didn't have money."

She blinked. "What kind of trouble?"

"The usual kind. Go out to the woods, get messed up, have sex."

"Last I checked, condoms and drugs cost money." She held on to Riley a little bit tighter. "Pretty sure you could have bought a movie ticket."

He lifted his shoulder. "Look, we pooled our money. We did what we did. Didn't worry about the future, didn't worry about anything."

"What changed?" Because obviously something had. He hadn't stayed here. He hadn't stayed aimless.

"One day I looked up and realized this was all I would ever have unless I changed something. Let me tell you, that's pretty sobering. A future of farming, barely making it, barely scraping by? That's what my dad had. And I hated it. I drank in the woods every night with my friends to avoid that reality. I didn't want to have my dad's life. So I made some changes. Not really soon enough to improve my grades or get myself a full scholarship, but I ended up moving to Seattle and getting myself an entry-level job with a PR firm."

"You just moved? You didn't know anybody?"

"No. I didn't know anyone. But I met people. And, it turned out, I was good at meeting people. Which was interesting because you don't meet very many new people in a small town that you've lived in your entire life. But in Seattle, no one knew me. No one knew who my father was, and no one had expectations for me. I was judged entirely on my own merit, and I could completely rewrite who I was. Not just some small-town deadbeat, but a young, bright kid who had a future in front of him."

The way he told that story, the very idea of it, was tantalizing to Danielle. The idea of starting over. Having a clean slate. Of course, with a baby in tow, a change like that would be much more difficult. But her association with Joshua would allow her to make it happen.

It was…shocking to realize he'd had to start over once. Incredibly encouraging, even though she was feeling annoyed with him at the moment.

She leaned forward and absently pressed a kiss to Riley's head. "That must've been incredible. And scary."

"The only scary thing was the idea of going back to where I came from without changing anything. So I didn't allow that to happen. I worked harder than everybody else. I set goals and I met them. And then I met Shannon."

Something ugly twisted inside of Danielle's stomach the moment he said the other woman's name. For the life of her she couldn't figure out why. She felt…curious. But in a desperate way. Like she needed to know everything about this other person. This person who had once shared Joshua's life. This person who had undoubtedly made him the man standing in front of her. If she didn't know about this woman, then she would never understand him.

"What, then? Who was Shannon?" Her desperation was evident in her words, and she didn't bother hiding it.

"She was my girlfriend. For four years, while I was getting established in Seattle. We lived together. I was going to ask her to marry me."

He looked away from her then, something in his blue eyes turning distant. "Then she found out she was pregnant, and I figured I could skip the elaborate proposal and move straight to the wedding."

She knew him well enough to know this story wasn't headed toward a happy ending. He didn't have a wife. He didn't have a child. In fact, she was willing to bet he'd never had a child. Based on the way he interacted with Riley. Or rather, the very practiced way he avoided interacting with Riley.

"That didn't happen," she said, because she didn't know what else to say, and part of her wanted to spare him having to tell the rest of the story. But, also, part of her needed to know.

"She wanted to plan the wedding. She wanted to wait until after the baby was born. You know, wedding dress sizes and stuff like that. So I agreed. She miscarried late, Danielle. Almost five months. It was…the most physically harrowing thing I've ever watched anyone go through. But the recovery was worse. And I didn't know what to do. So I went back to work. We had a nice apartment, we had a view of the city, and if I worked, she didn't have to. I could support her, I could buy her things. I could do my best to make her happy, keep her focused on the wedding."

He had moved so quickly through the devastating, painful revelation of his lost baby that she barely had time to process it. But she also realized he had to tell the story this way. There was no point lingering on the details. It was simple fact. He had been with a woman he loved very much. He had intended to marry her, had been expecting a child with her. And they had lost the baby.

She held on a little bit more tightly to Riley.

"She kept getting worse. Emotionally. She moved into a different bedroom, then she didn't get out of bed. She had a lot of pain. At first, I didn't question it, because it seemed reasonable that she'd need pain medication after what she went through. But then she kept taking it. And I wondered if that was okay. We had a fight about it. She said it wasn't right for me to question her pain—physical or otherwise—when all I did was work. And you know… I thought she was probably right. So I let it go. For a year, I let it go. And then I found out the situation with the prescription drugs was worse than I realized. But when I confronted Shannon, she just got angry."

It was so strange for Danielle to imagine what he was telling her. This whole other life he'd had. In a city where he had lived with a woman and loved her. Where he had dreamed of having a family. Of having a child. Where he had buried himself in work to avoid dealing with the pain of loss, while the woman he loved lost herself in a different way.

The tale seemed so far removed from the man he was now. From this place, from that hard set to his jaw, that sharp glitter in his eye, the way he held his shoulders straight. She couldn't imagine this man feeling at a loss. Feeling helpless.

"She got involved with another man, someone I worked with. Maybe it started before she left me, but I'm not entirely sure. All I know is she wasn't sleeping with me at the time, so even if she was with him before she moved out, it hardly felt like cheating. And anyway, the affair wasn't really the important part. That guy was into recreational drug use. It's how he functioned. And he made it all available to her."

"That's…that's awful, Joshua. I know how bad that stuff can be. I've seen it."

He shook his head. "Do you have any idea what it's

like? To have somebody come into your life who's beautiful, happy, and to watch her leave your life as something else entirely. Broken, an addict. I ruined her."

Danielle took a step back, feeling as though she had been struck by the impact of his words. "No, you didn't. It was drugs. It was…"

"I wasn't there for her. I didn't know how to be. I didn't like hard things, Danielle. I never did. I didn't want to stay in Copper Ridge and work the land—I didn't want to deal with a lifetime of scraping by, because it was too hard."

"Right. You're so lazy that you moved to Seattle and started from scratch and worked your way to the highest ranks of the company? I don't buy that."

"There's reward in that kind of work, though. And you don't have to deal with your life when it gets bad. You just go work more. And you can tell yourself it's fine because you're making more money. Because you're making your life easier, life for the other person easier, even while you let them sit on the couch slowly dying, waiting for you to help them. I convinced myself that what I was doing was important. It was the worst kind of narcissism, Danielle, and I'm not going to excuse it."

"But that was… It was a unique circumstance. And you're different. And…it's not like every future relationship…"

"And here's the problem. You don't know me. You don't even like me and yet you're trying to fix this. You're trying to convince me I should give relationships another try. It's your first instinct, and you don't even actually care. My father can't stop any more than you could stop yourself just now. So I did this." He gestured between the two of them. "I did this because he escalated it all the way to putting an ad in the paper. Because he won't listen to me. Because he knows my ex is a junkie somewhere living on the damned street, and that I feel responsible for that, and still he wants me to live his life. This life here, where he's never made a single mistake or let anyone down."

Danielle had no idea what to say to that. She imagined that his dad had made mistakes. But what did she know? She only knew about absentee fathers and mothers who treated their children like afterthoughts.

Her arms were starting to ache. Her chest ached too. All of her ached.

"I'm going to take Riley up to bed," she said, turning and heading up the stairs.

She didn't look back, but she could hear the heavy footfalls behind her, and she knew he was following her. Even if she didn't quite understand why.

She walked into her bedroom, and she left the door open. She crossed the space and set Riley down in the crib. He shifted for a moment, stretching his arms up above his head and kicking his feet out. But he didn't wake up. She was sweaty from having his warm little body pressed against her chest, but she was grateful for that feeling now. Thinking about Joshua and his loss made her feel especially grateful.

Joshua was standing in the doorway, looking at her. "Did you still want to argue with me?"

She shook her head. "I never wanted to argue with you."

She went to walk past him, but his big body blocked her path. She took a step toward him, and he refused to move, his blue eyes looking straight into hers.

"You seemed like you wanted to argue," he responded.

"No," she said, reaching up to press her hand against him, to push him out of the way. "I just wanted an explanation."

The moment her hand made contact with his shoulder, something raced through her. Something electric. Thrilling. Something that reached back to that feeling, that tightening low in her stomach when he'd first mentioned Shannon.

The two feelings were connected.

Jealousy. That was what she felt. Attraction. That was what this was.

She looked up, his chin in her line of sight. She saw a dusting of golden whiskers, and they looked prickly. His chin looked strong. The two things in combination—the strength and the prickliness—made her want to reach out and touch him, to test both of those hypotheses and see if either was true.

Touching him was craziness. She knew it was. So she curled her fingers into a fist and lowered her hand back down to her side.

"Tell me," he said, his voice rough. "After going through what you did, being pregnant. Being abandoned... You don't want to jump right back into relationships, do you?"

He didn't know the situation. And he didn't know it because she had purposefully kept it from him. Still, because of the circumstances surrounding Riley's birth, because of the way her mother had always conducted relationships with men, because of the way they had always ended, Danielle wanted to avoid romantic entanglements.

So she could find an honest answer in there somewhere.

"I don't want to jump into anything," she said, keeping

her voice even. "But there's a difference between being cautious and saying never."

"Is there?"

He had dipped his head slightly, and he seemed to loom over her, to fill her vision, to fill her senses. When she breathed in, the air was scented with him. When she felt warm, the warmth was from his body.

Her lips suddenly felt dry, and she licked them. Then became more aware of them than she'd ever been in her entire life. They felt...obvious. Needy.

She was afraid she knew exactly what they were needy for.

His mouth. His kiss.

The taste of him. The feel of him.

She wondered if he was thinking of their kiss too. Of course, for him, a kiss was probably a commonplace event.

For her, it had been singular.

"You can't honestly say you want to spend the rest of your life alone?"

"I'm only alone when I want to be," he said, his voice husky. "There's a big difference between wanting to share your life with somebody and wanting to share your bed sometimes." He tilted his head to the side. "Tell me. Have you shared your bed with anyone since you were with him?"

She shook her head, words, explanations, getting stuck in her throat. But before she knew it, she couldn't speak anyway, because he had closed the distance between them and claimed her mouth with his.

Chapter 6

He was hell bound, that much was certain. After everything that had happened tonight with his family, after Shannon, his fate had been set in stone. But if it hadn't been, then this kiss would have sealed that fate, padlocked it and flung it right down into the fire.

Danielle was young, she was vulnerable and contractually she was at his mercy to a certain degree. Kissing her, wanting to do more with her, was taking being jackass to extremes.

Right now, he didn't care.

If this was hell, he was happy to hang out for a while. If only he could keep kissing her, if only he could keep tasting her.

She held still against his body for a moment before angling her head, wrapping her arms around his neck, sliding her fingers through his hair and cupping the back of his head as if she was intent on holding him against her mouth.

As if she was concerned he might break the kiss. As if he was capable of that.

Sanity and reasonable decision making had exited the building the moment he had closed the distance between them. It wasn't coming back anytime soon. Not as long as she continued to make those sweet, kittenish noises. Not as long as she continued to stroke her tongue against his—tentatively at first and then with much more boldness.

He gripped the edge of the doorjamb, backing her against the frame, pressing his body against hers. He was hard, and he knew she would feel just how much he wanted her.

He slipped his hands around her waist, then down her behind to the hem of her dress. He shoved it upward, completely void of any sort of finesse. Void of anything beyond the need and desperation screaming inside of him to be inside her. To be buried so deep he wouldn't remember anything.

Not why he knew her. Why she was here. Not what had happened at his parents' house tonight. Not the horrific, unending sadness that had happened in his beautiful high-rise apartment overlooking the city he'd thought of as his. The penthouse that should have kept him above the struggle and insulated him from hardship.

Yeah, he didn't want to think about any of it.

He didn't want to think of anything but the way Danielle tasted. How soft her skin was to the touch.

Why the hell some skinny, bedraggled urchin had suddenly managed to light a fire inside of him was beyond him.

He didn't really care about the rationale right now. No. He just wanted to be burned.

He moved his hands around, then dipped one between her legs, rubbing his thumb against the silken fabric of her panties. She gasped, arching against him, wrenching her mouth away from his and letting her head fall back against the door frame.

That was an invitation to go further. He shifted his stance, drawing his hand upward and then down beneath the waistband of her underwear. He made contact with slick, damp skin that spoke of her desire for him. He had to clench his teeth to keep from embarrassing himself then and there.

He couldn't remember the last time a woman had affected him like this, if ever. When a simple touch, the promise of release, had pushed him so close to the edge.

When so little had felt like so much.

He stroked her, centering his attention on her most sensitive place. Her eyes flew open wide as if he had discovered something completely new. As if she was discovering something completely new. And that did things to him. Things it shouldn't do. Mattered in ways it shouldn't.

Because this shouldn't matter and neither should she.

He pressed his thumb against her chin, leaned forward and captured her open mouth with his.

"I have to have you," he said, the words rough, unpracticed, definitely not the way he usually propositioned a woman.

His words seemed to shock her. Like she had made contact with a naked wire. She went stiff in his arms, and then she pulled away, her eyes wide. "What are we doing?"

She was being utterly sincere, the words unsteady, her expression one of complete surprise and even…fear.

"I'm pretty sure we were about to make love," he said, using a more gentle terminology than he normally would have because of that strange vulnerability lurking in her eyes.

She shook her head, wiggling out of his hold and moving away from the door, backing toward the crib. "We can't do that. We can't." She pressed her hand against her cheek, and she looked so much like a stereotypical distressed female from some 1950s comic that he would have laughed if she hadn't successfully made him feel like he would be the villain in that piece. "It would be… It would be wrong."

"Why exactly?"

"Because. You're paying me to be here. You're paying me to play the part of your fiancée, and if things get physical between us, then I don't understand exactly what separates me from a prostitute."

"I'm not paying you for sex," he said. "I'm paying you to pretend to be my fiancée. I want you. And that's entirely separate from what we're doing here."

She shook her head, her eyes glistening. "Not to me. I already feel horrible. Like the worst person ever, after what I did to your family. After the way we tricked them tonight. After the way we will continue to trick them. I can't add sex to this situation. I have to walk away from this, Joshua. I have to walk away and not feel like I lost myself. I can't face the idea that I might finally sort out the money, where I'm going to live, how I'll survive… and lose the only thing I've always had. Myself. I just can't."

He had never begged a woman in his life, but he realized right then that he was on the verge of begging her to agree that it would feel good enough for whatever consequences to be damned. But as he looked behind her at the crib—the crib with the woman's baby in it, for heaven's sake—he realized the argument wasn't going to work with her.

She had been badly used, and though she had never really given him details, the evidence was obvious. She was alone. She had been abandoned at her most vulnerable. For her, the deepest consequences of sex were not hypothetical.

Though, they weren't for him either. And he was a stickler for safe sex, so there was that. Still, he couldn't blame her for not trusting him. And he should want nothing more than to find a woman who was less complicated. One who didn't have all the baggage that Danielle carried.

Still, he wanted to beg.

But he didn't.

"Sex isn't that big of a deal for me," he said. "If you're not into it, that's fine."

She nodded, the gesture jerky. "Good. That's probably another reason we shouldn't."

"I'm going to start interviewing nannies tomorrow," he said, abruptly changing the subject, because if he didn't, he would haul her back into his arms and finish what he had started.

"Okay," she said, looking shell-shocked.

"You'll have a little bit more freedom then. And we can go out riding."

She blinked. "Why? I just turned you down. Why do you want to do anything for me?"

"I already told you. None of this is a trade for sex. You turning me down doesn't change my intentions."

She frowned. "I don't understand." She looked down, picking at her thumbnail. "Everything has a price. There's no reason for you to do something for me when you're not looking for something in return."

"Not everything in life is a transaction, Danielle."

"I suppose it's not when you care about somebody." She tilted her head to the side. "But nobody's ever really cared about me."

If he hadn't already felt like a jerk, then her words would have done it. Because his family did care about him. His life had been filled with people doing things for him just because they wanted to give him something. They'd had no expectation of receiving anything in return.

But after Shannon, something had changed inside of him. He wanted to hold everybody at arm's length. Explaining himself felt impossible.

He hadn't wanted to give to anyone, connect with anyone, in a long time. But for some reason, he wanted to connect with Danielle. Wanted to give to that fragile, sweet girl.

It wasn't altruistic. Not really. She had so little that it was easy to step in and do something life altering. She didn't understand the smallest gesture of kindness, which meant the smallest gesture was enough.

"Tomorrow the interview process starts. I assume you want input?"

"Do I want input over who is going to be watching my baby? Yeah. That would be good."

She reached up, absently touching her lips, then lowered her hand quickly, wiggling her fingers slightly. "Good night," she said, the words coming out in a rush.

"Good night," he said, his voice hard. He turned, closing the door resolutely behind him, because if he didn't, he couldn't be responsible for what he might do.

He was going to leave her alone. He was going to do something nice for her. As if that would do something for his tarnished soul.

Well, maybe it wouldn't. But maybe it would do something for her. And for some reason, that mattered.

Maybe that meant he wasn't too far gone, after all.

Danielle had never interviewed anyone who was going to work for her. She had interviewed for several jobs herself, but she had never been on the reverse side. It was strange and infused her with an inordinate sense of power.

Which was nice, considering she rarely felt powerful.

Certainly not the other night when Joshua had kissed her. Then she had felt weak as a kitten. Ready to lie down and give him whatever he wanted.

Except she hadn't. She had said no. She was proud of herself for that, even while she mourned the loss of whatever pleasure she might have found with him.

It wasn't about pleasure. It was about pride.

Pride and self-preservation. What she had said to him had been true. If she walked away from this situation completely broken, unable to extricate herself from him, from his life, because she had allowed herself to get tangled up in ways she hadn't anticipated, then she would never forgive herself. If she had finally made her life easier in all the ways she'd always dreamed of, only to snare herself in a trap she knew would end in pain…

She would judge herself harshly for that.

Whatever she wanted to tell herself about Joshua— he was a tool, he didn't deserve the wonderful family he had—she was starting to feel things for him. Things she really couldn't afford to feel.

That story about his girlfriend had hit her hard and deep. Hit her in a place she normally kept well protected.

Dammit.

She took a deep breath and looked over at the new nanny, Janine, who had just started today, and who was going to watch Riley while Joshua and Danielle went for a ride.

She was nervous. Unsteady about leaving Riley for the first time in a while. Necessity had meant she'd had to leave him when she was working at the grocery store. Still, this felt different. Because it wasn't necessary. It made her feel guilty. Because she was leaving him to do something for herself.

She shook her head. Her reaction was ridiculous. But she supposed it was preferable to how her mother had operated. Which was to never think about her children at all. Her neglect of Danielle hadn't come close to her disinterest in her youngest child. Danielle supposed that by the time Riley was born, her mother had been fully burned-out. Had exhausted whatever maternal instinct she'd possessed.

Danielle shook her head. Then took a deep breath and turned to face Janine. "He should nap most of the time we're gone. And even if he wakes up, he's usually really happy."

Janine smiled. "He's just a baby. I've watched a lot of babies. Not that he isn't special," she said, as though she were trying to cover up some faux pas. "I just mean, I'm confident that I can handle him."

Danielle took a deep breath and nodded. Then Joshua

came into the room and the breath she had just drawn into her lungs rushed out.

He was wearing a dark blue button-down shirt and jeans, paired with a white cowboy hat that made him look like the hero in an old Western movie.

Do not get that stupid. He might be a hero, but he's not your hero.

No. Girls like her didn't get heroes. They had to be their own heroes. And that was fine. Honestly, it was.

If only she could tell her heart that. Her stupid heart, which was beating out of control.

It was far too easy to remember what it had been like to kiss him. To remember what it had felt like when his stubble-covered cheek scraped against hers. How sexy it had felt. How intoxicating it had been to touch a man like that. To experience the differences between men and women for the first time.

It was dangerous, was what it was. She had opened a door she had never intended to open, and now it was hard to close.

She shook her hands out, then balled them into fists, trying to banish the jitters that were racing through her veins.

"Are you ready?" he asked.

His eyes met hers and all she could think was how incredible it was that his eyes matched his shirt. They were a deep, perfect shade of navy.

There was something wrong with her. She had never been this stupid around a man before.

"Yes," she said, the answer coming out more as a squeak than an actual word. "I'm ready."

The corner of his mouth lifted into a lopsided grin. "You don't have to be nervous. I'll be gentle with you."

She nearly choked. "Good to know. But I'm more worried about the horse being gentle with me."

"She will be. Promise. I've never taught a girl how to ride before, but I'm pretty confident I can teach you."

His words ricocheted around inside of her, reaching the level of double entendre. Which wasn't fair. That wasn't how he'd meant it.

Or maybe it was.

He hadn't been shy about letting her know exactly what he wanted from her that night. He had put his hand between her legs. Touched her where no other man ever had. He'd made her see stars, tracked sparks over her skin.

It was understandable for her to be affected by the experience. But like he'd said, sex didn't really matter to him. It wasn't a big deal. So why he would be thinking of it now was beyond her. He had probably forgotten already. Probably that kiss had become an indistinct blur in his mind, mixed with all his other sexual encounters.

There were no other encounters for her. So there he was in her mind, and in front of her, far too sharp and far too clear.

"I'm ready," she said, the words rushed. "Totally ready."

"Great," he said. "Let's go."

Taking Danielle out riding was submitting himself to a particular kind of torture, that was for sure. But he was kind of into punishing himself...so he figured it fit his MO.

He hadn't stopped thinking about her since they had kissed—and more—in her bedroom the other night. He had done his best to throw himself into work, to avoid her, but still, he kept waking up with sweat slicked over his skin, his body hard and dreams of…her lips, her tongue, her scent…lingering in his thoughts.

Normally, the outdoors cleared his mind. Riding his horse along the length of the property was his therapy. Maneuvering her over the rolling hills, along the ridge line of the mountain, the evergreen trees rising behind them in a stately backdrop that left him feeling small within the greater context of the world. Which was something a man like him found refreshing some days.

But not today.

Today, he was obsessing. He was watching Danielle's behind as she rode her horse in front of him, the motion of the horse's gait making him think of what it would look like if the woman was riding him instead of his mare.

He couldn't understand this. Couldn't understand this obsession with her.

She wasn't the kind of sophisticated woman he tended to favor. In a lot of ways, she reminded him of the kind of girl he used to go for here in town, back when he had been a good-for-nothing teenager spending his free time drinking and getting laid out in the woods.

Back then he had liked hometown girls who wanted the same things he did. A few hours to escape, a little bit of fun.

The problem was, he already knew Danielle didn't want that. She didn't find casual hookups fun. And he didn't have anything to offer beyond a casual hookup.

The other problem was that the feelings he had for her were not casual. If they were, then he wouldn't be obsessing. But he was.

In the couple of weeks since she had come to live with him, she had started to fill out a bit. He could get a sense of her figure, of how she would look if she were thriving rather than simply surviving. She was naturally thin, but there was something elegant about her curves.

But even more appealing than the baser things, like the perky curve of her high breasts and the subtle slope of her hips, was the stubborn set of her jaw. The straight, brittle weight of her shoulders spoke of both strength and fragility.

While there was something unbreakable about her, he worried that if a man ever were to find her weakness, she would do more than just break. She would shatter.

He shook his head. And then he forced himself to look away from her, forced himself to look at the scenery. At the mountain spread out before them, and the ocean gray and fierce behind it.

"Am I doing okay?"

Danielle's question made it impossible to ignore her, and he found himself looking at her ass again. "You haven't fallen off yet," he said, perhaps a bit unkindly.

She snorted, then looked over her shoulder, a challenging light glittering in her brown eyes. "Yet? I'm not going to fall off, Joshua Grayson. It would take a hell of a lot to unseat me."

"Says the woman who was shaking when I helped her mount up earlier."

She surprised him by releasing her hold on the reins with one hand and waving it in the air. "Well, I'm getting the hang of it."

"You're a regular cowgirl," he said.

Suddenly, he wanted that to be true. It was the strangest thing. He wanted her to have this outlet, this freedom. Something more than a small apartment. Something more than struggle.

You're giving her that. That's what this entire bargain is for. Like she said, she's a gold digger, and you're giving her your gold.

Yes, but he wanted to give her more than that.

Just like he had told her the other day, what he wanted to give her wasn't about an exchange. He wanted her to have something for herself. Something for Riley.

Maybe it was a misguided attempt to atone for what he hadn't managed to give Shannon. What he hadn't ever been able to give the child he lost.

He swallowed hard, taking in a deep breath of the sharp pine and salt air, trying to ease the pressure in his chest.

She looked at him again, this time a dazzling smile on her lips. It took all that pressure in his chest and punched a hole right through it. He felt his lungs expand, all of him begin to expand.

He clenched his teeth, grinding them together so hard he was pretty sure his jaw was going to break. "Are you about ready to head back?"

"No. But I'm not sure I'm ever going to be ready to head back. This was… Thank you." She didn't look at him this time. But he had a feeling it was because she was a lot less comfortable with sincere connection than she was with sarcasm.

Well, that made two of them.

"You're welcome," he said, fixing his gaze on the line of trees beside them.

He maneuvered his horse around in front of hers so he could lead the way back down to the barn. They rode on in silence, but he could feel her staring holes into his back.

"Are you looking at my butt, Danielle?"

He heard a sputtering noise behind him. "No."

They rode up to the front of the barn and he dismounted, then walked over to her horse. "Liar. Do you need help?"

She frowned, her brows lowering. "Not from you. You called me a liar."

"Because you were looking at my butt and we both know it." He raised his hand up, extending it to her. "Now let me help you so you don't fall on your pretty face."

"Bah," she said, reaching out to him, her fingers brushing against his, sending an electrical current arcing between them. He chose to ignore it. Because there was no way in the whole damn world that the brush of a woman's fingertips against his should get him hot and bothered.

He grabbed hold of her and helped get her down from the horse, drawing her against him when her feet connected with the ground. And then it was over.

Pretending that this wasn't a long prelude to him kissing her again. Pretending that the last few days hadn't been foreplay. Pretending that every time either of them had thought about the kiss hadn't been easing them closer and closer to the inevitable.

She wanted him, he knew that. It was clear in the way she responded to him. She might have reservations about acting on it, and he had his own. But need was bigger than any of that right now, building between them, impossible to ignore.

He was a breath away from claiming her mouth with his when she shocked him by curving her fingers around his neck and stretching up on her toes.

Her kiss was soft, tentative. A question where his kiss would have been a command. But that made it all the sweeter. The fact that she had come to him. The fact that even though she was still conflicted about all of it, she couldn't resist any longer.

He cupped her cheek, calling on all his restraint—what little there was—to allow her to lead this, to allow her to guide the exploration. There was something so unpracticed about that pretty mouth of hers, something untutored about the way her lips skimmed over his. About the almost sweet, soft way her tongue tested his.

What he wanted to do was take it deep. Take it hard. What he wanted to do was grab hold of her hips and press her back against the barn. Push her jeans down her thighs and get his hand back between her gorgeous legs so he could feel all that soft, slick flesh.

What he wanted to press himself against her and slide in slowly, savoring the feel of her desire as it washed over him.

But he didn't.

And it was the damned hardest thing he had ever done. To wait. To let her lead. To let her believe she had the control here. Whatever she needed to do so she wouldn't get scared again. If he had to be patient, if he had to take it slow, he could. He would.

If it meant having her.

He had to have her. Had to exorcise the intense demon that had taken residence inside of him, that demanded he take her. Demanded he make her his own.

His horse snickered behind them, shifting her bulk, drawing Danielle's focus back to the present and away from him. Dammit all.

"Let me get them put away," he said.

He was going to do it quickly. And then he was going to get right back to tasting her. He half expected her to run to the house as he removed the tack from the animals and got them brushed down, but she didn't. Instead, she just stood there watching him, her eyes large, her expression one of absolute indecision.

Because she knew.

She knew that if she stayed down here, he wasn't going to leave it at a kiss. He wasn't going to leave it at all.

But he went about his tasks, slowing his movements, forcing himself not to rush. Forcing himself to draw it out. For her torture as well as his. He wanted her to need it, the way that he did.

And yes, he could see she wanted to run. He could also tell she wanted him, she wanted this. She was unbearably curious, even if she was also afraid.

And he was counting on that curiosity to win out.

Finally, she cleared her throat, shifting impatiently. "Are you going to take all day to do that?"

"You have to take good care of your horses, Danielle. I know a city girl like you doesn't understand how that works."

She squinted, then took a step forward, pulling his hat off his head and depositing it on her own. "Bull. You're playing with me."

He couldn't hold back the smile. "Not yet. But I plan to."

After that, he hurried a bit. He put the horses back in their paddock, then took hold of Danielle's hand, leading her deeper into the barn, to a ladder that went up to the loft.

"Can I show you something?"

She bit her lip, hesitating. "Why do I have a feeling that it isn't the loft you're going to show me?"

"I'm going to show you the loft. It's just not all I'm going to show you."

She took a step back, worrying her lip with her teeth. He reached out, cupping the back of her head and bringing his mouth down on hers, kissing her the way he had wanted to when she initiated the kiss outside. He didn't have patience anymore. And he wasn't going to let her lead. Not now.

He cupped her face, stroking her cheeks with his thumbs. "This has nothing to do with our agreement. It has nothing to do with the contract. Nothing to do with the ad or my father or anything other than the fact that I want you. Do you understand?"

She nodded slowly. "Yes," she said, the word coming out a whisper.

Adrenaline shot through him, a strange kind of triumph that came with a kick to the gut right behind it. He wanted her. He knew he didn't deserve her. But he wasn't going to stop himself from having her in spite of that.

Then he took her hand and led her up the ladder.

Chapter 7

Danielle's heart was pounding in her ears. It was all she could hear. The sound of her own heart beating as she climbed the rungs that led up to the loft.

It was different than she had imagined. It was clean. There was a haystack in one corner, but beyond that the floor was immaculate, every item stored and organized with precision. Which, knowing Joshua like she now did, wasn't too much of a surprise.

That made her smile, just a little. She did know him. In some ways, she felt like she knew him better than she knew anyone.

She wasn't sure what that said about her other relationships. For a while, she'd had friends, but they'd disappeared when she'd become consumed with caring for her pregnant mother and working as much as possible at the grocery store. And then no one had come back when Danielle ended up with full care of Riley.

In some ways, she didn't blame them. Life was hard enough without dealing with a friend who was juggling all of that. But just because she understood didn't mean she wasn't lonely.

She looked at Joshua, their eyes connecting. He had shared his past with her. But she was keeping something big from him. Even while she was prepared to give him her body, she was holding back secrets.

She took a breath, opening her mouth to speak, but something in his blue gaze stopped the words before they could form. Something sharp, predatory. Something that made her feel like she was the center of the world, or at least the center of his world.

It was intoxicating. She'd never experienced it before. She wanted more, all of it. Wherever it would lead.

And that was scary. Scarier than agreeing to do something she had never done before. Because she finally understood. Understood why her mother had traded her sanity, and her self-worth, for that moment when a man looked at you like you were his everything.

Danielle had spent so long being nothing to anyone. Nothing but a burden. Now, feeling like the solution rather than the problem was powerful, heady. She knew she couldn't turn back now no matter what.

Even if sanity tried to prevail, she would shove it aside. Because she needed this. Needed this balm for all the wounds that ran so deep inside of her.

Joshua walked across the immaculate space and opened up a cabinet. There were blankets inside, thick, woolen ones with geometric designs on them. He pulled out two and spread one on the ground.

She bit her lip, fighting a rising tide of hysteria, fighting a giggle that was climbing its way up her throat.

"I know this isn't exactly a fancy hotel suite."

She forced a smile. "It works for me."

He set the other blanket down on the end of the first one, still folded, then he reached out and took her hand, drawing her to him. He curved his fingers around her wrist, lifting her arm up, then shifted his hold, lacing his fingers through hers and dipping his head, pressing his lips to her own.

Her heart was still pounding that same, steady beat, and she was certain he must be able to hear it. Must be aware of just how he was affecting her.

There were all sorts of things she should tell him. About Riley's mother. About this being her first time.

But she didn't have the words.

She had her heartbeat. The way her limbs trembled. She could let him see that her eyes were filling with tears, and no matter how fiercely she blinked, they never quite went away.

She was good at manipulating conversation. At giving answers that walked the line between fact and fiction.

Her body could only tell the truth.

She hoped he could see it. That he understood. Later, they would talk. Later, there would be honesty between them. Because he would have questions. God knew. But for now, she would let the way her fingertips trailed down his back—uncertain and tentative—the way she peppered kisses along his jaw—clumsy and broken—say everything she couldn't.

"It doesn't need to be fancy," she said, her voice sounding thick even to her own ears.

"Maybe it should be," he said, his voice rough. "But if I was going to take you back to my bedroom, I expect I would have to wait until tonight. And I don't want to wait."

She shook her head. "It doesn't have to be fancy. It just has to be now. And it has to be you."

He drew his head back, inhaling sharply. And then he cupped her cheek and consumed her. His kiss was heat and fire, sparking against the dry, neglected things inside her and raging out of control.

She slid her hands up his arms, hanging on to his strong shoulders, using his steadiness to hold her fast even as her legs turned weak.

He lifted her up against him, then swept his arm beneath her legs, cradling her against his chest like she was a child. Then he set her down gently on the blanket, continuing to kiss her as he did so.

She was overwhelmed. Overwhelmed by the intensity of his gaze, by his focus. Overwhelmed by his closeness, his scent.

He was everywhere. His hands on her body, his face filling her vision.

She had spent the past few months caring for her half brother, pouring everything she had onto one little person she loved more than anything in the entire world. But in doing so, she had left herself empty. She had been giving continually, opening a vein and bleeding whenever necessary, and taking nothing in to refill herself.

But this… This was more than she had ever had. More than she'd ever thought she could have. Being the focus of a man's attention. Of his need.

This was a different kind of need than that of a child. Because it wasn't entirely selfish. Joshua's need gave her something in return; it compelled him to be close. Compelled him to kiss her, to skim his hands over her body, teasing and tormenting her with the promise of a pleasure she had never experienced.

Before she could think her actions through, she was pushing her fingertips beneath the hem of his shirt, his hard, flat stomach hot to the touch. And then it didn't matter what she had done before or what she hadn't done. Didn't matter that she was a virgin and this was an entirely new experience.

Need replaced everything except being skin to skin with him. Having nothing between them.

Suddenly, the years of feeling isolated, alone, cold and separate were simply too much. She needed his body over hers, his body inside hers. Whatever happened after that, whatever happened in the end, right now she couldn't care.

Because her desire outweighed the consequences. A wild, desperate thing starving to be fed. With his touch. With his possession.

She pushed his shirt up, and he helped her shrug it over his head. Her throat dried, her mouth opening slightly as she looked at him. His shoulders were broad, his chest well-defined and muscular, pale hair spreading over those glorious muscles, down his ridged abdomen, disappearing in a thin trail beneath the waistband of his low-slung jeans.

She had never seen a man who looked like him before, not in person. And she had never been this close to a man ever. She pressed her palm against his chest, relishing his heat and his hardness beneath her touch. His heart raging out of control, matching the beat of her own.

She parted her thighs and he settled between them. She could feel the hard ridge of his arousal pressing against that place where she was wet and needy for him. She was shocked at how hard he was, even through layers of clothing.

And she lost herself in his kiss, in the way he rocked his hips against hers. This moment, this experience was like everything she had missed growing up. Misspent teenage years when she should have been making out with boys in barns and hoping she didn't get caught. In reality, her mother wouldn't have cared.

This was a reclamation. More than that, it was something completely new. Something she had never even known she could want.

Joshua was something she had never known she could want.

It shouldn't make sense, the two of them. This brilliant businessman in his thirties who owned a ranch and seemed to shun most emotional connections. And her. Poor. In her twenties. Desperately clinging to any connection she could forge because each one was so rare and special.

But somehow they seemed to make sense. Kissing each other. Touching each other. For some reason, he was the only man that made sense.

Maybe it was because he had taught her to ride a horse. Maybe it was because he was giving her and Riley a ticket out of poverty. Maybe it was because he was handsome. She had a feeling this connection transcended all those things.

As his tongue traced a trail down her neck to the collar of her T-shirt, she was okay with not knowing. She didn't need to give this connection a name. She didn't even want to.

Her breath caught as he pushed her shirt up and over her head, then quickly dispensed with her bra using a skill not even she possessed. Her nipples tightened, and she was painfully aware of them and of the fact that she was a little lackluster in size.

If Joshua noticed, he didn't seem to mind.

Instead, he dipped his head, sucking one tightened bud between his lips. The move was so sudden, so shocking and so damned unexpected that she couldn't stop herself from arching into him, a cry on her lips.

He looked up, the smile on his face so damned cocky she should probably have been irritated. But she wasn't. She just allowed herself to get lost. In his heat. In the fire that flared between them. In the way he used his lips, his teeth and his tongue to draw a map of pleasure over her skin. All the way down to the waistband of her pants. He licked her. Just above the snap on her jeans. Another sensation so deliciously shocking she couldn't hold back the sound of pleasure on her lips.

She pressed her fist against her mouth, trying to keep herself from getting too vocal. From embarrassing herself. From revealing just how inexperienced she was. The noises she was making definitely announced the fact that these sensations were revelatory to her. And that made her feel a touch too vulnerable.

She was so used to holding people at a distance. So used to benign neglect and general apathy creating a shield around her feelings. Her secrets.

But there was no distance here.

And certainly none as he undid the button of her jeans and drew the zipper down slowly. As he pushed the rough denim down her legs, taking her panties with them.

If she had felt vulnerable a moment before, that was nothing compared to now. She felt so fragile. So exposed. And then he reached up, pressing his hand against her leg at the inside of her knee, spreading her wide so he could look his fill.

She wanted to snap her legs together. Wanted to cover up. But she was immobilized. Completely captive to whatever might happen next. She was so desperate to find out, and at the same time desperate to escape it.

Rough fingertips drifted down the tender skin on her inner thigh, brushing perilously close to her damp, needy flesh. And then he was there. His touch in no way gentle or tentative as he pressed his hand against her, the heel of his palm putting firm pressure on her most sensitive place before he pressed his fingers down and spread her wide.

He made his intentions clear as he lowered his head, tasting her deeply. She lifted her hips, a sharp sound on her lips, one she didn't even bother to hold back. He shifted his hold, gripping her hips, holding her just wide enough for his broad shoulders to fit right there, his sensual assault merciless.

Tension knotted her stomach like a fist, tighter and tighter with each pass of his tongue. Then he pressed his thumb against her at the same time as he flicked his tongue in the same spot. She grabbed hold of him, her fingernails digging into his back.

He drew his thumb down her crease, teasing the entrance of her body. She rocked her hips with the motion, desperate for something. Feeling suddenly empty and achy and needy in ways she never had before.

He rotated his hand, pressing his middle finger deep inside of her, and she gasped at the foreign invasion. But any discomfort passed quickly as her body grew wetter beneath the ministrations of his tongue. By the time he added a second finger, it slipped in easily.

He quickened his pace, and it felt like there was an earthquake starting inside her. A low, slow pull at her core that spread outward, her limbs trembling as the pressure at her center continued to mount.

His thumb joined with his tongue as he continued to pump his fingers inside her, and it was that added pressure that finally broke her. She was shaken. Rattled completely. The magnitude of measurable aftershocks rocking her long after the primary force had passed.

He moved into a sitting position, undoing his belt and the button on his jeans. Then he stood for a moment, drawing the zipper down slowly and pushing the denim down his muscular thighs.

She had never seen a naked man in person before, and the stark, thick evidence of his arousal standing out from his body was a clear reminder that they weren't finished, no matter how wrung out and replete she felt.

Except, even though she felt satisfied, limp from the intensity of her release, she did want more. Because there was more to have. Because she wanted to be close to him. Because she wanted to give him even an ounce of the satisfaction that she had just experienced.

He knelt back down, pulling his jeans closer and taking his wallet out of his back pocket. He produced a condom packet and she gave thanks for his presence of mind. She knew better than to have unprotected sex with someone. For myriad reasons. But still, she wondered if she would have remembered if he had not.

Thank God one of them was thinking. She was too overwhelmed. Too swamped by the release that had overtaken her, and by the enormity of what was about to happen. When he positioned himself at the entrance of her body and pressed against her, she gasped in shock.

It *hurt*. Dear God it hurt. His fingers hadn't prepared her for the rest of him.

He noticed her hesitation and slowed his movements, pressing inside her inch by excruciating inch. She held on to his shoulders, closing her eyes and burying her face in his neck as he jerked his hips forward, fully seating himself inside her.

She did her best to breathe through it. But she was in a daze. Joshua was inside her, and she wasn't a virgin anymore. It felt... Well, it didn't feel like losing anything. It felt like gaining something. Gaining a whole lot.

The pain began to recede and she looked up, at his face, at the extreme concentration there, at the set of his jaw, the veins in his neck standing out.

"Are you okay?" he asked, his voice strangled.

She nodded wordlessly, then flexed her hips experimentally.

He groaned, lowering his head, pressing his forehead against hers, before kissing her. Then he began to move.

Soon, that same sweet tension began to build again in her stomach, need replacing the bone-deep satisfaction that she had only just experienced. She didn't know how it was possible to be back in that needy place only moments after feeling fulfilled.

But she was. And then she was lost in the rhythm, lost in the feeling of his thick length stroking in and out of her, all of the pain gone now, only pleasure remaining. It was so foreign, so singular and unlike anything she had ever experienced. And she loved it. Reveled in it.

But even more than her own pleasure, she reveled in watching his unraveling.

Because he had pulled her apart in a million astounding ways, and she didn't know if she could ever be reassembled. So it was only fair that he lost himself too. Only fair that she be his undoing in some way.

Sweat beaded on his brow, trickled down his back. She reveled in the feel of it beneath her fingertips. In the obvious evidence of what this did to him.

His breathing became more labored, his muscles shaking as each thrust became less gentle. As he began to pound into her. And just as he needed to go harder, go faster, so did she.

Her own pleasure wound around his, inextricably linked.

On a harsh growl he buried his face in her neck, his arms shaking as he thrust into her one last time, slamming into her, breaking a wave of pleasure over her body as he found his own release.

He tried to pull away, but she wrapped her arms around him, holding him close. Because the sooner he separated from her body, the sooner they would have to talk. And she wasn't exactly sure she wanted to talk.

But when he lifted his head, his blue eyes glinting in the dim light, she could tell that whether or not she wanted to talk, they were going to.

He rolled away from her, pushing into a sitting position. "Are you going to explain all of this to me? Or are you going to make me guess?"

"What?" She sounded overly innocent, her eyes wider than necessary.

"Danielle, I'm going to ask you a question, and I need you to answer me honestly. Were you a virgin?"

Joshua's blood was still running hot through his veins, arousal still burning beneath the surface of his skin. And he knew the question he had just asked her was probably insane. He could explain her discomfort as pain because she hadn't taken a man to her bed since she'd given birth.

But that wasn't it. It wasn't.

The more credence he gave to his virgin theory, the more everything about her started to make sense. The way she responded to his kiss, the way she acted when he touched her.

Her reaction had been about more than simple attraction, more than pleasure. There had been wonder there. A sense of discovery.

But that meant Riley wasn't her son. And it meant she had been lying to him.

"Well, Joshua, given that this is not a New Testament kind of situation…"

He reached out, grabbing hold of her wrist and tugging her upward, drawing her toward him. "Don't lie to me."

"Why would you think that?" she asked, her words small. Admission enough as far as he was concerned.

"A lot of reasons. But I have had sex with a virgin before. More accurately, Sadie Miller and I took each other's virginity in the woods some eighteen years ago. You don't forget that. And, I grant you, there could be other reasons for the fact that it hurt you, for the fact that you were tight." A flush spread over her skin, her cheeks turning beet red. "But I don't think any of those reasons are the truth. So what's going on? Who is Riley's mother?"

A tear slid down her cheek, her expression mutinous and angry. "I am," she said, her voice trembling. "At least, I might as well be. I should be."

"You didn't give birth to Riley."

She sniffed loudly, another tear sliding down her cheek. "No. I didn't."

"Are you running from somebody? Is there something I need to know?"

"It's not like that. I'm not hiding. I didn't steal him. I have legal custody of Riley. But my situation was problematic. At least, as far as Child Services was concerned. I lost my job because of the babysitting situation and I needed money."

She suddenly looked so incredibly young, so vulnerable... And he felt like the biggest jerk on planet Earth.

She had lied to him. She had most definitely led him to believe she was in an entirely different circumstance than she was, and still, he was mostly angry at himself.

Because the picture she was painting was even more desperate than the one he had been led to believe. Because she had been a virgin and he had just roughly dispensed with that.

She had been desperate. Utterly desperate. And had taken this post with him because she hadn't seen another option. Whatever he'd thought of her before, he was forced to revise it, and there was no way that revision didn't include recasting himself as the villain.

"Whose baby is he?"

She swallowed hard, drawing her knees up to her chest, covering her nudity. "Riley is my half brother. My mother showed up at my place about a year ago pregnant and desperate. She needed someone to help her out. When she came to me, she sounded pretty determined to take care of him. She even named him. She told me she would do better for him than she had for me, because she was done with men now and all of that. But she broke her promises. She had the baby, she met somebody else. I didn't know it at first. I didn't realize she was leaving Riley in the apartment alone sometimes while I was at work."

She took a deep, shuddering breath, then continued. "I didn't mess around when I found out. I didn't wait for her to decide to abandon him. I called Child Services. And I got temporary guardianship. My mother left. But then things started to fall apart with the work, and I didn't know how I was going to pay for the apartment... Then I saw your ad."

He swore. "You should have told me."

"Maybe. But I needed the money, Joshua. And I didn't want to do anything to jeopardize your offer. I could tell you were uncomfortable that I brought a baby with me, and now I know why. But, regardless, at the time, I didn't want to do anything that might compromise our arrangement."

He felt like the jackass he undoubtedly was. The worst part was, it shone a light on all the BS he'd put her through. Regardless of Riley's parentage, she'd been desperate and he'd taken advantage of that. Less so when he'd been keeping his hands to himself. At least then it had been feasible to pretend it was an even exchange.

But now?

Now he'd slept with her and it was impossible to keep pretending.

And frankly, he didn't want to.

He'd been wrestling with this feeling from the moment they'd gone out riding today, or maybe since they'd left his parents' house last week.

But today...when he'd looked at her, seen her smile... noticed the way she'd gained weight after being in a place where she felt secure...

He'd wanted to give her more of that.

He'd wanted to do more good than harm. Had wanted to fix something instead of break it.

It was too late for Shannon. But he could help Danielle. He could make sure she always felt safe. That she and Riley were always protected.

The realization would have made him want to laugh if it didn't all feel too damned grim. Somehow his father's ad had brought him to this place when he'd been determined to teach the old man a lesson.

But Joshua hadn't counted on Danielle.

Hadn't counted on how she would make him feel. That she'd wake something inside him he'd thought had been asleep for good.

It wasn't just chemistry. Wasn't just sex. It was the desire to make her happy. To give her things.

To fix what was broken.

He knew the solution wouldn't come from him personally, but his money could sure as hell fix her problems. And they did have chemistry. The kind that wasn't common. It sure as hell went beyond anything he'd ever experienced before.

"The truth doesn't change anything," she said, lowering her face into her arms, her words muffled. "It doesn't."

He reached out, taking her chin between his thumb and forefinger, tilting her face back up. "It does. Even if it shouldn't. Though, maybe it's not Riley that changes it. Maybe it's just the two of us."

She shook her head. "It doesn't have to change anything."

"Danielle... I can't..."

She lurched forward, grabbing his arm, her eyes wide, her expression wild. "Joshua, please. I need this money.

I can't go back to where we were. I'm being held to a harsher standard than his biological mother would be and I can't lose him."

He grabbed her chin again, steadying her face, looking into those glistening brown eyes. "Danielle, I would never let you lose him. I want to protect you. Both of you."

She tilted her head to the side, her expression growing suspicious. "You…do?"

"I've been thinking. I was thinking this earlier when we were riding, but now, knowing your whole story… I want you and Riley to stay with me."

She blinked. "What?"

"Danielle, I want you to marry me."

Chapter 8

Danielle couldn't process any of this.

She had expected him to be angry. Had expected him to get mad because she'd lied to him.

She hadn't expected a marriage proposal.

At least, she was pretty sure that was what had just happened. "You want to…marry me? For real marry me?"

"Yes," he said, his tone hard, decisive. "You don't feel good about fooling my family—neither do I. You need money and security and, hell, I have both. We have chemistry. I want… I don't want to send you back into the world alone. You don't even know where you're going."

He wasn't wrong. And dammit his offer was tempting. They were both naked, and he was so beautiful, and she wanted to kiss him again. Touch him again. But more than that, she wanted him to hold her in his arms again.

She wanted to be close to him. Bonded to him.

She wanted—so desperately—to not be alone.

But there had to be a catch.

There was always a catch. He could say whatever he wanted about how all of this wasn't a transaction, how he had taken her riding just to take her riding. But then they'd had sex. And he'd had a condom in his wallet.

So he'd been prepared.

That made her stomach sour.

"Did you plan this?" she asked. "The horse-riding seduction?"

"No, I didn't plan it. I carry a condom because I like to be prepared to have sex. You never know. You can get mad at me for that if you want, but then, we did need one, so it seems a little hypocritical."

"Are you tricking me?" she asked, feeling desperate and panicky. "Is this a trick? Because I don't understand how it benefits you to marry me. To keep Riley and me here. You don't even like Riley, Joshua. You can't stand to be in the same room with him."

"I broke Shannon," he said, his voice hard. "I ruined her. I did that. But I won't break you. I want to fix this."

"You can't slap duct tape and a wedding band on me and call it done," she said, her voice trembling. "I'm not a leaky faucet."

"I didn't say you were. But you need something I have and I... Danielle, I need you." His voice was rough, intense. "I'm not offering you love, but I can be faithful. I was ready to be a husband years ago, that part doesn't faze me. I can take care of you. I can keep you safe. And if I send you out into the world with nothing more than money and something happens to you or Riley, I won't forgive myself. So stay with me. Marry me."

It was crazy. He was crazy.

And she was crazy for sitting there fully considering everything he was offering.

But she was imagining a life here. For her, for Riley. On Joshua's ranch, in his beautiful house.

And she knew—she absolutely knew—that what she had felt physically with him, what had just happened, was a huge reason why they were having this conversation at all.

More than the pleasure, the closeness drew her in. Actually, that was the most dangerous part of his offer. The idea that she could go through life with somebody by her side. To raise Riley with this strong man backing her up.

Something clenched tight in her chest, working its way down to her stomach. Riley. He could have a father figure. She didn't know exactly what function Joshua would play in his life. Joshua had trouble with the baby right now. But she knew Joshua was a good man, and that he would never freeze Riley out intentionally. Not when he was offering them a life together.

"What about Riley?" she asked, her throat dry. She swallowed hard. She had to know what he was thinking.

"What about him?"

"This offer extends to him too. And I mean…not just protection and support. But would you… Would you teach him things? Would your father be a grandfather to him? Would your brothers be uncles and your sister be an aunt? I understand that having a child around might be hard for you, after you lost your chance at being a father. And I understand you want to fix me, my situation. And it's tempting, Joshua, it's very tempting. But I need to know if that support, if all of that, extends to Riley."

Joshua's face looked as though it had been cast in

stone. "I'm not sure if I would be a good father, Danielle. I was going to be a father, and so I was going to figure it out—how to do that, how to be that. I suppose I can apply that same intent here. I can't guarantee that I'll be the best, but I'll try. And you're right. I have my family to back me up. And he has you."

That was it.

That was the reason she couldn't say no. Because if she walked away from Joshua now, Riley would have her. Only her. She loved him, but she was just one person. If she stayed here with Joshua, Riley would have grandparents. Aunts and uncles. Family. People who knew how to be a family. She was doing the very best she could, but her idea of family was somewhere between cold neglectful nightmare and a TV sitcom.

The Grayson family knew—Joshua knew—what it meant to be a family. If she said yes, she could give that to Riley.

She swallowed again, trying to alleviate the scratchy feeling in her throat.

"I guess... I guess I can't really say no to that." She straightened, still naked, and not even a little bit embarrassed. There were bigger things going on here than the fact that he could see her breasts. "Okay, Joshua. I'll marry you."

Chapter 9

The biggest problem with this sudden change in plan was the fact that Joshua had deliberately set out to make his family dislike Danielle. And now he was marrying her for real.

Of course, the flaw in his original plan was that Danielle *hadn't* been roundly hated by his family. They'd distrusted the whole situation, certainly, but his family was simply too fair, too nice to hate her.

Still, guilt clutched at him, and he knew he was going to have to do something to fix this. Which was why he found himself down at the Gray Bear Construction office rather than working from home. Because he knew Faith and Isaiah would be in, and he needed to have a talk with his siblings.

The office was a newly constructed building fashioned to look like a log cabin. It was down at the edge of town, by where Rona's diner used to be, a former greasy spoon that had been transformed into a series of smaller, hipper shops that were more in line with the interests of Copper Ridge's tourists.

It was a great office space with a prime view of the ocean, but still, Joshua typically preferred to work in the privacy of his own home, secluded in the mountains.

Isaiah did too, which was why it was notable that his brother was in the office today, but he'd had a meeting of some kind, so he'd put on a decent shirt and a pair of nice jeans and gotten himself out of his hermitage.

Faith, being the bright, sharp creature she was, always came into the office, always dressed in some variation of her personal uniform. Black pants and a black top—a sweater today because of the chilly weather.

"What are you doing here?" Faith asked, her expression scrutinizing.

"I came here to talk to you," he said.

"I'll make coffee." Joshua turned and saw Poppy standing there. Strange, he hadn't noticed. But then, Poppy usually stayed in the background. He couldn't remember running the business without her, but like useful office supplies, you really only noticed them when they didn't work. And Poppy always worked.

"Thanks, Poppy," Faith said.

Isaiah folded his arms over his chest and leaned back in his chair. "What's up?"

"I'm getting married in two weeks."

Faith made a scoffing sound. "To that child you're dating?"

"She's your age," he said. "And yes. Just like I said I was."

"Which begs the question," Isaiah said. "Why are you telling us again?"

"Because. The first time I was lying. Dad put that ad in the paper trying to find a wife for me, and I selected Danielle in order to teach him a lesson. The joke's on me it turns out." Damn was it ever.

"Good God, Joshua. You're such a jerk," Faith said, leaning against the wall, her arms folded, mirroring Isaiah's stance. "I knew something was up, but of all the things I suspected, you tricking our mother and father was not one of them."

"What did you suspect?"

"That you were thinking with your… Well. And now I'm back to that conclusion. Because why are you marrying her?"

"I care about her. And believe me when I say she's had it rough."

"You've slept with her?" This question came from Isaiah, and there was absolutely no tact in it. But then, Isaiah himself possessed absolutely no tact. Which was why he handled money and not people.

"Yes," Joshua said.

"She must be good. But I'm not sure that's going to convince either of us you're thinking with your big brain." His brother stood up, not unfolding his arms.

"Well, you're obnoxious," Joshua returned. "The sex has nothing to do with it. I can get sex whenever I want."

Faith made a hissing sound. He tossed his younger sister a glance. "You can stop hissing and settle down," he said to her. "You were the one who brought sex into it, I'm just clarifying. You know what I went through with Shannon, what I put Shannon through. If I send Danielle and her baby back out into the world and something happens to them, I'll never forgive myself."

"Well, Joshua, that kind of implies you aren't already living in a perpetual state of self-flagellation," Faith said.

"Do you want to see if it can get worse?"

She shook her head. "No, but marrying some random woman you found through an ad seems like an extreme way to go about searching for atonement. Can't you do some Hail Marys or something?"

"If it were that simple, I would have done it a long time ago." He took a deep breath. "I'm not going to tell Mom and Dad the whole story. But I'm telling you because I need you to be nice about Danielle. However it looked when I brought her by to introduce her to the family... I threw her under the bus, and now I want to drag her back out from under it."

Isaiah shook his head. "You're a contrary son of a gun."

"Well, usually that's your function. I figured it was my turn."

The door to the office opened and in walked their business partner, Jonathan Bear, who ran the construction side of the firm. He looked around the room, clearly confused by the fact that they were all in residence. "Is there a meeting I didn't know about?"

"Joshua is getting married," Faith said, looking sullen.

"Congratulations," Jonathan said, smiling, which was unusual for the other man, who was typically pretty taciturn. "I can highly recommend it."

Jonathan had married the pastor's daughter, Hayley Thompson, in a small ceremony recently.

In the past, Jonathan had walked around like he had his own personal storm cloud overhead, and since meeting Hayley, he had most definitely changed. Maybe there was something to that whole marriage thing. Maybe

Joshua's idea of atonement wasn't as outrageous as it might have initially seemed.

"There," Joshua said. "Jonathan recommends it. So you two can stop looking at me suspiciously."

Jonathan shrugged and walked through the main area and into the back, toward his office, leaving Joshua alone with his siblings.

Faith tucked her hair behind her ear. "Honestly, whatever you need, whatever you want, I'll help. But I don't want you to get hurt."

"And I appreciate that," he said. "But the thing is, you can only get hurt if there's love involved. I don't love her."

Faith looked wounded by that. "Then what's the point? I'm not trying to argue. I just don't understand."

"Love is not the be-all and end-all, Faith. Sometimes just committing to taking care of somebody else is enough. I loved Shannon, but I still didn't do the right thing for her. I'm older now. And I know what's important. I'm going to keep Danielle safe. I'm going to keep Riley safe. What's more important than that?" He shook his head. "I'm sure Shannon would have rather had that than any expression of love."

"Fine," she said. "I support you. I'm in."

"So you aren't going to be a persnickety brat?"

A small smile quirked her lips upward. "I didn't say that. I said I would support you. But as a younger sister, I feel the need to remind you that being a persnickety brat is sometimes part of my support."

He shot Isaiah a baleful look. "I suppose you're still going to be obnoxious?"

"Obviously."

Joshua smiled then. Because that was the best he was going to get from his siblings. But it was a step toward making sure Danielle felt like she had a place in the family, rather than feeling like an outsider.

And if he wanted that with an intensity that wasn't strictly normal or healthy, he would ignore that. He had never pretended to be normal or healthy. He wasn't going to start now.

Danielle was getting fluttery waiting for Joshua to come home. The anticipation was a strange feeling. It had been a long time since she'd looked forward to someone coming home. She remembered being young, when it was hard to be alone. But she hadn't exactly wished for her mother to come home, because she knew that when her mother arrived, she would be drunk. And Danielle would be tasked with managing her in some way.

That was the story of her life. Not being alone meant taking care of somebody. Being alone meant isolation, but at least she had time to herself.

But Joshua wasn't like that. Being with him didn't mean she had to manage him.

She thought of their time together in the barn, and the memory made her shiver. She had gone to bed in her own room last night, and he hadn't made any move toward her since his proposal. She had a feeling his hesitation had something to do with her inexperience.

But she was ready for him again. Ready for more.

She shook her hands out, feeling jittery. And a little scared.

It was so easy to want him. To dream about him coming home, how she would embrace him, kiss him. And maybe even learn to cook, so she could make him dinner. Learn to do something other than warm up Pop-Tarts.

Although, he liked Pop-Tarts, and so did she.

Maybe they should have Pop-Tarts at their wedding. That was the kind of thing couples did. Incorporate the cute foundations of their relationships into their wedding ceremonies.

She made a small sound that was halfway between a whimper and a growl. She was getting loopy about him. About a guy. Which she had promised herself she would never do. But it was hard *not* to get loopy. He had offered her support, a family for Riley, a house to live in. He had become her lover, and then he had asked to become her husband.

And in those few short moments, her entire vision for the rest of her life had changed. It had become something so much warmer, so much more secure than she had ever imagined it could be. She just wasn't strong enough to reject that vision.

Honestly, she didn't know a woman who would be strong enough. Joshua was hot. And he was nice. Well, sometimes he was kind of a jerk, but mostly, at his core, he was nice and he had wonderful taste in breakfast food.

That seemed like as good a foundation for a marriage as any.

She heard the front door open and shut, and as it slammed, her heart lurched against her breastbone.

Joshua walked in looking so intensely handsome in a light blue button-up shirt, the sleeves pushed up his arms, that she wanted to swoon for the first time in her entire life.

"Do you think they can make a wedding cake out of Pop-Tarts?" She didn't know why that was the first thing that came out of her mouth. Probably, it would have been better if she had said something about how she couldn't wait to tear his clothes off.

But no. She had led with toaster pastry.

"I don't know. But we're getting married in two weeks, so if you can stack Pop-Tarts and call them a cake, I suppose it might save time and money."

"I could probably do that. I promise that's not all I thought about today, but for some reason it's what came out of my mouth."

"How about I keep your mouth busy for a while," he said, his blue gaze getting sharp. He crossed the space between them, wrapping his arm around her waist and drawing her against him. And then he kissed her.

It was so deep, so warm, and she felt so...sheltered. Enveloped completely in his arms, in his strength. Who cared if she was lost in a fantasy right now? It would be the first time. She had never had the luxury of dreaming about men like him, or passion this intense.

It seemed right, only fair, that she have the fantasy. If only for a while. To have a moment where she actually dreamed about a wedding with cake. Where she fantasized about a man walking in the door and kissing her like this, wanting her like this.

"Is Janine here?" he asked, breaking the kiss just long enough to pose the question.

"No," she said, barely managing to answer before he slammed his lips back down on hers.

Then she found herself being lifted and carried from the entryway into the living room, deposited on the couch. And somehow, as he set her down, he managed to raise her shirt up over her head.

She stared at him, dazed, while he divested himself of his own shirt. "You're very good at this," she said. "I assume you've had a lot of practice?"

He lifted an eyebrow, his hands going to his belt buckle. "Is this a conversation you want to have?"

She felt…bemused rather than jealous. "I don't know. I'm just curious."

"I got into a lot of trouble when I was a teenager. I think I mentioned the incident with my virginity in the woods."

She nodded. "You did. And since I lost my virginity in a barn, I suppose I have to reserve judgment."

"Probably. Then I moved to Seattle. And I was even worse, because suddenly I was surrounded by women I hadn't known my whole life."

Danielle nodded gravely. "I can see how that would be an issue."

He smiled. Then finished undoing his belt, button and zipper before shoving his pants down to the floor. He stood in front of her naked, aroused and beautiful.

"Then I got myself into a long-term relationship, and it turns out I'm good at that. Well, at the being faithful part."

"That's a relief."

"In terms of promiscuity, though, my behavior has been somewhat appalling for the past five years. I have picked up a particular set of skills."

She wrinkled her nose. "I suppose that's something."

"You asked."

She straightened. "And I wanted to know."

He reached behind her back, undoing her bra, pulling it off and throwing it somewhere behind him. "Well, now you do." He pressed his hands against the back of the couch, bracketing her in. "You still want to marry me?"

"I had a very tempting proposal from the UPS man

today. He asked me to sign for a package. So I guess you could say it's getting kind of serious."

"I don't think the UPS man makes you feel like this." He captured her mouth with his, and she found herself being pressed into the cushions, sliding to the side, until he'd maneuvered her so they were both lying flat on the couch.

He wrapped his fingers around her wrists, lifting them up over her head as he bent to kiss her neck, her collarbone, to draw one nipple inside his mouth.

She bucked against him, and he shifted, pushing his hand beneath her jeans, under the fabric of her panties, discovering just how wet and ready she was for him.

She rolled her hips upward, moving in time with the rhythm of his strokes, lights beginning to flash behind her eyelids, orgasm barreling down on her at an embarrassingly quick rate.

Danielle sucked in a deep breath, trying her best to hold her climax at bay. Because how embarrassing would it be to come from a kiss? A brief bit of attention to her breast and a quick stroke between the legs?

But then she opened her eyes and met his gaze. His lips curved into a wicked smile as he turned his wrist, sliding one finger deep inside as he flicked his thumb over her.

All she could do then was hold on tight and ride out the explosion. He never looked away from her, and as much as she wanted to, she couldn't look away from him.

It felt too intense, too raw and much too intimate.

But she was trapped in it, drowning in it, and there was nothing she could do to stop it. She just had to surrender.

While she was still recovering from her orgasm,

Joshua made quick work of her jeans, flinging them in the same direction her bra had gone.

Then, still looking right at her, he stroked her, over the thin fabric of her panties, the tease against her overly sensitized skin almost too much to handle.

Then he traced the edge of the fabric at the crease of her thigh, dipping one finger beneath her underwear, touching slick flesh.

He hooked his finger around the fabric, pulling her panties off and casting them aside. And here she was, just as she'd been the first time, completely open and vulnerable to him. At his mercy.

It wasn't as though she didn't want that. There was something wonderful about it. Something incredible about the way he lavished attention on her, about being his sole focus.

But she wanted more. She wanted to be... She wanted to be equal to him in some way.

He was practiced. And he had skill. He'd had a lot of lovers. Realistically, she imagined he didn't even know exactly how many.

She didn't have skill. She hadn't been tutored in the art of love by anyone. But she *wanted*.

If desire could equal skill, then she could rival any woman he'd ever been with. Because the depth of her need, the depth of her passion, reached places inside her she hadn't known existed.

She pressed her hands down on the couch cushions, launching herself into a sitting position. His eyes widened, and she reveled in the fact that she had surprised him. She reached out, resting one palm against his chest, luxuriating in the feel of all that heat, that muscle, that masculine hair that tickled her sensitive skin.

"Danielle," he said, his tone filled with warning.

She didn't care about his warnings.

She was going to marry this man. He was going to be her husband. That thought filled her with such a strange sense of elation.

He had all the power. He had the money. He had the beautiful house. What he was giving her…it bordered on charity. If she was ever going to feel like she belonged—like this place was really hers—they needed to be equals in some regard.

She had to give him something too.

And if it started here, then it started here.

She leaned in, cautiously tasting his neck, tracing a line down to his nipple. He jerked beneath her touch, his reaction satisfying her in a way that went well beyond the physical.

He was beautiful, and she reveled in the chance to explore him. To run her fingertips over each well-defined muscle. Over his abs and the hard cut inward just below his hip bone.

But she didn't stop there. No, she wasn't even remotely finished with him.

He had made her shake. He had made her tremble. He had made her lose her mind.

And she was going to return the favor.

She took a deep breath and kissed his stomach. Just one easy thing before she moved on to what she wanted, even though it scared her.

She lifted her head, meeting his gaze as she wrapped her fingers around him and squeezed. His eyes glittered like ice on fire, and he said nothing. He just sat there, his jaw held tight, his expression one of absolute concentration.

Then she looked away from his face, bringing her attention to that most masculine part of him. She was hungry for him. There was no other word for it.

She was starving for a taste.

And that hunger overtook everything else.

She flicked her tongue out and tasted him, his skin salty and hot. But the true eroticism was in his response. His head fell back, his breath hissing sharply through his teeth. And he reached out, pressing his hand to her back, spreading his fingers wide at the center of her shoulder blades.

Maybe she didn't have skill. Maybe she didn't know what she was doing. But he liked it. And that made her feel powerful. It made her feel needed.

She slid her hand down his shaft, gripping the base before taking him more deeply into her mouth. His groan sounded torn from him, wild and untamed, and she loved it.

Because Joshua was all about control. Had been from the moment she'd first met him.

That was what all this was, after all. From the ad in the paper to his marriage proposal—all of it was him trying to bend the situation to his will. To bend those around him to his will, to make them see he was right, that his way was the best way.

But right now he was losing control. He was at her mercy. Shaking. Because of her.

And even though she was the one pleasuring him, she felt an immense sense of satisfaction flood her as she continued to taste him. As she continued to make him tremble.

He needed her. He wanted her. After a lifetime of feeling like nobody wanted her at all, this was the most brilliant and beautiful thing she could ever imagine.

She'd heard her friends talk about giving guys blow jobs before. They laughed about it. Or said it was gross. Or said it was a great way to control their boyfriends.

They hadn't said what an incredible thing it was to make a big, strong alpha male sweat and shake. They hadn't said it could make you feel so desired, so beloved. Or that giving someone else pleasure was even better—in some ways—than being on the receiving end of the attention.

She swallowed more of him, and his hand jerked up to her hair, tugging her head back. "Careful," he said, his tone hard and thin.

"Why?"

"You keep doing that and I'm going to come," he said, not bothering to sugarcoat it.

"So what? When you did it for me, that's what I did."

"Yes. But you're a woman. And you can have as many orgasms as I can give you without time off in between. I don't want it to end like this."

She was about to protest, but then he pulled her forward, kissing her hard and deep, stealing not just her ability to speak, but her ability to think of words.

He left her for a moment, retrieving his wallet and the protection in it, making quick work of putting the condom on before he laid her back down on the couch.

"Wait," she said, the word husky, rough. "I want… Can I be on top?"

He drew back, arching one brow. "Since you asked so nicely."

He gripped her hips, reversing their position, bringing her to sit astride him. He was hard beneath her, and she shifted back and forth experimentally, rubbing her slick folds over him before positioning him at the entrance of her body.

She bit her lip, lowering herself onto him, taking it slow, relishing that moment of him filling her so utterly and completely.

"I don't know what I'm doing," she whispered when he was buried fully inside of her.

He reached up, brushing his fingertips over her cheek before lowering his hand to grip both her hips tightly, lift her, then impale her on his hard length again.

"Just do what feels good," he ground out, the words strained.

She rocked her hips, then lifted herself slightly before taking him inside again. She repeated the motion. Again and again. Finding the speed and rhythm that made him gasp and made her moan. Finding just the right angle, just the right pressure, to please them both.

Pleasure began to ripple through her, the now somewhat familiar pressure of impending orgasm building inside her. She rolled her hips, making contact right where she needed it. He grabbed her chin, drawing her head down to kiss her. Deep, wet.

And that was it. She was done.

Pleasure burst behind her eyes, her internal muscles gripping him tight as her orgasm rocked her.

She found herself being rolled onto her back and Joshua began to pound into her, chasing his own release with a raw ferocity that made her whole body feel like it was on fire with passion.

He was undone. Completely. Because of her.

He growled, reaching beneath her to cup her behind, drawing her hard against him, forcing her to meet his every thrust. And that was when he proved himself right. She really could come as many times as he could make her.

She lost it then, shaking and shivering as her second orgasm overtook her already sensitized body.

He lowered his head, his teeth scraping against her collarbone as he froze against her, finding his own release.

He lay against her for a moment, his face buried in her neck, and she sifted her fingers through his hair, a small smile touching her lips as ripples of lingering pleasure continued to fan out through her body.

He looked at her, then brushed his lips gently over hers. She found herself being lifted up, cradled against his chest as he carried her from the couch to the stairs.

"Time for bed," he said, the words husky and rough.

She reached up and touched his face. "Okay."

He carried her to his room, laid her down on the expansive mattress, the blanket decadent and soft beneath her bare skin.

This would be their room. A room they would share.

For some reason, that thought made tears sting her eyes. She had spent so long being alone that the idea of so much closeness was almost overwhelming. But no matter what, she wanted it.

Wanted it so badly it was like a physical hunger.

Joshua joined her on the bed and she was overwhelmed by the urge to simply fold herself into his embrace. To enjoy the closeness.

But then he was naked. And so was she. So the desire for closeness fought with her desire to play with him a little more.

He pressed his hand against her lower back, then slid it down to her butt, squeezing tight. And he smiled.

Something intense and sharp filled her chest. It was almost painful.

Happiness, she realized. She was happy.

She knew in that moment that she never really had been happy before. At least, not without an equally weighty worry to balance it. To warn her that on the other side of the happiness could easily lie tragedy.

But she wasn't thinking of tragedy now. She couldn't.

Joshua filled her vision, and he filled her brain, and for now—just for now—everything in her world felt right.

For a while, she wanted that to be the whole story.

So she blocked out every other thought, every single what-if, and she kissed him again.

When Joshua woke up, the bedroom was dark. There was a woman wrapped around him. And he wasn't entirely sure what had pulled him out of his deep slumber.

Danielle was sleeping peacefully. Her dark hair was wrapped around her face like a spiderweb, and he reached down to push it back. She flinched, pursing her lips and shifting against him, tightening her arms around his waist.

She was exhausted. Probably because he was an animal who had taken her three, maybe four times before they'd finally both fallen asleep.

He looked at her, and the hunger was immediate. Visceral. And he wondered if he was fooling himself pretending, even for a moment, that any of this was for her.

That he had any kind of higher purpose.

He wondered if he had any purpose at all beyond trying to satisfy himself with her.

And then he realized what had woken him up.

He heard a high, keening cry that barely filtered through the open bedroom door. Riley.

He looked down at Danielle, who was still fast asleep, and who would no doubt be upset that they had forgotten to bring the baby monitor into the room. Joshua had barely been able to remember his own name, much less a baby monitor.

He extricated himself from her hold, scrubbing his hand over his face. Then he walked over to his closet, grabbing a pair of jeans and pulling them on with nothing underneath.

He had no idea what in the hell to do with the baby. But Danielle was exhausted, because of him, and he didn't want to wake her up.

The cries got louder as he made his way down the hall, and he walked into the room to see flailing movement coming from the crib. The baby was very unhappy, whatever the reason.

Joshua walked across the room and stood above the crib, looking down. If he was going to marry Danielle, then that meant Riley was his responsibility too.

Riley would be his son.

Something prickled at the back of his throat, making it tight. So much had happened after Shannon lost the baby that he didn't tend to think too much about what might have been. But it was impossible not to think about it right now.

His son would have been five.

He swallowed hard, trying to combat the rising tide of emotion in his chest. That emotion was why he avoided contact with Riley. Joshua wasn't so out of touch with his feelings that he didn't know that.

But his son wasn't here. He'd never had the chance to be born.

Riley was here.

And Joshua could be there for him.

He reached down, placing his hand on the baby's chest. His little body started, but he stopped crying.

Joshua didn't know the first thing about babies. He'd never had to learn. He'd never had the chance to hold his son. Never gone through a sleepless night because of crying.

He reached down, picking up the small boy from his crib, holding the baby close to his chest and supporting Riley's downy head.

There weren't very many situations in life that caused Joshua to doubt himself. Mostly because he took great care to ensure he was only ever in situations where he had the utmost control.

But holding this tiny creature in his arms made him feel at a loss. Made him feel like his strength might be a liability rather than an asset. Because at the moment, he felt like this little boy could be far too easily broken. Like he might crush the baby somehow.

Either with his hands or with his inadequacy.

Though, he supposed that was the good thing about babies. Right now, Riley didn't seem to need him to be perfect. He just needed Joshua to be there. Being there he could handle.

He made his way to the rocking chair in the corner and sat down, pressing Riley to his chest as he rocked back and forth.

"You might be hungry," Joshua said, keeping his voice soft. "I didn't ask."

Riley turned his head back and forth, leaving a small

trail of drool behind on Joshua's skin. He had a feeling if his brother could see him now, he would mock him mercilessly. But then, he couldn't imagine Isaiah with a baby at all. Devlin, yes. But only since he had married Mia. She had changed Devlin completely. Made him more relaxed. Made him a better man.

Joshua thought of Danielle, sleeping soundly back in his room. Of just how insatiable he'd been for her earlier. Of how utterly trapped she was, and more or less at his mercy.

He had to wonder if there was any way she could make him a better man, all things considered.

Though, he supposed he'd kind of started to become a better man already. Since he had taken her on. And Riley.

He had to be the man who could take care of them, if he was so intent on fixing things.

Maybe they can fix you too.

Even though there was no one in the room but the baby, Joshua shook his head. That wasn't a fair thing to put on either of them.

"Joshua?"

He looked up and saw Danielle standing in the doorway. She was wearing one of his T-shirts, the hem falling to the top of her thighs. He couldn't see her expression in the darkened room.

"Over here."

"Are you holding Riley?" She moved deeper into the room and stopped in front of him, the moonlight streaming through the window shadowing one side of her face. With her long, dark hair hanging loose around her shoulders, and that silver light casting her in a glow, she looked ethereal. He wondered how he had ever thought she was pitiful. How he had ever imagined she wasn't beautiful.

"He was crying," he responded.

"I can take him."

He shook his head, for some reason reluctant to give him up. "That's okay."

A smile curved her lips. "Okay. I can make him a bottle."

He nodded, moving his hand up and down on the baby's back. "Okay."

Danielle rummaged around for a moment and then went across the room to the changing station, where he assumed she kept the bottle-making supplies. Warmers and filtered water and all of that. He didn't know much about it, only that he had arranged to have it all delivered to the house to make things easier for her.

She returned a moment later, bottle in hand. She tilted it upside down and tested it on the inside of her wrist. "It's all good. Do you want to give it to him?"

He nodded slowly and reached up. "Sure."

He shifted his hold on Riley, repositioning him in the crook of his arm so he could offer him the bottle.

"Do you have a lot of experience with babies?"

"None," he said.

"You could have fooled me. Although, I didn't really have any experience with babies until Riley was born. I didn't figure I would ever have experience with them."

"No?"

She shook her head. "No. I was never going to get married, Joshua. I knew all about men, you see. My mother got pregnant with me when she was fourteen. Needless to say, things didn't get off to the best start. I never knew my father. My upbringing was…unstable.

My mother just wasn't ready to have a baby, and honestly, I don't know how she could have been. She didn't have a good home life, and she was so young. I think she wanted to keep me, wanted to do the right thing—it was just hard. She was always looking for something else. Looking for love."

"Not in the right places, I assume."

She bit her lip. "No. To say the least. She had a lot of boyfriends, and we lived with some of them. Sometimes that was better. Sometimes they were more established than us and had better homes. The older I got, the less like a mom my mom seemed. I started to really understand how young she was. When she would get her heart broken, I comforted her more like a friend than like a daughter. When she would go out and get drunk, I would put her to bed like I was the parent." Danielle took a deep breath. "I just didn't want that for myself. I didn't want to depend on anybody, or have anyone depend on me. I didn't want to pin my hopes on someone else. And I never saw a relationship that looked like anything else when I was growing up."

"But here you are," he said, his chest feeling tight. "And you're marrying me."

"I don't know if you can possibly understand what this is like," she said, laughing, a kind of shaky nervous sound. "Having this idea of what your life will be and just…changing that. I was so certain about what I would have, and what I wouldn't have. I would never get married. I would never have children. I would never have…a beautiful house or a yard." Her words got thick, her throat sounding tight. "Then there was Riley. And then there was your ad. And then there was you. And suddenly everything I want is different, everything I expect is different. I actually hope for things. It's kind of a miracle."

He wanted to tell her that he wasn't a miracle. That whatever she expected from him, he was sure to disappoint her in some way. But what she was describing was too close to his own truth.

He had written off having a wife. He had written off having children. That was the whole part of being human he'd decided wasn't for him. And yet here he was, feeding a baby at three in the morning staring at a woman who had just come from his bed. A woman who was wearing his ring.

The way Joshua needed it, the way he wanted to cling to his new reality, to make sure that it was real and that it would last, shocked him with its ferocity.

A moment later, he heard a strange sucking sound and realized the bottle was empty.

"Am I supposed to burp him?"

Danielle laughed. "Yes. But I'll do that."

"I'm not helpless."

"He's probably going to spit up on your hot and sexy chest. Better to have him do it on your T-shirt." She reached out. "I got this."

She took Riley from him and he sat back and admired the expert way she handled the little boy. She rocked him over her shoulder, patting his back lightly until he made a sound that most definitely suggested he had spit up on the T-shirt she was wearing.

Joshua had found her to be such a strange creature when he had first seen her. Brittle and pointed. Fragile.

But she was made of iron. He could see that now.

No one had been there to raise her, not really. And then she had stepped in to make sure that her half brother was taken care of. Had upended every plan she'd made for her life and decided to become a mother at twenty-two.

"What?" she asked, and he realized he had been sitting there staring at her.

"You're an amazing woman, Danielle Kelly. And if no one's ever told you that, it's about time someone did."

She was so bright, so beautiful, so fearless.

All this time she had been a burning flame no one had taken the time to look at. But she had come to him, answered his ad and started a wildfire in his life.

It didn't seem fair, the way the world saw each of them. He was a celebrated businessman, and she… Well, hadn't he chosen her because he knew his family would simply see her as a poor, unwed mother?

She was worth ten of him.

She blinked rapidly and wasn't quite able to stop a tear from tracking down her cheek. "Why…why do you think that?"

"Not very many people would have done what you did. Taking your brother. Not after everything your mother already put you through. Not after spending your whole life taking care of the one person who should have been taking care of you. And then you came here and answered my ad."

"Some people might argue that the last part was taking the easy way out."

"Right. Except that I could have been a serial killer."

"Or made me dress like a teddy bear," she said, keeping her tone completely serious. "I actually feel like that last one is more likely."

"Do you?"

"There are more furries than there are serial killers, thank God."

"I guess, lucky for you, I'm neither one." He wasn't sure he was the great hope she seemed to think he was. But right now, he wanted to be.

"Very lucky for me," she said. "Oh… Joshua, imagine if someone were both."

"I'd rather not."

She went to the changing table and quickly set about getting Riley a new diaper before placing him back in the crib. Then she straightened and hesitated. "I guess I could… I can just stay in here. Or…"

"Get the baby monitor," he said. "You're coming back to my bed."

She smiled, and she did just that.

The next day there were wedding dresses in Danielle's room. Not just a couple of wedding dresses. At least ten, all in her size.

She turned in a circle, looking at all of the garment bags with heavy white satin, beads and chiffon showing through.

Joshua walked into the room behind her, his arms folded over his chest. She raised her eyebrows, gesturing wildly at the dresses. "What is this?"

"We are getting married in less than two weeks. You need a dress."

"A fancy dress to eat my Pop-Tart cake in," she said, moving to a joke because if she didn't she might cry. Because the man had ordered wedding dresses and brought them into the house.

And because if she were normal, she might have friends to share this occasion with her. Or her mother. Instead, she was standing in her bedroom, where her baby was napping, and her fiancé was the only potential spectator.

"You aren't supposed to see the dresses, though," she said.

"I promise you I cannot make any sense out of them based on how they look stuffed into those bags. I called the bridal store in town and described your figure and had her send dresses accordingly."

Her eyes flew wide, her mouth dropping open. "You described my figure?"

"To give her an idea of what would suit you."

"I'm going to need a play-by-play of this description. How did you describe my figure, Joshua? This is very important."

"Elfin," he said, surprising her because he didn't seem to be joking. And that was a downright fanciful description coming from him.

"Elfin?"

A smile tipped his lips upward. "Yes. You're like an elf. Or a nymph."

"Nympho, maybe. And I blame you for that."

He reached out then, hooking his arm around her waist and drawing her toward him. "Danielle, I am serious."

She swallowed hard. "Okay," she said, because she didn't really know what else to say.

"You're beautiful."

Hearing him say that made her throat feel all dry and scratchy, made her eyes feel like they were burning. "You don't have to do that," she said.

"You think I'm lying? Why would I lie about that? Also, men can't fake this." He grabbed her hand and pressed it up against the front of his jeans, against the hardness there.

"You're asking me to believe your penis? Because penises are notoriously indiscriminate."

"You have a point. Plus, mine is pretty damn famously indiscriminate. By my own admission. But the one good thing about that is you can trust I know the difference between generalized lust and when a woman has reached down inside of me and grabbed hold of something I didn't even know was there. I told you, I like it easy. I told you... I don't deal with difficult situations or difficult people. That was my past failing. A huge failing, and I don't know if I'm ever going to forgive myself for it. But what we have here makes me feel like maybe I can make up for it."

There were a lot of nice words in there. A lot of beautiful sentiments tangled up in something that made her feel, well, kind of gross.

But he was looking at her with all that intensity, and there were wedding dresses hung up all around her, his ring glittering on her finger. And she just didn't want to examine the bad feelings. She was so tired of bad feelings.

Joshua—all of this—was like a fantasy. She wanted to live in the fantasy for as long as she could.

Was that wrong? After everything she had been through, she couldn't believe that it was.

"Well, get your penis out of here. The rest of you too. I'm going to try on dresses."

"I don't get to watch?"

"I grant you nothing about our relationship has been typical so far, but I would like to surprise you with my dress choice."

"That's fair. Why don't you let me take Riley for a while?"

"Janine is going to be here soon."

He shrugged. "I'll take him until then." He strode across the room and picked Riley up, and Riley flashed a small, gummy smile that might have been nothing more than a facial twitch but still made Danielle's heart do something fluttery and funny.

Joshua's confidence with Riley was increasing, and he made a massive effort to be proactive when it came to taking care of the baby.

Watching Joshua stand there with Riley banished any lingering gross feelings about being considered difficult, and when Joshua left the room and Danielle turned to face the array of gowns, she pushed every last one of her doubts to the side.

Maybe Joshua wasn't perfect. Maybe there were some issues. But all of this, with him, was a damn sight better than anything she'd had before.

And a girl like her couldn't afford to be too picky.

She took a deep breath and unzipped the first dress.

Chapter 10

The day of the wedding was drawing closer and Danielle was drawing closer to a potential nervous breakdown. She was happy, in a way. When Joshua kissed her, when he took her to bed, when he spent the whole night holding her in his strong arms, everything felt great.

It was the in-between hours. The quiet moments she spent with herself, rocking Riley in that gray time before dawn. That was when she pulled those bad feelings out and began to examine them.

She had two days until the wedding, and her dress had been professionally altered to fit her—a glorious, heavy satin gown with a deep V in the back and buttons that ran down the full skirt—and if for no other reason than that, she couldn't back out.

The thought of backing out sent a burst of pain blooming through her chest. Unfurling, spreading, expanding. No. She didn't want to leave Joshua. No matter the strange, imbalanced feelings between them, she wanted to be with him. She felt almost desperate to be with him.

She looked over at him now, sitting in the driver's seat of what was still the nicest car she had ever touched, much less ridden in, as they pulled up to the front of his parents' house.

Sometimes looking at him hurt. And sometimes looking away from him hurt. Sometimes everything hurt. The need to be near him, the need for distance.

Maybe she really had lost her mind.

It took her a moment to realize she was still sitting motionless in the passenger seat, and Joshua had already put the car in Park and retrieved Riley from the back seat. He didn't bother to bring the car seat inside this time. Instead, he wrapped the baby in a blanket and cradled him in his arms.

Oh, that hurt her in a whole different way.

Joshua was sexy. All the time. There was no question about that. But the way he was with Riley... Well, she was surprised that any woman who walked by him when he was holding Riley didn't fall immediately at his feet.

She nearly did. Every damned time.

She followed him to the front door, looking down to focus on the way the gravel crunched beneath her boots—new boots courtesy of Joshua that didn't have holes in them, and didn't need three pairs of socks to keep her toes from turning into icicles—because otherwise she was going to get swallowed up by the nerves that were riding through her.

His mother had insisted on making a prewedding dinner for them, and this was Danielle's second chance to make a first impression. Now it was real and she felt an immense amount of pressure to be better than she was, rather than simply sliding into the lowest expectation people like his family had of someone like her, as she'd done before.

She looked over at him when she realized he was staring at her. "You're going to be fine," he said.

Then he bent down and kissed her. She closed her eyes, her breath rushing from her lungs as she gave herself over to his kiss.

That, of course, was when the front door opened.

"You're here!"

Nancy Grayson actually looked happy to see them both, and even happier that she had caught them making out on the front porch.

Danielle tucked a stray lock of hair behind her ear. "Thank you for doing this," she said, jarred by the change in her role, but desperate to do a good job.

"Of course," the older woman said. "Now, let me hold my grandbaby."

Those words made Danielle pause, made her freeze up. Made her want to cry. Actually, she *was* crying. Tears were rolling down her cheeks without even giving her a chance to hold them back.

Joshua's mother frowned. "What's wrong, honey?"

Danielle swallowed hard. "I didn't ever expect that he would have grandparents. That he would have a family." She took a deep breath. "I mean like this. It means a lot to me."

Nancy took Riley from Joshua's arms. But then she reached out and put her hand on Danielle's shoulder. "He's not the only one who has a family. You do too."

Throughout the evening Danielle was stunned by the warm acceptance of Joshua's entire family. By the way his sister-in-law, Mia, made an effort to get to know her, and by the complete absence of antagonism coming from his younger sister, Faith.

But what really surprised her was when Joshua's father came and sat next to her on the couch during dessert. Joshua was engaged in conversation with his brothers across the room while Mia, Faith and Joshua's mother were busy playing with Riley.

"I knew you would be good for him," Mr. Grayson said.

Danielle looked up at the older man. "A wife, you mean," she said, her voice soft. She didn't know why she had challenged his assertion, why she'd done anything but blandly agree. Except she knew she wasn't the woman he would have chosen for his son, and she didn't want him to pretend otherwise.

He shook his head. "I'm not talking about the ad. I know what he did. I know that he placed another ad looking for somebody he could use to get back at me. But the minute I met you, I knew you were exactly what he needed. Somebody unexpected. Somebody who would push him out of his comfort zone. It's real now, isn't it?"

It's real now.

Those words echoed inside of her. What did real mean? They were really getting married, but was their relationship real?

He didn't love her. He wanted to fix her. And somehow, through fixing her, he believed he would fix himself.

Maybe that wasn't any less real than what most people had. Maybe it was just more honest.

"Yes," she said, her voice a whisper. "It's real."

"I know that my meddling upset him. I'm not stupid.

And I know he felt like I wasn't listening to him. But he has been so lost in all that pain, and I knew… I knew he just needed to love somebody again. He thought everything I did, everything I said was because I don't understand a life that goes beyond what we have here." He gestured around the living room—small, cozy, essentially a stereotype of the happy, rural family. "But that's not it. Doesn't matter what a life looks like, a man needs love. And *that* man needs love more than most. He always was stubborn, difficult. Never could get him to talk about much of anything. He needs someone he can talk to. Someone who can see the good in him so he can start to see it too."

"Love," Danielle said softly, the word a revelation she had been trying to avoid.

That was why it hurt. When she looked at him. When she was with him. When she looked away from him. When he was gone.

That was the intense, building pressure inside her that felt almost too large for her body to contain.

It was every beautiful, hopeful feeling she'd had since meeting him.

She loved him.

And he didn't love her. That absence was the cause of the dark disquiet she'd felt sometimes. He wanted to use her as a substitute for his girlfriend, the one he thought he had failed.

"Every man needs love," Todd said. "Successful businessmen and humble farmers. Trust me. It's the thing that makes life run. The thing that keeps you going when crops don't grow and the weather doesn't cooperate. The thing that pulls you up from the dark pit when you can't find the light. I'm glad he found his light."

But he hadn't.

She had found hers.

For him, she was a Band-Aid he was trying to put over a wound that would end up being fatal if he didn't do something to treat it. If he didn't do something more than simply cover it up.

She took a deep breath. "I don't…"

"Are you ready to go home?"

Danielle looked up and saw Joshua standing in front of her. And those words…

Him asking if she wanted to go home, meaning to his house, with him, like that house belonged to her. Like he belonged to her…

Well, his question allowed her to erase all the doubts that had just washed through her. Allowed her to put herself back in the fantasy she'd been living in since she'd agreed to his proposal.

"Sure," she said, pushing herself up from the couch.

She watched as he said goodbye to his family, as he collected Riley and slung the diaper bag over his shoulder. Yes. She loved him.

She was an absolute and total lost cause for him. In love. Something she had thought she could never be.

The only problem was, she was in love alone.

It was his wedding day.

Thankfully, only his family would be in attendance. A small wedding in Copper Ridge's Baptist church, which was already decorated for Christmas and so saved everyone time and hassle.

Which was a good thing, since he had already harassed local baker Alison Donnelly to the point where she was ready to assault him with a spatula over his demands related to a Pop-Tart cake.

It was the one thing Danielle had said she wanted, and even if she had been joking, he wanted to make it happen for her.

He liked doing things for her. Whether it was teaching her how to ride horses, pleasuring her in the bedroom or fixing her nice meals, she always expressed a deep and sweet gratitude that transcended anything he had ever experienced before.

Her appreciation affected him. He couldn't pretend it didn't.

She affected him.

He walked into the empty church, looking up at the steeply pitched roof and the thick, curved beams of wood that ran the length of it, currently decked with actual boughs of holly.

Everything looked like it was set up and ready, all there was to do now was wait for the ceremony to start.

Suddenly, the doors that led to the fellowship hall opened wide and in burst Danielle. If he had thought she looked ethereal before, it was nothing compared to how she looked at this moment. Her dark hair was swept back in a loose bun, sprigs of baby's breath woven into it, some tendrils hanging around her face.

And the dress…

The bodice was fitted, showing off her slim figure, and the skirt billowed out around her, shimmering with each and every step. She was holding a bouquet of dark red roses, her lips painted a deep crimson to match.

"I didn't think I was supposed to see you until the wedding?" It was a stupid thing to say, but it was about the only thing he could think of.

"Yes. I know. I was here getting ready, and I was going to hide until everything started. Stay in the dressing room." She shook her head. "I need to talk to you, though. And I was already wearing this dress, and all of the layers of underwear that you have to wear underneath it to make it do this." She kicked her foot out, causing the skirt to flare.

"To make it do what?"

"You need a crinoline. Otherwise your skirt is like a wilted tulip. That's something I learned when the wedding store lady came this morning to help me get ready. But that's not what I wanted to talk to you about."

He wasn't sure if her clarification was a relief or not. He wasn't an expert on the subject of crinolines, but it seemed like an innocuous subject. Anything else that had drawn her out of hiding before the ceremony probably wasn't.

"Then talk."

She took a deep breath, wringing her hands around the stem of her bouquet. "Okay. I will talk. I'm going to. In just a second."

He shook his head. "Danielle Kelly, you stormed into my house with a baby and pretty much refused to leave until I agreed to give you what you wanted—don't act like you're afraid of me now."

"That was different. I wasn't afraid of losing you then." She looked up at him, her dark eyes liquid. "I'm afraid right now."

"You?" He couldn't imagine this brave, wonderfully strong woman being afraid of anything.

"I've never had anything that I wanted to keep. Or I guess, I never did before Riley. Once I had him, the thought of losing him was one of the things that scared me. It was the first time I'd ever felt anything like it. And now…it's the same with you. Do you know what you have in common with Riley?"

"The occasional tantrum?" His chest was tight. He knew that was the wrong thing to say, knew it was wrong to make light of the situation when she was so obviously serious and trembling.

"Fair enough," she said. Then she took a deep breath. "I love you. That's what you have in common with Riley. That's why I'm afraid of losing you. Because you matter. Because you more than matter. You're…everything."

Her words were like a sucker punch straight to the gut. "Danielle…"

He was such a jerk. Of course she thought she was in love with him. He was her first lover, the first man to ever give her an orgasm. He had offered her a place to live and he was promising a certain amount of financial security, the kind she'd never had before.

Of course such a vulnerable, lonely woman would confuse those feelings of gratitude with love.

She frowned. "Don't use that tone with me. I know you're about to act like you're the older and wiser of the two of us. You're about to explain why I don't understand what I'm talking about. Remember when you told me about your penis?"

He looked over his shoulder, then back at Danielle. "Okay, I'm not usually a prude, but we are in a church."

She let out an exasperated sound. "Sorry. But the thing is, remember when you told me that because you had been indiscriminate you knew the difference between common, garden-variety sex—"

"Danielle, Pastor John is around here somewhere."

She straightened her arms at her sides, the flowers

in her hand trembling with her unsuppressed irritation. "Who cares? This is our life. Anyway, what little I've read in the Bible was pretty honest about people. Everything I'm talking about—it's all part of being a person. I'm not embarrassed about any of it." She tilted her chin up, looking defiant. "My point is, I don't need you telling me what you think I feel. I have spent so much time alone, so much time without love, that I've had a lot of time to think about what it might feel like. About what it might mean."

He lowered his voice and took a step toward her. "Danielle, feeling cared for isn't the same as love. Pleasure isn't the same as love."

"I know that!" Her words echoed in the empty sanctuary. "Trust me. If I thought being taken care of was the same thing as love, I probably would have repeated my mother's pattern for my entire life. But I didn't. I waited. I waited until I found a man who was worth being an idiot over. Here I am in a wedding dress yelling at the man I'm supposed to marry in an hour, wanting him to understand that I love him. You can't be much more of an idiot than that, Joshua."

"It's okay if you love me," he said, even though it made his stomach feel tight. Even though it wasn't okay at all. "But I don't know what you expect me to do with that."

She stamped her foot, the sound ricocheting around them. "Love me back, dammit."

He felt like someone had grabbed hold of his heart and squeezed it hard. "Danielle, I can't do that. I can't. And honestly, it's better if you don't feel that way about me. I think we can have a partnership. I'm good with those. I'm good with making agreements, shaking hands, holding up my end of the deal. But feelings, all that stuff in between… I would tell you to call Shannon and ask her about that, but I don't think she has a phone right now, because I'm pretty sure she's homeless."

"You can't take the blame for that. You can't take the blame for her mistakes. I mean, I guess you can, you've been doing a great job of it for the past five years. And I get that. You lost a child. And then you lost your fiancée, the woman you loved. And you're holding on to that pain to try to insulate yourself from more."

He shook his head. "That's not it. It would be damned irresponsible of me not to pay attention to what I did to her. To what being with me can do to a woman." He cleared his throat. "She needed something that I couldn't give. I did love her—you're right. But it wasn't enough."

"You're wrong about that too," she said. "You loved her enough. But sometimes, Joshua, you can love somebody and love somebody, but unless they do something with that love it goes fallow. You can sow the seeds all you want, but if they don't water them, if they don't nurture them, you can't fix it for them."

"I didn't do enough," he said, tightening his jaw, hardening his heart.

"Maybe you were difficult. Maybe you did some wrong things. But at some point, she needed to reach out and tell you that. But she didn't. She shut down. Love can be everything, but it can't all be coming from one direction. The other person has to accept it. You can't love someone into being whole. They have to love themselves enough to want to be whole. And they have to love you enough to lay down their pain, to lay down their selfishness, and change—even when it's hard."

"I can't say she was selfish," he said, his voice rough. "I can't say she did anything wrong."

"What about my mother? God knows she had it hard, Joshua. I can't imagine having a baby at fourteen. It's hard enough having one at twenty-two. She has a lot of excuses. And they're valid. She went through hell, but the fact of the matter is she's choosing to go through it at this point. She has spent her whole life searching for the kind of love that either one of her children would have given her for nothing. I couldn't have loved her more. Riley is a baby, completely and totally dependent on whoever might take care of him. Could we have loved her more? Could we have made her stay?"

"That's different."

She stamped her foot again. "It is not!"

He didn't bother to yell at her about them being in a church again. "I understand that all of this is new to you," he said, fighting to keep his voice steady. "And honestly? It feels good, selfishly good, to know you see all this in me. It's tempting to lie to you, Danielle. But I can't do that. What I offered you is the beginning and end of what I have. Either you accept our partnership or you walk away."

She wouldn't.

She needed him too much. That was the part that made him a monster.

He knew he had all the power here, and he knew she would ultimately see things his way. She would have to.

And then what? Would she wither away living with him? Wanting something that he refused to give her?

The situation looked too familiar.

He tightened his jaw, steeling himself for her response.

What he didn't expect was to find a bouquet of flowers tossed at him. He caught them, and her petite shoulders lifted up, then lowered as she let out a shuddering breath. "I guess you're the next one to get married, then. Congratulations. You caught the flowers."

"Of course I damn well am," he said, tightening his fist around the roses, ignoring the thorn that bit into his palm. "Our wedding is in an hour."

Her eyes filled with tears, and she shook her head. Then she turned and ran out of the room, pausing only to kick her shoes off and leave them lying on the floor like she was Cinderella.

And he just stood there, holding on to the flowers, a trickle of blood from the thorn dripping down his wrist as he watched the first ray of light, the first bit of hope he'd had in years, disappear from his life.

Of course, her exit didn't stop him from standing at the altar and waiting. Didn't stop him from acting like the wedding would continue without a hitch.

He knew she hadn't gone far, mostly because Janine was still at the church with Riley, and while Danielle's actions were painful and mystifying at the moment, he knew her well enough to know she wasn't going to leave without Riley.

But the music began to play and no bride materialized.

There he was, a fool in a suit, waiting for a woman who wasn't going to come.

His family looked at each other, trading expressions filled with a mix of pity and anger. But it was his father who spoke up. "What in hell did you do, boy?"

A damned good question.

Unfortunately, he knew the answer to it.

"Why are you blaming him?" Faith asked, his younger

sister defending him to the bitter end, even when he didn't deserve it.

"Because that girl loves him," his father said, his tone full of confidence, "and she wouldn't have left him standing there if he hadn't done something."

Pastor John raised his hands, the gesture clearly meant to placate. "If there are any doubts about a marriage, it's definitely best to stop and consider those doubts, as it is a union meant for life."

"And she was certain," Joshua's father said. "Which means he messed it up."

"When two people love each other..." The rest of Pastor John's words were swallowed up by Joshua's family, but those first six hit Joshua and pierced him right in the chest.

When two people love each other.

Two people. Loving each other.

Love going both ways. Giving and taking.

And he understood then. He really understood.

Why she couldn't submit to living in a relationship that she thought might be one-sided. Because she had already endured it once. Because she'd already lived it with her mother.

Danielle was willing to walk away from everything he'd offered her. From the house, from the money, from the security. Even from his family. Because for some reason his love meant that much to her.

That realization nearly brought him to his knees.

He had thought his love insufficient. Had thought it destructive. And as she had stood there, pleading with him to love her back, he had thought his love unimportant.

But to her, it was everything.

How dare he question her feelings for him? Love, to Danielle, was more than a ranch and good sex. And she had proved it, because she was clearly willing to sacrifice the ranch and the sex to have him return her love.

"It was my fault," he said, his voice sounding like a stranger's as it echoed through the room. "She said she loved me. And I told her I couldn't love her back."

"Well," Faith said, "not even I can defend you now."

His mother looked stricken, his father angry. His brothers seemed completely unsurprised.

"You do love her, though," his father said, his tone steady. "So why did you tell her you didn't?"

Of course, Joshua realized right then something else she'd been right about. He was afraid.

Afraid of wanting this life he really had always dreamed of but had written off because he messed up his first attempt so badly. Afraid because the first time had been so painful, had gone so horribly wrong.

"Because I'm a coward," he said. "But I'm not going to be one anymore."

He walked down off the stage and to the front pew, picking up the bouquet. "I'm going to go find her," he said. "I know she's not far, since Riley is here."

Suddenly, he knew exactly where she was.

"Do you have any other weddings today, Pastor?"

Pastor John shook his head. "No. This is the only thing I have on my schedule today. Not many people get married on a Thursday."

"Hopefully, if I don't mess this up, we'll need you."

Chapter 11

It was cold. And Danielle's bare feet were starting to ache. But there had been no way in hell she could run in those high heels. She would have broken her neck.

Of course, if she had broken her neck, she might have fully severed her spinal cord and then not been able to feel anything. A broken heart sadly didn't work that way. She felt everything. Pain, deep and unending. Pain that spread from her chest out to the tips of her fingers and toes.

She wiggled her toes. In fairness, they might just be frostbitten.

She knew she was being pathetic. Lying down on that Pendleton blanket in the loft. The place where Joshua had first made love to her. Hiding.

Facing everyone—facing Joshua again—was inevitable. She was going to have to get Riley. Pack up her things. Figure out life without Joshua's money. Go back to working a cash register at a grocery store somewhere. Wrestling with childcare problems.

She expected terror to clutch her at the thought. Expected to feel deep sadness about her impending poverty. But those feelings didn't come.

She really didn't care about any of that.

Well, she probably would care once she was neck deep in it again, but right now all she cared about was that she wouldn't have Joshua.

If he had no money, if he was struggling just like her, she would have wanted to struggle right along with him.

But money or no money, struggle or no struggle, she needed him to love her. Otherwise...

She closed her eyes and took in a breath of sharp, cold air.

She had been bound and determined to ignore all of the little warnings she'd felt in her soul when she'd thought about their relationship. But in the end, she couldn't.

She knew far too well what it was like to pour love out and never get it back. And for a while it had been easy to pretend. That his support, and the sex, was the same as getting something back.

But they were temporary.

The kinds of things that would fade over the years.

If none of his choices were rooted in love, if none of it was founded in love, then what they had couldn't last.

She was saving herself hideous heartbreak down the road by stabbing herself in the chest now.

She snorted. Right now, she kind of wondered what the point was.

Pride?

"Screw pride," she croaked.

She heard the barn door open, heard footsteps down below, and she curled up into a ball, the crinoline under her dress scratching her legs. She buried her face in her arm, like a child. As if whoever had just walked into the barn wouldn't be able to see her as long as she couldn't see him.

Then she heard footsteps on the ladder rungs, the sound of calloused hands sliding over the metal. She knew who it was. Oh well. She had already embarrassed herself in front of him earlier. It was not like him seeing her sprawled in a tragic heap in a barn was any worse than her stamping her foot like a dramatic silent-film heroine.

"I thought I might find you here."

She didn't look up when she heard his voice. Instead, she curled into a tighter, even more resolute ball.

She felt him getting closer, which was ridiculous. She knew she couldn't actually feel the heat radiating from his body.

"I got you that Pop-Tart cake," he said. "I mean, I had Alison from Pie in the Sky make one. And I have to tell you, it looks disgusting. I mean, she did a great job, but I can't imagine that it's edible."

She uncurled as a sudden spout of rage flooded through her and she pushed herself into a sitting position. "Screw your Pop-Tart cake, Joshua."

"I thought we both liked Pop-Tarts."

"Yes. But I don't like lies. And your Pop-Tarts would taste like lies."

"Actually," he said slowly, "I think the Pop-Tart cake is closer to the truth than anything I said to you back in the church. You said a lot of things that were true. I'm a coward, Danielle. And guilt is a hell of a lot easier than grief."

"What the hell does that mean?" She drew her arm underneath her nose, wiping snot and tears away, tempted to ask him where his elfin princess was now. "Don't tease me. Don't talk in riddles. I'm ready to walk away from you if I need to, but I don't want to do it. So please, don't tempt me to hurt myself like that if you aren't..."

"I love you," he said, his voice rough. "And my saying so now isn't because I was afraid you were a gold digger and you proved you weren't by walking away. I realize what I'm about to say could be confused for that, but don't be confused. Because loving you has nothing to do with that. If you need my money... I've never blamed you for going after it. I've never blamed you for wanting to make your and Riley's lives easier. But the fact that you *were* willing to walk away from everything over three words... How can I pretend they aren't important? How can I pretend that I don't need your love when you demonstrated that you need my love more than financial security. More than sex. How can I doubt you and the strength of your feelings? How can I excuse my unwillingness to open myself up to you? My unwillingness to make myself bleed for you?"

He reached out, taking hold of her hands, down on his knees with her.

"You're going to get your suit dirty," she said inanely.

"Your dress is filthy," he returned.

She looked down at the dirt and smudges on the beautiful white satin. "Crap."

He took hold of her chin, tilting her face up to look at him. "I don't care. It doesn't matter. Because I would marry you in blue jeans, or I would marry you in this barn. I would sure as hell marry you in that dirty wedding dress. I... You are right about everything.

"It was easy to martyr myself over Shannon's pain. To blame myself so I didn't have to try again. So I didn't have to hurt again. Old pain is easier. The pain from that time in my life isn't gone, but it's dull. It throbs sometimes. It aches. When I look at Riley, he reminds me of my son, who never took a breath, and it hurts down deep. But I know that if I were to lose either of you now... That would be fresh pain. A fresh hell. And I have some idea of what that hell would be like because of what I've been through before.

"But it would be worse now. And... I was protecting myself from it. But now, I don't care about the pain, the fear. I want it all. I want you.

"I love you. Whatever might happen, whatever might come our way in the future... I love you. And I am going to do the hard yards for you, Danielle."

His expression was so fierce, his words so raw and real, all she could do was stare at him, listening as he said all the things she had never imagined she would hear.

"I was young and stupid the last time I tried love. Selfish. I made mistakes. I can't take credit for everything that went wrong. Some of it was fate. Some of it was her choices. But when things get hard this time, you have my word I won't pull away. I'm not going to let you shut me out. If you close the door on me, I'm going to kick it down. Because what we have is special. It's real. It's hope. And I will fight with everything I have to hold on to it."

She lurched forward, wrapping her arms around his neck, making them both fall backward. "I'll never shut you out." She squeezed her eyes closed, tears tracking down her cheeks. "Finding you has been the best thing that's ever happened to me. I don't feel alone, Joshua. Can you possibly understand what that means to me?"

He nodded gravely, kissing her lips. "I do understand," he said. "Because I've been alone in my own swamp for a long damned time. And you're the first person who made me feel like it was worth it to wade out."

"I love you," she said.

"I love you too. Do you still want to marry me?"

"Hell yeah."

"Good." He maneuvered them both so they were upright, taking her hand and leading her to the ladder. They climbed down, and she hopped from foot to foot on the cold cement floor. "Come on," he said, grabbing her hand and leading her through the open double doors.

She stopped when she saw that his whole family, Janine and Riley, and Pastor John were standing out there in the gravel.

Joshua's mother was holding the bouquet of roses, and she reached out, handing it back to Danielle. Then Joshua went to Janine and took Riley from her arms, holding the baby in the crook of his own. Then Joshua went back to Danielle, taking both of her hands with his free one.

"I look bedraggled," she said.

"You look perfect to me."

She smiled, gazing at everyone, at her new family. At this new life she was going to have.

And then she looked back at the man she loved with all her heart. "Well," she said, "okay, then. Marry me, cowboy."

Epilogue

December 5, 2017
FOUND A WIFE—

Local rancher Todd Grayson and his wife, Nancy, are pleased to announce the marriage of their son, a wealthy former bachelor, Joshua Grayson (no longer irritated with his father) to Danielle Kelly, formerly of Portland, now of Copper Ridge and the daughter of their hearts. Mr. Grayson knew his son would need a partner who was strong, determined and able to handle an extremely stubborn cuss, which she does beautifully. But best of all, she loves him with her whole heart, which is all his meddling parents ever wanted for him.

* * * * *

A VERY INTIMATE TAKEOVER

LaQuette

To sixteen-year-old LaQuette,
who never believed she'd see herself in the pages
of a Harlequin category romance, and to Charles G.
for convincing her it was time to rectify that.

To the late Ms. Diahann Carroll
for gifting the world with Dominique Deveraux.
Thank you for being brave enough to embrace
becoming "the first Black bitch on television."

Chapter 1

"Jordan Dylan Devereaux III."

Trey froze midstep, thwarted in her attempt to quietly slip through the reception area of DD Enterprises' executive suites. Five minutes of peace before this meeting was all she wanted. But when she heard the boom of her father's voice, she knew it wasn't to be. She tried to pretend she didn't hear him as she turned toward her office.

"Trey! Don't make me call your government name again. Bring yourself into my office."

Trey sighed and looked toward the ceiling, hoping to calm the shivers plaguing her body. Those tremors—more a sign of her rage than fear—persisted beyond the usual deep breath she took to get control of herself.

Remember, he's your daddy and you're too pretty to go to jail for patricide. She took one final breath and made the left turn to enter his office.

She walked into the large room with sunlight beaming

through the floor-to-ceiling windows that ran the length of three walls and looked at her father. He reminded her of the East River as he stood there watching, deceptively calm at first glance, but filled with angry currents that could drag you down into darkness at the drop of a hat.

"Did you hear me calling you?" His tone was unemotional, but she hadn't been the daughter of Jordan Dylan "Deuce" Devereaux II for thirty-two years not to know this was the calm before the storm.

"Daddy, everyone on this floor heard you calling me." She closed his office door to give them more privacy. If he was using her full name, things would probably get much louder very soon. "What's on your mind?"

"We lost the Singleton bid."

She stiffened. She knew this was coming. Deuce Devereaux didn't tolerate failure from anyone, not even his baby girl. "I'm aware, Daddy. It was out of my control."

"Out of your control? Correct me if I'm wrong, but aren't you my VP? And isn't the mergers and acquisitions department under your direct supervision?"

He knew very well she was and it was. He'd promoted her into the position four years ago because she had a keen eye for recognizing when businesses were ripe for the picking. Since then, she'd landed deal after deal, making him an obscene amount of money and putting his investment management firm, DD Enterprises, neck and neck with his number one competitor, Devereaux Incorporated. *His* father's investment firm.

Deuce turned away from his perch at the window and faced her. A tall Black man with the same smooth, deep brown skin and eyes he'd blessed Trey with, he always pulled the attention of a room. His dark close-cropped tight curls and thick, neatly trimmed mustache gave him a seasoned confidence only someone with significant life experience possessed. He wasn't a man you could fool. Only logic and reason won you any sway with him, and by the way his narrowed eyes locked on to hers, she knew he wasn't seeing the logic in her statement.

"I told you I wanted those shares at any cost, no matter how long it took."

"Daddy, in less than six months I've acquired thirty-three of the fifty-one percent of the shares needed to complete our takeover. Singleton is the only holdout. I gave our people permission to pay him four times what his Devereaux Inc. shares were worth. We both know he's in a financial hole and those shares are the only means he has to getting back on his feet. But at the last minute, he backed out with no explanation."

"You're too impulsive, Trey. Singleton isn't like the rest of the people you dangled money in front of. He's an old hand like my father, Ace. They came up together in business. He knows how to play the long game. Without his shares, my chance to take back what Ace stole from me—"

"Is only temporarily postponed. You'll have it. I promise," she answered quickly, hoping he'd remember how often she'd kept similar promises like this one in the past. "Singleton got spooked. But I'll make sure our reps get him back on track. Everyone has a price, Daddy. I just have to figure out what his is."

"I told you not to push him too hard. You don't know how to finesse people, Trey, only steamroll over them."

She threw her hand up in the air and let it fall back against her thick thigh, snug in her pencil skirt. "Here we go again. You're the one who taught me not to be anyone's chump. Placating people's nonsense is the biggest chump move you can make. Any of that sound familiar, Daddy, or did you forget who you raised me to be?"

Her father folded his arms over his chest and squinted at her, proof he wasn't thrilled with her tone. "I have forgotten nothing, but obviously you have if you're not taking this as seriously as I am."

She took another breath, trying to get her head together again. "Ace fired you and threw you out of the Devereaux family at twenty-two for loving my mother. He believed someone from her humble East New York beginnings could only be after the Devereaux money, or worse, was trying to get her hooks into his beloved company. He didn't give a damn how his cruelty would impact the daughter growing in her womb. That daughter was me. I haven't forgotten, Daddy. I will make him pay for loving that company more than he did his own blood and for choosing it over his own son and unborn grandchild. Even if I have to buy the damn thing from him myself."

Her father walked closer to her, pointing his finger in her direction and stabbing the air as he spoke. "Don't even joke like that. Stay away from Ace. He's treacherous."

"Fine, I'll stay away from him." Her acquiescence brought Deuce visible relief as the tension in the tight lines of his face melted away. Challenging her father on business matters was one thing. But she dared not test his unbreakable rule concerning her grandfather. "I promise I'll find another way. I always do, don't I?"

"How, Trey? Everyone else on that board is a member of Ace's family or in his pocket. They will never sell to an outsider. How do you propose we secure those shares now? My way was the only way of getting everything I've worked so hard for. And you in your infinite wisdom just screwed that up."

The little girl in her who ached for her father's approval crumbled a little. But the grown-ass woman in her refused to let her father have that satisfaction, so she placed her hands on her hips and straightened her posture.

"If you think I'm not doing a good enough job, then fire me. Otherwise, I've got a desk full of things I need to handle before the end of business today."

She turned on her skinny heel, opened the door, and closed it quietly behind her. She wouldn't slam it and show that he'd gotten to her. No one got the better of Trey Devereaux, not even the father she adored.

She walked across the hall to her own office and slipped inside. Sliding behind her desk, she placed her Hermès Black Box tote on a nearby side table. The moment the plush material of her chair cradled her body, she let an audible sigh spill from her slightly parted lips. Relief bled through her. This was her sanctuary. From this desk, she could create miracles. No matter the struggle, when she was here, in the quiet room that fueled her creativity with pops of vibrant red, gray, black and white, she could handle it all.

Then act like it.

She abruptly stopped the nervous tapping of her fingernail on the glass tabletop and looked at the pile of unopened mail. Fortified with a sip of her favorite iced coffee and a letter opener, Trey got to work distracting herself.

Halfway through the pile her secretary, Anisha, popped her head in the door and waved an envelope. "A courier delivered this letter before you came in. It looks important. He made me sign for it in triplicate before he'd hand it over. Unfortunately, I can't tell if it's for you or your dad. There's no designation on it."

Trey shrugged. When you bore a name shared by many generations, confusion was common. "I really wish people understood the 'III' at the end of my name isn't optional." Most women didn't have to deal with this problem since it was customary for sons to carry their father's names. But Deuce Devereaux insisted gender had no bearing on birthright and had proudly bestowed his name—what he saw as the only thing his father, Ace, couldn't strip him of—onto his daughter.

She waved Anisha in. "I'll take it. If it's for my dad, I'll walk it over later." Anisha gave her the letter, then disappeared into the hall.

"It's almost too pretty to open." Trey looked at the return address trying to surmise who J. Benton from St. James Place in Brooklyn, New York, was. The envelope was smooth yet had enough texture that she took her time sliding her finger across it. The deep sandalwood beige, trimmed in a dark mahogany and gold foil, had enough flare to let you know the sender cared about making a good impression, but not so much that it was gaudy.

She opened the envelope and pulled out the folded paper carefully. She was curious to see what this J. Benton had to say.

Dear Mr. Jordan Dylan Devereaux,
I'm Jeremiah Benton, the COO at Devereaux Incorporated.
    Please forgive my forwardness in sending you a physical letter. However, I needed to confirm delivery of this message while ensuring our communication remained private. What I have to say is too important to risk getting lost in your spam folder or intercepted by prying eyes. The elder Mr.

Devereaux has forbidden me to share this with you, but I felt that as his son, you needed to know. I regret to inform you that Ace has fallen ill. Ill enough that his physicians have determined he may have less than six months of life remaining. I know I am a stranger, and this is a personal topic, but your father and his business need you now as his next of kin. If left to his sister, Martha Devereaux-Smith, Devereaux Incorporated will suffer. You are the only person who can stop her. Please don't delay. For your father, and his legacy, I beg you to return to Devereaux Manor immediately.

Sincerely,

J. Benton

Trey rose in one quick movement, heading for her father's office. When she arrived, she immediately paused. The grandfather she'd seen nowhere but on television and in business magazines was dying. She tried to process what this new knowledge made her feel, and all she could identify was numbness. But her father, having spent the first twenty-two years of his life at his father's side, might feel something more than the nothingness that spread through her veins.

The door was slightly ajar. She was about to knock when she heard her parents' voices.

"Destiny, she's too quick to act. I've told her she couldn't rely solely on her usual tactics, and she ignored everything I said and did it her way instead. Now, she can't make this right." Her father's words cut deep, like a heated blade. He was still angry with her, his focus so fused to her failure, he couldn't see her ability to get this job done.

"Deuce, practically from the moment we found out I was carrying Trey, you have demanded greatness from her. You used to place your head on my belly every night when she would kick me so hard I couldn't sleep and say the same thing over and over until she calmed down. 'Trey, you are Deuce Devereaux's daughter, and there isn't a man or woman that can stand against you.' You believed that then, and in all this time she's never given you reason to doubt her."

"This is different, Des. This was her test, to prove to me she could handle everything I'm leaving to her. Now, after this disaster, I can't retire. I can't leave DD Enterprises until I know she's ready. I'm so tired, baby." The hitch in his voice yanked at Trey's heart. His lack of faith in her might have raised her blood pressure, but hearing him this way, so fragile, so hopeless, felt like something crushing her from the inside out. "I've been fighting this fight with Ace for over thirty years. It's taken so much away from my life with you. I'd thought I could retire early and leave it all to her, but now…"

"Don't doubt her, Deuce. She will find a way."

The letter she was holding pressed against her palm like a million pounds of sand. So tiny and insignificant from a glance, but the information inside it had the power to completely change their situation. A plan began to form in her mind. She'd promised her father she'd deliver Devereaux Incorporated to him; she would keep that promise.

Trey returned to her office, unfolding the letter again and looking at the information it contained with new eyes. She'd promised her father she'd win this fight for him, and suddenly she realized she held the key to victory right there in her hand.

Chapter 2

"What are you up to, Jeremiah?"

Jeremiah Benton smiled, then released a long breath as he looked up from his phone. His assistant had just sent him confirmation of a meeting he'd thought would never happen. "Nothing you should be concerned with, Ace."

Jeremiah watched as the older man, in his black silk pajamas, sat up against the headboard in his large four-poster bed. With tightly curled white hair on the sides of his head, and a smooth reddish-brown complexion that belied his seventy-five years, even on his sickbed, Ace Devereaux knew how to look the part of a seasoned, debonair statesman. "If you're being this secretive, it must involve a woman."

He chuckled. If only it was something as trivial as his love life. No, this meeting was about business—saving Ace's to be exact. "You know I don't have time to worry about women. I'm too busy making money for you."

Ace shrugged, his smile dropping a bit. "I love Devereaux Incorporated, Jeremiah. But the most fulfilling thing in my life was my beloved, Alva. And trust me, no amount of money in the world could compare to what it felt like to be loved by her."

Ace opened his arms, and Jeremiah stood from the bedside chair and sat beside the older man, falling into his embrace. It didn't matter that Ace was older and his body frail from time and the cancer they'd discovered a month ago. His hugs still made Jeremiah feel loved, safe and cared for in a way nothing else had in his life.

"You, my dear boy, work too hard. Until I close my eyes to this world, I'm your boss. Take some time to find someone who loves you the way my Alva loved me—completely, without fear and with a fierceness that both frightened me and comforted me in ways I'd never known before."

Ace placed a strong kiss on Jeremiah's cheek, releasing him from the embrace, and breaking the comforting spell that always came whenever the older man put his arms around him. The thought of having only a finite number of those famous Ace hugs remaining spread like ice in his soul—cold, hard and numbing.

"Is there anything else I can do for you before I go, old man? Ms. Alicia is downstairs, and you can call her if you need anything."

"I'll be gone in six months, maybe less," Ace answered. "All that anyone can do for me has already been done. I just want you to live your life. From the moment I pulled you off that street corner at sixteen, it was all I ever wanted. For you to live and thrive. I gave you a home, and all that comes with it, so you would reach your full potential. Not so you could wait on me hand and foot, Jeremiah."

"Ace, I owe you so much."

"You owe me nothing."

Jeremiah didn't argue. Actions had a much greater impact with Ace, so he pulled the precious folded document sitting in his jacket's breast pocket out and gave it to Ace. "I know you told me I didn't have to do this," he said, changing the subject abruptly. "But I had Amara start the process of changing my last name to Devereaux. Once I sign and file these papers, it's done."

When Ace tried to interrupt, Jeremiah lifted a finger to silence him. "I know I didn't have to, but I wanted to. You've given me so much, Ace. You've been like a father to me. And although you tried to hide it from me, I know the only reason you didn't adopt me and become my legal father was because my mother wouldn't give up her parental rights to me. Considering all that, the least I could do was take your name to honor you now."

"I'm speechless, Jeremiah."

"No need to say anything. Look over the papers, think it over, and decide if you want to give me your blessing. It's your name. I won't do this unless you agree."

Ace patted Jeremiah's cheek. His brown eyes shimmered with unshed tears as they gazed into Jeremiah's. "You are a gift I never deserved. At no time did I blame your mother for not wanting to give up that last piece of you and neither should you. She did the best she could with what she had. She did right by you when she let you come stay with me. But asking her to relinquish parental rights was too much for her ailing heart to bear."

"I know that."

Jeremiah felt much more compassion now than when

he'd discovered his mother's refusal back then. But she was long dead, and holding on to so much pain would've stopped him from enjoying the love Ace bestowed on him.

"Speaking of other things I know," Jeremiah continued. "David asked me to talk to you about the will again. Ace, you either need to talk to Deuce or remove the clause that says he or his descendants have to show up at the reading of your will to claim your forty percent of Devereaux Inc."

Ace waved his hand to dismiss Jeremiah and as much as he loved the older man, he also wanted to reach out and strangle him.

"Ace, the way the will is worded, if Deuce or his descendents don't claim it, Martha will become the largest single shareholder in the company. All she'd need is to acquire eleven percent more of the shares in support to take control of the company, or worse, chop it up and sell it off. Is that what you want?"

Ace turned away from Jeremiah, staring at nothing. "It's not what I want, but it's the right thing to do. I know you don't understand, but I'm trying to set things right in my death that I couldn't fix in my life."

Jeremiah groaned in frustration. Ace was usually stubborn, but his actions were always grounded in logic. This made no sense at all.

"Change the will, Ace. Leave the shares to Amara, Lyric, Stephan or me." He pleaded. "We've stood by you, given you everything—especially our loyalty. Don't do this to us."

Ace closed his eyes, and when he opened them again, they were muddied with sadness and guilt. "I'm sorry. But I can't do what you're asking."

Ace took a moment to clear his throat before he spoke again. "Now, as I was saying before you tried to distract me with talk about my will, my only wish for you is an abundant life. I've lived mine. No." He stopped, his eyes falling on the framed picture of his son as a young boy resting on the nearby nightstand. More than the cancer eating away at him, memories of his son always revealed the hurt Ace still carried over their estrangement. It was an obvious pain, a deep cut that was his chronic source of agony. Resolute, he placed his hand against Jeremiah's cheek. "I've wasted mine. I have so many regrets. Don't be like me. Be better than me. Live yours. Live, Jeremiah."

The calendar alarm dinged on Jeremiah's phone, and he knew he had to leave. He brooked the disappointment flooding his chest and turned his face to kiss the withered palm Ace held against his cheek. He would do as the man instructed. He always did. Ace's sage advice had taken him from being a street hustler to the chief operating officer of a billion-dollar business.

But first, he had to make sure he wiped away the look of anguish from the old man's face. He might not save Ace's life, but he would do all he could to give him peace in these last few days. And a meeting with Deuce Devereaux, Ace's estranged son, was the first step in making that happen.

"I'll be back to check on you this evening, Ace. Don't give Ms. Alicia a hard time."

Ace winked, indicating he would do what he damn well pleased regardless of who was around. It was hard to be mad at that. Especially when he'd used that same will to create Devereaux Incorporated.

Jeremiah left the room with a smile that slipped off his

face as soon as the door closed behind him. He felt the familiar resentment he kept buried so deep that he often tricked himself into believing it wasn't there.

It should be yours.

He closed his eyes, trying to force his troubling thoughts back into the shadows of his mind. Ace had given him too much. Who was he to question why the man wouldn't choose Jeremiah as his heir, even when Jeremiah had dedicated his entire career to making Devereaux Inc. thrive?

He stepped out onto Clinton Avenue, still determined to preserve Ace's legacy at all costs, even at the risk of his own professional aspirations. This meeting with Deuce Devereaux would work. Jeremiah wouldn't let it happen any other way.

Jeremiah sat in the back at The Vault, an exclusive VIP lounge in Brooklyn, waiting for Jordan Dylan "Deuce" Devereaux II to arrive. God, that was a mouthful. Thank goodness father and son went by Ace and Deuce respectively, otherwise saying that every day might get tiresome real fast. He leaned forward, picked up his lowball filled with two fingers of the house's best whiskey, and gently shook the glass until the amber liquid swirled inside the tumbler. He pulled the glass to his lips and took a slow, deliberate sip of his drink and let the whiskey's heat spread through him.

Business matters rarely bothered Jeremiah to the point that he reached for a drink to calm down. With data, analysis and a plan of execution, he could usually deal with anything the business world threw at him. But the success of what he planned to do here tonight depended on the whims of another human being. The preservation of Ace's legacy could go sideways if Deuce said no to Jeremiah's proposition.

He glanced at his Rolex and watched the second hand tick until it was the agreed upon meeting time. The door opened, flooding the warm reddish glow of the lounge with bright streaks of white from the streetlights outside. A tall woman in silhouette filled the threshold. He should've attempted to look past her to see if Deuce would follow, but her curves trapped his gaze and wouldn't let go.

Thankfully, she stepped inside the lounge, letting the door close and giving him the fuller view he silently prayed for of her deep brown skin and flawless body. She moved farther into the lounge, stopping to glance around the room before heading in his direction. With each step she took, the red, single-breasted pantsuit and black mesh bustier revealed new delights, making him regret the fact that he was here for business instead of the pleasure of just watching her walk. But he didn't have time to consider his predicament further, because before he knew it, she was standing at his table smiling down at him.

Her smile was as intriguing as the sensual strut she'd used to glide across the room. Strong, bright, peppered with a bit of mischief. It was everything he never knew he needed a woman's smile to be. It was sexy as hell; she was sexy as hell, a goddess gracing the mere mortals around her with her presence. Making sure his cool-calm-and-collected facade was in place, he sipped his whiskey and carefully balanced it on his knee when he finished.

"Can I help you with something, miss?"

Her smile spread wider. "I think I'm here to help you."

She unbuttoned her jacket. The two flaps opened, giving him a better view of her full breasts cradled in her bustier, making him envious of the strappy material's proximity to her skin.

"I really wish that were true," he responded, taking another moment to let his gaze slide over her. "But I'm here for a business meeting, and as much as I wish it, you're not the person I'm expecting."

"You sure about that?"

She sat down next to him on the wide chaise, crossing one thick leg over the other as she leaned back against the cushions. A hint of a spiced, floral aroma wafted off her skin. He wanted to lean in and follow it, press his nose as close to her flesh as she'd allow and breathe her in. *Keep it together, J.* Forever the gentleman, he cleared his throat, fighting the need building deep in his belly, sending ripples of electricity that prickled his skin, and lifted his eyes to meet hers.

Big mistake. Her body might have set his senses on fire, but the spark in her deep brown gaze hypnotized him, making him want to fly closer to her flame.

The sound of the door opening again broke the spell. He looked toward the entryway, praying that Deuce had found his way here, because the predatory look in this sexy stranger's eyes both alarmed and titillated him. When another young woman walked in, he paused, attempting to fortify himself before he dared look back at the stranger next to him.

"Trust me," he pushed the words past his suddenly dry lips. "I'd rather spend my evening…" He tugged his bottom lip into his mouth trying to keep himself from saying something that would get him slapped, or worse, cause this goddess to walk away. But when a sly smile tilted her lips, the notion of censoring himself disappeared into the heated air sparking around them. "I was going to say talking to you. But the truth is, if you bless me with your time tonight, there won't be much talking going on."

"You don't mince words." A spark of excitement flashed across her eyes as she cocked her head and let her smile grow wider. "I like a man who says what he wants. And by the looks of you—" she let her heated gaze travel up and down his seated body "—I think I'd enjoy hearing more of what you want. But before we do that, we should get our intended purpose out of the way first."

"Unless you're a fifty-something-year-old man named Jordan Devereaux, I think you're looking for someone else. But if you're wondering, I'd be glad to be anyone you want tonight."

She beamed at him, like she was privy to something he wasn't, and extended her hand for him to shake it. When he grabbed it, her handshake was firm and confident. It was all business. But even still, he ached to let his palm remain in her possession. "I'm Trey, but my given name is Jordan Devereaux." Her smile shone brighter as she finally pulled her hand from his. "The third," she added with a flippant wave of her hand as if it were an afterthought. "That fifty-something-year-old man you mentioned is my father, Deuce. According to your letter, you wanted his help. He couldn't be here, so he sent the next best thing. Me."

Jeremiah didn't respond. He couldn't. This was not what he'd asked for. He was about to tell her so when she held up a finger to stop him. "So, Mr. Benton—" her voice was deep and sultry, soothing even "—do you want my help or not?" She leaned in closer, the sweet and decadent scent of her driving him insane. "Or are we going to forget about your letter and find somewhere to get… better acquainted?"

He scrutinized her to see if she was joking, but the way she sat back, letting her tongue dart out and caress her bottom lip like she was hunting for a tasty snack, told him she was serious.

Tempting, but not the smartest move you could make. Sure you wanna hit that?

Hell yeah, he was sure. He could feel his traitorous cock thickening behind his zipper now.

You know this will end badly. What happens to Ace's company then?

Damn his common sense for intruding on his baser needs. Because there was no way any self-respecting Brooklyn playa would willingly walk away from this woman.

"To be clear," she gave him a sheepish smile peppered with equal measures of sass and heat, "I'm game with either scenario." She winked at him and licked her bottom lip again, and the ambient temperature crept up. Jeremiah loosened his tie. This meeting wasn't going how he'd planned and he'd be damned if he even wanted to get it back on track.

"You," he said to her as he pointed a single finger over the top of the empty tumbler in his hand, "are a problem."

Chapter 3

"Jeremiah, are you listening to me?"

Jeremiah blinked at the mention of his name and met Amara Devereaux-Rodriguez's gaze. Ace's grandniece was one of the two lawyers in the family on the business's legal team. She and Jeremiah had met as teenagers and become fast friends the moment Ace brought him home.

"I heard everything you said." He smiled when she glared at him. "You said Trey's background check came back clean. She is who she says she is, and therefore can lay claim to Ace's shares if her father refuses. Deuce sending Trey instead of showing up himself could be a sign he still wants nothing to do with Ace. Therefore, Trey's our best option. Since she's primed to take over DD Enterprises, she'd probably be a safer bet than Deuce anyway, and would be more likely to sell me the shares than her father."

Dev's bemused smile lit up her face. "I will never know how you do that."

"Do what?" he asked.

"Stay present while obviously thinking of something else." She shook her head and took a deep breath. "But back to securing Uncle Ace's shares." Jeremiah repositioned himself in his leather office chair, trying not to let his frustration show. "You shouldn't have to go through this to get what you've earned. It's not right, J."

"Amara—"

She held up a hand and interrupted him, then stood and walked around to his side of the desk and sat on the corner to face him. "Jeremiah, those shares should be yours."

"Amara, that's not what Ace's will says."

"I also know that there's an easy fix for that. All Uncle Ace has to do is change the will. You've been more son to him than his own flesh and blood. It's not right and if you won't say something about all of this, I sure as hell will because—"

"Amara, enough!" Jeremiah slammed his hand down on the desk, instantly regretting the loss of control. "Yes, I deserve those shares. But I won't beg for what should be mine. Not from Ace, not from anyone." Only children threw tantrums when they didn't get what they wanted. Grown men sucked it up and dealt with it. "So, please let this go. I've been with the man since I was sixteen. If he hasn't changed the will in all that time, he has to have a reason for it. It's not for any of us to question what Ace does with his shares."

He swallowed the bitterness settling on his tongue, attempting to temper his anger and get Amara to drop the subject. "Whatever our feelings, the only thing that matters is what Ace wants. Are we clear?"

He rarely pulled rank on Amara. She'd been a vital partner in his success at Devereaux Inc. But on this he would not budge. He would give Ace what he'd longed for all these years, even if it meant he had to step aside to make it happen.

"Now." He closed his eyes and pinched the bridge of his nose. "You're certain Trey can legally claim the shares if Deuce fails, and I can buy them from her once she does?"

When he opened his eyes again, he noticed Amara studying him before she answered. "Yes. But I can tell by the pensive crease in your forehead you're worried about bringing Trey in."

He nodded. "She's never been around him. Who knows what Deuce has told her about Ace? Is she really here to help or take the only opportunity she's ever had to spit in the old man's face? What if she's just as greedy and manipulative as Martha and refuses to sell me the shares after she claims them? There are so many unknowns."

Amara reached out and placed her hand on Jeremiah's. "I can't answer that. Everything my investigator could find in the short time between last night and this morning suggests she's on the level. I can't give you any guarantees beyond that."

He lifted a skeptical brow. "Then what's your suggestion? How do I let her help but protect Ace too?"

"Limit her access," she responded. "Keep her out of Devereaux Inc. for now. Start by introducing her to Ace. Her interaction with him will tell you how to proceed." She dropped her gaze for a second and when she lifted it again, the shine of unshed tears filled her eyes. "We don't have time. Uncle Ace can't hold on for much longer."

Jeremiah let out an audible sigh. As usual, Amara wasn't wrong. They had few options left at this point, and he had to act if he was to save his family and his mentor. He closed the folders sitting open on the table and returned them to Amara. She slipped them into her nearby briefcase and stood when the doorbell chimed. Jeremiah attempted to stand, but Amara held out a hand.

"Let me welcome her, please. Anyone who can twist the ever-cool Jeremiah Benton into knots has got to be one hell of a woman."

More than you know.

Trey stood on the curb at Clinton and Gates Avenues, staring in awe. The eggshell double mansion with its early twentieth-century Beaux Arts architecture stood out on the busy Brooklyn street like a large sparkly jewel in the night. Deuce had forbade her ever going near it as a child, and the close watch her parents kept on her during adolescence left little time for her to explore the grandeur of Devereaux Manor. But here it still sat, the home where at one time two generations of Devereauxs once lived.

A ripple of uncertainty made her stiffen as she replayed her plan in her head. She was breaking her father's explicit mandate of staying away from Ace, not to mention, she was here to steal a dying man's company.

Not just any dying man, your grandfather.

Trey shuddered. She was ruthless in her usual business dealings. But it was always business, never personal. This was different. The stakes were higher. Being her father's unknowing instrument of retribution, she'd hand Deuce his rightful legacy while proving she was capable of going to any lengths to get the job done for DD Enterprises.

Before her conscience made her change her mind, she took one shaky step and then another until she was standing before the double doors. She straightened her spine, took one final fortifying breath and rang the bell.

Jeremiah hadn't explained any details regarding why he wanted to meet her here. Trey didn't have any clue what or whom she'd encounter once inside. The door opened quickly and a beautiful woman with familiar features stared at Trey with a wide smile. Trey, slightly in awe of seeing anyone who looked like her besides her father, stood with her mouth agape. The same deep brown eyes, high cheekbones and matching dimples stared back at her, confirming that the mythical side of her family she'd only heard tales of really existed. "Hi, I'm Amara. I'm your second cousin."

Trey extended her hand and continued to stare for a moment longer before she caught the knowing smile on Amara's face. "I understand," the woman continued. "Those Devereaux genes are something else. Even though my grandfather is nearly a decade younger than yours, they look like twins. The same is true for my mom and me. I'm assuming you look like your dad spit you out too."

The delight and natural curiosity on Amara's face made a bubble of laughter spread through Trey's chest. "Much to my mother's disappointment, I am a carbon copy of my father. Let her tell it, not only am I his twin, but I act too much like him too."

Amara laughed. "Unfortunately, it's the plight of anyone who procreates with a Devereaux." Amara waved her in, opening the door wider so Trey could step inside the foyer. She waited for Amara to escort her inside, but the young woman remained still, smiling as she looked at Trey. "Uncle Ace will be thrilled to see you. I know there's tension surrounding the split between him and your dad. But believe me, you being here now will mean so much to him."

Trey wasn't sure how to process that. Ace Devereaux had abandoned her father when Deuce had needed him most. How could someone so callous celebrate the return of his long-lost granddaughter?

"Jeremiah is waiting in the living room. It's the first doorway on your right."

Trey nodded and turned to walk in the direction Amara indicated. A gentle touch on her arm stopped her, forcing her to look back at her new second cousin.

"Trey, Uncle Ace isn't the only one glad you're here. I am too. I look forward to getting to know you and becoming real cousins, real friends." She reached into her pocket and pulled out a business card and gave it to Trey. "If you need someone to explain this unusual family to you, or you just want to talk, don't hesitate to dial my number."

Trey smiled. She wasn't sure what she was expecting when she'd walked into this place, into this family. But Amara being the first Devereaux she met was definitely a good thing. She heard the door shut behind Amara and stared at her card. An uneasy chill spread through her as she remembered her reason for being here. It wasn't to make friends or embrace the family that disowned the father she loved. It was to make them pay in the most painful way possible. Making friends wouldn't help that goal, regardless of her genuine desire to get to know Amara.

"I hope Amara didn't scare you. She can be a bit much to deal with this early in the morning."

Trey shook herself from her musings and followed the deep baritone voice to its source. Jeremiah Benton stood tall and strong in the high-arched doorway. Yesterday evening he'd been impeccable in a tailor-made Armani suit. Today he wore slacks and a fitted button-down shirt whose first two buttons were open, giving her a peak at a curl or two of dark brown hair.

Bald, with a neat goatee and piercing rich brown eyes, he presented a calm and controlled power that both alarmed and enticed her. Her mission was to get revenge. Thirsting after her grandfather's right-hand man wasn't part of the plan.

She cleared her throat and put on a practiced smile. "Not at all. I wasn't sure what kind of reception I'd have coming here this morning. Amara was exactly what I needed." He stood aside and waved her into the living room. The scent of something spicy wafted off his skin and tickled her senses as she walked past him. She kept her composure, fighting against her desire to move closer to him and sniff his inviting fragrance.

When she stepped inside the room, a large painting hanging over the fireplace drew her attention. She'd seen it before, not the painting, but the photograph version. It was her father as a young man graduating college.

"Did you put this here for my benefit?" She noted a confused look on Jeremiah's face. "The picture of my father?"

He stepped closer, taking his phone out, and tapped on it before handing it to her. On its screen was a picture of Ace by the fireplace with the picture hanging in the same place.

"Tap the picture to see the details."

She did as instructed and saw a timestamp of two years ago.

"Ace took me in twenty-two years ago. From the moment I arrived, that picture has always hung in the middle of this room."

She returned his phone to him and looked at the portrait of her father once more. Ace was her foresworn enemy, but in this moment, she couldn't help but feel a little spark of something unidentifiable for him. She turned in a circle as she looked at other portraits of years gone by in the Devereaux clan. These people were the source of her father's anguish. But part of her still marveled at the novelty of seeing people who bore such a strong resemblance to her and her dad.

If things hadn't gone sideways all those years ago, there might be pictures of her on one of these large walls too.

Jeremiah pointed to the sitting area, and she sat on a large sofa near the window. "I'm assuming you asked to meet here instead of the office so you don't tip your hand about my possible involvement in whatever this situation is."

"I see you've inherited your grandfather's habit of cutting to the chase."

"It saves time. So, what's the problem and what kind of help do you want from my father?" He'd been very light on the details last night, asking her to come here to discuss the matter further in the morning.

His eyes lingered on her, as if he were considering how much he should say. "Last night was just to see if you were interested."

He was smart to be cautious. Trey smiled, hoping to

ease Jeremiah's hesitation, and leaned back into the sofa cushions. "If I don't know what's wrong, I can't help."

"Your grandfather owns forty percent of Devereaux Inc. With his illness progressing so quickly, I started trying to get all of his end-of-life documents together and discovered that his will leaves the future of the company on shaky ground. Simply put, your father or one of his direct descendants has to claim Ace's shares. If they don't, they go to Ace's closest blood relative, his sister, Martha."

She nodded her head. "I'm guessing there's some reason Ace can't have the will rewritten or file an addendum to eliminate the possibility of Martha from getting her hands on the shares?"

"He could, and I even asked him to as a last resort. But changing a will this close to his presumed death could run the risk of it being overturned if anyone contested it. And knowing Martha, she would."

Trey tilted her head, narrowing her gaze as she pieced together the unspoken meaning of his words.

"So, you're hoping my father will show up to the reading of the will and take ownership of the shares? That's betting a lot on a perfect stranger who hasn't spoken to his father in more than thirty years. Aren't there any other blood relatives? What about Amara?"

"It's not merely a matter of blood relation," he replied. "But rather consanguinity or how proximal your relationship is to Ace. The exact wording of the clause is that the heir must be a direct descendant of Jordan Dylan Devereaux the first. If no such person stipulates a claim, the shares go to the closest proximal relative. That's not Amara."

"I presume there's something wrong with dear old Auntie Martha if you're seeking help from my father?"

"Aside from her being a bitter and mean bully, she doesn't have the best business acumen and she's already expressed a desire to liquidate the company. She's currently the head of our lifestyle brand, Inkosi."

"Inkosi? How does the Zulu word for *king* translate to a lifestyle brand?"

"As in 'made for a king.' Everything we make, promote or invest in has to be of the highest quality. It has to be as strong, valuable, powerful and as close to perfection as humanly possible. Only the best for the king."

She nodded, impressed with his explanation. "That's hellified brand recognition. But it also raises the bar very high."

"We know."

"Then why would you put someone who doesn't have the best business acumen in that position?"

"Martha is phenomenal when it comes to style, symbolism and packaging a product or campaign so that it snatches the attention of the consumer. And before you think I'm being chauvinistic and assigning gender roles, I'm not. Her skills are invaluable to us. We couldn't launch half of our ventures without Martha's contributions."

She crossed her leg and tapped her knee with her finger as she thought about Jeremiah's revelations so far. "So, because he doesn't want his sister to take over, Ace asked you to fetch my father to pull his company out of the fire? The old man is an entitled SOB, I'll give him that."

"He is, in most cases. But not with your father. Ace's greatest shame was turning your father away for marrying your mother. He carries unimaginable guilt because of it. He would never ask for your father's help."

"Because he thinks he's too good?"

Jeremiah shook his head before he quietly replied, "Because he doesn't believe he deserves it."

Whatever answer she was expecting, it wasn't that. A lump of uncomfortable emotion formed in her throat. She pulled her gaze from Jeremiah's and took a second to compose herself before speaking again.

"So, reaching out for my father's help, that was all your idea?"

He nodded. "Ace has no clue I tried to contact your father."

"Why would you do it then? Especially when I suspect you'd rather have the shares yourself." He stared at her, the look on his face confirming her assumption.

"You're right. I do want the shares for myself," he admitted, looking directly into her eyes. "And as soon as either of you claim them, I plan to make you an offer for a ridiculous amount of money for them."

He had balls. She had to give him that. There wasn't any sign of subterfuge in his statement. "But even if I can't convince either of you to sell them to me, that would still be a more acceptable option than Martha getting a hold of them. Ace saved me once when I was a hardheaded sixteen-year-old hustler on the streets of East New York. It's only fair I do the same for him as a hardheaded old man."

She could relate to this fierce love for a father figure; it was almost identical to the love she possessed for her dad. But the small gleam of admiration building for Jeremiah commingled with a distinct thread of fear. She'd have to watch Jeremiah Benton carefully, and not because he was the most beautiful specimen of a man she'd ever laid eyes on. If his devotion to Ace was as strong as hers to her father, he'd do anything to protect the man. She needed to be careful. Because his affection for Ace made him the enemy.

"On that note, why don't you introduce me to my grandfather?"

Chapter 4

"Ace, I have a visitor for you. Are you up for company?"

Trey waited patiently for an answer to Jeremiah's question as they stood outside her grandfather's bedroom. The thought of being turned away somehow brought a mix of relief and disappointment.

"That depends," Ace answered, "on whether it's that damnable nurse who comes only to poke and prod me each week."

Trey bowed her head slightly and smiled. Ace's voice was gravelly, worn with time and sickness, but his mental faculties were obviously still intact.

Jeremiah turned to her and whispered, "Cancer hasn't made him any less of a smart-ass, I'm afraid."

As far as she was concerned, anyone who had to battle with that horrid disease had a right to be as cantankerous as they wanted.

He cracked the door and poked his head inside. "It's not the nurse," Jeremiah responded. "Can we come in?"

Trey didn't hear Ace's response, but he must have given his permission, because Jeremiah slowly opened the door and stepped inside, then waved her on to follow him.

Whatever Trey was expecting, it hadn't prepared her for the scene unfolding before her eyes. Ace sat in his large bed, propped up against a mountain of pillows. He didn't look sick. Even from bed he appeared to command a recognizable power that hummed throughout the room.

He fixed her with his penetrating gaze. She was a stranger to him; of course he would look her up and down to understand who she was and what she wanted.

"Jordan Dylan Devereaux III." Ace stated her name as fact. She glanced at Jeremiah to ask if he'd told Ace about her, but before she could form the words, he was shaking his head and shrugging.

"You know who I am?"

A warm smile spread across the old man's face as he beckoned her with a wave of his hand. She gave Jeremiah another quick glance, and watched as he slipped from the room. Once he was gone, she stepped closer to the bed and sat down in the chair by Ace's side.

"I would recognize my blood anywhere. You are the spitting image of your father who is the spitting image of me."

"But how did you know my name? You haven't spoken to my father in over thirty years when you disowned him for marrying the poor girl from the wrong side of Brooklyn."

He winced at that last part, dropping his eyes for a second and then returning his gaze to hers with a widened smile. As he leaned forward, his eyes twinkled with a spark of wonder, as if he were encountering a miracle of sorts.

"I may have foolishly let too much time pass between your father and me. That doesn't mean I didn't keep track of him and you."

He leaned over, opening the nightstand drawer and plucking a small book from it before handing it to her. She wasn't sure what to make of it, but when Ace nodded, she flipped it open.

A breath caught in her throat when she saw the familiar picture of her mother holding Trey as a newborn in Brooklyn Hospital. Her father was standing beside them, his proud smile still shining like a beacon despite the faded colors of the image.

She continued to flip through the book, finding pictures that tracked her from her infancy up to her latest public acquisition, which had been plastered all over the news and social media.

She attempted to speak, but her tongue felt heavy and thick under the mountain of emotion falling down on her. This was wrong. She hadn't come here for this. She was here to right a wrong, not allow her emotions to cloud her head.

She closed the book and closed her eyes, needing a moment to get herself together. She was stronger than this. A few sentimental pictures shouldn't have bothered her this much.

"How did you get these photos?"

"Your mother sent them. Your father was understandably angry for so many years. I'd done that to him. I didn't want to inflict any more pain on him by forcing my way back into his life before he was ready. But your mother wanted me to know my only grandchild, my namesake, my legacy. So, every few months I'd receive new pictures from her chronicling your life until you were grown up. I have countless photo albums around this house filled with your face."

His smile was sad. As if he were cataloging the disappointing parts of his past. "I didn't deserve that kindness from her. But I'll go to my grave being grateful for Destiny's compassion and insistence I be allowed to witness your life, even from afar."

Trey was quiet for a long time, torn between compassion for a sick old man and anger over the destruction he'd caused in her family. Because sitting with this man now, witnessing the regret in his eyes, Trey understood she'd lost something precious for nothing more than the pride of stubborn men.

He glanced at the door with anticipation. She'd caught him doing that every so often when she'd look up from the pictures. "If you want me to get Jeremiah, I can," she said.

He shook his head. "I think he wants us to have time alone. But I wasn't looking for him anyway."

"Then who?"

He smoothed shaky hands over his linen-covered legs before raising his eyes to her again. "Did my son come with you?"

Discomfort lodged itself in her chest, almost robbing her of breath as she attempted to speak. She didn't even know this man, but the hopeful expectation etched into his shaky smile was almost her undoing.

"No. He's not with me."

"Does that mean he's not with you today, or he's not coming at all?"

"There's a lot of bad blood between the two of you. I

don't know if he'll ever get to the place where he'll want to be in the same room with you again. But who knows what could happen. I never thought I'd be here, sitting next to you while you told me all about my life. I guess that means anything is possible."

He watched her carefully, seeming to take stock of her every word. Eventually he nodded and gave her the same bright smile he'd offered her when she first walked in.

"You're right. I'll just count this time with you as a blessing and let the rest unfold as it will."

There was an awkward pause, unspoken emotion filling the room like the thick, hot air of a muggy New York summer day. Needing to break free of its hold, she cleared her throat and smiled at him in return.

"Well, it seems you know a lot about me, Ace. Why don't you tell me about you?"

Jeremiah left Ace and Trey to talk. The Devereauxs finally coming together was both beautiful and painful to watch. He'd known how much Ace had missed taking part in his son's and Trey's lives, but it had never been more palpable than when his estranged granddaughter sat in the chair next to him, gazing back at the older man with pain of her own etched on her face.

He walked downstairs to the kitchen, trying to find something to keep himself busy. Every part of him wanted to be inside that room to monitor how things were going. He was too protective of Ace to guarantee he wouldn't lose his shit if Trey showed the old man the least bit of disrespect.

Ace needs this. Hold your tongue and swallow your pride. Do whatever needs to be done to give him what he needs.

He was too wired to work. Aside from the gym, the kitchen was the best place for him to get out all of this anxious energy. After eating takeout for two weeks straight when he'd first arrived at Ace's, his new benefactor had told him he wasn't indulging his fast-food habit any longer. Jeremiah had thought that meant Ace would be cooking. He did. But as always when it came to Ace, he didn't give you anything without teaching you how to get it for yourself.

The old man had made sixteen-year-old Jeremiah stand at his side and mirror his every move as they made their first dinner together. And to this day, Jeremiah couldn't remember having more fun or feeling more welcomed in his life.

Sadness suddenly gripped him. The thought of losing precious moments like that to this evil disease made him want to break something.

Now's not the time, J. Get it together.

After shoring himself up, he put his hands on his waist and pondered what he should make for lunch. He wasn't certain what kind of food Trey liked or how long this visit would last, so he decided on something simple. Panini sandwiches with a side of French onion soup would do. Ace's appetite was often nonexistent. Sometimes soup was all he could get the man to swallow. So, even though it was a hot summer day in Brooklyn, Jeremiah set out to make the warm dish.

As he moved around in the kitchen, he finally let his mind process the sight of Trey in these hallowed halls.

She wore a loose-fitting camisole and a lightweight cardigan paired with skinny jeans and wedged sandals. Whether she was in the designer business attire he'd seen her in last night or casual chic, she still couldn't hide how damn sexy she was.

If he'd thought their first meeting was a fluke, he now realized how wrong he was. Last night she'd caught him off guard. In the dark depths of the lounge, she was sultry and intriguing. In the light of day, she was regal and captivating. What other reason could there have been for him to stare at her so openly as she looked around at the art in the living room when she'd first arrived?

He decided belaboring that thought wouldn't lead his mind to good places, so he focused on stirring the simmering soup and checking the sandwich grill to see if it was ready for the panini.

He set a covered plate on a tray for Ace, carried it upstairs and knocked softly on his door before entering. Trey was sitting in the same chair as when he'd left her. Her expression was guarded, like she was fighting to keep her thoughts to herself. Apprehension began to build until he glanced at a smiling Ace.

"You ready to eat, Ace?"

"I'm actually a little tired." He pointed a weary finger at the contents of the tray. "Will it keep until I wake up?"

"Sure. I'll put it up for you. As soon as you're ready for it, just text me."

Trey waved goodbye to Ace, then stood and followed Jeremiah out of the room and downstairs to the kitchen. After he put Ace's food away, he turned to find her still standing in the doorway.

His gaze slid down her body, appreciating the glorious vision she made bathed in the glow of sunlight streaming through a nearby window.

She was a sight to behold. Thick, curvy and confident. What man could resist that combination?

"It smells good in here. What did you make?"

He swallowed, forcing his mind and his eyes to focus on her face and not how much he appreciated her shapely form.

"Turkey and tomato panini with French onion soup. I know it's warm outside, but soft foods and liquids are easier for Ace to eat."

She shrugged. "That's what central air-conditioning is for. Although with a building this old, I shouldn't assume that Ace necessarily went through the hassle of refitting the house."

"He did," Jeremiah quickly commented as he plated their food, then set it on the eat-in counter along with two glasses of lemonade. "It was tricky getting it done, but he was able to keep the original shell and architecture of this building and managed to update the wiring and heating systems too."

She nodded as she looked around the state-of-the-art kitchen. "Good," she replied. "That means I can enjoy the soup and not worry about my braid-out turning into an unruly mop of curls."

She sat down at the counter and stared out the nearby window as she spoke. "I think talking about all the years we've missed together tired him out."

Jeremiah should've insisted they go back upstairs where Ace, even in sleep, would act as a buffer between them. He was about to do that when she pulled her gaze from the window and met his. Something akin to sadness and despair muddied her bright brown eyes, making them look softer, more enchanting than they had when she'd first arrived this morning.

He should be the cool and controlled COO Ace had trained him to be. But in the presence of this woman, nothing seemed to be in his control. Not his heart that was beating faster than it should, and not the need he'd been trying to ignore since he discovered her identity last night.

"So," he began, hating the uncertainty in his voice. "What's Deuce's position on all of this?" He sat down next to her and focused on the food, pretending it was the most interesting thing in the room.

She reached for the glass of lemonade with her left hand while he simultaneously reached for his fork with his right and their shoulders and elbows bumped together. A spark of something indescribable passed between them, something exciting and risky that a smart man would walk away from if he had the chance.

Their eyes met, and she gave him an apologetic smile. She didn't move, though. Instead, she held her arm still next to him for a moment longer than necessary, but nowhere near long enough for his taste.

"My father is still very angry. He's not ready to deal with Ace. That's why he sent me."

"So, is he washing his hands of the whole issue? Is he just going to toss his inheritance aside?"

She shrugged, taking another sip of her lemonade before speaking. "My father built DD Enterprises from the ground up so he would never have to be concerned with Devereaux Inc. That means I'm all you've got. It's either me or nothing."

There was something in her tone that seemed off. He couldn't tell if she was holding back, or the pressure of the situation was beginning to get to her. "Was talking to Ace rough? You seem a little out of sorts." He hadn't meant to blurt that out. It was like being next to this woman kept him from exerting his usual good sense.

"Not sure if *rough* is the way I'd describe it." She leaned over the table as she carefully brought a spoonful of soup to her mouth. "It was good, but also strange. I kept feeling as if I were in some kind of movie. Like this was happening to someone else. There are so many things to process, but so little time to do it in."

Time seemed to stop as he watched her purse her lips to blow on the warm broth. When she placed the spoon in her mouth, he had to force his gaze back to his food to keep from turning into the creep his lecherous mind told him he was.

She was meeting her grandfather for the first time. The last thing she needed was him perving on her as she sipped soup.

Maybe Ace is right. Maybe I should find someone to spend a little time with.

"I'm glad you came to meet him. Thank you for doing that."

"It's so strange to have you thank me for doing something for my grandfather. It should really be the other way around. I guess that's what happens when anger and pettiness win out over love."

He could see the streak of sadness in her expression. But he also got the sense she was holding back. There was still something in the way she walled herself off when talking about Ace and her father that made him suspicious.

Or it could just be you're looking for a reason not to like her because she may end up owning the shares that should be yours.

Despite his suspicion, he couldn't ignore his need to take away her sorrow. He reached across the table and rested his hand on hers. Without hesitation, she closed her fingers around his and gave them a squeeze. She was warm and strong, everything about her essence calling to something unfamiliar in him.

"I don't think anger and pettiness have won out, Trey. If they had, you wouldn't be sitting here with me now."

Chapter 5

Trey sat in her Cadillac Escalade with a direct view of Junior's across the street. She'd spent yesterday with her estranged grandfather and his sexy COO. That alone warranted the fat slice of cheesecake she planned to order. As far as she was concerned, settling on a single slice was a remarkable show of self-restraint. Frankly, she deserved the whole damn cheesecake.

She tried to feel excitement at the thought of strawberry sauce dripping over the creamy confection, but couldn't find the slightest spark. Hell, sitting in her ride didn't even do anything for her today. Usually, whenever she sat in its plush imported black leather seats and ran her hands across the custom woodgrain paneling on the steering wheel and console, decadent pride practically oozed out of her.

She closed her eyes and rubbed her temples, trying

to get her head right so she could go in there and get her damn dessert. It was a new day and she should be over whatever happened yesterday. The only problem was, she couldn't figure out what *had* actually occurred.

She'd walked into that house intent on destroying the man who'd abandoned her father. But somewhere between meeting her grandfather, and sitting in the kitchen with Jeremiah, her motivation didn't seem so clear anymore.

If Ace's revelations had surprised her, Jeremiah's kindness as they sat and ate outright shocked her. They didn't know each other well, and yet, when he'd placed his hand on hers, it was like laying the weight of the world at his feet and watching as he'd willingly taken up the burden just to give her a reprieve.

What kind of man was this?

This wasn't happening the way she planned. It was early, sure. But even now she could see things were going off the rails. Her emotions were all over the place. She was intrigued by the grandfather she'd never known, and angry with him out of loyalty to her father. And her father would not be pleased with her at all.

No, he wouldn't be pleased with any of this. And Trey felt guilty; even in his anger at Ace, the daughter in her wondered if she was depriving him of the opportunity to say goodbye to his father. Six months wasn't long. However, it was long enough for them to reconnect. Trying to answer that question had kept her tossing and turning all night. Was she doing the right thing by keeping her father in the dark about Ace's illness?

She knew for a fact she'd want every remaining moment with her father if she were in his position. But

Deuce's anger was so deep-seated, so vivid and bright, she couldn't be certain he would feel the same.

She looked up to the roof of her car, then closed her eyes. "What should I do? Tell me what to do?" she murmured.

As if she'd somehow conjured him up, her phone rang with her father's picture filling the large screen of her smartphone.

"Afternoon, Daddy." Her voice was rough with hesitation. She wasn't sure what to expect from this call after the way they'd left things two days ago.

"Afternoon, pumpkin." His greeting washed over her like a soothing balm. He called her pumpkin only when he was contrite or sentimental. She waited a beat to determine which version of him she was speaking to. "I don't like it when we fight, Trey. And since you wouldn't call me, I knew I couldn't let any more time pass before I reached out. I want nothing to separate me from you, baby girl."

"Daddy…"

"Pumpkin, I was wrong. I let old hurts get the better of me and I took it out on you. You always come through. I gotta trust you to do the same now."

Her chest filled with emotions she dared not speak, making it hard to breathe. When she didn't respond, her father continued.

"Trey, you're the best thing that's ever happened to me. And as mad as I was two days ago, it hit me when your assistant said you wouldn't be coming back to work for the next four weeks that maybe I could've pushed you too far this time."

"Daddy, that's not why I didn't come back to work. You and I have had blowouts before. They've never stopped me from coming into DD Enterprises and doing the job I love. I realized I needed to take some time off for self-care. With nothing pressing on my agenda, now seemed like the perfect time." Besides, who could put in a full day's work and execute complicated revenge schemes while navigating messy family drama at the same time? Certainly not her.

When she heard his audible sigh through the phone, her heart dropped. Despite her anger, she'd never intended to upset him. His father had abandoned him. He shouldn't have to worry about his daughter leaving too.

"It doesn't matter why. What matters is that you know there is nothing you could ever do that would make me turn you away. I am not my father and I would never do to you what he did to me."

Warmth spread through her. Even in anger, she'd never doubted her father's love. It had been the single most important force in her life. She ached for him, knowing he couldn't say the same about his father.

"Daddy, speaking of Ace—" she hedged her words, careful not to give too much away "—would you ever consider talking to him again? I know what he did to you was unforgivable. But what if he were sick or dying? Would that change things?"

The line was quiet for a long time before her father finally took a slow, loud breath. "To me, Ace Devereaux died a long time ago. There will never be a good enough reason to dig up those old bones."

"Daddy, you don't mean that."

"I do. He can't get the time of day from me. The last interaction we will have is when I snatch Devereaux Incorporated from his clutches and prove to him I'm the better husband, father, business executive and man."

Trey ended the call and her heart sank a little. As of now, all that remained was her self-appointed mission to get Ace to give her his shares. It was too soon for her to ask for them outright. She'd have to get to know him better, get him to trust her so she could influence his decision.

She took a breath, trying to ease the anxiety building inside of her. The old man's charm wasn't lost on her. He was smooth, and she could end up liking him. But she couldn't get caught up with Ace or the other Devereauxs and let anyone in that family take what should rightfully belong to her father whether Ace was alive or dead.

That was unacceptable.

No matter how charming Ace was she had to remember he'd hurt her father and the only retribution that would suffice would be his total and complete destruction.

The memory of Jeremiah wrapping his hand around hers to comfort her flittered through her mind. Regret toiled inside her stomach and she prayed she could do this without falling victim to a self-inflicted wound. She grabbed her Louis Vuitton Vertical Trunk Pochette and left the car, getting a ticket from the parking meter and putting it on her dashboard when she returned. As she crossed DeKalb Avenue, she wondered how she would live with herself when this was all over. Because if spending a day with those two men had her questioning her life choices, she was almost afraid to imagine how tied up in knots she'd be if she were in their ranks for much longer.

Jeremiah was standing at the corner of Flatbush and DeKalb Avenues when he glimpsed Trey sitting in her luxury SUV. Black and bold with sleek lines and chrome accents, it was the perfect representation of Trey.

Even from this distance, her power radiated from the inside of her vehicle to where he stood on the busy Brooklyn street. Whenever she was near, his body went on alert.

He'd assumed it was the novelty of just meeting her and her ties to Ace and the company that had him so wound up. But as she exited the SUV and stepped onto the curb, her endless brown legs exposed by the denim shorts she wore, Jeremiah understood Trey's effect on him had nothing to do with novelty and everything to do with this woman being a force of nature he desperately wanted to tangle with.

He smiled as he watched her head toward Junior's. He had a front-row seat to this perfect vision of Brooklyn glam in a crisp red graphic T-shirt that caressed her ample breasts. Thank goodness for the Melanin Poppin' message on its front. It gave him an excuse for staring at her much longer than good manners allowed.

Her long dark curls were piled into a neat pineapple style on top of her head. Thin gold hoops hung from her ears, accenting a graceful neck. He let his gaze travel farther down until it rested on her white Nike Air Force 1s.

His smile broadened as he heard the lyrics to LL Cool J's "Around the Way Girl" playing in his head. That was precisely the vibe Trey was giving off. Except for her car, she didn't look like money. She blended into concrete sidewalks and the urban, understated magnificence of her surroundings the way most people on the street did. She represented the beauty of Brooklyn, really, its wealth hidden from those who discounted the importance of cultural expression for the vast array of ethnicities and nationalities that made up each neighborhood.

"You've certainly got the casual chic thing going on today," he said, finally catching up with her just as she got to the door of the restaurant.

She looked up from the phone in her hand and followed the sound of his voice until her eyes met his.

She looked down at herself and back at him. "Anytime I don't have to be at work or an event, I'm dressed like this. Brooklyn chic is my thing."

"A woman after my own heart."

"How so?"

He pointed down to her sneakers. "Your sneaker game is tight. Only a sneaker connoisseur would know that a classic athletic shoe like the Air Force 1s never goes out of style." Especially the pair she was wearing. The Remade x ACU Nike Air Force 1s were four grand at a bargain price.

Her gaze panned down until she was looking at his shoes. "If those Dior Jordans are any indication, I'm not the only one with a sneaker fetish."

He shrugged. "Guilty as charged. I have an entire room in my brownstone dedicated to my love of Jordans."

"Your brownstone? You mean you don't live at Devereaux Manor?"

"No," he confirmed. "I still have a room there from when I came to live with Ace. But I have a place four blocks up on St. James and Greene."

He stepped aside, holding the door open and motioned for her to enter Junior's. "I was gonna stop in for a drink. Care to join me?"

Trey glanced down at the Tiffany Art Deco 2-Hand watch on her wrist before returning her gaze to his.

"Sure," she replied. "We're both here. No sense in wasting two tables, right?"

She stepped in front of him and he thanked every deity he could remember for the opportunity to watch all that ass in those shorts. "Makes perfect sense to me."

Trey bit the inside of her lip to keep herself from saying something she shouldn't. Jeremiah was gorgeous. There was no getting around that. Whether in an Armani suit or the sleeveless tank and gray sweatpants he wore now, Jeremiah's body was a thing of beauty.

"You hungry, Trey?"

Jeremiah held out her seat for her, and once she took it, he sat down in his own, grabbing his menu. She swallowed, trying to drag her mind out of the gutter and bring it back to a respectable place where she didn't have to worry about her lascivious thoughts making her say inappropriate things.

"Not for food."

He closed his menu, giving her his full, heated attention. "If not food, then what?"

You need to stop playing and gon' and tell that man you want to do dirty things to him with your mouth.

She pressed her eyelids shut in an effort to keep that thought from spilling out of her head. "Cheesecake," she breathed on a long sigh. "I don't want food as in a meal. I just had a hankering for cheesecake."

She opened her eyes in time to see his full lips pull into a wide grin and all the heaviness Trey had been carrying since yesterday dissipated. In its place, a rush of heat flooded her.

"Whatever the lady wants, the lady gets." He bowed

in deference to her, and one glance at his strong, broad shoulders had her falling under his spell.

She rested her elbows on the tabletop and leaned forward. "Are you having any?"

Playing with fire isn't a smart thing to do, Trey.

"Probably a to-go order," he responded. "I usually drop in for the pancakes."

"It's way beyond the hour for pancakes."

"It's never too late for pancakes." He pointed a finger at her. "Maybe you should try some. Then whatever had you looking so serious in your car probably wouldn't bother you so much."

"You were watching me?"

"Not in the creepy way your question suggests."

She should have felt uncomfortable with his accurate observation. But somehow, her need to conceal herself was absent in that moment.

"You think pancakes have that kind of magic in them?"

"There is nothing a hot stack, a hot cup of coffee and a conversation can't fix. Whatever it is, I guarantee hotcakes will make you feel better." He gave her a wink before he dropped his eyes to his menu.

She tried to ignore all the signs that she should probably get out of Dodge. Becoming too familiar with the COO of her grandfather's company was a bad idea. But as Jeremiah's rich, decadent smile called to her, she pushed her misgivings aside and hoped like hell they wouldn't come back to haunt her. Because as any adult knows, avoiding your problems was always the best way to resolve them, right?

Chapter 6

"You came back."

Trey smiled politely at her grandfather as she entered his bedroom.

"I said I would," she responded. "A Devereaux—"

"Is only as good as their word," he continued. He lifted a shaky hand and beckoned her to step closer to him. "My daddy taught me that and I taught it to yours. I'm glad he taught it to you too."

Today, he sat in his wheelchair positioned by large bay windows trimmed by a cushioned bench. In the glow of the summer rays the gray tinge to his skin that she'd noted on her last visit was gone. For a moment she could almost forget he was an ailing man.

"How is Deuce?"

His directness pulled her mouth into a smile. *So, this is where I get it from?* "He's well. I spoke to him this morning. We had a good talk."

"About me?" He turned to her slowly. Expectation tinged the air and it made her uncomfortable.

She leaned back into the cushions and crossed her legs, buying herself some time before she answered. "Your name came up in the conversation."

Where the hell did that evasive maneuver come from?

In business, she could handle anything. But sitting here watching hope grow in this old man's eyes was twisting something inside of her gut. She didn't want to tell the cold, hard truth for once.

"My son still isn't ready to forgive me, is he?"

She saw the sadness etched into his face but could also tell from the proud jut of his jaw he didn't want her pity. If their roles were reversed, she probably wouldn't want his, either.

She slowly placed her hand atop his. "I told you, he's not there yet, Ace." She traced reassuring circles on the back of his hand as she spoke. "But to be fair, you haven't actually asked for his forgiveness. You've let many years pass and to my knowledge, you've never reached out to him to express your remorse. Maybe if he heard that from you, he might see his way around his anger."

Ace smiled at her, his eyes filling with unshed tears. "You're honest, but you've got a big heart. I can tell. Never stop telling the truth, Trey. It's your greatest asset."

She knew she didn't deserve his encouragement, especially since she'd been lying to him since they'd met. But warmth spread through her as he smiled at her, like a soothing blanket protecting her from something she couldn't even name. She'd known this man, her grandfather, for less than forty-eight hours, his affection made her feel seen in ways she'd never dared to share with another living soul.

Every man in her life from her father to business associates, even the men she'd dated, acted like her inability to entertain nonsense for the sake of politeness was a flaw. She was too brash, too aggressive. But for once, there was someone telling her to be herself. How ironic that when that moment came, she was stuck pretending to be something she wasn't.

Their visit continued in much the same fashion as the previous one, where Ace would draw connections she never knew existed between her upbringing and her dad's. Like explaining to her why all the lights and electronics had to be turned off in the house during a thunderstorm when she was a kid. Her father would always say, "When the Lord is taking care of His business, you let yours go undone." After speaking to Ace, she realized that was a superstition that stretched back into the Devereaux lineage for ages.

After a while, Ace yawned. Fatigue made his eyelids droop when he looked at her. "Forgive me, Trey." He squeezed her hand lightly. "I'm a little worn out. I think it might be time for a nap."

"That's fine." She looked at her watch, realizing two hours had lapsed during their visit. "I didn't mean to stay so long and tire you out."

"No," he answered. "I was thrilled to have you here. I was hoping I could get Jeremiah to take me out on a walk so I could show you some of the significant places in the neighborhood that were part of Deuce's childhood." He yawned again, this time rubbing his eyes like a weary child. "Today would've been a great day to walk you over to Devereaux Inc." He held up a finger and picked up a cell phone sitting on a nearby table. He tapped the screen and waited for a second before he spoke. "Jeremiah, after talking Trey's ear off, I'm gonna take a nap. Why don't you take my granddaughter for a walk and show her the neighborhood before she goes home? You could even take her to Devereaux Inc. if she's up to it."

He disconnected the call and smiled at her. "Jeremiah is a good egg. He'll see to you."

"That's unnecessary, Ace. I don't need a babysitter. I've lived in Brooklyn all my life."

"Humor me," he answered as his home health aide entered the room and pushed his wheelchair closer to the bed. "He's great at taking care of the things that mean the most to me. Outside of your father, there's no one I'd trust more with your well-being."

She stood up to leave. As she walked out the door, he called her name again. "A beautiful girl like you need not stay inside with an old man on a pretty summer day." He winked at her, revealing more mischief in his spirit than a man his age should probably be allowed. "Besides," he hedged. "I'm sure you'll find J is much better company too."

Jeremiah made the left turn from Clinton Avenue onto Gates Avenue as he and Trey walked through Clinton Hill.

He glanced over at Trey. She'd been quiet since they'd left Devereaux Manor, keeping her eyes on their concrete path as their long gait ate up the blocks.

It was off. She was off. He'd noticed it when she'd come downstairs from Ace's room. Everything about Trey was bold and loud in the best ways, from the bright red T-shirt she wore, to the tricked-out SUV she drove. It all screamed, *I have arrived, and you can't handle me.*

This unnatural quiet didn't suit her, and it made him wonder what had occurred when she was with Ace.

He could be a difficult pill to swallow. He said exactly what he was thinking and sometimes the old coot couldn't muster up enough give-a-damn to ration out a bit of tact.

"You seem quiet. Is everything all right?"

She took her time paying him a glance. But she'd heard him, he was certain of it. Trey was a natural predator, aware of her surroundings at all times. It was one thing that made it so damn difficult not to allow his baser self to step forward.

And watching the taut muscles of her thighs contract with each step made him ache desperately to let his inner hound off the leash. But again, there were more pressing matters at hand, and discovering what all that deep brown skin she had on display tasted like would have to take a back seat to more pertinent issues.

"Trey?"

"Everything is fine." She pulled her stare away from his and looked ahead of her. "I'm processing all that's going on. I never expected to meet Ace in my lifetime. He always seemed like this larger-than-life fable that made my dad, the strongest man I know, tremble with anger and fear. And yet trying to reconcile what I know of him with the man I've spent the last two days with is difficult. I can't believe he's the same person."

Jeremiah chuckled. "Ace is a lot of things. He's a ruthless businessman and a charmer. His natural charisma compels you to follow him to the ends of the earth. But the detached coldness he's able to unleash keeps most people, like your father for instance, at arm's length."

"You have an interesting perspective on my grandfather, Jeremiah."

"It's been over twenty years since Ace pulled me off the streets. In all that time, I've met no one who made you want to back away with extreme caution while simultaneously luring you into his web like he does." He paused and tried his best to keep his thoughts contained.

He let his gaze fall over her and for the briefest moment, let himself imagine what it would be like to set himself free and reach for what he desired.

"Until you," he added.

She stepped closer, the fruity scent of her perfume gnawing at the precarious control he had over his libido at the moment.

"What exactly does that mean, Mr. Benton?" Her voice was low and sultry as she spoke his name.

"It means you both know how to reel people in. All that remains is determining whether you'll use that to your advantage or not."

She licked her bottom lip and the hairs on the back of his neck stood up from the zap of electricity. She stepped closer. So close, only air could pass between them.

"First rule of business, take every advantage you can. That's how you win."

Everything in him demanded he lean in and press his mouth to hers repeatedly until she opened to him and he could finally answer the question he'd ached to know.

How sweet does she taste?

"Is me winning what has you all tied in knots? Are you afraid I will hurt Ace's business?"

And without warning, cold spilled down his spine like a bucket of ice water over the head. In the New York summer heat, the cool sensation flooding his insides should be a relief. But her voicing his greatest fear made his spine snap straight and his eyes focus.

"What makes you say that?"

"It's been three days since you asked for my help and two since I arrived on Ace's doorstep. I've spent time with Ace, or with you talking about Ace, but other than you needing me or my dad to claim the shares, you haven't told me anything about Devereaux Inc."

He didn't correct her. Why should he? It was obvious they both knew it was true.

"Don't worry." Her voice dropped lower. "The moment I want more than what's being offered to me, I'll make it my business to let you know."

She was on the hunt. He'd seen it from the moment she stepped into The Vault and first locked eyes with him. She'd known exactly where everyone and everything was in that dimly lit room. You only moved with that kind of confidence when you knew exactly what you came for. The question remained, was she here to help Ace, or herself? And would knowing the answer stop this inconvenient—and possibly dangerous—desire he had to possess her?

Chapter 7

"I cannot believe you beat those kids so badly."

Jeremiah smiled as they stood next to Trey's SUV parked in front of Devereaux Manor. On their return from their walk, they'd encountered a group of kids playing double Dutch. Trey asked for a jump, and one of the teenagers made the mistake of hinting Trey might be too old.

She shrugged as her mouth curved into that delicious smile he was becoming all too familiar with. "It works to my benefit when people underestimate me. I've been jumping rope since I could toddle. It's a rite of passage for a Brooklyn girl. You pair experience with skill and the outcome is inevitable. Those kids didn't know who they were dealing with."

His gaze slid down her body. He was fascinated by the woman before him, while cognizant of the threat she posed. Trey was like a bullet. Gleaming and sleek, in its state of rest no more dangerous than a pen on a table. But when you paired it with a firearm, its lethal potential was exponential.

He nodded his agreement while Trey leaned against the rear passenger door. "They sure didn't. But, they're kids. I can't imagine any adult who can walk and chew gum at the same time to be incapable of seeing you for anything other than what you are."

She turned around, only to playfully look back over her shoulder and cast him a questioning look. "What do you think I am, Mr. Benton?"

"Dangerous," he answered. He swallowed and shoved his hands in his pockets to steel himself against the shiver of need passing through him. Why the hell did his formal name sound so damn sexy on this woman's lips? The way her sultry voice wrapped around each syllable made his body tense. And considering how he was wearing sweatpants, he needed to get it together before he embarrassed himself in front of this woman.

"Like most things with a potential for danger, I'm only a problem if you mess with me. Otherwise, I'm as harmless as a butterfly."

As graceful and vibrant as one, yes. But there was nothing harmless about Trey. Not the way she looked, not the brilliant mind shining through her bright brown eyes, and certainly not the way she made his body burn with only her velvety voice.

Devilry crinkled her eyes as her full lips spread into a bold and sexy smirk. Yeah, she was as harmless as a heart attack. And if he didn't watch out, he was certain his desire for her would cause cardiac arrest.

If you don't trust her, maybe you should do something to change that.

The thought was loud, crowding all of the space in his head. He realized that was lust talking. It certainly couldn't be his common sense. If he were being sensible, he'd stay the hell away from her instead of leaning in closer to get a whiff of her intoxicating scent.

"You're dangerous, Trey," he repeated, "and reckless too, the way you keep looking at me like that."

She tugged her bottom lip between her teeth and it took all of his control to keep from reaching out and sliding his thumb across it.

"How exactly am I looking at you, Jeremiah?"

"Like I'm ice water in the desert."

Her gaze raked over him before she lifted her eyes to his. "I'd be lying if I said I wasn't feeling a little parched right now."

"I'm trying to keep things professional. You're not helping, woman."

She shrugged.

"Smart money says you should. This isn't what either of us are here for."

He watched her carefully, trying to anticipate her next words. If she wanted to put a stop to this, now was the time because there was no way he would ignore the opportunity to have her if she offered.

"But scared money don't make no money. So, if you're willing to take the risk, I'm down too."

It should've been a simple kiss. But the moment she leaned into him, running her fingers up his chest, Jeremiah pressed his body against hers.

Trey didn't shy away from him. She gave as good as she received. The firm placement of her hands as they caressed his bare scalp set a blaze that traveled from his head directly to his cock. He ground his hips into hers, trying desperately to get as much friction as he could, and her resulting groan against his mouth lit his blood on fire.

It wasn't until she tore her lips away, panting, looking up at him with fire burning in her eyes that he recognized how far gone they both were.

"How long have you been waiting to do that?" Her question floated on a slightly breathless whisper.

"From the moment I watched you walk into that lounge."

"I hope it was everything you hoped for."

"Better than," he answered.

He stepped back, smoothing his hand down his T-shirt. He felt the hungry pull of her gaze slide down his body, as if she was visually devouring him inch by inch.

"You really need to stop that."

Her brow furrowed. "Stop what?"

"Tempting me beyond restraint," he huffed. "I have work to do tonight, and everything about this moment makes me want to shirk my duties and find a quiet place where I can kiss you instead."

"That's all you'd like to do? Kiss me?"

He pressed his eyes shut, trying his best to get his cock to behave. "You're not playing fair, Trey."

"I never do when it comes to something I want."

"You are so dangerous, woman."

"We've already established that, Jeremiah."

He chuckled. He was fast learning Trey always had a comeback. He looked at her again. There was a flicker of something unrecognizable in her eyes that fostered his need to pull her into his arms and keep her there, safe and protected from whatever was chasing away the playful mood they shared.

"If you're uncomfortable with this, it's more than all right." The last thing he wanted was for her to feel pressured.

"It's not that," she replied. "But I think we both need to admit us getting involved probably isn't the smartest thing we could do."

Fine, smart, rational and not afraid to tackle the hard topics, including the consequences of him kissing her in public against her vehicle.

Real classy, J. Stop thinking with your dick and at least pretend to pay attention to what the woman is saying.

"Trey." He said her name like a whispered prayer, reverent, powerful, filled with hope and need. "There are many ramifications to it. But I don't think I could ignore this if I tried."

A chill passed through him as disappointment took root with each moment she didn't speak. He hadn't known her a full week. He wasn't an expert on Trey at all. But her silence made him worry that maybe he'd moved too far too fast.

He pulled away, and she gripped his waist. "We just came together like kindling during that kiss, and I'd be lying if I said I didn't want to feel that again. I think the situation is too complicated for us to think about anything substantive happening between us, though."

Her words scraped across his insides like metal against metal, making him flinch.

"But we'd be foolish to try to ignore this chemistry, at least on a physical basis," she finally added.

He tilted his head to the side and squinted. "So, you'll fuck me, but nothing more?"

She nodded. "Keeping it simple might be the only way all of this doesn't go tits up."

He wished she were wrong. But with so much at stake, getting emotionally involved might make this messier than necessary.

"Agreed. No strings attached." He kissed her again. He could drink from this woman all day and would certainly try if he didn't have a mountain of work waiting for him at home. He gentled the kiss, nipping at her bottom lip as he smiled. "I would love to stay here with my arms around you while I figure out all the ways I can get you to moan so pretty for me. Unfortunately, work is calling." He lifted her chin with his finger and smiled. "Have dinner with me tomorrow night?"

"I've shared meals with you for the last couple of days. Why the need to ask now?"

He could see the faux confusion plastered across her smooth features. "Granted, it's been a while since I've done this, between taking care of Ace and running the business. But I know my game can't be that bad you don't recognize when I'm asking you out on a date."

She playfully shrugged. "I'm a girl who likes plain words. Tell me what you want and I'm more inclined to give it to you."

He groaned again. This woman's mouth was like dynamite and if he didn't pull away from her orbit soon, he would end up crashing right into her.

"Does that mean you agree to let me take you out tomorrow?"

"I thought we just agreed to no strings attached. Doesn't dating count as strings?"

"Not if we don't want it to. What do you say?"

She remained silent. If it wasn't for the devilish gleam

in her eye, he would've thought she was ignoring him. She slid her hands down his back until they were firm on the curve of his ass. She squeezed his cheeks and brought her hands to the side of his legs where his pockets were. She slipped her hand inside the left one, removing his phone and handing it to him as she waited for him to unlock it with the facial recognition feature. When he finished, he handed the phone back to her. She turned around in his arms so the curve of her ass fit perfectly over his erection, and the image of her bent over the arm of his favorite chair while he stood behind her, buried balls deep inside, burned behind his lids.

She found her name in his contacts, added her address, then returned the phone to him once she updated the entry. Facing him again, pulling his body close to hers, she settled against him.

"Pick me up at eight," she whispered. "Any particular attire required?"

"Something comfortable," he answered. "And for my sake, please let it be something that won't get me arrested for public lewdness."

She laughed at his edict as she placed a tiny peck against the corner of his mouth. "Ahh baby, you don't understand what kind of challenge you just laid down."

Good Lord, have mercy.

Chapter 8

Jeremiah was in the home stretch. As soon as this meeting with his assistant ended, he'd head out to get ready for his evening with Trey.

"Jeremiah, Global Hyatt is waiting for the valuation of the hotel chain they're interested in acquiring."

He winked at his assistant, Sharon, and tapped a few keys on his keyboard. "It's done. Just sent a copy to your inbox. Schedule a meeting with them first thing next week."

"Okay," she confirmed. "That's it for our agenda." Sharon closed her tablet case and stood. "Do you need me to do anything else before you get out of here for the day?"

He waved a finger. "No thanks. I'm headed out soon. That means you should be leaving too, Sharon."

"Yes, sir." She closed the door quietly behind her, leaving him alone to wrestle with his thoughts of Trey.

The excitement flowing through his body concerned him. Trey wasn't the first beautiful woman he'd had this sort of a liaison with. Someone as busy as he was didn't have time for relationships. He shouldn't let Trey take more of his attention than any random woman he'd had a few hours of fun with.

But that was the problem. Trey wasn't random. She was Ace's granddaughter. That fact alone made her important. She also possessed the ability to screw with his life in very unpleasant ways if she desired. His place in Ace's life had never been a question. But seeing how enamored Ace was becoming with his only grandchild, he knew it would crush the old man if Jeremiah hurt her.

And Ace's disappointment wasn't the only issue. He still didn't know if he could trust Trey's motivations where Ace and Devereaux Inc. were concerned. If he let her get too close, let her learn too much, and entrusted her with too much power, she could destroy everything he and Ace had built together. That alone should make him stay away from her.

But instead of keeping a safe distance, he kept treading closer. He wanted more. And knowing Trey wanted only his body grated on his nerves. It shouldn't. Her "no strings" edict should relieve him. But deep down it made him flinch.

The intrusive ring of his office phone cut into his thoughts.

"What is it, Sharon?"

"Mrs. Devereaux-Smith is here to see you. Are you available?"

Jeremiah rubbed his temple. The mention of Martha's name made his head hurt.

He tapped his finger against his large mahogany desk

and pondered whether ignoring Martha was an option. It wasn't like he hadn't done it before, but she was relentless, and the last thing he needed tonight was his phone interrupting him when he was with Trey.

"Send her in, Sharon."

He braced himself as he awaited her entrance. Even if he hadn't been staring at the door, he still would've known the moment she stepped inside the room.

His office was large, with high ceilings and grand floor-to-ceiling windows that flooded the room with light. And yet, as soon as Martha crossed the threshold of the plush carpeting that lined the floor, the room felt small and suffocating, making him aware of every breath he took.

Martha was a slim woman, fond of designer dresses and suits that looked like a throwback to the 1980s. Everything she owned seemed to be pencil thin with wide shoulders, made from some shimmering material.

She had her shoulder-length white tresses pulled into a severe bun that made her cheekbones more prominent. Her angled face was heavily contoured with makeup that produced a light brown glow. She was in her early seventies, but thanks to Black girl magic mixed with what he'd bet was a bit of plastic surgery, she didn't look older than her late fifties.

"Martha, to what do I owe the pleasure?"

She cut her eyes at him before taking one of the two high-backed chairs on the opposite side of his desk, serving him her usual disapproving glare.

"Jeremiah, I called Sharon yesterday asking for the company's second quarter reports. Your secretary refused to provide them to me. So, I'm here in person to retrieve them."

He lifted a brow and offered an insincere smile. "Martha, we only dispense those reports to the CEO, the COO, the CFO and the board of directors. You're the executive director of the lifestyle brand. That does not entitle you to the company's quarterly earnings report. You know this. So, why are you really here?"

The corner of her mouth hitched in a sinister smile before she spoke. "Your days of telling me what I am and am not entitled to are ending, Jeremiah. My brother is dying. I'm his next of kin."

"His son is still living."

"His ungrateful offspring abandoned Ace and any claim he had to Ace's legacy over thirty years ago. This company is my birthright to do with as I please. Once cancer is finished with Ace, it will be mine."

Jeremiah could feel the tension building in his jaw as it locked in place. It would feel so good to call Martha on her petty nonsense, but he couldn't risk giving anything away.

"Why do you hate him so much? All Ace has ever done was love this family, you included."

She tightened her hands around the armrests on her chair and leaned slightly forward before speaking.

"I don't need his brand of love. What he took from me can never be replaced. The only restitution I'll accept is the complete and utter destruction of the one thing he's ever loved."

"When the time comes that Ace closes his eyes to this world, his shares will end up with a blood relative. Only time will tell if that's you."

"Enjoy whatever power you have right now. I promise you, my first order of business will be to get the board to fire you. You're an interloper. The trust my brother has instilled in you is proof he's no longer fit to lead. When he's gone, I plan to rectify his mistake."

Jeremiah shrugged. "Trust me, if it ever comes to that, you'll have my resignation long before you have the power to fire me. But until then, I am COO of this company by Ace's authority. As such, I'll ask you to go back to your office and do what Devereaux Inc. actually pays you to do. Leave the running of the company to those of us tasked with doing it."

He pressed the intercom button on his office phone and waited for his assistant to answer. "Yes, Mr. Benton?"

"Sharon, Mrs. Devereaux-Smith was just leaving, please see her to the front door."

"Yes, Mr. Benton."

He turned his gaze back to Martha's and marveled at her ability to keep her rage concealed underneath the mask of respectability she'd worn ever since he'd known her. She was a piece of work for sure, but she was also as bitter as she was petty. A bad combination that made his job more difficult with each passing day.

She stood and sauntered toward the door. Before she opened it, she looked over her shoulder and offered him a chilling smile. "Your days are numbered, Jeremiah. Remember that." She opened the door, closing it quietly behind her and leaving her threat lingering in the air.

Dread conjured the image of Trey in his mind. It was time for him to lay his cards on the table and move to the next phase of his plan. He had to push her to claim those shares and stop Martha once and for all. And if his luck held, he'd have those shares in his hand when this was all said and done. Otherwise, Devereaux Inc. was doomed.

Chapter 9

Jeremiah stood in the lobby of Trey's building ready to get their date underway. The doorman directed him to the reception desk where a smiling young man greeted him, had him sign the visitor's log and informed him Trey would be downstairs momentarily. He looked around the spacious lobby, its floor covered in large black tiles, the walls made of wood paneling, creating a warm yet sleek and modern look.

A quiet ding pulled his gaze toward the small bank of elevators, and he planted his feet to prepare himself for whatever Trey had on. He'd seen her in a business suit, and casual wear, and every time, her devastating curves made him weak.

Tonight was no different. She wore a bright pink, one-shouldered T-shirt that bore a jewel-embossed crown with the words *Queens Are Born in Brooklyn* under it. The shirt hugged her torso. Her wide hips gave way to a pair of white leggings. She was breathtaking. But when he saw a pair of white retro Jordans with a bright pink sole and matching accents, a chuckle spilled from his lips.

"You look amazing, Trey."

"You said dress casual for our date. I hope this is okay."

He gave her an appreciative look, stopping at her athletic footwear. "Woman, your sneaker game is so tight. Turn around and let me get a look at those."

She turned around, doing her best impression of a sneaker model as he inspected her footwear.

"Those are Generation Twelves. But I don't remember this white and hot-pink color combination."

She nodded. "Unless you had a young child you were buying them for, you wouldn't. They were regrettably only made available to the public in girl's sizes. One of my best friends from back in the day is an executive for Nike. I get custom stuff that will never hit the market all the time."

He looked up, placing both hands on her shoulders, caressing them in a firm embrace. "Did you just tell me you have a hook-up at Nike?"

She let a gentle bubble of laughter escape her lips. "I did. And if you play your cards right, I might even contact my connection for you. But that's only if you act right."

She pulled a small white Louis Vuitton backpack from her shoulder and dropped her keys inside it before heading for the door, looking over her shoulder at him. She winked and angled her head toward the exit. "You gonna act right, Jeremiah?"

Hell yes, he would. He didn't need to know what "acting right" entailed. The promise of what was to come painted across her smile was enough to tempt him into submission. Anything this woman wanted him to do, short of committing a crime—and even that was debatable—he was already game for.

As he caught up to her, he refused to think about how irresponsible it was to follow this woman blindly. Hypnotized by the motion of her rounded hips, thick thighs and shapely ass, the only thought he would entertain was how quickly he could peel those tights off her legs and bury himself between them.

"Hmm, that's funny." Trey eased back into the soft black leather of Jeremiah's silver Lexus LS.

"What?"

She watched his profile as he directed the car through downtown Brooklyn. "I would've pictured you more in a Jag. Maybe even something sporty and fast like a Ferrari."

He spared her a brief glance and returned his gaze to the road. "In Brooklyn, where there's a stoplight on every corner? Nah. I may wear Hugo Boss and Armani, but I'm still a homie from East New York at heart. If it's not a Lexus, Beamer, Benz or an Escalade, I can't drive it."

"Spoken like a true Brooklynite." She laughed loudly as she remembered her youth in East New York. "Back in the day, if a brother was riding in anything but one of those cars, or an Acura Legend, his rep was trash on the block."

"You do not understand how heartbroken I was when they discontinued the Acura Legend in 1995." He held his hand to his chest like he was wounded. "Devastated my little twelve-year-old soul when I realized they'd likely be obsolete by the time I could get a license."

"You seem to have gotten over the disappointment."

He nodded. "Only because your grandfather found a mint condition '95 for me and kept it in storage until I was old enough to get my license. He surprised me with it when I graduated with honors from Brooklyn Tech."

"You went to Tech?"

She noted his faraway expression. From his profile she wondered if he was really that focused on the road or if his mind had drifted somewhere she couldn't reach.

"I was sixteen when I met Ace. I was hustling on a corner when he pulled up and asked me if I wanted more for my life. At the time, it meant not ending up like some of my crew—dead or in jail. I'd been truant for so long at that point, I couldn't even tell you what grade I was in. But Ace saw that I was smart and pulled some strings to get me into Tech. I'm sure he had to have donated a building or something to get me admitted. No way they would've accepted me otherwise. But within two years of being there and busting my ass every single day with the private tutor Ace hired for me, I went from high school dropout to graduating with honors from a specialized high school, to entering the freshman class at Howard University."

She sat quietly as she added up the small pieces of Jeremiah's history that she knew. Ace hadn't merely pulled him off the street. The man had fathered him, given him the best of chances and allowed the benefit of generational wealth to course correct Jeremiah's life.

"It seems like Ace did more than pull you off the street. He gave you the keys to success in a system stacked against you."

He nodded. "He did. I owe him my life."

"It's so ironic how our lives have run parallel because of this thing between my grandfather and father."

"How so?"

She thought about it before answering. "We've basically lived on both sides of the same coin because of their rift. I grew up in East New York with my mother's family. My father scrimped and saved every penny he could to build DD Enterprises from nothing. It's an international success now, but only because my father was determined to prove he could make it without my grandfather's help. We're about six years apart, right?"

"Yeah," he answered.

"It seems when Ace was pulling you off the streets, my father was moving me into a penthouse. It was then I understood and experienced the impact of wealth on a person's life. I went to Tech and Howard too. They're legacy schools for the Devereaux clan. Generations of us have attended both schools, according to my dad. Ace wasn't being nice to you. He was making you part of the family."

He slowed the car down, and she realized the streets looked very familiar. They were almost at the end of Atlantic Avenue. He made the right turn on to Furman Street and she released the breath she was holding. A few hundred feet in the opposite direction and she would be at DD Enterprises headquarters.

Too close for comfort, huh?

While she was wrestling with her conscience, he made another turn and slid into an available parking space near the East River. He cut the ignition and reached across the console to grab her hand.

"Thank you for telling me that. I didn't know that about Tech and Howard. Ace has always been good to me. But I didn't know how gracious he was until this moment. I'll never understand why he chose a hustler with

no future to pluck off the street. But I'm forever grateful he did."

She leaned in close, her smile growing. "Ace saw what
I see, a compassionate man who has the power to do
great things. There's no more reason needed than that."

He kissed her. It was soft and sweet. More comforting than sensual, revealing a vulnerability in him she'd
seen only when he was in the presence of her grandfather.
Jeremiah was strong, powerful and always in control of
his situation from everything she'd seen in the past few
days. But the way he touched her, as if he needed an an-
chor in that moment, was like a bolt of electricity awak-
ening every cell in her body.

When he pulled away from her, something had shifted.
He felt it too. He stared at her, as if he was trying to
make sense of what was happening between them. Too
afraid to let them explore it, she cleared her throat to cut
the tension.

"So, we're at Brooklyn Bridge Park. Are we headed to
a restaurant?" She gave a cursory wave down her body
and then his. "If we are, I don't think our current fashion
choices will work in any of the establishments around
here."

"No, they're not." He spared her a brief smile and
kissed her again. She settled back into the seat. Kissing
this man was fast becoming one of her favorite pastimes.
"We're going to the marina. I figured we could have a
quiet night on my yacht."

She raised an eyebrow. "You own a yacht?"

He held his thumb and his forefinger less than an inch
apart. "A small one. It's only sixty-five feet."

He winked at her, got out of the car and came around
to open the door for her. The wicked twinkle in his eye

was still there when he offered her a hand and helped her out. It was there, between his devastating smile, and the shameless lust filling his eyes, that she realized she was in so much trouble. Deep, world-changing trouble, and she had no regrets as she willingly walked head-first into it.

They walked in silence as they reached a slip in the middle of the docks. Holding his offered hand, Trey stepped aboard the luxury vessel and took in the beauty of it. The main cabin was an elongated oval with sleek curves. The flooring and paneling were a rich wood grain in deep chestnut that was a perfect contrast to the two white sofas and benches running the length of the port and starboard sides on the yacht. The pilot's area sat proudly at the bow, its own little separated enclave from the rest of the open-design room.

"This is beautiful, Jeremiah." A proud smile spread across his face and she could've sworn she saw his chest puff out the slightest bit. "I don't know many people from Brooklyn, or in all of New York City even, who have yachts docked in the five boroughs."

"Thank you. This is my little slice of heaven in the concrete jungle. It's not easy or cheap keeping her close. But at least I can come here whenever I want to get away and take a moment to breathe."

She could see the advantages. The lulling motion of the boat was already relaxing her.

"Come on—" he motioned toward the small winding staircase "—let me show you the rest of her." He showed her the upper deck with its bow and starboard lounges, where you could take in the skyline unobstructed. Then he took her to the lower deck where the galley and staterooms were. "There are three staterooms." He pointed to their individual doors.

"Which one is yours?"

He pointed behind him. "That would be the master suite."

"Good to know." She took him by his hand and headed toward the room. For a cabin on a yacht, it was spacious. There was a large bed with an elaborate headboard against one wall and a curved bench and cabinet with a television atop it on the other side. There was an en suite bath; she could see a longish shower stall through the open door.

"Nice digs, Mr. Benton."

She moved over to the bed, sitting down and placing her small backpack next to her before looking up at him and smiling.

"Make yourself comfortable. The remote to the TV is in the nightstand. I'm gonna whip us up something to eat."

"Actually." Her voice halted his motion toward the door. She leaned down, removing her sneakers before looking up at him again. "I have a better idea. How about you join me on this comfy bed of yours and we work up an appetite? You can feed me later."

He sighed. "I am trying my best to be a gentleman, Trey. You're making it hard."

"I certainly hope so."

He chuckled. "You're not gonna let me finesse you, huh?"

She slid up to the head of the bed and rested against the decorated pillows. "I finesse myself enough. That's not what I want right now."

He moved closer to her and leaned in. "What is it you want, then?"

She looked into the depths of his brown eyes, molten lust making tiny flecks of gold appear in the soft yellow light surrounding them. "You."

One word was all it took to switch from the playful banter they were engaging in to something much more intense.

"We don't have to do this, Trey. I'd be happy to spend an evening watching TV and cooking your dinner."

She shrugged and dropped a peck on his irresistible lips. "I know you've got this gentleman thing going on and it's admittedly one of the sexiest things about you." She changed positions until she straddled his lap, and they both let out a long moan when she settled over his hard cock. "But I'm here on this bed with you because I have every intention of knowing what you feel like sliding inside of me. If that's not what you want, I'm cool with the TV scenario. But I so hope the getting-naked-with-me plan appeals to you more."

"God, yes." He pulled her forward and buried his mouth in the curve of her neck as his hands slid down her back. One moved under the hem of her T-shirt while the other burrowed beneath the elastic waistband of her leggings. The sensation of his fingers on her flesh made the low simmer of arousal she'd started with blaze into a full-on flame.

She thought about slowing things down to savor the moment. But when he grabbed a handful of her ass and pulled her over his obvious bulge, taking her time lost its appeal. She wanted every inch of this man now.

She pulled away from his glorious mouth and found the hem of his shirt, tugging until he finally got with the program and lifted his arms to let her remove the offending garment. She made quick work of taking off hers and then resumed the kiss. With ease, he rolled her over onto her back and settled himself between her thighs.

From there, time and motion blended together, and they became a mix of tangled limbs and desperate touches. His teeth lightly grazing her nipple while the play of his fingers between her folds was nearly her undoing. His touch was like everything else she knew to be true about Jeremiah Benton: tender but firm, considerate but determined, and talented and sexy as fuck.

By the time he slid down her body and settled his head between her thighs, Trey was already on edge, like an exposed nerve too susceptible to the slightest stimulus. The first swipe of his tongue made her body quake. He paused and placed a firm hand atop her mound to keep her pinned to the mattress. That was the last moment of reprieve he allowed her.

Though she undulated beneath him, demanding more, he took his time, devouring her at a leisurely pace that nearly destroyed her. When he finally slid his skilled fingers inside her and closed those talented lips over her responsive clitoris, her body yielded, and the dam broke under the powerful wave of pleasure crashing down on her. Jeremiah could've had the decency to let her wallow in her glorious destruction unbothered, but he granted her no such quarter. His fingers and tongue continued their onslaught until she was at her breaking point again. Before this wave took her over, she glanced down at him, at the sight of his bald head trapped between her thighs, and let that delectable image coupled with his incredible touch take her under again.

He kissed his way back up her body and reached

over her, opening a nightstand drawer. He pressed a foil packet in her hand and smiled down at her with a wicked grin. "You still down, or do you need a break?"

Yeah, she could do with a break after those explosive orgasms he'd gifted her with. Probably a nap too. But damn if she was about to let him know that.

She found the strength and dexterity to lift her arms and roll the condom down his hard length before locking eyes with him. "I'm down for anything you've got."

The low growl rumbling up from his chest should've told her she'd bitten off more than she could chew. But Trey was known for pushing past the point of caution, and she saw no reason this should be any different. She didn't give up or give in, and neither did Jeremiah apparently.

After the slow stretch he allowed her as he entered her body, all bets were off. The force of his strokes, the rhythm and pace of his hips' thrusts, the depth of pleasure he gave them both—it was almost too much to bear. The position didn't matter. Whether they were facing each other in missionary, or she was straddling him from on top, or whether she was bent over on all fours, every time he entered her and rubbed deliberately against her hidden bundle of nerves, her body clung to his in desperation, trembling in anticipation of her release. And when she thought she would collapse from the onslaught of unyielding pleasure, she felt his grasp tighten on her shoulders and his body stiffen behind her a second before he let out a moan suffused in both anguish and relief. Then he collapsed on top of her, covering her entire body with his before whispering in her ear, "You hungry yet? Or do you need me to put in more work?"

Chapter 10

Trey purred as Jeremiah leaned across the console and nuzzled the sensitive curve of her neck. He'd found that spot last night during their lovemaking and seemed determine to keep abusing it for as long as she allowed.

"If this is how you drop a girl off after a date, I might be inclined to go out with you again."

He removed his mouth from her neck and tracked tiny kisses up the side of her jaw until his lips were teasing hers. "If that's an invitation, I'm all in. We could go upstairs to your place and discuss the details."

Trey purred again, her lady parts tingling at the promise in his words. "I'd love for you to come upstairs. But didn't you say you have to check in on Ace, then head to the office?"

He groaned, tearing his mouth from hers and falling back against his seat. "Using your grandfather to cockblock is not cool, Trey."

"True," she laughed. "But it's effective."

He cut his eyes at her in a sharp slant and she exploded into laughter. "Fine, I'll behave. Let me see you inside and I'll be on my way."

He stepped out of the car and walked around to her side. Offering his hand to help her out, he pulled her against him, sliding his hand around to the small of her back. "Do I at least get a raincheck for the amazing amount of restraint I'm displaying right now?"

She lifted up on her tiptoes and hugged his neck. "Not only do you get a raincheck—" she placed her mouth against his, nipping at his full bottom lip with her teeth "—you get a reward."

She could feel his body tremble against hers. Satisfied with his reactions, she gave him a quick peck on the lips and broke free of his embrace. "Come on." She curled her finger at him. "The sooner you leave, the sooner you can meet me here for dinner tonight."

He moaned, but his expectant smile was unmistakable. He was as excited about receiving her invitation as she was giving it. He gently covered her hand in his and caressed the back of it before lacing his fingers through hers. The simple act felt significant, like something much more special than the aftermath of a good night of screwing each other's brains out.

She closed her eyes and pushed the thought out of her mind. Thinking about it too much would cause her to question her plans. And if she thought about them long enough, she'd have to admit she was so far off course, finding her way back to her original path might be impossible. She couldn't let that happen. Above all else, even this thing sparking between them, Trey's plans to serve Devereaux Inc. to her father on a silver platter had to come to fruition.

Infiltrating the Devereauxs had taken less effort than she'd thought. But sleeping with Jeremiah, might make her endgame harder. If their new intimacy made him trust her, it might make the next leg of her plan easier to execute. But would she be able to willingly sacrifice this thing growing between them? She wasn't sure, and that terrified her.

They walked in silence, and before she was ready, they were already in the lobby of her building.

"Trey, thank you for last night."

An awkward giggle escaped her lips. "I don't think a man's ever thanked me for sex before. I'm not sure what the protocol is for something like that."

His shoulders shook with quiet laughter. "Don't get it twisted. That part was great, but I wasn't really referring to that. I was talking about getting a chance to relax with you. Since Ace has been sick, I've spent all of my time between taking care of him and running Devereaux Inc. I didn't even realize how much I needed a night of simple fun and good company. So yes, thanks for the great sex, but more importantly, thanks for getting me out of my head for a bit."

Too conflicted to speak, she smiled instead, and was grateful when he placed a gentle peck on her lips. "See you tonight," he said after breaking the kiss and unraveling his fingers from hers. She watched as he left, his Brooklyn swag evident in his graceful gait. Jeremiah was poise tinged with a bit of roughness that enticed her.

If she wasn't careful, temptation would definitely be her downfall. The best thing she could do was stay away from him, keep him at arm's length. So, for the life of her, she couldn't understand why she called his name. He turned around; his brow lifted as his questioning gaze locked on hers. The appropriate thing would've been to say something like "Drive safe," or "See you soon." Instead, her words betrayed her. "Bring a bag."

That sexy mouth of his curved into the most tantalizing smile, and she damn near melted while standing at the elevators. He said nothing, simply nodded and continued his way around the corner and through the lobby. Too rung out to examine her actions, she pulled her keycard out of her bag and tapped it against the digital sensor to open her private elevator.

By the time the elevator dinged and opened on her private floor, she still didn't have an answer. Determined to push the thoughts out of her head, she opened her door. The second she closed it, the familiar cinnamon and woody scent of Clive Christian X masculine perfume struck her. It was smooth and manly, and expensive as hell. And there was only one person she knew who wore it religiously.

She stepped into her apartment as anxiety and annoyance mixed uncomfortably in her gut. When she rounded the corner, her eyes settled on what her nose already knew. Sitting there at her eat-in kitchen counter was none other than her father.

"Daddy? What are you doing here?"

He looked up with a welcoming smile, as if it was normal for her to walk in and find him sitting in her apartment uninvited. Then he stood and opened his arms. "I'm here to see my baby girl, of course."

She dropped her bag on the counter and crossed her arms over her chest. "You know I'm always glad to see you, but you aren't supposed to just let yourself in with the spare keys I gave you. Am I going to have to change the locks?"

Deuce laughed, an apologetic smile gracing his face. He held up his hands in mock surrender as he returned to his seat at the counter. "I'm sorry, baby girl. You know your mother and I respect your privacy. But you've been uncharacteristically absent and all my calls are going to voicemail. I needed to make sure you were all right. That's all, Trey. I promise I won't make a habit of intruding on your privacy."

She gifted him with a relieved smile before walking to her father and grabbing him in one of their usual tight hugs. When she stepped back, he looked at her with a tinge of amusement. "So, you wanna tell me what you were up to that has you walking in at nine in the morning?"

"Not particularly."

He nodded and smiled. "You can't blame a father for trying." He laughed at himself. Trey's independence was never up for discussion outside the confines of DD Enterprises. There he was her boss. But in the real world, Trey answered to no one. Her parents thankfully respected that, which helped foster their close relationship.

"At least tell me this. Are you enjoying your time off?"

"I really am. I hadn't realized how much I needed this down time."

"Your mother pointed out the last vacation you took was a year ago. That was before you started working on the Devereaux Inc. takeover."

She nodded. There was no question it had consumed her life. The fact that she was using her time off now to still pursue it was proof of that.

"Listen, Trey, I never meant for my obsession with my

father's company to become yours. If that smile you've got on your face is any indication, it shows me how much pressure I've been putting on you."

"How'd you come to that conclusion?"

"Trey, I haven't seen you smile like this, so free and effortless, since you started working on acquiring Devereaux Inc. A few days away from the job and you come home looking rested and unbothered. What else am I supposed to think?"

She waved a dismissive hand and leaned into the counter. "Daddy, I'm your second-in-command. I knew this job would be high-pressure when I accepted it. You don't need to apologize for that."

"No, you're wrong. This isn't like any other takeover we've handled before. I've been pushing this one more than I should because of my history with my father. I shouldn't have done that to you. But, no worries. I'm gonna fix that, starting right now."

She clapped her hands together and rubbed them back and forth. "What, am I getting a raise? You know I won't turn down an extra juicy bonus."

Her father threw his head back in a loud chuckle and her heart danced. It had been such a long time since she'd seen him let loose like this.

"You get paid more than a fair wage, baby girl. But seriously, I've been too hard on you. So, to make up for it, I'm giving you two extra weeks off. Take your time and recharge, Trey. When you come back, we'll figure out a new way to gain control of Devereaux Inc. that doesn't take up so much of your life."

Guilt bled into this happy moment they were sharing. She was lying to him, even if it was to accomplish something he wanted. Her conscience was screaming she should be ashamed of herself.

"Daddy, maybe we've been looking at this Devereaux Inc. thing all wrong. Instead of scheming, maybe Ace would talk to us and we could work this thing out. I could even act as an intermediary if you wanted. Maybe his lack of history with me would make it easier for him to see how wrong he was all those years ago."

Her father groaned, the laughing smile dropping from his face. "Trey, I want nothing to do with that man. He's no good. Promise me you'll stay away from Ace. He will destroy you, if for no other reason than you're my child."

She swallowed her guilt and mustered a sympathetic smile. "Yes, Daddy," she agreed.

Her father's tense shoulders relaxed, and the corners of his mouth curved into a grin.

"That's my baby girl." He planted a loud, smacking kiss on her cheek the way he used to when she was a kid. Still guilt ridden, she placed her head on his chest and waited for him to envelop her in his embrace.

She might not deserve his adoration for the crap she was pulling, but that didn't mean she wouldn't take it. Because if he ever found out what she was truly doing with her time off, she might not get another one of his famous daddy hugs for a long time to come.

Chapter 11

In short time Jeremiah made it from the sign-in log at the front desk to Trey's penthouse. The black marble tiles on the floor were a stark contrast to the white walls of the hallway. On one side of the hall there was what he assumed was a damn good replica of Faith Ringgold's *The Bitter Nest, Part II: The Harlem Renaissance.* The tapestry's mix of red, brown and black was eye-catching against the stark white wall.

He was still admiring it when he heard the black metal door slide open and saw Trey stick her head out into the hall.

"There you are." Her lips pulled into a wide grin that displayed her perfect white teeth. "I thought you'd gotten lost."

"On a private elevator that only stops at the garage, the first floor and the penthouse? I've had a long day, but not that long."

He pointed to the tapestry on the wall. "That's an amazing replica. I'm no art aficionado, but it looks real."

She slid her hand into his and guided him toward the door. "It is real."

"Isn't it supposed to be at the Smithsonian?"

"It was, but I bought it a few years ago."

"You can buy exhibits from the Smithsonian?"

She winked and turned back the way she'd come. "You can buy anything if you've got enough money and clout. Fortunately, I have both."

They stepped inside and she closed the door before escorting him down the small hallway that opened up into a ridiculously wide room with reddish-brown hand-scraped hardwood floors. The walls inside the apartment were the same shade of stark white, and acted as a backdrop to more artwork in varying red, gold, green and black patterns.

There were several throw rugs in specific locations: under the glass coffee table, near the bay window with the red bench, in front of the fireplace. They created eye-catching focal points.

"It's gorgeous in here. How on earth did you find an apartment this size in downtown Brooklyn?"

"It's technically Brooklyn Heights, but same difference." She relieved him of his overnight bag and disappeared down another hall to the right, quickly returning and leading him toward a large leather couch against a long wall.

"Well, it started out as three apartments, one at each corner of the hall and one in the center. I had them remodeled into one penthouse."

He continued to glance around the room, taking in

its vibrant decor that mixed modern construction with a more traditional Afrocentric style. "So, this is you, huh?"

She tucked her feet underneath her on the couch and pitched her head as she smiled. "Yeah, it's me. A perfect mix of the old and the new."

"I like it. I may have to borrow your interior decorator. I wouldn't mind having a few pieces that celebrate our connection to the motherland."

"That would be my mom." Her face lit up and her voice was tinged with a softness he hadn't noticed before. "She's really into Pan-Africanism. One of the first things she did when we were finally earning enough from the business to live comfortably was take me to see art by Black creatives all over the world. She wanted me to understand our people created beauty in this world. It must have stuck because now when I see authentic art that reflects the Black experience, I can't pass it up."

"She carved out a beautiful space for you, Trey. It's warm, welcoming and uplifting."

He took her hand in his and pulled her over to straddle him. His strong, tight arms circled her waist until they were filled with nothing but Trey. Her natural heat was comforting, a balm for the emotional exhaustion he couldn't shake off.

"I missed you."

She pulled back from nuzzling the curve of his neck and looked down at him. "Did you, now?"

"Yeah, the office has been intense these last couple of days."

She nodded as she placed both hands on the sides of his face. "Ah, I thought I recognized that look."

"What look?"

She chuckled. "The work-is-kicking-my-ass look. I have the perfect remedy for it."

He drew his brows together as he watched playfulness light up her face.

"Oh yeah? What's that?"

"Me."

He stole a soft kiss, pulling away before it became deeper. He let his head sag against the back of the couch as he looked up into her eyes.

"I have no doubt you could fix all that ails me. But instead of indulging in this glorious body of yours, I really need to talk to you about Devereaux Inc."

Trey shook her head and pressed a finger against his lips.

"Nope," she replied. "Not until I get you relaxed." She snaked her hands under the hem of his sweatshirt and tugged until it was over his head. She quickly tossed it aside on the sofa before moving off his lap. She knelt, removing his sneakers, and then looked up at him. "Do you need an invitation to get rid of the rest of your clothes?"

"You are so damn bossy." He stood and stripped off his remaining garments before sitting again.

"I think that's exactly what you need tonight." She ran her hands up his thighs and his muscles twitched in anticipation beneath her touch. "Someone who will care for you for once."

"What do you mean?"

She moved her hands lightly over his abs and he shivered from the tantalizing spark her light caress stirred in him.

"You've been taking care of my grandfather and running his company with no help, all while you try to fight off his viper of a sister. When are you going to let someone do the same for you?"

Her fingers grazed his nipple, sending an electric current through him as he sank into the soft cushions of the sofa. He felt her hand cup his cheek, rubbing her delicate thumb over his stubble, the simple gesture making his blood simmer and cock tighten.

"You trust me to take care of you, Mr. Benton?"

He shouldn't. She was unpredictable and worse, uncontrollable. Everything could blow up in his face. Trusting her wasn't smart. Especially before he had a chance to talk to her about whether her father, or Trey herself, would help secure the leadership of Devereaux Inc.

He made the mistake of looking into her smoldering brown eyes and all rational thought left his mind. There was only one word ringing in his head that his mouth would let him speak.

"Yes."

He was tired and more than a little aggravated with his day, and yet a simple touch from her made his body burn. Whether he'd let himself admit his heart was involved or not, he knew he would have a hard time letting this feeling go when it ended. And he knew it would end. It was cute for her to indulge in adult play with her grandfather's second-in-command when she didn't have any involvement with the family company. But if she or her father joined the company, a woman like Trey wouldn't compromise her reputation or her ability to command respect by sleeping with an employee.

He closed his eyes, trying to ignore the thought of becoming just another employee at Devereaux Inc. He'd served Ace so diligently all these years, and when the old man was finally gone, he might end up just the way

Ace had found him, jobless, with no real family unit to speak of.

He could feel despair tugging him away from the oasis Trey was attempting to create. But as she wrapped her hand around his erection, he knew one thing: Trey Devereaux was fast becoming an addiction he wouldn't easily break.

The warmth of her caress made him spread his legs, giving her room to work. It was an invitation. His way of saying, *Have your way.*

Her palm was soft and firm, and its first stroke was the thing dreams were made of. Or so he thought before the hot weight of her tongue licked a path from his sac up the length of his cock that stole his breath. By the time the wet heat of her mouth closed around his crown, his lungs burned with the need to breathe.

When she took him completely into her mouth, he spoke her name on a long, low moan of pleasure as her tongue cupped the underside of his length.

His fingers found their way into the full, thick strands of her hair, burying themselves there. She picked up the pace, adding a twist to her hand at the base of his cock, driving him out of his mind. He was near the tipping point, his body tightening, begging for release as she swallowed around him.

"Fuck, Trey." She glanced up, her eyes leveling a delicious challenge. The vision of her handling him—correction, owning him—made it impossible for him to keep himself in check.

She paused and ran her tongue across her bruised lips. He used the opportunity to turn the tables and re-gain control.

He grabbed her to him and plastered his mouth against

those gorgeous pouty lips of hers and savored the taste of him on her. Before she protested, he twisted them around until she was lying beneath him on the sofa. He found his sweatshirt in a frantic grasp and pulled his wallet out of it, searching for the emergency condom he always kept there.

Relieved when his fingers grazed the foil, he snatched it out, threw the wallet to the floor, opened the packet and sheathed himself.

He lifted her satin lounge shirt up over her chest to find her blessedly naked beneath it. He guided himself to her slick opening, and pushed inside in one stroke, as he whispered, "I promise I'll make this up to you later. I just need…"

She circled her legs around his waist and tightened her heat around him, breaking his will. Unable to hold back the driving need to move, he snapped his hips. His movements were punishing and wild, and if all his blood hadn't drained from his brain at the moment, he might have been able to add a little more finesse to his touch. But Trey's actions had reduced him to a grunting caveman, and he couldn't find the decency to be the least bit ashamed of it.

He looked down at her and saw she was waging her own battle. Her nails bit into his flesh, clawing at him as she chased release. The lines of her face pulled tightly while her muscles clenched around him like a searing vice, and when she arched her back and screamed his name, he was lost. Lost to the demands of her body, lost to the need she stirred inside him, and most frighteningly he was lost to the pull Trey had on his soul.

His body betrayed him before that thought could latch on. The orgasm wouldn't be denied or delayed any longer. The tightness at the bottom of his spine gave way and torturous bliss claimed him as he pulsed his release into the latex sheath covering him.

He'd come to her irritated, exhausted and worried about work. And now, after she'd bled his body of its essence, all he could focus on was how right it felt to be taken care of by the woman in his arms.

Trey watched a sleeping Jeremiah settled in her king-size bed, one leg bent, the other stretched out, taking up most of the space. She chuckled, realizing she didn't care. The serene picture he made, his nearness and contentment, made her happy. That was all that mattered.

I want more. The thought made her body stiffen with regret. *What have you done to me, Jeremiah, that I could even consider letting my father down just to be with you?* Whatever magic it was he wielded, the force of its power made her tremble. *Are you worth my father's disappointment?*

Her father's reaction to losing the Singleton bid would be mild in comparison to the explosion she knew would come if he ever found out how far into enemy territory she'd crossed. He'd be mad as hell that she was pursuing her own plan for taking over Ace's company without consulting him, one that involved direct contact with the man he'd forbidden her to have contact with. But Deuce would consider it a personal betrayal that she'd allowed herself to develop a deep fondness for the father Deuce hated. If he knew she'd also permitted herself to become emotionally attached to Ace's second-in-command, he'd probably disown her.

Deuce promised there was nothing in this world that could separate him from the love he bore for her. But was she willing to put that declaration to the test for more time with this powerful, beautiful man hogging the covers in her bed? Was she really willing to betray the man who gave her life for the man who made her feel alive?

Is he worth hurting your daddy?

Her heart clenched at even the imagined loss of her father's love. Deuce was her hero. He'd raised her to fear nothing and no one. Without his daily affirmations of her power and ability, would she be bold enough to even consider taking what she wanted? Would she be someone Jeremiah would want?

The question thudded against her brain again. *Is Jeremiah Benton worth the trouble?*

He turned in his sleep, his body instinctively looking for hers. When he gathered her in his arms, everything became clear and there was only one answer she could give.

Yes, he is.

Chapter 12

The tempting sensation of warmth against his skin pulled Jeremiah from sleep. He opened his eyes to find Trey's naked form flattened against him in the shadows.

Slightly disoriented, he reached for his phone on the nearby nightstand. It was nine in the morning, but the deceptive darkness caused by the blackout curtains made him want to stay in bed with an armful of Trey for many more hours.

He thought of their night together. It was more than sex. It was comfort and concern. It was Trey taking care of him in a way he wasn't exactly certain how to process.

Jeremiah had never experienced this kind of connection. Merely being in her presence made him feel better.

"Stop thinking so loud. You're disturbing my sleep."

Her groggy voice made him chuckle as she pulled the covers up over her shoulders and repositioned her bonnet-covered head on the pillow.

He leaned down, running a finger over the black satin garment pulled down over her ears. "I will never understand the mystical power Black women possess when it comes to these things. You make them appear out of thin air."

"You can't possibly think of starting this day by taking shots at my sleep bonnet."

He snuggled down closer to her, wrapping his arm around her thickness and tugging until there was no space between them.

"Not at all. I'm actually in awe. And also, a little proud you feel comfortable enough with me to let me see you in it. I like that there's no pretense between us."

She turned around in his arms until she was facing him. Her face free of makeup, her hair covered by the bonnet, she was the picture of confidence, someone comfortable in her own skin. And he couldn't get enough of her.

"You think my bonnet is sexy?" Her face was lit up with amusement. "Because I have 'em in an assortment of colors. If I ever pull out the red one, know it's about to be on."

"Is that so? Well, I'm not sure I could take it if things were even more *on* than they were last night. God, how am I satisfied, thoroughly relaxed and exhausted too?"

She shrugged a shoulder. "That's simple. I've got that good-good."

Without missing a beat, he replied, "You ain't ever lied. Your sex is damn near lethal. I can't imagine what would've happened if I were a lesser man."

"A lesser man wouldn't have been here. You've got skills. I'm not mad at them. You know how to handle your business."

Guilt quickly replaced desire as concern for Ace's

legacy grew. "Speaking of, I need to talk to you about Devereaux Inc."

She lifted up on her elbow to meet his gaze. "Is something wrong?"

"Martha came to the office before I left to get ready for our date. She wanted to inform me that when Ace is dead and his shares are hers, I'm out on my ass."

"Is that why you're so determined to stop her? You're worried about your job?"

He shook his head. "Do I want to leave Devereaux Inc.? No. Unfortunately, it's not as simple as that." He certainly wished it were. "As a boss you'll understand this more than most. There are certain people who seek power who should never be allowed to have it."

She nodded. "Because absolute power corrupts absolutely."

"Exactly," he replied. "She's always been entitled. Even raising her late son as the heir apparent to Ace's throne. Planning out his life so when the time came, Devereaux Inc. would be his. But when he died two years ago, it's like those failed dreams consumed her. And I fear if I don't stop her, if Ace dies and neither your father nor you claim your birthright, Martha's misplaced pain and ambition may consume us all."

Trey swirled a finger in the space between his pecs. He'd told her Devereaux Inc. could very well be lost and her response was to playfully slide her finger over his skin. He didn't know whether to be unnerved or relieved.

He looked up and saw the fire burning deep in her brown eyes. He went to speak again, and she placed a lone finger over his mouth. "Let's make a deal. Instead of worrying about something you have no control over, how about you spend the morning with me? I'll take you to have some of the best pancakes in Brooklyn, and everything will be fine."

He lifted a brow. "The best pancakes I've ever had I cooked. You saying these are better than mine?"

She gave him a conspiratorial wink. "Baby, nothing's better than yours."

God help him, the way she said that, the conviction that saturated her voice, it rocked him. It made him want to forget about all of his responsibilities, to bask in all of her power.

"Trey, I just told you Martha is a real threat. I won't be able to relax until I know if you or your father will stop her from getting her hooks into Devereaux Inc."

"No, Jeremiah. Martha is an annoyance. I'm the threat."

He was thinking this was simply bravado, but then he felt her spine stiffen underneath his palm and he knew this was so much more than that.

"My name is Jordan Dylan Devereaux III. There's not a man or woman born who can stand against me. That name is my birthright, as are the power and legacy attached to it. Martha and whatever schemes she has in the works will fail because of one simple reason. Whatever sacrifice is necessary, I will not rest until Devereaux Inc. is safely where it belongs."

She leaned down to kiss him, the kiss sparking this peculiar fusion of relief and concern. He believed Trey would beat Martha. Nothing he'd ever known about the other woman could compare to the blaze of power Jeremiah could feel burning through Trey's touch. But somewhere in the back of his mind he worried whether that same power wouldn't consume him and Devereaux Inc. too.

* * *

Trey watched in delight as Jeremiah devoured the stack of Amaretto pancakes on his plate as they sat in Le Petit Café. In all her years, she'd met no one who seemed to derive such pleasure from fried bread covered in syrup. But when he moaned his satisfaction as he placed the last forkful in his mouth, Trey decided she would make certain he ate pancakes every day if it meant she got to experience him making those sinful faces and delicious sounds as he dined.

"What? Do I have food on my face?"

"No," she laughed. "Simply thinking I've never known a man who could make eating pancakes look as sexy as you do. It could easily become a favorite pastime of mine."

He grabbed his napkin and wiped at his mouth before he swallowed and graced her with a smile. "What can I say? I love pancakes. Especially when they're this good and I didn't have to make them myself."

He swallowed his coffee before bringing his gaze back up to hers. "So, from our conversation this morning, I got the feeling you had a plan to stop Martha. Is that true or just wishful thinking on my part?"

She placed her hand over his, trying to burn the feel of his skin into her memory. *Please don't make me think about this now. I'm not ready to give this up. And I'm not ready to betray my father and all the promises I've made to him.*

As if the universe wanted to remind her she was out of time, she heard the soulful voice of Sam Cooke as he crooned the sad and mournful "A Change Gonna Come" over the restaurant's audio system.

No matter what I do, I'm gonna hurt someone I love.

"Trey? Did you hear me?"

She nodded. "I have a plan to get Martha off your back now." He opened his mouth to speak but she quieted him with a raised hand. "We'll discuss it when we're with Ace. He needs to weigh in on this. I also need to run this by my father."

"Seems like whatever you've got planned you think your father will disapprove." He paused, his brow furrowed as he awaited her response.

"My father wants nothing to do with Ace." It was the truth, but only a small sliver of it. "He can't get past Ace's transgressions, not in time to handle Martha, anyway."

Jeremiah scratched at his beard as he fixed his questioning gaze on her. "So, it's likely he won't be thrilled with whatever this plan is as a result?"

She shrugged. She knew damn well Deuce wouldn't be happy about any of this. Not about knowing she was lying to him, not about her spending time with Ace, and certainly not about sleeping with a man he would no doubt count as his enemy. And not about the precarious position she'd be putting herself in with the SEC if anyone ever connected the dots about her hostile takeover plans and the plan she was going to lay before Ace today. But what choice did she have?

"Let me worry about my father."

Her stomach sank as she thought of all the ways things could blow up in her face. But she couldn't worry about any of that now. She was in too deep. No place to go but forward. Her feelings for Jeremiah wouldn't allow her to walk away. Even if her saving Ace's shares meant Jeremiah would hate her in the end for the way she did it.

"Come on." She waved for the check. "Let's get back to Ace's so we can get to work."

Chapter 13

Trey cut the ignition of her Escalade and sat back in her seat, letting the supple leather caress her. Once she exited her vehicle and walked around the corner, things would change. This would no longer be a hustle in theory. The moment she spoke to Ace, and she took his shares, she would pass the point of no return.

"Hey, what's on your mind?" Jeremiah asked.

You're going to hate me when you realize I've been lying all along.

"Trey?"

She managed a small smile and nodded. "I'm fine."

He picked up her hand and placed a gentle kiss on the back of it. She felt unworthy of his comfort but it still soothed her. It was one more item in a long list of things she was stealing.

"I promise this will be all right, Trey. I've no doubt you can handle yourself against any foe. But I'm here if you need me. I won't let you drown trying to save Ace's legacy."

His gaze was so intense. It comforted her, yes, but also abraded the protective layer she'd told herself would keep her safe when her plans took root.

"Don't make promises you can't keep, Jeremiah. Otherwise, I'll have to remind you when all hell breaks loose."

He seemed thrown by her comment, confusion swimming in those whiskey-colored eyes.

"Trey?"

"Shhh," she whispered against his full lips. "Let me have this moment. The rest will work itself out in its own time."

She could still see the unanswered questions plaguing him, but he leaned in, hooking his fingers firmly behind her neck, and answered, "Whatever you need."

She lost herself in his kiss, in the scrape of his fingers against her nape, in the sweet taste of maple syrup and Amaretto that remained after brunch. She needed to remember everything about this moment. Because there was no way it could survive once they stepped out of her car.

They left her SUV and made it up the porch stairs and into the house. Trey stepped into Ace's room and like every time before, the weight of his gaze on her made her conscience twist into tight knots.

When she'd started this, she was certain this was justified retribution. Ace had kicked her father out of the Devereaux family, stripping him of all the power, access and stability attached to the name. Ace's actions had left her father broke and homeless with a new wife and a baby on the way and no immediate means of providing for them.

But Deuce had survived. He'd toiled by day to put food on the table and worked all night to build the company that would one day rival his father's.

After watching her father live through that, the righteousness of her motives seemed apparent. But watching the brittle old man sitting propped up on his mountain of pillows in his bed with a frail smile, all of this felt wrong. Really wrong.

He waved a welcoming hand and then patted the space on the bed next to him, asking her to join him. The hope in the old man's eyes pierced something inside of her, making her pull away from his gaze and search Jeremiah's for comfort.

Wrong move again, Trey. As soon as her eyes met Jeremiah's, the guilt continued to pour on.

She managed a small smile, hoping she didn't look like a guilty fool. What she wouldn't give to be back in her apartment, wrapped up with Jeremiah under her sheets. But that seemed like a lifetime ago, and now they were here. Even though regret festered in the pit of her soul, she couldn't stop this machine now. Too much had happened.

"There's my grandbaby."

Are you really going to steal this dying old man's company, Trey?

She sat down on the bed and Ace covered her hand with his, giving it a soft pat. "Ace, I have something to talk to you about. Do you know why Jeremiah found me in the first place?"

The man nodded. "He was trying to help an old fool feel better before leaving this world."

She looked at Jeremiah and could see the love and admiration he had for Ace in the depths of his deep brown gaze.

"That's partly true," she replied. "He also brought me here because Martha is lying in wait for your company, Ace. Are you aware of that? Is that what you want? Jeremiah thinks I can stop her. But before I even attempt to, I need to know if that's what you really want. Is this worth the energy I'd need to invest?"

"You mean, is it worth the turmoil it will cause between you and my son?"

A proud grin crept onto her mouth. A glint of mischief and clarity sparked on his face and reminded her again so much of who she was, who her father was. They both came from this man.

"My father won't be happy about this, Ace. You're his direct competitor. By helping you save your company I'd be risking my relationship with him if I continue down this path. Is it worth it?"

He scanned her face, as if he was trying to not only see her but see through her and gauge her sincerity.

"I built this company for my son and the heirs he would bring forth. Martha is my sister and I love her, but she can't have what I created. Do whatever you must to stop her and do it fast. She called before you arrived. She's up to something. I don't know what. But it can't be good."

A knock came from the opened door, breaking the spell. Amara walked in holding a mug in her hand. "Uncle Ace," she began once she walked over to the opposite side of the bed, placing the steaming mug on the nightstand before turning to him. "I'm sorry. I couldn't help but overhear your conversation as I came upstairs.

Are you sure about involving Trey? Shoving Martha at her is a lot for anyone, let alone someone who's just walking in to all this mess."

Ace threw his head back and his laughter filled the room.

"My dear, Amara. Just like your mom and your grand-daddy, always worrying about the outcomes. No need to worry about the outcomes if you plan things right. Trey has nothing to fear from Martha."

"You can't know that, Uncle Ace." Her displeasure was notable in the annoyed grimace she offered him. "No offense, but you don't know that much about Trey beyond the few visits you've had with her. How can you place so much faith in her?"

It was a fair question, one Trey would definitely ask if she was in Amara's position as the family attorney.

But a spark of excitement mixed with certainty swirled in the elderly man's eyes, once brown but now graying with age. That spark jumped from him, electrifying the room around them. Even Trey could feel the jolt of confidence light her own fire.

"Amara, she's my namesake. There's not a man or woman born who can stand against her."

Trey narrowed her gaze as she watched her grandfather's smiling face. "My father has spoken those exact words to me for as long as I can remember. My mom says he used to say that into her belly when she carried me. How could you have known?"

Ace smiled at her, pride and comfort flushing the gray pallor from his face and infusing his skin with a red blush. "Where do you think Deuce got it from? I spoke that phrase to him while he was in the womb and every day of his life until we parted ways. I spoke his power into existence, and he did the same for you. The strength in our name flows through you. That force, that ability, that's the true legacy of the Devereaux clan and Devereaux Incorporated. Martha can't win. Because you won't let her."

Her throat felt tight. His words made her tremble and yet, she'd never felt stronger or more capable in her life.

"You're right, I won't let her win. But I will need something from you to nullify any power she has to contest the contents of your will."

He didn't ask what. He simply nodded as if he already knew what she was thinking. He probably did, but she still needed to speak the words to make certain they were on the same page.

"I need you to sell me all the shares you own in Devereaux Incorporated."

Chapter 14

Jeremiah sat paralyzed as he processed Trey's demand. When no one said anything to counter her ridiculous ask, he turned his laser focus on Trey.

He'd brought her in for her help, presuming she or Deuce would claim Ace's shares upon his death. But this was not what he had in mind. This would mean stripping Ace of his stake in a company he'd built from nothing.

"You can't be serious."

"I am," she answered. Her voice was smooth and matter-of-fact, all business with little room for anything else including the closeness they'd shared a few hours ago. "Jeremiah, it's the only way."

He stood up. "Like hell it is. There is always another way. This can't be your brilliant plan."

"It's the only one that's guaranteed to prevent Martha from getting her hands on the shares," she responded in a cool tone that pissed him off.

"That's bullshit and you know it." His barked reply was loud and sharp enough to make even him wince, but Trey simply sat still on Ace's bed.

"Jeremiah, it's the only way."

She kept saying that like it would somehow click in his head that she was right, and he'd go along with it. But there was no way in hell that was happening. He'd worked too hard to protect Ace from all threats. He didn't want to imagine Trey could be one of them, especially not after the time they'd spent together recently. But what else could he believe if her plan amounted to Ace losing his life's work.

"Ace giving away everything he's worked for is the brilliant plan you've come up with? There's no way I'm letting him do this. Come up with something else." When Trey said nothing, and everyone else remained quiet, he locked gazes with Amara. "Amara, you can't be on board with this nonsense."

She ran a palm across her forehead. "I don't like this, J. But Trey's right. This is an option. Martha can't contest the will if the shares have already been sold before Ace's death."

Trey stood and walked toward the footboard where there was more space. She motioned for Jeremiah to meet her there. Her gaze was strong and unwavering, with no hint of guilt or fear. It was clear she was serious about this plan of hers.

"Jeremiah." He could feel his anger deflating just from the sound of his name on her lips. Being angry with her was the only way he could fight her. *Dammit, how did you let this happen. When did you let her get under your skin like this?*

"Trey, I can't stand by and let him give everything away."

"I didn't say give. I said sell."

"It's a billion-dollar business. His shares total forty percent of the company. You've got four hundred million dollars lying around to spend at a moment's notice on this harebrained scheme?"

Trey stiffened her back and narrowed her eyes before giving him a sarcastic grin. "Would you prefer a check or a wire transfer? I'd offer you cash, but with all those pesky banking rules, it would take a few days to complete the transaction."

God, she was hot when she was pissing him off. The same fire he'd seen in her the night she'd shown up at The Vault filled her eyes. Their dark brown color had transformed to the same shade of fiery amber they were in bed. *This is not the time to be thinking about this, Jeremiah.*

He averted his gaze and stepped away from her, needing to break free of her orbit and regain his illusive control.

"Jeremiah." The soft sound of her voice chiseled away at the last bit of restraint he had. "I asked you last night if you trusted me. You said yes. Trust me now. I promise you, I will keep Ace's company out of Martha's hands."

The pleading in her voice undid him like a loose thread on the edge of a sweater. With little effort and maximum effect, she'd broken through his defenses and reached that place he'd sworn no one would ever enter: his heart. And the realization was shocking.

He placed his hands on his waist and shook his head. "You'll own forty percent of Devereaux Inc. That makes you the largest shareholder, but it doesn't mean you win by default."

She shrugged her shoulders as if the subject of their conversation amounted to where they'd have a quick bite to eat instead of the control and the fate of a Fortune 500 company.

"It's been my experience that people will follow the majority. With my forty percent and presumably your sixteen, I have no doubt I'd be able to stop any of Martha's attempts to destroy Devereaux Inc. Also, his lawyer is standing right here along with you as another witness to testify to Ace's state of mind. If he gives me those shares, a woman he hasn't known very long, he looks unstable. If he makes a sound business deal that nets his company four hundred million dollars, he looks like the mogul he is. It's a foolproof plan."

It was, and Jeremiah knew it. But in admitting it, he'd have to admit his subsequent discovery: he'd fallen for Ace's granddaughter. And now he couldn't tell if he was helping his mentor or serving him up on a platter.

"Amara, help me out here. You can't possibly agree with this." He waited for Amara to throw him a lifeline. But when he heard her expel a loud huff of air from her lungs, he didn't hold out much hope.

"I don't like it any more than you do, J." Amara's voice broke when she spoke his name. He couldn't remember a time where she looked so fragile in all the years he'd known her, and it tore at something in his heart. He loved Amara. She'd been the closest thing he'd ever had to a sibling. Seeing her hurt didn't sit right with him. "But Trey is right. If she buys his shares, it will stop Martha in her tracks."

Amara looked at him with fierce devotion and Trey

with compassion. Both women seemed to understand his need to fight and his refusal to give in. All he'd wanted was to save Ace like the man had saved him, and if Jeremiah was reckless, Ace would end up losing everything. He turned to his mentor, hoping that his brilliant mind was working ten steps ahead of them like it always seemed to be. But when he saw the shimmer of unshed tears in the man's eyes, Jeremiah knew he'd lost this battle.

"Jeremiah, I know you're trying to fight for me. And I love you for it. But this is as it should be. Whether any of us likes it, my days are numbered. What good will these shares do me if I can't use them to stop Martha?"

And that was the real problem. Fighting for Ace's business wasn't about doing something for the older man. It was about refusing to let go of him as the cancer took a little more of him away each day. He was running out of time. But when Trey stepped closer to him and placed a calm, gentle hand on his arm, the fear ebbed, and for a moment, he could see clearly.

"Fine," Jeremiah relented. "If this is the only way, this is what we'll do. But there is one contractual stipulation." Trey waited for his demand, her eyes flitting as she anticipated his next words. "The shares can only be gifted, willed or sold to a blood relative who is your eponym or namesake and a direct descendant of Jordan Dylan Devereaux I. Your father or your heirs, Trey. No one else. Even though there are outside shareholders, Devereaux Inc. is a family business and it must always remain so."

If he couldn't save Ace, the least he could do was ensure that his dream of passing his legacy from parent to child would endure beyond Trey's generation.

"Agreed." The conviction in her voice rocked him. He wasn't ready to speak, so he simply nodded in agreement.

"Amara." Trey turned toward her cousin, extending a hand to her. "Why don't we go downstairs, and I can put you in contact with my attorney and we can get the sale underway."

Amara gave Trey a weak smile and walked across to Trey, taking her hand and leading her out of the room, so that Jeremiah and Ace were now alone.

"She's magnificent, isn't she?"

Ace's words caught Jeremiah off guard. He cocked his head to the side as he tried to make sense of the question.

"Who, Amara? She's always been amazing."

Ace lifted his brow and chuckled. "Yes, my great-niece is amazing. But I think we both know I wasn't talking about her. I was speaking of my granddaughter, Trey. She'll take over the world one day, one heart at a time." The old man smiled and shook an accusing finger at Jeremiah. "And it seems like she's started with yours."

The lie was on the tip of his tongue. But he was raw and rung out, and he didn't have the energy it would take to deceive such a wise person as Ace.

"I think you might be right, old man."

Ace laughed again. "So, what do you plan on doing about it?"

Jeremiah shrugged, then he walked over to the side of Ace's bed and slumped into a nearby chair.

"The hell if I know."

The old man had another laugh at Jeremiah's expense. If he hadn't spent so many years showering Jeremiah with kindness, Jeremiah would call Ace cruel.

"Listen, young'un. It happens to the best of us. Love puts you on your ass and you can do one of two things. Fight about it or surrender and ask for mercy. Does she know?"

Jeremiah shook his head. How could Trey know when he was just finding out himself?

"Young people make things so difficult. I met my Alva and two months later she was my bride. You fellas have no game."

"Well, since you know so much, old man, how about you school me?"

Ace waved a dismissive hand. "I'm trying if you'd quit interrupting me." Jeremiah pretended to pull a zipper closed across his mouth as he sat up and made a show of giving Ace his undivided attention. "Why don't you start by taking her to the Legacy Ball?"

Jeremiah thought about the annual celebration that brought Devereaux Inc. executives and employees together to celebrate their leader and the company's success. It was a formal night filled with fun, food and more libations than anyone could ever want.

"All the board members will be in town," Ace continued, "for the ball. The sale of my shares will be completed by then. It will give you a chance to show Trey around and school her on who all the major players are, while she takes the time to dazzle some of them before the meeting."

Jeremiah had to admit it. Ace's advice was practical with the right touch of romance to it. No wonder the man was so successful. He always knew what to say with that silver tongue of his.

Jeremiah was about to get up and leave the room when Ace held up a hand. "I wanted to talk to you."

He gave Ace his entire focus. His tone was heavy, and Jeremiah could tell whatever it was his mentor wanted to say was important.

"What is it?"

Ace leaned over and pulled the familiar document Jeremiah had given him just before he'd brought Trey into the fold.

"You asked that I take time to consider whether I'd give my blessing for your name change. And I did."

His chest tightened with anticipation as he waited for Ace's next word.

"The moment I brought you home with me, you were family. You've always been a Devereaux to me."

"But?" Jeremiah questioned him.

"I don't need you to change your name officially to make me love you." Ace beckoned Jeremiah with a wave of his hand and patted the bed next him. Jeremiah heeded the man's request and sat next to him with his heart thudding hard against his rib cage, waiting for Ace to finish. Ace took Jeremiah's hand in his and gifted him with his signature full smile. "But it would make me damn proud if you bore it. Because you, Jeremiah Benton Devereaux, are the best of the best, son. And that means you belong to this family and have claim to its legacy and power."

"If that's true, why wouldn't you bequeath the shares to me in your will?"

To hear Ace use the official name he'd chosen on those documents meant everything to him. But just as love swelled inside him, that dark pocket of envy nipped at the back of his mind keeping him from embracing this wonderful moment in its entirety.

Surprise lit up Ace's face. His spine stiffened and he tightened his hold on Jeremiah's hands. "Jeremiah, there are things you don't understand."

"I understand Deuce has been gone for more than thirty years and yet you refuse to change your will, so he can step in and assume the throne whenever he wants.

My loyalty to you and the company has never wavered. And yet, you would leave it all to him, even when you know doing so might destroy everything. I've tried to understand it, Ace. But the only thing that makes sense is I'm not as much family as you claim."

Ace took a deep breath, placing a shaky hand against his chest as if speaking actually hurt. "There has never been a question in my mind that you were deserving of my shares. There were many times over the years when I came very close to changing the will so you could inherit them. But ultimately, I couldn't."

"Because of Deuce." Jeremiah's voice was harsh as it passed through his clenched teeth.

"No," Ace answered. "Because of his mother, Alva." Ace repositioned himself in the bed before he spoke again. "My wife was an only child when her mother died. When her father remarried, his new wife saw my Alva as a nuisance. By the time Alva was a teenager, her stepmother pushed to have her sent away. To keep the peace, Alva's father sent her to Brooklyn to live with his sister. Alva was never welcomed in her own home or family again. And when the father died, her stepmother cut her out of her father's will.

"Although it hurt her, she made peace with her father sending her here. But completely erasing her claim to his legacy, like she never existed, it broke her heart. She never wanted something like that to happen to Deuce. And when we built this company, she made me promise no matter what happened to my relationship with Deuce that he'd always maintain his claim to my legacy as my firstborn. That his heirs would always be able to inherit it even if Deuce himself didn't want it or wasn't here to claim it."

"So, the will—"

"Was a way to ensure I kept my promise to the love of my life. It was never about a lack of faith in you or love for you. You are mine, Jeremiah Benton Devereaux." He sniffled, still fighting to keep his composure. "And even my love for my estranged son can't change that. Now, is that all right with you?"

It was more than all right, because Ace, his hero, his father figure, loved him. "Yes, it is," was all he could manage as he pursed his lips, trying to keep the tears from falling.

"You have made my dream come true and secured the future of my legacy. I can never thank you enough or love you enough for all you've gifted me with now, and throughout all the years I've been blessed to watch you grow. I'm terribly sorry if for even a second I made you feel unloved or unwanted. That was never my intention."

Ace leaned forward, and his weathered cheek, still wet with tears, touched the side of Jeremiah's face. He dragged in a shaky breath and then whispered the most precious words in Jeremiah's ear. "I love you, young Master Devereaux, and I only have one request left to ask of you." Ace's teary smile spread, lighting those spaces where doubt and envy rotted inside Jeremiah. "Love Trey as fiercely as you've loved me."

He leaned back against his pillows, still smiling, still holding Jeremiah's hand. "Do you think you can do that for a dying old man?"

He wanted to say yes without a single shred of uncertainty or hesitation. Loving Trey wasn't the problem. He was already there. Trusting her, however, especially once Ace's shares were hers, he wasn't sure he could do.

Chapter 15

"Trey, when you said you had the perfect designer in mind for our outfits for this ball, I was thinking more couture." He looked around the familiar neighborhood with its row houses and cracked concrete sidewalks and lifted a skeptical brow. "Not homemade 'hood chic."

She laughed. "Let me find out you've been living the good life too long and have forgotten your humble beginnings."

"Not at all. I still come by once in a while to connect with some of my people. But Trey, nothing about East New York says red carpet ready. Why are we here?"

She nodded and threw up her hands. "Because you and I are both products of this neighborhood. Money may have brought us opportunity, but our foundations were built here. There's strength and beauty in this place. And inside that building right there is Mrs. Ndiaye, a friend of my mom's family. She makes gorgeous clothes that make powerful statements about who the wearer is. Trust me. You will not regret this."

There she went again, asking him to trust her. Each time, his brain itched with the tiniest bit of hesitancy, but like before, she smiled at him or touched him and he forgot his concerns.

"Speaking of regret, are you sure about your decision to attend the ball? How'd your dad take it?"

"He doesn't know yet. I plan to talk to him, though. Getting to spend the evening with you and taking my place in the family, I just couldn't pass it up."

They made their way from the car to the front door of a gray building in the middle of the block. Trey rang the bell, and a full-figured woman with glowing deep brown skin opened the door, gifting them with a big smile.

"Trey! It's been way too long. I should take you over my knee for not visiting me sooner." Trey was about to speak, but Mrs. Ndiaye held up her hand and turned to Jeremiah. "Eh-eh, what's this? You brought me a handsome man to dress?"

Trey giggled as the older woman looked Jeremiah up and down with an expression that simultaneously made him feel appreciated and slightly threatened.

"Well, what are you waiting on? Come inside so I can make you beautiful."

She took them inside, and they entered a room with two long tables against the wall filled with regal, colorful fabric. There were mannequins and measuring tapes all over the place, along with a few industrial sewing machines.

"Trey, when you called and told me about this event and the meaning you wanted your ensemble to speak, I pulled some swatches for you."

"Meaning?" Jeremiah asked.

"Clothes, and specifically the color combinations of the fabrics, possess meaning." She waved them over to a far corner and showed them three swatches of gold, black and purple fabrics. "Purple is the color of royalty, nobility and grandeur. As the new leaders of the Devereaux empire, you and Trey are the new monarchs. Black is the color of strength, power and authority. Without it, you cannot rule. And gold—gold is the color of courage, compassion, wealth and wisdom." She nodded matter-of-factly. "Without those attributes, no ruler can govern their people properly. So, I will fashion glorious garments of gold, black and purple that will speak these things so anyone in your path will know without a doubt that the Devereaux tribe is in benevolent, powerful and capable hands."

"Mrs. Ndiaye, your vision is beautiful."

"Eh-eh? I think I like this one, Trey."

Trey bumped shoulders with Jeremiah before sliding her hand around his waist and snuggling into his side. "He definitely grows on you."

"Good, good. Now, let us select the Adinkra symbols you want added to the design. I will use the purple material to embroider the symbols onto your garments."

"Adinkra symbols?"

Trey placed a gentle hand on his chest and smiled. "They're aphorisms, quotes or sayings that have origins in the Ashanti people in Ghana. They usually speak to spiritual aspects people wish to embody. They're added to clothing, pottery and artwork. You said you liked my Pan-African vibe. I thought this might be a nice way to share it with you."

Trey left his side as Mrs. Ndiaye beckoned her and

pointed to a framed poster with columns and rows of what looked like ancient symbols. "For you, my emerging queen, I think there is only one symbol to be worn." She pointed toward a symbol that looked like two machete swords crossed to make an X with a heart on its left, a crescent moon on its right and a star at its bottom. "The Akofena symbolizes authority, legitimacy, legality and heroism."

She shook a finger at him. "For you, the new queen's consort, I have something else in mind."

He really should've corrected her. But the spark of pride he felt as being seen as worthy enough to stand at this woman's side kept his tongue still.

But he knew the truth: he wasn't Trey's anything. She'd never asked for more than the good time they seemed to be having. To be fair, he hadn't exactly made any declarations yet, either. Nevertheless, the more time they spent together, the closer he knew he was to doing just that.

"This is Nsoroma," she continued, pointing to an eight-point star with a circular hole in its middle. "It means you are born of heaven. It is a symbol of patronage and loyalty. And the way you've been looking at my Trey since I opened the door tells me she never has to question if you'll be there for her."

Whether it was mysticism, or merely living long enough to read people well, Mrs. Ndiaye was partially right. He wanted to give Trey his loyalty, but there was something keeping him from going that last mile even though she already had his heart.

Jeremiah stepped off the elevator onto Trey's penthouse floor. He took one step toward her door, then turned around to the closed mirrored doors of the elevator behind him to check his appearance first. The rich gold tuxedo jacket trimmed with black lapels was a stunning contrast against his dark skin and the black material of his tuxedo shirt, pants and the black patent leather Armani Derby shoes that completed the look. The purple Nsoroma Adinkra symbols embroidered onto the gold were the perfect representation of his loyalty and service to the Devereaux family, its patriarch, and now to Trey.

He rang the bell and Trey answered the door quickly.

"Jeremiah, you're early. I was about to put my dress on."

Her face, artfully made up in different hues of purple, that ranged from deep to light, including the royal purple on her full lips, made him ache to press his mouth against hers. Her long thick mane of curls was pressed bone straight and swept to one side, resting against her shoulder. His fingers itched to examine the softness of her tresses while his mind cautioned him about messing up a look that probably took a full workday to achieve.

"You're gorgeous," he whispered as he stepped across the threshold.

"In a robe?"

"In your bare skin."

She pointed a reprimanding finger at him as she grinned. "Don't start none, won't be none. We don't have the time to get into any of the naughty things your eyes tell me you wish we were doing."

She was right. But that didn't stop him from wanting to peel the soft, slippery material off her and slide his hands against her supple flesh. "Fine, go get dressed. I'll wait in the living room."

He stood in her living room, trying to tamp down his anxious nerves. He wasn't a jittery person by nature, but he desperately wanted to see Trey in her dress. If Mrs. Ndiaye could make him look so regal, he knew Trey would be an utter vision.

The distinctive click-clack of high-heeled shoes against the hardwood floor pulled his attention toward the hall.

"I'm ready. What do you think?"

Think? How the hell was he expected to think coherent thoughts when he was standing before beauty so enchanting. Her dress was a royal purple. Its bodice was a strapless ruffled neckline that gracefully fanned out across her ample bosom, tapering into a fitted waistline that flared slightly into a miniskirt that stopped midthigh. That alone would've made her the best-dressed person at the ball. But the sweeping floor-length train that spilled from her waistline was made for a queen. His queen. The train was in the same royal purple silk satin of the bodice, lined with the same gold material used for his tuxedo jacket, with her purple Akofena Adinkra symbol signaling her purpose, her status, her right.

"Jeremiah? Should I change? Is this too much?"

"I've never seen a woman look more beautiful in my life."

She went to say something else, but he held up a finger to stop her as he walked toward her. He took one long look down from the hair, to her regal gown, to the black Christian Louboutin peep-toe platform heels on her feet. He'd been wrong. He'd thought she'd be a vision; but he hadn't counted on her transforming into a goddess.

"Everything in me wants to worship you right now. With my hands, my lips…my soul."

He saw the shock creasing her smooth features. If his confession surprised her, she didn't understand how unexpected it was for him to feel that way too. But it was the truth, the unadulterated truth. And he meant every word of it.

"Introducing you tonight as the majority stockholder of Devereaux Inc. is necessary to put an end to Martha's antics. But as soon as we're done with our obligations, I will bring you back here. And if you allow me, I will do everything within my power to show you the depth of my patronage."

Her breath was ragged, but she held her poised stance, and he yearned for the moment he could test that resolve. But now wasn't the time. Now they needed to save Ace's company.

"I see your neck is bare."

She swallowed slowly, sticking her tongue out to moisten her lips. "I'm not really a fan of jewelry around my neck."

He nodded, and pulled a thin circular velvet box from his pocket to give to her. "When I went for my final fitting, Mrs. Ndiaye told me you didn't like neck pieces, but made me promise to get you some kind of statement jewelry that would tie your regal look together."

Trey opened it slowly, and he watched surprise light up her smooth features. "Jeremiah, is this?"

"A five-carat pear-shaped black diamond encased in an eighteen-carat gold bracelet? Why yes, yes, it is."

"Jeremiah." She extended a shaky hand toward the bracelet as she said his name. "This is not costume jewelry. This had to have cost you more money than some people make in a year. Are you sure you wanna give this to someone—"

He wasn't sure what she was about to say, but he knew he wouldn't like the sound of it. She was everything, deserved everything, and he wouldn't let anyone state otherwise. Not even her. Carefully, he snaked his hand around her neck and pulled her close. "You couldn't possibly be fixing your lips to imply I don't know what I want and who I want, could you?"

"Don't say things you don't mean. We said this was nothing more than fun…after tonight things could get very messy professionally. Aren't you worried about being seen together publicly? Will being together openly bring professional scrutiny?"

He'd braced himself internally for the impact of those words, but they still stung. She was right about all of it. And even though Ace had explained his reasoning for not changing the will that would allow Trey to assume power in Devereaux Inc., part of him still resented the fact that it wouldn't be him. Despite that, he still wanted more from Trey.

He realized they'd never promised each other more than a good time. Yet somewhere along the way she'd become necessary to him.

"You once told me when you wanted more, you would ask for it. Trey, that's all I'm trying to do. This is me telling you the circumstances don't matter. I want more. When we walk into that ballroom tonight, I want everyone to know you're mine and I'm yours." He removed the slender piece from its cushioned bed before casually tossing the box on a nearby table. "I wanted you to have something from me to remind you of how I see you— Black, beautiful, strong, regal and precious."

He closed the clasp and returned his gaze to hers. "If you decide to end things because of your newly acquired shares, that is your right. But please know, that's not what I want."

Overwhelmed with emotion, she blinked away the tears that threatened to destroy the artfully applied makeup she wore. "I would kiss you, but then I'd have to fix my lipstick."

He chuckled. "Don't worry, baby. There'll be plenty of time for me to mess it up tonight."

Chapter 16

Trey's heart pounded in her chest as Jeremiah pulled his Lexus onto Pier 41 in Red Hook. This wasn't her first time at the Liberty Warehouse. The high-end event space was a converted warehouse with the most spectacular view of New York Harbor. When you came from one of the wealthiest families in Brooklyn, attending parties here was par for the course. So, what was different about tonight?

You know what's different. The tall broad-shouldered fine-ass Black man sitting next to you changes the game. Yeah, but there's also the little matter of you finally avenging your father even though you had to commit a little bit of insider trading.

It wasn't a little bit and she knew it. But she couldn't focus on that right now. Tonight, she took her place as the largest shareholder in her grandfather's company. It should feel great. But knowing her father secretly owned thirty-three percent of the company before she'd ever stepped foot inside Devereaux Manor tainted what should've been one of the happiest moments of her life. And knowing she'd been the one to acquire that thirty-three percent for Deuce made her sink deeper inside her thoughts as she wallowed in her guilt.

"You okay? You've been unusually quiet since we left your place." As always, his observation was spot on. She wasn't all right. But she couldn't voice that.

She ran her thumb over the large black diamond on her wrist hoping it would somehow calm the uneasiness settling in her bones. The bracelet was more than a bauble. It was proof this unexpectedly beautiful thing she shared with Jeremiah was real. It was real, which meant she could lose it.

You mean will. You will lose it once he finds out what you are planning.

She let a quiet breath escape her. She was tired of lying. "I'm fine. This is a big night. I'm trying to take it all in."

"You're number two at DD Enterprises. Becoming the largest shareholder at Devereaux Inc. can't feel all that different. Speaking of, how'd he take it when you told him about the shares?"

She twisted her fingers in her lap as she considered her answer. "I haven't told him yet. I told myself I'd tell him before the ball… This thing with Ace, he just can't get past it. And I don't want to have that fight tonight."

He spared her a quick glance. "No matter how mad he is with Ace, I can't imagine he wouldn't want to see you being introduced to the Devereaux world. Besides, this is covered by the press. It won't be difficult for him to find out."

She continued to twist her fingers, hoping the movement would settle her nerves. "Well, tonight's date night for my parents. Hopefully that will keep them away from their devices long enough for them to remain unaware until I can find a quiet space inside and call them with the news."

When he gave her a cautionary glance, she nodded. "I know, Jeremiah. I just don't want to ruin this night."

"Why are you so nervous about people knowing you bought the shares, Trey?"

"It's not just the shares." She hesitated for a moment but decided if she couldn't be honest about everything that was bothering her, she'd at least tell him the truth about her feelings. "It's taking my place in the Devereaux clan. But more than that, it's realizing that of all the assets I've gained, none of them are as meaningful to me as what's grown between me and you. I've never feared anything, Jeremiah. But the thought of losing it terrifies me."

He grabbed her hand, pressing a gentle kiss across her knuckles that made her shudder. "I've already told you I'm not going anywhere. If that's what you're worried about, don't."

"There are things in my past," she began. "My immediate past that would send you running from me. You should know what you're getting into. I can't selfishly accept the gift of you until you know who you're getting involved with."

They were one car away from the valet station. She needed to get this out before the valet interrupted them. "Jeremiah—"

"Trey, stop."

"But—"

"No," he answered, his tone final. "I'm no angel and I have no right to convict you for your past, either. I want you. All of you. It doesn't matter in the least who you were before you walked into my life. How we feel right now is all I'm concerned about. Everything else is moot."

She could hear the chorus of Patti LaBelle's "If Only You Knew" playing on repeat in her head, and not in the good way the singer intended, either. If he knew, he'd leave, and she'd more than likely lose all the people who'd become important to her recently, namely her grandfather and her cousin Amara.

"From the moment we step inside, we're victors, Trey. No one can stop us."

The certainty illuminating his dark eyes made her shiver. She wanted it, needed everything it promised her. Too afraid to lose it to lies, she resolved she'd tell him…soon.

Tonight, she would take it all in, his affection and adoration and the pride she felt at assuming her rightful place among the Devereauxs. She'd risked too much to get to this moment to let guilt rob her of all that awaited her inside. With renewed commitment strengthening her, she pulled her shoulders back, summoned her best smile, and let the confidence that was her birthright take over. She was Jordan Dylan Devereaux III and there was nothing in that ballroom she couldn't handle.

Jeremiah watched Trey from across the room as she charmed the board members and the Devereaux family, including Ace's brother, David. All the family members and most of the executives she'd met were eating out of her hand. All except one person, Martha. With her signature pinched brow and sharply set mouth, she hovered around the room on her imaginary broom, seething at Trey.

If he wasn't certain of Trey's plan, he might've worried what harsh thoughts were swirling around in the woman's head. But knowing the sale was completed and Trey was now the largest shareholder put him at cautious ease. It didn't give her an outright majority, but her shares paired with his gave her more than enough power to stop Martha.

"If you think dragging that outsider here will accomplish anything, you're wrong. Whether she smiles pretty for everyone in this room or not, once I have Ace's shares, this little performance will be meaningless."

Jeremiah caught sight of a server carrying a tray of champagne and reached for a flute. Knowing Martha hated to be kept waiting, he slowly sipped from his glass to piss her off before giving her his attention.

"Good evening to you too, Martha. Are you having a good time?"

She squinted, her eyes cold and hard, revealing her frustration. "Don't get in my way, Jeremiah. You will regret it if you do and she will too."

"Martha." He said her name through the stiff set of his jaw as he stepped closer to her, leaning down so she could hear him over the loud music blasting from the DJ's speakers. "I have mostly tolerated you over the years because you're Ace's sister. But understand this. If you so much as look crossways at Trey, there's no family connection on this earth that will spare you my wrath." He stepped back to look at her again, her rapidly shifting eyes scanning his face with a wild mixture of surprise and fear.

When she didn't respond, he lifted an eyebrow and asked, "You feel me?"

The muscle in her jaw ticked as she dropped her eyes

and stepped back from him. Without another look, she turned and sauntered away.

He watched her disappear across the crowded dance floor before he looked for Trey. Standing next to Ace, she met his gaze across the room, waving a hand, beckoning him to come over.

A few quick strides and he was slipping his arm around her waist and pulling her into his side. He stole a quick kiss before smiling down at his mentor. "How are my two favorite Devereauxs enjoying the evening?"

Ace gave them a knowing glance. It was a nod of approval Jeremiah hadn't realized he'd been waiting for. It felt good to know the man he had so much respect for supported whatever this thing was he and Trey were building. And even though they hadn't sat down and detailed the ins and outs of their connection, he needed to see it grow beyond this moment.

"Ace is leaving soon." Trey answered. "He wants to make the announcement now."

The chorus of Sly and the Family Stone's "Family Affair" filled the room, and Jeremiah's heartbeat thudded loudly in his ears. The Devereaux clan was truly a family this year. With the addition of Trey, they were stronger, fuller and better connected than Jeremiah could ever recall. Jeremiah knew having Deuce there would've been the icing on the cake for Ace. But the joy he'd found in his granddaughter helped visibly lessen Ace's pain.

He went to help Ace to the stage and the older man waved him off. He pulled an elegant walking stick from a nearby seat and stood. "Your job is to assist my granddaughter now, not me. Be her support, Jeremiah. Protect her with the same fierce loyalty you've gifted me."

Jeremiah said nothing, simply nodded and stepped

aside for Ace to walk to the stage. Ms. Alicia followed him to the foot of the stairs and two ushers dressed in black tuxedos assisted the elderly man safely up the steps and followed closely behind him until he was standing at the Plexiglas podium in the center of the stage.

"I haven't known him long enough to know if this is true." Trey said, appearing at Jeremiah's side, "but he seems happier tonight than usual."

Jeremiah couldn't help the smile tugging at his lips as he looked down into her soulful eyes. "Listen, we both know the only thing that could make him happier than he is now is if your father was taking that stage with you. I'm sorry we couldn't make that happen for him." She nodded, her lids drooping as she tried to clear the hint of sadness from her eyes.

"You were right back in the car. After seeing how happy Ace is, I know my cowardice where my dad is concerned robbed Ace of the opportunity to set things right. I can't let this go on any longer. As soon as we get off that stage, I'm gonna call Deuce."

He smiled, pulling her tighter against him as Ace began his speech.

"I built Devereaux Incorporated for one reason, so that every one of my direct heirs would have something in this world that was theirs by birthright. Something no one, regardless how hard they tried, could take away. With so few certainties in this world, especially for a Black man from Brooklyn born in the '40s, it was important that my legacy would live beyond me while keeping my family safe and provided for.

"It's no secret I'm not long for this world. And when a leader leaves, it can be difficult for everyone else to determine the next steps. But don't worry. Devereaux Inc.'s future and my legacy are more certain than ever. And that's all because of one woman. It is with great pride I introduce to you my granddaughter and the largest shareholder of Devereaux Inc., Jordan Dylan Devereaux III."

Thunderous applause filled the room, and if Jeremiah didn't have his arm secured around Trey's waist, he would've joined in. Instead, he leaned into her, speaking directly into her ear. "May I escort you to the stage so you can address your family and your company?"

She turned to him, and the confident slant of her eye and the half-turned smile revealed what he'd known from the moment he'd laid eyes on her: this woman was a force the world wasn't ready for.

Trey offered him her hand. He kissed it before tucking it under his arm and walking her to the stage. He didn't give a damn if people saw his open affection for her. In fact, he wanted everyone to know they were a united front. Nothing would penetrate their alliance. And as he walked her to the podium, he placed another delicate kiss on her cheek before stepping behind her. With a quick scan of the audience, he found Martha standing on the other side of the room with her arms folded and her face pulled into sharp, angry lines. He'd proven his point. Trey was the future of Devereaux Inc., and Jeremiah would do everything he could to serve and protect her.

Mission accomplished.

Anxious had never been a word Trey used to describe herself. She was bold, strong and decisive in all things. But the force of the booming applause coupled with the pride she saw in Jeremiah's eyes almost buckled her knees. It should have sent her scampering away. But something inside her knew all along this was where she was supposed to be. Among family, surrounded by love. Jeremiah's love.

He hadn't said those exact words yet, but she could see it in the gleam in his eye when his gaze met hers. She could feel it in the way he touched her, like she was something precious and necessary in his life. And as he stood behind her, far enough to give her the space she needed to lead and yet close enough to support her if she asked, she knew she loved him too. She'd come here to steal her grandfather's company, and Jeremiah had stolen her heart instead.

Is that what you're gonna tell your dad?

Worries about her father's reaction tried to intrude on the peace washing over her. But one glance at Jeremiah's smiling face pushed them away.

I'm gonna soak it all up and do my damnedest to be worthy from this moment on.

"Thank you, Ace, and all of you for that wonderful welcome," she said into the microphone. "As many of you probably know, I've only been around very recently. But knowing Ace even for this short time has taught me one thing. There's always a place for you among family. You can always go home."

She glanced over at Ace as he stood on the stage in the distance, glowing with pride. "I won't take up much of your time tonight. Monday will come soon enough, and we'll have time to talk of my plans for Devereaux Inc. then. Tonight is for rejoicing and we are fortunate to have so much to celebrate. Namely, our leader, and his dedication to this family and this company.

"My grandfather has built an indestructible foundation. My job is to care for it, nurture it and help it become even greater. I promise you, Grandfather, your legacy won't simply survive you. It will stand as a living testament to your greatness far beyond my lifetime. Generations to come will know your name and that you built a matchless legacy of strength for the Devereaux family to stand on. So, before we move into the future, let's take this moment to honor the strength, ingenuity and conviction of the man who started it all, our patriarch, our leader, Jordan Dylan Devereaux I, our very own Ace."

The applause was much louder than the two hundred attendees should've been able to generate in that ballroom. Their raucous celebration could have filled a stadium, and she realized at that moment, if she weren't the person speaking at the podium, she would've gladly joined in. She was proud to be a Devereaux. Always had been. But knowing Ace, even for the short span of time she'd been in his life, had deepened her respect for him and appreciation for her heritage.

A brief flash of guilt tried to invade the space where her growing affection for her grandfather bloomed. She'd betrayed Deuce. Not so much in taking the shares. That was always the plan. But because after tonight, she knew she couldn't destroy Devereaux Inc., and Deuce would never abide by that.

Jeremiah returned to her side, placing a comforting hand at the base of her spine. She fell in step behind Ace and disappeared through the wing of the stage and outside the hidden door that brought them to the lobby of the lavish catering hall. She attempted to walk around to the main entrance of the ballroom, but before she could reach it, the press swarmed her and Jeremiah with their loud and fast questions and blinding camera flashes.

She answered questions carefully, giving the reporters enough sound bites to put on a good show, but revealing nothing substantive that could hurt her family. Her gaze fell on Jeremiah and her heart fluttered as she realized she included him in that number.

It's time to come clean, girl.

Jeremiah finally extracted her from the press and when she asked for a quiet space where she could call her dad, he took her to a set of private rooms the event space had set up for them. They walked all the way down the hall to a door at the end.

The sound of a familiar deep baritone made Trey tense and stopped her in her tracks. She looked over her shoulder and saw her father looming large as he walked down the hall toward them. He wore a Tom Ford ivory tuxedo jacket with satin lapels. It was a sharp contrast to the black pants, shoes and handkerchief neatly folded in his chest pocket.

To anyone who didn't know him, his face was pleasant. But she could tell from the fire in his fixed gaze that he was furious. Her mother was walking next to him, and had her hand on his forearm. Trey had seen that gesture plenty of times before. It was meant to soothe him. But the heat she felt coming from down the hall was a clear sign her mother's trick wasn't working.

Her father stopped in front of her, his gaze still heavy and angry. "I'd ask you what you're doing here, Trey. But I think the answer is obvious."

"My brotha, I think you're getting a little too close to my lady. Can I help you with…?"

Jeremiah stepped in front of her, creating distance between Trey and her father.

Dear God, this is bad.

Panic rose up in her throat. How had she let this get

so out of hand that one of the two people she cared so deeply for would need to protect her from the other.

Get it together, girl, before this gets worse.

She grabbed Jeremiah's forearm, much like her mother still clung to her father's, praying it would have more impact on him than it seemed to have on Deuce.

"Jeremiah, this is my father."

His eyes searched hers for an explanation, but she didn't have one. How could she? Deuce had blindsided her by showing up here.

"At least you're protective of my daughter." He gave Jeremiah a tight smile and extended his hand.

Jeremiah gave Trey one more questioning look before he accepted it. "My apologies, Mr. Devereaux. I didn't recognize you."

"Call me Deuce," he responded. "And you are?"

"Jeremiah Benton, sir. I'm—"

"Ace's second-in-command," Deuce interrupted. "If you're as protective of him as you seem to be of my daughter, it's no wonder Devereaux Inc. has flourished all these years."

Jeremiah held her hand tighter and a proud smile lit up his face. "I care for my people."

"Believe me," Deuce answered as he formed what Trey called his polite business smile. "I appreciate it." He continued with his fake smile as he released Jeremiah's hand. "I can see you two had other plans, but could I borrow my daughter for a minute? I need to have a word with her."

Jeremiah looked to Trey, presumably to see if she was all right with it. When she nodded, he leaned in and placed a light kiss at her temple before returning his gaze to her father.

"I hope you'll consider visiting Ace. He's probably in one of the first rooms up the hall. I know it would mean the world to him to see you."

Deuce kept his practiced smile in place as he answered Jeremiah. "I won't be here that long, I'm afraid," he replied. "I only intended to stay long enough to surprise my baby girl and congratulate her on her latest accomplishment."

Jeremiah nodded and gave Trey's hand a quick squeeze before he made his way through the suite doors.

"Deuce." The pleading Trey heard in her mother's voice didn't do much to ease her worry that this was about to get way out of hand.

"Destiny, please go inside and get to know the young man our daughter seems to be well acquainted with. I need to talk to her alone."

"Fine," she huffed. "But if I hear you so much as raise your voice once, you'll have to deal with me. Everybody in this building doesn't need to know our business." He nodded then waited for her mother to give Trey a comforting hug before she closed the door to the suite Jeremiah had entered a few moments ago.

"Are you going to explain yourself, young lady?"

"Not particularly. I think once you put two and two together things are pretty obvious."

"I forbade you to get involved with Ace, Trey. And yet, I find you looking cozy with my father's COO."

Trey crossed her arms and let out a loud breath through her flared nostrils. This was the problem with working for your father. There was this blurred line between parent and child and employer and employee that made conversations like this impossible.

"I know what I'm doing, Daddy. For once, just trust me."

"You know what you're doing? That's impossible," he huffed. "Whatever game you think you're playing, I can promise you, Ace sees right through it and is playing you to his advantage. He will destroy you to get to me. And he wouldn't think twice about using his errand boy to do it."

She pinched the bridge of her nose. *Lord, please let me remember that I love and respect this man.*

"Daddy, I need a little while longer and everything will work out fine."

He whispered in her ear. A fact she was grateful for because they were still standing out in the open hall where anyone could happen by. "Trey, you can't win this way. I may not know the details of your plan, but it's obvious why you're here. If you're found out, you could lose everything. Including your freedom. I will not let you risk this for me."

If it were only that simple. When this began, her father's vindication was all she was concerned about. But somewhere between making love to Jeremiah all night and watching him eat pancakes the following morning, she'd known she couldn't go any further. "It's beyond that now, Daddy. There's so much going on. So much I haven't had the chance to share with you. I have to do this, Daddy. There's no other way."

His stern features softened, and he placed a loving hand against her jaw, brushing his thumb against her cheek before pulling her into his embrace.

"What kind of father would I be if I let you sacrifice yourself because of this war between Ace and me?"

She patted his back and stepped slowly out of his embrace. "It's not about the war anymore. I've gotta make this right."

He nodded and then kissed her cheek, the action deflating most of his pent-up rage. "Be careful, Trey. I—"

"Deuce?"

Her father stood to his full height, turning slowly at the sound of Ace speaking his name.

"Son?" Ace stepped closer until he was standing next to Trey and Deuce. He went to extend his hand to touch Deuce, but her father successfully avoided the attempt by stepping back.

"Let's leave it at Deuce," he responded. "No need to pretend there's any real connection between us other than our names."

Ace wobbled as if he'd been struck. "Daddy, is that really necessary?" Trey asked.

It was Deuce's turn to reel back. "You would defend him in front of me? What the hell has he been telling you, Trey? What could he have possibly said to you to make you believe he deserves anything but your contempt?"

"Daddy—"

"Hold on, Trey. Your father is right. You shouldn't be defending me after everything I did to him and your mother. I was so stubborn and wrong."

She watched the muscle in Deuce's jaw twitch beneath his deep brown skin and knew that was a sign shit was about to go wrong.

"Daddy?"

"You're sorry?" Deuce spoke through clenched teeth. "Is that supposed to fix what you did?"

"Daddy." She placed a hand on her father's arm, hoping to draw his attention away from Ace. "This isn't the time or the place."

"She's right," Ace said. "Maybe you and Destiny could

drop by the house and we could talk this thing out. I have so much I have to say."

Deuce chuckled low in his throat. "What makes you think I give a damn about what you want after you tossed me on the street and disowned me for loving my wife?"

"I deserve that," Ace whispered as his shoulders drooped.

"You deserve a whole lot worse than my scorn, Ace. But I promised my wife I wouldn't show my ass in public, so the only thing I'll say is go to hell."

"There's a one-way trip planned in my very near future, so you'll get your wish."

Deuce looked at Trey for an explanation. She shook her head and hoped he wouldn't say anything more to hurt Ace.

"Ace," she said as sweetly as she could. "Why don't you go back to your suite?" She rubbed his back, hoping it would soothe some of the pain she felt radiating from his body. "I promise, Jeremiah and I will be in shortly."

Ace closed his eyes and nodded. She placed a gentle kiss on his cheek then helped him back to the suite.

"What did he mean by that?" Trey turned to see her father standing right behind her.

"Oh, so now you care? Two minutes ago, you were ready to spit on him. But suddenly you give a damn about his well-being?"

He swallowed hard, his intense glare bearing down on her. "Trey," he huffed. "I deserved that. But I still want to know what he meant. Is he okay?"

"No," she whispered. "He has cancer. He doesn't have much longer to live. That might've been his only opportunity to beg your forgiveness and you gave him your ass to kiss. I love you, Daddy. But you should know I've never been more ashamed of you."

She left him standing there, slack-jawed, and retraced her steps to the room Jeremiah and her mother were in. When she opened the door, Jeremiah was already standing on the other side of it. He took one look at her and stepped into the hall to pull her into his embrace. "You okay?"

She fought to keep her practiced smile steady. "I am now that you're here."

She looked back to find her father still standing in the middle of the hall with his mouth open, poised to speak.

"Martha, I said no!"

The sharp and forceful sound of Ace's voice grabbed their attention, causing them all to head for the room she'd seen Ace enter.

When they walked inside, Ace was shaking with anger as he and Martha engaged in what was clearly an argument. Even without yelling, the intensity in both their voices filled the room.

"What the hell are you doing, Martha?" Jeremiah left Trey's side to stand near Ace. Her father and mother came and stood with her.

"Stay out of this, Jeremiah. You're my brother's lackey. You have no place in things that concern the family."

"Well," Trey interrupted as she moved to her grandfather's side too. "That means I should definitely be invited to this little chat, right?"

"Young lady—"

Trey felt her mother step forward in Martha's direction and realized things were about to get out of hand. The one thing you didn't do in Destiny Devereaux's presence was disrespect her husband or daughter. Martha was about to open up a whole can of whoop-ass she really wanted no part of.

Trey blocked her mother's path, and positioned herself in front of Martha. "So, you're Martha. I've heard so many things about you." Martha's cocky smile made Trey want to snatch the smug look off her face, but Martha wasn't worth messing up her pretty manicure for. "Since this is our first time meeting, I'll let that 'young lady' thing pass. But I think if we're going to get along, we'd better get some rules straight."

Trey held up a single finger in front of her. "First, as Ace's granddaughter, if I ever catch you harassing him like that again, you'll be out on your ass faster than you can fix your lips to say my name."

Martha swallowed as she straightened her spine, making some last-ditch attempt to recoup the appearance of control. "I've been at this company since its inception. You would threaten me? You've been a part of this company and family for all of five minutes. Who the hell do you think you are?"

"Didn't you hear the announcement? I'm the largest shareholder in the company. With Jeremiah's support, I've got control of Devereaux Inc. So, if I wanted to, I could spend my time making your life hell."

Martha folded her arms, jutting a hip out as she leaned to the side. "I don't know how you stole my brother's shares, but I'll fix this."

"I think you'll have difficulty doing that, but carry on if you must."

"You," Martha spat the word as if it tasted foul and putrid in her mouth, "won't get away with this. If it's the last thing I do, Trey, I will take back what you stole from me."

"You mean what my absence allowed you to have?" Deuce said, coming to stand next to Trey and glaring at Martha in much the same manner as his daughter. Cool and unbothered, but poised for attack.

"You left, Deuce."

"I did." He leaned in with his hands in his pockets. "But I'm back. And worse for you, my daughter is with me. Trust me, Auntie, you don't want to tangle with her. If she says you don't have a chance, then you don't."

Pride swelled in her chest. Her father had no clue whether she'd purchased Ace's shares, not yet anyway. But even still, he'd proven what she'd somehow forgotten in all of this mess with Ace. He was her daddy, and he would always have her back.

Martha glared at Trey one last time before she stormed off toward the side exit door and disappeared into the hall.

Trey took a deep, satisfying breath as she looked at Jeremiah, her parents and then her grandfather. "Good ridda—" When she made eye contact with Ace, there was fear there. Before she could respond, his eyes rolled upward into his head and he began to topple.

It was all happening in slow motion. Her screaming Ace's name, Jeremiah catching him, her father running to help Jeremiah, all three men falling to the floor. Trey getting down on her knees next to them, trying her best to jostle Ace back into consciousness. And the only clear thought running through her mind was, *God, please don't take him now. Not when I've finally found him, not when my daddy is finally here.*

Chapter 17

Jeremiah stood just outside the hospital lobby trying to let the night air calm his soul. The doctors were working on Ace, and staying in that tiny waiting room was driving him up a wall. Destiny and Deuce had promised to look after Trey while he stretched his legs for a bit.

"You're worried about him." Jeremiah turned to find Deuce standing next to him.

"He's in the hospital. Of course I'm worried. Are you?" He narrowed his gaze at Deuce. "I heard what you said to Ace in that hallway. I know you two have had a difficult past, and I know Ace was responsible for it. But if you're here simply to kick him while he's literally down, then you'll have to go through me to do it."

To Deuce's credit, the older man didn't flinch. He looked at Jeremiah, sizing him up the way any man confident in his own skin would. "Is this the part where we come to fisticuffs over Ace?" He lifted a sharp brow.

"Cause if it is, I gotta tell you. I paid way too much money for this Tom Ford tuxedo to be rolling around on the concrete with you."

Jeremiah cut his eyes at Deuce before letting laughter fill him. "I've got a couple of those in my closet so I feel you, man." He turned to Deuce. "I'm sorry. I was out of line talking to you like that. I…I'm just not ready to lose him. He's been all I've had for such a long time. I'm not ready to let go. I know I'm not his son, but he's the only father I've ever had. I'll move heaven and earth to protect him from anything and anyone."

Jeremiah cleared his throat and looked out into the empty night as both their phones chimed. Before he could pull his out, Deuce was already holding his, scrolling through a text message.

"That's Trey. She says Ace is awake and asking for his sons. We should get back."

"I know things have been problematic between you and your father. I wouldn't want to intrude on your reunion."

Deuce stepped closer to him. The two were a match in height, so their gazes were equal. "I let my anger cost me a relationship with my father. And while I was out proving to the world that I was nothing like Ace, you were there caring for him and showing him the love I should've been."

Deuce raised his hands and placed them carefully on Jeremiah's shoulders. "My father asked for his sons, plural. My vote is that we give the old man what he wants and show him his family is here for whatever time he has left."

Jeremiah's throat tightened, making it hard to think and breathe concurrently. What was it about the Devereaux men that they could turn his life upside down with only their words?

Before his mind could conjure an answer, Deuce pulled Jeremiah into a tight hug and smacked him on the back as he rocked them back and forth. "You've born the weight of my absence for far too long, Jeremiah. Let me lighten the load for you. It's the least I can do after letting my pride keep me away for so long."

Jeremiah clamped his arms around Deuce and clung to the older man. The walls he'd been holding up for so long crumbled around him, and it was only this man's strength that kept him upright.

They were perfect strangers and yet both connected to the same great man. Deuce, like no other person in the world, understood how devastating this impending loss would be. So, without the slightest bit of shame, he stood in front of that hospital with a man he hardly knew and let grief and fatigue wash over him.

He was with family after all. And what was family for if you couldn't let down your guard and commiserate with them?

Trey watched her father as he and Jeremiah walked into the hospital room. Whatever had transpired in the time they'd been gone, something was different with Jeremiah. He seemed lighter and more centered. The same was true of her father. When he laid eyes on Ace, the layers of anger he'd always worn seemed to fall away.

"Deuce, Jeremiah?"

The two men sat carefully on the edge of either side of the bed. "We're here, Daddy."

"Where we both belong," Jeremiah added as he looked down at Ace.

Ace's eyes widened. As he fixed his gaze on them, she could see disbelief and doubt muting the rich brown of his eyes.

"Son, I...I—"

"Shhh," Deuce soothed him. "Nothing else matters. Whatever happened in the past is done. All I want is to be here with you and Jeremiah, and Des and Trey. That's all that's important."

Ace looked slowly from Deuce and cast his gaze on Trey's mother. "Destiny. I was so wrong. I'm so, so sorry."

"Hush." Her mother's soothing tone did more than calm Ace, it lifted the heaviness of the more than thirty-year-old cloud cast over her family. "Worry about resting."

Ace closed his eyes as a weak smile curled the corners of his mouth. "I want to go home, Jeremiah. Take me home."

Her father brought Ace's weathered hand to his cheek. The tender way he cradled it to his flesh almost broke Trey.

Her father looked to Jeremiah sitting on the opposite side of the bed with respect. The newfound kinship between the two men was on display for everyone to see. "Jeremiah, our father wants to go home. Would you stay with him while I find a doctor?"

Jeremiah smiled, then leaned down to place a soft kiss on Ace's head. He stood up, with the same sad but determined smile as he looked at Deuce. "I'll go. You stay here with him. He needs you."

Jeremiah left and she followed behind him, grabbing his hand to get his attention. When he turned to her, she closed the distance between them, bringing their lips together in a hard, quick kiss.

"What was that for?" His question made sense. They were in a hospital ward, and this wasn't the most romantic place for PDA.

She took a deep breath and let it slip out slowly into the air before answering him. "The father I love and the grandfather I've come to love have reunited. None of that would be possible if it wasn't for you. With all that's happened, I can't imagine how different my life would be if you hadn't stumbled into it."

"Trey," he whispered. "Don't say it if you don't mean it."

She placed a firm hand behind his neck and drew him closer. "Jeremiah," she said, her voice stern even though she couldn't keep the growing smile off her face, "you couldn't possibly be fixing your lips to imply I don't know what I want and who I want, could you?"

"Nah, shorty," he answered before letting his tongue swipe across that sexy bottom lip of his. "I wouldn't dare make a mistake like that. If you want me, I'm yours."

She cupped his face, stroking the neatly trimmed line of his goatee. "Good," she responded. "In case you didn't notice, we Devereauxs like to stamp our names across our things."

"As long as there's mutual stamping, I don't see a problem with that in the least."

Chapter 18

Trey found Jeremiah waiting at the bottom of the ground floor steps at Devereaux Manor. When she arrived at the last step, he pulled her against him and let his mouth slide easily against her lips.

"Mmm, I've missed you." He moaned his words against her mouth, tempting her to chase the touch of his lips against hers when he pulled away.

"I've been in the house with you for the last two days. How can you miss me?"

He tightened his hand around her waist, steadying her as she leaned against him. "We've been in the house taking care of Ace and your parents during that time. That hasn't exactly left us any time alone together."

She leaned in for another kiss and chuckled against his lips. "Are you really complaining about not getting any as we care for my ailing grandfather?"

"Woman, have you looked in the mirror? Every second I can't touch you is sheer torture."

God, this playfulness was everything her battered soul needed right now. Between Ace being rushed to the hospital the night of the Legacy Ball, getting him transported home in the wee hours of the morning, and playing nursemaid to Ace and support system for her parents, there had been little time for herself.

"Thank you for making me smile."

"It's what I'm here for." He pulled his hand from her waist and slid his thumb lightly across her cheek. "Are you okay?"

"As okay as I can be in this situation. It's so strange. Two days ago, I thought Ace might leave us. But since he's been home and my mom and dad haven't left his side, he seems…better. When Uncle David arrived a little while ago, Ace looked like he was having the best time. Does that make sense?"

"Yeah," he replied as she smoothed her hand through her hair. "Ace has spent so much time regretting his actions and aching for the son he pushed away. It doesn't surprise me he won't allow even cancer to ruin the gift of family."

"I worried how my dad returning might impact you." He noted the swift change in subject and lifted a questioning eyebrow as she continued. "You've been with Ace for over two decades. I didn't want my dad to make you feel you were being pushed out."

He shrugged his shoulders in that easy way he had. "I love Ace and I know he loves me. Nothing changes that. And if I were more concerned with my ego than doing what's right for this man who's been so good to me, then I wouldn't be worthy of Ace's love or yours."

God, what this man does to my senses with those intense words of his. "If there wasn't a houseful of family upstairs, the things I would do to you right now."

He chuckled as he stole a quick kiss. "Then I suggest maybe we skip out and go back to my place to recharge."

Yes was on the tip of her tongue when the sound of Jeremiah's phone interrupted her, and he pulled back slightly to answer the phone.

"Hey, Amara." He smiled at Trey as he spoke to her cousin. "I was about to get into something. I hope you can make this quick."

Jeremiah gave her a quick wink, but as he returned his attention to the call, his body went from relaxed and playful to stiff and serious.

"What the hell do you mean?" He was quiet for another moment before he said, "That's an hour from now. I can't…look…whatever… I'm gonna run home and change now. Stall until I get there, Amara."

Before he could slide his phone back into his pocket, Trey was at his side. "What's wrong?"

"It's the board. Martha's convened them without my knowledge."

"For what purpose?" She moved her finger back and forth between them. "You and I hold the majority of shares. They don't have a quorum without us."

His agitation didn't subside. "It's not about votes right now. It's about influence. Martha might not have the majority. But that doesn't mean she can't gain influence and make our lives a living hell. We don't want to have to fight for every gain. And we certainly don't want to make the other shareholders feel like their voices aren't heard. We need to get down there and see what she's up to."

Her pulse sped up. "Jeremiah, Ace was in the hospital

two days ago. My family's found its way back together only now. We won't have very many more moments like this when Ace…"

"Hey." His tone was soothing as if trying to reassure her. "I understand. You're right. You and I together have the majority and there isn't a quorum without us. I'll go check things out. You stay here and watch out for the family."

He pulled her into his arms and hugged her to him. But the tidal wave of guilt building in her gut meant there was no way she could find comfort, even in his strong arms.

"Baby, it's gonna be fine. I'll handle it."

She nodded, and he kissed her swiftly before turning away and walking out of the front door. She refused to watch him leave for fear she'd do something stupid like follow him and destroy the fragile bliss they'd woven in their short time together.

"Why did you refuse to go with him?" Deuce stood at the top of the stairs. She walked up to meet him plopping down on a wooden stair as her father eased into the open space next to her. She could barely meet his eyes when he looked at her.

"It's not important, Daddy. The only thing that is important is how terrible I feel about lying to you all this time. I should've forced you to come when Jeremiah first wrote to you. Instead, I wimped out and stole your birthright from behind your back."

He sighed loudly, placing an arm around her shoulder. "Was that your intent? To take my birthright? Or was it to protect Devereaux Inc.?"

"The latter."

"You did what was right, Trey. I was the foolish one.

You don't have to apologize. The truth is, I'm glad it's you. You're the one who's done all this work to heal a festering wound. You've earned this inheritance." He gave her a squeeze with his arm, letting her snuggle into his side like she used to when she was little. And just like back then, her tears began to fall.

"Talk to me, honey. What's going on?"

Her lips began to quiver, as her tears ran faster.

"If I go, he'll know I lied and I'm not ready for him to know." She blurted out in one breath. "I'll destroy it all if he discovers what I've done. Not to mention, he'd have enough circumstantial evidence to have the SEC look into me."

"Damn, Trey, I warned you."

"This wasn't my plan. My plan was to schmooze Ace and get him to give me the shares. But to prevent the share transfer from being contested, buying them was the only way to make it look like—"

"Ace made a sound business decision."

She cried harder then, letting her father's shirt soak up all of her tears.

"Sounds like you've got yourself into a pickle, young lady," Ace interjected. Panic filled her as she caught sight of David pushing her grandfather's wheelchair through the door of his bedroom into the hall.

"Ace, I—"

"Planned to steal my company?" he interrupted. "I know. I knew that from the moment you arrived."

Trey stared blankly. She looked at her father, and with a coy smile he gestured for her to go to Ace.

She ambled to him, staring down in awe as Ace smiled up at her.

"How could you have known and if you did, why didn't you say anything?"

"Trey, your father may have taught you everything he knows about business. But who do you think taught him?" She turned back to her father, who was still sitting on the top step with a knowing smile. The entire scene was so confusing. Why was everyone so calm when all hell was breaking loose? "My actuary recognized that someone was buying up small amounts of shares of my company. So, I had a forensic accountant follow the money and discovered those shell companies were subsidiaries of DD Enterprises. I kept it quiet and pulled all the disclosure reports so Jeremiah wouldn't find them. I let you buy thirty-three percent and then pulled the plug on your little operation by making Singleton refuse your bid."

Her chest was hurting as all the pieces fell into place. How could this be happening? "So, you knew why I was here, and you let me buy your shares and commit insider trading as some sort of payback in this game between you and my father?"

Ace lifted a brow as the smile dripped from his face. "Isn't that what you deserve after coming here to steal my company, young lady?"

"Yes, but I—"

"Changed your mind?" He narrowed his gaze, daring her to lie.

"I did." She dropped her head in shame as she spoke. "I came here to destroy you. But once I met you, knew you, I couldn't go through with it. I'd decided to end the plan, but Martha wouldn't stop. I'm sorry."

The hot tears sliding down her face seared her shame into her flesh. She'd allowed retribution to corrupt her and put everything at risk—her relationship with her grandfather, her freedom, and most of all, the love she shared with Jeremiah.

Comforting strong hands covered her shoulders as her father stood behind her, willing her his strength. "All these years I've carried that angry young man in my heart. But the moment I walked into that hospital room and my father called me son, it all disappeared. And now we've mended fences and you're left to deal with the fallout. This is my fault, Trey. I shouldn't have poured my hatred into you."

Her tears fell faster. Partly because she was thrilled her father and grandfather had reconciled, but also because fear and shame lurked in her heart too.

It wasn't until Ace's warm hand covered hers that she could bring herself to open her eyes and face what she'd done.

"You came to destroy, but love made you sacrifice yourself to save me instead. And because of that, I'm gonna do what all good grandfathers do—spare you the rod, clean up your mess and make it all better."

"But how? My takeover bid through DD Enterprises and then my purchasing your shares for my personal portfolio is proof of insider knowledge of the company." Trey's questions fell on Ace's smiling face.

"Your uncle David heads the legal department for Devereaux Inc." David stood straighter, offering Trey a smile similar to Ace's. "David," Ace called to him. "Would you explain the legality of how we'll make this all disappear for my granddaughter?"

"I signed papers and paid you money for those shares, Ace. There's no undoing that."

"There is," David answered. "As long as no sale actually took place. You signed papers, and we insisted on a check as payment. I never filed those papers and Ace never cashed your check."

Her head was spinning. She couldn't figure out what these two old men were trying to pull. "I received ownership certificates. I am the owner of Ace's forty percent."

David nodded. "You are. But not because you bought them, because Ace gifted them to you. And because of that, technically, no crime was committed. With the thirty-three percent owned by DD Enterprises backing you, you control seventy-three percent of Devereaux Inc. No one on that board can stop you."

If her father hadn't been standing behind her, she would've fallen over. This old man, this mastermind, had not only played her, but saved her too.

"But what about Martha contesting the shares being gifted? Aren't you still worried about that?"

"Trey." Ace's voice grew stern and serious. "Martha can't win. Between DD Enterprises' shares, Jeremiah's shares and David's, the majority is on our side. Take a proxy for the thirty-three percent DD Enterprises owns and…"

"Call a vote and install a new CEO." Her response garnered a nod from Ace. "But when this is over, you must tell Jeremiah the truth. Trust is important to him. And if you love him like I think you do, there's no room for deceit between you."

"He'll hate me," she answered.

"He'll be angry with you. But you're a Devereaux. He couldn't stop loving you if he tried. Tell him yourself. Because if he finds out about this from anyone else, it will destroy him."

Ace was right. Her fear notwithstanding, she had to come clean.

"So," Ace continued. "You have under an hour to make it to that meeting. You think you can get home and grab a power suit in that time?"

Trey wiped her tears and straightened her spine as doubt left her. Looking at the three men surrounding her—her father, her great-uncle and her grandfather—she'd never before felt this much power running through her.

"I'm a Devereaux," she responded. "I'm always prepared."

Chapter 19

"She's a total stranger! How could Ace hand the company over to her without discussing it with the board first?"

As the COO, Jeremiah sat at the head of the table in Ace's absence, surveying all the Armani suits in varying shades of black, gray and navy blue. At this point, the board members were all acting like angry villagers carrying pitchforks and torches as they called for the capture and burning of the newly discovered witch.

As the man in Trey's life, all of his protective instincts were on high alert. But if he was to win this day, he knew he had to get control of his anger.

The current suit yelling at him was Jason Singleton. He was an old-school businessman who believed money and power should always remain in the hands of the elders. He was also a staunch supporter of Martha's, so him leading the charge against Trey wasn't surprising. It didn't make it any less annoying, however.

"She's had Ace's shares for a hot second," Singleton barked. "And you're going to let her come in here and take the CEO spot? We don't know anything about this woman."

"Jason," Jeremiah replied. "No decisions have been made about who the new CEO will be. But if she did decide to reach for it, I don't doubt she could do the job. This is a lateral move for her from DD Enterprises."

"Our shareholders are having a fit, Jeremiah," Jason continued, and the other board members nodded in solidarity. "If we allow this long-lost granddaughter to take the helm, shareholders might unload their stock quicker than we can say Devereaux Incorporated. No, we need someone familiar, someone who's been here since the beginning. We need Martha."

Jeremiah's gaze zeroed in on the opposite end of the table to a smiling and confident Martha. Poised and elegant, she definitely looked the part of a CEO. But he knew she didn't have what it took to bring Devereaux Inc. into the future. Not with her heart blackened by injuries from the past.

"Jason, I respect your position. However, I think we need to look at the facts. Although Martha has done a wonderful job with our lifestyle brand, that is not the same thing as running a multinational business like Devereaux Incorporated. She doesn't have the experience or credentials."

"We don't know her and we can't trust her. The fact that you sit here defending her tells me what I've always known. We can't trust you, either, Jeremiah." Martha's comment drew everyone's attention in her direction. And by the way the corners of her mouth curled into a sinister grin, Jeremiah knew she was enjoying it. "She hasn't proven her loyalty to this family, our business or our legacy. Hell, she didn't bother to show up at this meeting to speak on her own behalf about whether she intends to install herself as CEO or not. Instead, she sent my brother's loyal puppy to do it."

"Loyalty is a quality to be revered, not ridiculed, Martha. You could use a lesson in practicing it," a familiar voice interjected from behind him.

Jeremiah instinctively responded to the sound of that rich, empowered voice. It had tempted him beyond his senses and ignited an inextinguishable blaze of passion deep in his core.

He turned to find Trey standing in the doorway. She was wearing a knee-length, draped, one-sleeve dress with a fitted silhouette that put every one of her luscious curves on display. Its cheetah print signaled her predatory and powerful instincts. She was here to dominate, and anyone who didn't understand that had already lost.

In her black patent-leather pumps, she ate up the ground beneath her feet, giving her hips the perfect confident sway as she walked across the room and stood next to him.

He smiled at her. "You came."

She gave him a playful wink. "Was there ever any doubt I'd take my place in the Devereaux legacy?"

He may have doubted her attendance at this meeting, but from the day he'd laid eyes on her, he'd known that she would be the person to carry this company into the future. And there was no time like the present to usher in the new era. He stood, giving her his seat, stepping aside to let her do what she did best: lead.

"Ladies and gentlemen of the board, I'm Ms. Devereaux, but my friends call me Trey. The outcome of this meeting will determine what you get to call me." She sat down in the executive chair and crossed one knee over the other before flipping the sleek strands of her hair behind her shoulder. "I don't have time to waste on platitudes. From what I gathered from the door, Martha called this little meeting to tell you I planned to take over as CEO. Well, she's absolutely right." Like falling dominoes, each person's jaw dropped in an almost synchronous rhythm. "I am the rightful leader of this company and this family. To my mind, there is no question about it."

"With all due respect, young lady—" Jason Singleton never got the chance to finish his thought. She raised up a single finger, silencing him immediately.

"I've already told you, my name is Trey, depending on whether you're friendly or not. Calling me young lady to shut me up means you either call me by my formal given name, or you don't address me at all. Second, I don't need your respect. Yours, nor anyone else's on this board."

"Why? Because you've got Jeremiah in your pocket and he's just gonna roll over for you?"

Trey pressed delicate fingers to her temple as she focused on Martha.

"Auntie, does it ever get exhausting being this much of a pain? The answer to your question is yes and no. Yes, Jeremiah and I hold the majority. No, I don't plan to install a CEO today."

Jeremiah's questioning gaze fell heavily on her. She twisted in her seat, winking before she returned her attention to Martha and the board. "I plan to install two. Jeremiah and myself."

She leaned back in the chair and folded her arms over her chest. She was the picture of calm among the red-faced board members whose heads looked ready to explode all over the large glass conference table.

"So," she continued, a slick smile on her gorgeous, matte red lips, "we can go ahead with this sham of a meeting, or we can get on with the rest of our day and accept that Jeremiah and I are the co-CEOs of Devereaux Incorporated."

Martha shot up out of her chair, slamming her hands hard enough against the table that anyone touching the glass could surely feel the vibrations. "How did you steal my brother's company?"

Trey tilted her head; her body language was relaxed and unbothered while tension and anger flared in Martha's every sinew. "Since you've never actually owned any part of the company as far as I can tell, I don't think that's any of your business, Martha." She waved a dismissive hand in the air before continuing. "Anyhow—" she returned her attention to the rest of the board "—the fact remains that any vote would be moot with fifty-six percent of it in our hands. The only purpose it would serve is to show us who to count as an enemy. Is that really how we want to start our working relationship?"

Jeremiah noted a good deal of fidgeting around the table, and none of it was coming from Trey. Hot damn, she'd done it. She'd saved Ace's shares, taken her rightful place in her grandfather's company, and still managed to acknowledge all of Jeremiah's hard work and dedication and cemented his place in Devereaux Inc.'s leadership. She'd done it all and looked deliciously edible the whole time. *God, I love this woman.*

"Welcome, Madame CEO." Jason Singleton spoke

through clenched teeth. He was pissed as hell, but he wasn't stupid. Marking himself as an enemy of one of the new leaders and largest shareholder of the company would be a lethal mistake.

Martha sauntered up to Trey in a way that made Jeremiah uneasy. Her face was cold, devoid of any emotion. "This isn't over, great-niece. I'm owed a pound of flesh from Ace and the only payment I'll accept is this damned company. Getting in my way isn't smart."

Trey gave her a polite nod. "Well, I'll make sure to inform Ace you're seeking payment. But until the next time we meet," Trey beamed. "you have a lovely day."

And just like that, his woman had put on her cape and saved the day.

Black women always get the job done.

"You are amazing!" Trey couldn't respond before Jeremiah pressed her against his desk and captured her mouth with his. "God, I've seen nothing sexier than you dressed to kill, owning every soul in that room."

Again, she attempted to respond, but he kissed her once more, this time parting her lips with his tongue and licking inside her mouth. The sure strokes made heat pool at her center, spreading slowly throughout her body.

"Who are you wearing?"

She let a soft chuckle escape her lips at his question. Only in rarified circles did people ask "who" and not "what" someone was wearing.

"Christian Siriano. Why?"

He placed another peck on her lips. "Because I'm gonna buy as many of his dresses for you as I can so I can simply sit back and marvel at how his creations caress your curves."

"A man who wants to buy me pretty dresses is never a bad thing. But it's not a requirement, though."

With his hands around her waist he pulled her tighter into his embrace. "Oh yeah? What is then?"

"That he knows how to take care of me when I'm out of the dress."

He growled before leaning over and pushing the intercom button on his phone.

"Sharon, please cancel my appointments for the rest of the day." He gave Trey a pointed stare. "I'll be putting in a good deal of work from home."

That promise made all of her tingle. Jeremiah was detailed and determined. To be the focal point of all of his attention was both powerful and terrifying. Particularly when she knew she had to tell Jeremiah some very difficult truths.

"Does that include your meeting with Mrs. Devereaux-Smith? She stopped by my desk a few minutes ago to confirm the time. She was insistent you give her the quarterly numbers for the lifestyle department."

Trey's smile momentarily slipped. Martha wouldn't quit, it appeared. When Jeremiah opened his mouth to respond, Trey placed a soft finger across his lips, silencing him.

"Sharon, this is Ms. Devereaux. Please tell my great-aunt Jeremiah won't be meeting with her today. He'll leave a printout of the data on his desk. You can give it to her when she arrives."

"Yes ma'am, Ms. Devereaux. I'll handle that immediately."

"Thank you, Sharon." Trey disconnected the call and stared up at a smiling Jeremiah. "What?"

He smiled as if he were marveling at a real-life miracle.

"Nothing. Merely impressed as hell once again at how you always devise the best plans."

A lump formed at the base of her throat as she fought to push down her guilt. Although she tried to ignore it, it kept stabbing at her insides.

How do I tell him what I've done without losing him? He'll hate me.

Trey closed her eyes and leaned in to place a gentle kiss on his lips.

You tell him the truth, no matter what.

"Print those reports for Martha so I can show you the other areas where my plans work too."

Jeremiah let them in his front door and quickly grabbed Trey's hand. "I'll give you the two-cent tour later. Right now, I wanna show you something."

She hurried as quickly as her Christian Louboutins would carry her, following him up a grand central staircase. *Two-cent tour, my ass.* The neoclassical architecture and high vaulted ceilings were impressive, to say the least.

When they reached the second floor, he opened a door, and she stepped inside. She expected to see a bedroom, but when he clicked on the lights, she was delightfully surprised to find she was wrong.

It was a room filled with display cases containing shoes. Everything from dress shoes to sandals lined the walls. She gasped when she faced the largest and longest wall in the room. It was an athletic footwear fiend's dream.

"You weren't kidding when you said you loved Jordans, were you?"

He stepped close behind her, enveloping her in his

embrace. He leaned down and placed a sweet kiss on the curve of her neck.

"No, I wasn't." His laugh was easy, but there was a seriousness embedded in his voice that caused her to turn around and look into his eyes. "The night I met you in that lounge, I knew I wanted you, Trey. You were sexy as sin in those heels, that pantsuit and corset. But when I ran into you at Junior's in a pair of Air Force 1s, I knew I had to have you. Any woman who could appreciate a classic shoe like that and make them look so good paired with those tempting denim shorts understood the beauty of history and legacy."

She still wasn't sure where he was going with this. But the sound of his voice, the emotion in his words made her skin tingle with anticipation.

"Today, when you sauntered into that boardroom sexy, confident and powerful, ready to slap down any foe as if they were a mild annoyance, I knew it wasn't the clothes or the shoes. It was you. Everything about you called to me. Everything about you unlocks some door inside me I didn't even realize was closed. I love you, Trey. And never more so than when you saved us all from Martha's clutches and made me your equal in leadership."

The hot burn of her tears spilled down her cheeks. When his gaze bore down on her, she closed her eyes from the onslaught of guilt welling up inside her.

"Jeremiah, you—"

"Are the luckiest man in the world if you feel for me even a fraction of what I feel for you. Tell me I'm not imagining this, baby."

"I. Love. You." She said those words with as much passion and certainty as her shaky soul could muster. "You're everything, Jeremiah. You're worth everything.

And I would willingly risk all I have to keep you safe and happy. No matter the cost."

It was the deepest truth she possessed. She might very well have risked it all in that board meeting today. But she'd done it anyway because he needed her.

Tell him.

She couldn't escape the truth. But standing here in his arms with all of his love and pride showering down on her, she couldn't, wouldn't destroy the beauty of this moment with the ugliness of her foolish choices.

He smiled at her, then leaned in to press his lips to hers before pulling her to another door inside the room. When he opened it, they were standing inside his bedroom. This time, she didn't spare any of her attention on the decor. The only thing worth seeing was Jeremiah as he removed his Hugo Boss suit jacket and tossed it irreverently on the floor. His remaining clothing suffered the same fate and soon he stood proud and gloriously naked before her.

He sat on the edge of the high four-poster bed and gestured for her to join him. Without hesitation, she went to him. He found the side zipper to her dress and pulled it down. Within seconds, it pooled around her ankles, crumpled in a heap, and she didn't care one damn bit. All that mattered was him.

"Jeremiah, always remember, whatever I've done, it's because I love you. For the rest of my life that will always be the answer to every question about me."

His Adam's apple bobbed as he visibly tried to contain his reaction to her words. He wasn't successful, though. The way he stared at her, the way his breathing ticked up in ragged puffs proved this moment was shredding him to pieces too.

He slid his hands up the sides of her thighs and gripped her full hips, pulling her toward him.

"If it's all about me, Trey, show me."

It was like a starter pistol went off inside her head. With ease, she tossed aside her shoes and underwear, and she was straddling him. By the time her lips touched his, she was burned ash. Heat consumed her, driving her to touch and taste him wherever her fingers could reach.

They were naked and horizontal on his bed, and the need to grind on his thickness was primal and instinctive.

"Condom, now," she commanded.

"Nightstand, top drawer."

She broke their connection to lean over and find what she desperately needed. She removed it from its foil packaging and with deft fingers covered him quickly.

She planted her hands on his large pecs as she lifted her hips high enough to angle him at her opening. She kissed him once more, then slid down, devouring him inch by glorious inch, delighting in the stretch of her body around his.

The sensation of him inside her went beyond physical pleasure. It was joy and need and life. A life she wished to hold on to, a life whose possibility was fragile and nebulous.

The thought of losing this connection, of never being given the permission to touch him like this, brought tears to her eyes.

"Baby?" He stopped moving, sitting up and running a gentle thumb across her cheek to collect her tears.

"I'm fine. I just love you so much, love us so much."

He placed a firm hand behind her neck as he plastered his mouth over hers. They came together in a clash of lips, tongues and teeth as they resumed their punishing rhythm. He circled his arms around her, bringing her back down to the pillows with him. He planted his feet into the mattress and pistoned his hips, hitting the perfect angle. Her soul shattered and her body followed close behind, breaking apart under his expert touch as pleasure consumed her in a blaze of heat.

As her release crested, he deepened his angle again, sparking another orgasm that demanded she dig into his shoulders as she held on to him, her source, her strength, her heart.

And while he destroyed her with pleasure, she felt his rhythm hitch, his corded muscles bunching beneath her. When her name spilled from his lips, she swallowed it in a searing kiss, desperate to keep their connection for as long as she could.

When they were both sated, she took a moment to look at his features, smoothed out by bliss and physical satisfaction.

You need to tell him now.

Her conscience was right. But she couldn't. Not now. Not when this moment between them was perfect.

She lifted her hips, and he disposed of the condom in a nearby wastebasket, pulling her into his arms with a firm, possessive grip when he returned. Her conscience tried to warn her again, but she ignored it. The power of his embrace made it impossible for her to think beyond the pleasure he gifted her with. Common sense or right or wrong didn't even factor into the equation. So, she snuggled closer and made a bargain with herself she knew she'd regret.

Tomorrow. I'll tell him everything tomorrow.

* * *

Jeremiah walked downstairs, ready to make his famous pancakes for the beautiful woman lying in his bed. After the work they both put in sexing all hours of the night, carbo-loading was probably a good thing.

He was about to turn down the hall toward his kitchen when the chimes from his doorbell alerted him to a visitor.

His good mood tanked when he opened the door. "Why are you here, Martha?"

"Can I come in?"

"No. What do you want?"

"This is important, Jeremiah. I came as soon as I had proof."

"Of what?"

"Proof that your girlfriend is trying to steal my brother's company."

Jeremiah huffed. "Are we back to this again? Let it go Martha, you lost."

She shook her head as she looked through her over-size purse and removed a folder. "I didn't lose, Jeremiah. I was cheated."

She smacked the folder against his chest. Determined not to let her ruin his good mood, he didn't respond. Instead, he opened the folder and read. It was a holdings report, one he'd seen before.

"Why are you showing me this? I already know how the shares are divided up and who owns them."

"Are you sure?"

The satisfied smirk on her face told him he was missing something. He read further, digging into the actuary's report until he found the smoking gun Martha apparently wanted him to see.

There were several companies listed that owned small

pieces of Devereaux Inc. He was ready to ignore Martha until he read the shareholder's disclosure report. If this report was to be believed, DD Enterprises owned those smaller companies.

He could feel his anger rising, making his stomach roil. "Where did you get this?"

Martha smiled and cold spilled down his spine. If she was that happy, it could only mean chaos was coming to his life.

"From our actuary, of course. When Trey wouldn't tell me how she acquired the company, Singleton suggested I go to the actuary for the information. Imagine my surprise when I discovered he was right."

He fought back the anger clawing its way up from his gut. The hopeful smile on her face meant losing his control was exactly what Martha wanted. He refused to give her that satisfaction.

"Well," Martha quipped. "Are you gonna call the SEC or am I?"

He closed the file and stepped out onto the porch. "You are an employee of Devereaux Incorporated, not a shareholder. This is not your concern."

"You're going to just—"

He stepped down onto the stoop and leaned in, making sure he was close enough for her to hear him. "Not. Your. Concern."

Without waiting for a response, he left her standing where he'd found her and headed back into the house.

Instinct told him to charge up the stairs and wake Trey and demand an explanation, but his need to find the lie in Martha's accusation sent him into his living room, spreading papers across his coffee table in quick frantic passes of his hand.

He searched for the out, the thing that would vindicate Trey and make it okay for him to love her, keep riding this blissful wave of passion, sex and emotion.

He sat long enough, pouring over the documents, until his hope gave way to tacit acceptance and the resulting hurt burned into a blazing ball of acrimony.

"There was no lie." He growled through clenched teeth as he pushed the words into the air. "She did it."

"Who did what? Wait, are we talking about Martha again?"

The sound of Trey's voice was like hot blades of metal slicing through his skin, leaving him raw and exposed to the world.

"For once, it's not Martha."

She tilted her head. "If not her then who?"

He stood and walked over to her, letting his glare travel her face before saying, "You, Trey. It's you."

Chapter 20

Trey watched Jeremiah. He was hot, and this wasn't the sexy kind of hot she preferred. It was the "I'm-mad-enough-to-set-shit-ablaze variety."

"Jeremiah?"

"How could you do this, Trey?" His calm voice and easy words belied the rage she saw spreading throughout his tense body.

"I'm not exactly—"

He raised a finger, silencing her. "The truth, Trey. Don't try to handle me like one of your employees."

For half a second, she thought to remind him they were peers now. But the way the muscle in his tight jaw flexed, she figured that might not be the best approach to take with this situation.

You were brave enough to implement this plan. Don't punk out now, girl.

"Jeremiah, this wasn't supposed to happen."

"What, you inadvertently stealing Ace's company?"

She straightened her shoulders, bracing for his fury. She was a woman who'd been taught from birth that she was destined to control her fate and the fate of those around her. But standing under the angry heat of Jeremiah's fixed stare made her quake. Not with fear, because Trey feared no man. No, this was shame.

"No, I had every intention of taking Ace's company. But I had no idea I'd fall in love with you."

He scoffed, the sound of his laughter knocking against the walls of the large room. "This ain't love, Trey. Love doesn't lie. Love doesn't steal. But most of all, love doesn't manipulate, and that's exactly what you did to Ace and me. You played us and the worst part of this situation is I let you."

Pain and anger pulled the smooth lines of his face into a grimace, forcing her to fight her instinct to soothe him.

"Jeremiah, I didn't play you or him. I didn't. I stole nothing. Yes, I planned to take the company from him. But once I knew you, there was no way I could go through with it."

"Then why did you?"

"Because you asked for my help and there was no other way I could."

"So, this is my fault, Trey?" His voice boomed loud enough to rattle the hanging chandelier in the nearby hall. "Are you really gonna try to sell this bullshit?"

"It's not bullshit," she countered calmly. Meeting his fire with her own would get her nowhere. She needed to get through to him. And if keeping her cool and giving him the space to express his anger without policing him would help, she would remain calm through this entire ordeal. "I'd already decided to end it. But you said Devereaux Inc. needed my help. Buying those shares was the only way."

He paced as if he needed to move around to process what she was saying.

"Even if I believed you, the shit you pulled could get you in hot water with the SEC. Was getting back at Ace worth your freedom?"

She stepped closer to him, placing a careful hand on his arm to still him so he'd look at her and hopefully see her truth. "For revenge? No. But to help the man I love, help the grandfather who'd come to mean so much to me, yes."

His gaze traveled from where her hand rested on his bicep to her face until their eyes met. She saw a spark of something hopeful. She squeezed the muscles bunched beneath her hand. When he didn't pull away, she stepped into his space, lifting her other hand to his face as she savored the prickle of his goatee beneath her thumb.

God knows if I'll ever get to do this again.

"I love you, Jeremiah." Her voice trembled with fear and hope simultaneously. "I'd do anything to make you happy. Aside from my initial motivations, this was real. Please don't doubt me."

He leaned into her touch, causing her anticipation to swell. Then he pressed his lips gently against hers but pulled back when she tried to chase his retreating mouth. Attempting to understand the loss of physical connection, she looked into his eyes again and found sadness where there had briefly been a spark of hope.

"But that's the problem, Trey. I'm aware of your lies and I can't trust you anymore."

His words felt like a slash of hot fire against her skin.

She stepped away from him and tilted her head as she assessed him.

"You can't trust me?" She crossed her arms and tapped her fingers against her bicep to keep herself calm. "Jeremiah, I'm not denying I fucked up. But don't act as if you're some innocent party I used and discarded."

"So, is this the point in the argument where you start deflecting? Is that how your daddy taught you to behave when you got caught?"

"First of all, keep my daddy's name out of your mouth. This is between you and me. Leave him out of it." This was going from bad to worse quickly. She took a breath and tried to shake off the angry, red curtain of rage attempting to drape itself over her brain.

"Jeremiah, are you telling me you didn't think sleeping with me would influence me to stay and do what you wanted?"

He laughed, then leveled his pointed gaze at her. "You're really trying to mitigate what you did by saying I dickmatized you? I mean, I knew my stroke game was good. But I never knew it was *that* good."

His stroke game was *that* good. But it wasn't the reason for her actions. Even she wouldn't tell that lie.

"I'm not saying it makes what I did right. I'm not even saying you set out to seduce me to get the result you wanted. But you're a smart man. Part of you had to hope us becoming so close would make me stay."

He nodded. "You're correct. I hoped you'd stay because of what was growing between us. But I never actively worked to take your choice away from you. You entered my life under false pretenses and used our connection to swindle a dying, elderly man out of his company. There's no explaining that away."

He stepped around her and headed toward the hall. When he reached the doorway, he turned to her and called her name in a voice that was both foreign and cold.

"I'm going out to clear my head. Please be gone when I return."

Jeremiah walked around the neighborhood, unsuccessfully attempting to cool down.

His worst nightmare had happened. He'd been wrong about Trey. The consequences of his error haunted his mind.

Why the hell didn't I see it?

The answer settled into his consciousness without hesitation.

Because you didn't want to.

He'd wanted her so badly, and in the haze of his unquenchable lust, he'd given Trey the keys to the kingdom and allowed her to steal everything right from under his nose.

His rage was still burning when he turned the corner and realized he'd been instinctively walking toward Devereaux Manor.

God, he didn't want to be there right now. But Ace was his mentor and his family. He owed everything to him, including the truth of how he lost the man's company.

He let himself into the house and found Ace sitting up in his bed while Ms. Alicia tidied the room. She stopped fluffing a pillow long enough to take a cautious glance at Jeremiah before placing the pillow back on the chair and quietly exiting the room.

"What's got you looking so hangdog about the face, young'un."

He didn't even try to deny it. His head was throbbing,

and his hands were aching from being in clenched fists from the moment he'd left his home.

"It's all my fault, Ace."

"What happened, Jeremiah?" The alarm in his mentor's voice stoked his anger even more.

"When I reached out to Deuce for help, I thought it was the safest option. I thought I could control the outcome. I was so wrong. She lied to me, Ace. She lied to all of us."

Ace threaded his eyebrows together as if understanding had finally dawned on him before beckoning Jeremiah to his bedside.

"Trey—"

"She lied about her motives for being here."

Jeremiah eased down onto the bed next to Ace, wondering why he was the only one who seemed to be bothered by this news.

"You knew?"

Ace chuckled and waved a dismissive hand. "I've been on this earth a long time. It's hard to pull a fast one on me. That young lady came here with revenge in mind, but she wound up with love in her heart. Love for me and love for you too. Or are you too angry to see that?"

Angry didn't begin to describe how he felt. Betrayed, furious, gutted—all of those fit the dark pit of feelings trying to swallow him whole from the inside.

"She played me, and I let her steal your company."

"Trey can't steal what was already hers. Even if Deuce had taken over the company, eventually, when he retired or passed away, it would've wound up in her hands anyway." Ace shrugged it off as if this was no big deal, and Jeremiah couldn't tell if he should be relieved or angry. "This cancer and my sister's plotting only sped up the timetable."

"I don't understand how you can be so cavalier about this." His tone was more forceful than he'd ever dared use with Ace. But dammit, this was important, and Ace wasn't listening. "She swindled you out of your company. I'm mad as hell about that. Why aren't you?"

Ace leaned forward, placing his hands on either side of Jeremiah's face, forcing him to look directly into the ailing man's eyes. "Son, you set out to save my legacy and to help heal the rift between my son and me. You accomplished that and found something special with my granddaughter while doing it. Everything happened the way it was supposed to. I can see that. And if you'd put your anger down, you'd see it too."

"She stole everything from you."

Ace shook his head and smiled. "She gave me everything that matters to me. My son, my daughter-in-law, my grandbaby. And she gave me the opportunity to see you happy, Jeremiah. The company is just a thing. But the bond that holds us together, that makes all of us family, that's what matters."

"She came to hurt you and I let her."

"She came to help her father heal a wound I inflicted. Don't make me out to be an innocent in any of this. Regardless of how it started, she changed her motives."

There was certainty in the old man's eyes that Jeremiah desperately wished to cling to. He was drowning in pain and would give anything to pull himself to the surface.

"How can you be so sure she changed?"

"Because she loved you, Jeremiah. And let me tell you from personal experience, loving you and being loved by you is a life-changing event that no one forgets. My love for you made me worthy of my son's and granddaughter's love. Your love for me has single-handedly brought my family back together. That was something even I couldn't do. So, don't tell me loving you didn't change my granddaughter's heart."

Jeremiah wanted to believe it. But she'd lied and knowing that fueled his anger, stoking it into a mighty blaze. This close, he was sure Ace couldn't help but feel the heat of it. But instead of shying away, he came closer to Jeremiah and smiled again.

"Don't let your hurt pride cost you a lifetime with Trey. Trust me, we wouldn't even be in this position if I'd had a better handle on mine. Don't be like me. Be better."

Jeremiah swallowed the lump in his throat, closing his eyes because he didn't want to see the love and adoration Ace held for him devolve into disappointment when he said, "I'm not sure I can."

Chapter 21

Trey walked into Ace's bedroom and found her father sitting at his bedside. The two looked as if they'd been waiting for her, like they'd been practicing the inquisition she knew would go down as soon as she closed the door.

Two weeks had passed since Jeremiah discovered her treachery. Although she'd talked to her father and grandfather during that time, she'd purposely kept her distance, using the excuse she was busy getting acclimated to her new job at Devereaux Inc.

"All right, Granddaddy. You insisted I visit after work. What's going on?"

Ace patted the space on his bed next to him. And like an obedient granddaughter, she went to him. She stopped for a moment to hug and kiss her father before she settled next to her grandfather on the bed.

"How are you, Trey?" Ace's question barely registered as she struggled to keep the memories of her and Jeremiah and their brief time together spent taking care of Ace in this room.

"I'm fine." She pasted on her work smile, the one that hid her feelings when she couldn't afford to appear weak. "Transitioning into my new role at Devereaux Inc. has been time-consuming, but smooth."

"Including working with Jeremiah?" That question came from her father. She didn't look at him. He knew her too well, and if he had an inkling how wrecked she was after her blowup with Jeremiah, he'd go into full papa bear mode. No one needed that.

"Jeremiah has been efficient. He's an asset to Devereaux Inc. and I can see why you selected him as your second."

She smiled at Ace again and congratulated herself for being able to keep the tremble off her lips and out of her voice. She was fine. Almost normal, even, until Ace's eyes pooled with sympathy and concern as he opened his frail arms to her. In an instant, her hard-fought resolve crumbled as she leaned into Ace's embrace.

Her face flamed as her tears spilled hot and furious down her cheeks and onto Ace's silk pajama top.

"Granddaddy, I ruined everything," she openly sobbed. "Unless it's about business, Jeremiah refuses to speak to me." Her breath hitched in her chest when she tried to stop the flow of tears. "He's so hurt, and I can't fix this."

"He's hurt," Ace agreed. "He's only stopped by a handful of days over the last two weeks. I figured you two were still having a rough time."

She finally staunched the flow of her tears and quieted her breathing. "It's not a rough time. He wants nothing to do with me."

"Baby girl," her father laughed before continuing,

"take it from someone who has messed up a lot during his marriage. Things are never as bad as they seem. Believe it or not, what you did rates very low on the things-that-can't-be-forgiven scale. You can fix this."

Usually her father's words inspired unwavering confidence. If he said it, it was the truth. But this time, she worried his assessment of the situation was skewed.

Her grandfather laughed too, and Trey couldn't decide if both men had lost their minds or if she was missing a key piece of this conversation. Because nothing was funny about any of this.

"Your father's right, sweetie. I've watched you and Jeremiah grow close. I think you have the makings of forever. You just have to get out of your own way."

"How on earth am I supposed to do that?"

Ace grinned, further confusing her. "Honey, you're a Devereaux and we are powerful people, who through sheer will can shape the world. But there's something else we do really well for the people we love."

Her interest piqued, she raised a brow as she leaned in a little closer. If there was anything she could do to fix things with Jeremiah, she was game.

The two men shared a knowing glance before they each gifted her with a smile and said in unison, "Grovel."

Jeremiah was two seconds from stepping out onto his stoop to head to work when his cell phone vibrated in his pocket.

"Hey, Ace, what's up. I'm trying to get to the office."

"Good," his mentor crooned. "I caught you at the perfect time. Look here. I've got a taste for your pancakes. Why don't you come over and make me some?"

Jeremiah groaned in frustration. He could not be serious.

"Listen, Ace. I've got some important stuff to handle at the office. How about I come over this evening and we'll have breakfast for dinner like we did when I first came to live with you?"

There was silence on the phone before Ace let out a prolonged sigh. "Young man, tonight is not promised. You need to stop working so much. But never mind that. I figured you wouldn't come here willingly, the way you've been working lately. That's why Trey is downstairs making 'em for me as we speak."

Jeremiah thought about the beautiful white marble surfaces in Ace's custom kitchen and cringed.

"Trey can barely make toast without burning it. She'll destroy that kitchen. But then you know that. So, I can only assume this is about getting me to come over and see her."

Ace laughed over the line. "Possibly, but the why doesn't matter. If you don't come here immediately and stop her, there's no tellin' what kind of mess she'll make in your favorite space."

"You wouldn't. You didn't, old man."

"Boy, when have you ever known me to not speak plain?"

Jeremiah thought about his statement for a moment, and realized Ace wasn't bluffing. "You're playing dirty."

"True," Ace answered. "But I've told you before, it's the only way to win."

"Nothing's gonna fix this, Ace. Not even your meddling."

"Humor me," he said. "Come and talk to her. There's

nothing that can't be solved over a hot stack and a cup of coffee. Isn't that what you always say?"

He did always say that, and knowing Ace was using his words against him was pissing him the hell off.

"Does she even know you're trying to play match-maker?"

"She'll find out when you get here."

"Dammit, Ace." That was his mentor, always ten steps ahead of everyone else. Always certain he could pull strings and get what he wanted.

Too bad Jeremiah didn't share those same assurances.

"Shit!" Trey watched the smoke billow from the skillet, signaling she'd burned yet another godforsaken pancake.

"What the hell happened? Are you trying to burn the house down?"

Jeremiah. At least it sounded like him. With all the smoke irritating her eyes, she couldn't be 100 percent sure. He moved past her, opening a few windows and the back door to clear the smoke out.

"As good as you are at everything else, you're terrible at cooking."

"You ain't ever lied."

The flash of laughter in his eyes sparked her own laughter too. A relieved sigh escaped her lips. He was beautiful. Tall, dressed in a dark blue Brooks Brothers single-breasted suit that reminded her of how sculpted his body was. It wasn't like she needed that reminder. She'd relived the images of their time together over and over in her head. There wasn't an inch of him she didn't know…intimately.

"Not that I'm complaining, but what are you doing here?"

He shrugged. "Your grandfather hijacked my morning and told me to come here and stop you from burning down the kitchen."

Embarrassment warmed her face. *That old busybody.*

"I'm sorry about that. I didn't ask Ace to call you. I know I'm not your favorite person right now."

"Trey—" he began, but stopped when she raised her hands palm-side up to interrupt.

"Don't answer. I know it's true. I hurt you and now you're forced to work with a woman you hate."

"Yes, you hurt me," he replied. "And I'm pissed about it. But hating you…" He laid his hand on his chest, a sign of how much pain he was in. "It's not something I'm capable of."

"Does that mean there's a chance you'll forgive me?"

He made an exasperated sound that stayed her breath. Worried she'd pushed too far this time, she waited for his answer.

"I don't know if we can ever fix this, Trey. You broke us. But I haven't felt joy since I held you two weeks ago. I can't get used to this ache you left me with."

"Does that mean you still love me?"

He ran a hand over his goatee before sighing. "I don't know how to stop loving you. You found your way into my life and buried yourself under my skin. I'm changed and I can't reset and get back to who I used to be."

There was a long pause after he stopped talking. A gap filled with tension and awkwardness that heightened her ache to turn back time.

He's not ready, Trey. Don't push him. She wiped her messy hands on the Busy Making My Ancestors Proud apron to give her fingers something to do. When they were free of most of the flour and dough, she decided this was torture and neither of them needed to endure it any longer.

"I won't keep you. I'll go order Ace some pancakes from Grubhub."

She made it to the door when she heard, "Apparently you don't know how to reset, either, because the woman I fell in love with wouldn't give up so easily."

Heat spread through her, bringing life to the cold, empty parts of her haunted soul. *Don't play with me, Jeremiah Benton.* She turned around intending to speak but struggled to respond as a glimmer of hope planted itself in her heart. It was foolish, but the minor gesture made a seedling of optimism sprout up inside.

She took a few steps in his direction and extended a hesitant hand toward him. He didn't hesitate to grab it in his. "Ace and my daddy say I gotta grovel to make things right. If that's what you need, I'll gladly do it."

He let his thumb caress the back of her hand, sending sparks of electricity through her body. Her breath hitched, and she savored the excited buzz of energy flowing from him to her.

"Queens don't grovel, Trey. Especially not my queen. They lead. They rule."

"Queens also take responsibility when they fall short of their duty. I was wrong, Jeremiah. I'll never be able to express how sorry I am for lying to you and hurting you."

He tilted his head. "But it wasn't just about me. You broke the law, Trey."

"It's complicated. I would have agreed with that assessment if we'd had this conversation before the board meeting. But as always, my grandfather, even from his sickbed, is a mastermind. He never cashed my check. He destroyed it and gifted the shares to me instead."

"I don't understand."

Until Ace had explained it all to her, she hadn't, either. "Apparently, my grandfather knew about DD Enterprises' hostile takeover plans. He blocked them and when I showed up on his doorstep, he knew why I'd come."

"I know that. Ace already told me."

"So," she continued, "when I was willing to sacrifice myself to save his company from Martha's control, he knew I'd done it because my heart was in the right place."

"Then there's nothing hanging over your head?"

"Technically, no crime was committed, so—"

Before the next word could slip through her lips, his mouth was on her and the world tilted. Touching him, tasting him, it was relief and desperation mixed up into one messy ball of emotion. When he broke the kiss and fixed his gaze on her, she shivered under its power.

She snuggled into his chest, taking her time to recover.

God, I never want this to end. Especially not this moment.

She leaned back and saw a flour fingerprint where she'd gripped his lapel while they were kissing. It reminded her of what she was doing in the kitchen in the first place. Ace still needed his pancakes.

She moved to wipe the flour off, but Jeremiah playfully pulled her hand away and caressed it with a light kiss. She smiled up at him and asked, "You hungry? If you are, maybe we could stop in for a bite ourselves while we pick up Ace's pancakes." His grin still in place, he narrowed his gaze as he stared at her.

"I'm told," she continued. "There's nothing a hot stack and a hot cup of coffee can't fix."

"You and your grandfather are gonna stop using my words against me."

"Maybe we've both come to realize you're the smartest one among us and we should listen to your wisdom more."

He wrapped his arms around her, pulling her closer. "I will remind you you said that at my annual performance review. Until then, I'll let you treat me to some pancakes."

"I truly hope you'll let me treat you to a lot more than pancakes." She let her hands slide over his shoulders, down his strong back until they were palming his ass. She gave both cheeks an inviting squeeze and nearly melted when he pressed his pelvis into hers, not caring about her messy apron ruining his expensive suit.

She offered him a coy smile and pulled him down into a languid kiss. There was no need to rush this time. He was here with her. He was willing to look beyond her faults, and most importantly, he was hers and she was his. Beyond that, nothing else mattered.

Epilogue

Two weeks later

A quick succession of taps on the door pulled her attention from the spreadsheet she was reading.

"Sorry to interrupt. I'm here to file a complaint about my woman's new manager."

She chuckled at Jeremiah's pretense. This was one way he kept things light between them, even while they spent most of their days working together and most of their evenings taking care of Ace.

"Please, come inside and I'll help you as best I can." He took long strides from the door and sat down. "First, let's start with the most important thing. What's your woman's name?"

"Trey, and she works for a taskmaster named Jordan Dylan Devereaux III."

Trey pretended to scribble on a notepad as Jeremiah continued.

"And what exactly is your grievance against Ms. Devereaux?"

He leaned back in the chair, his complexion as smooth as the silk tie around his neck. "She works my lady way too hard. Trey has no time to relax and enjoy herself. She has no time for me."

"Ahh, so this is more about your needs instead of Trey's?"

He shook his head. "No ma'am. Trey's needs are always my first priority."

"She's very fortunate to have you then."

"That's exactly what I keep telling her."

Their eyes met across the desk and their charade crumbled into a fit of laughter.

"You're a mess. You know that, right?"

He shrugged. "I'm your mess, though." He stood up, walked to her side of the desk and knelt before her. "As such, I'm always here for you."

His tone changed, the timber of his voice deepening. "All jokes aside, baby. You mean the world to me."

She leaned forward and stroked his goatee. "The feeling's mutual, Mr. Benton."

He held up a finger, "About that. It's Mr. Devereaux." He moved his head from side to side casually. "Actually, it will be Mr. Devereaux once you decide which method I should take to make it official."

He pulled a folded legal document from his inside jacket pocket and placed it carefully in her hand.

She opened it, her eyes scanning the pages quickly, attempting to weed through the legalese to find meaning.

"You're legally changing your name to Devereaux?"

She glanced at the last page containing his signature, along with the signatures of her father and grandfather acting as his witnesses. "I'm not understanding what you're trying to say."

He gave her a knowing smile as he leaned in and kissed her. "Ace is more than a mentor to me. He's family. He made me family, and I wanted to honor him. I didn't know if he and Deuce would ever reconcile. In case that never happened, I wanted to change my name to Devereaux so someone who loved him would remain in this world, carrying his name, his legacy. He gave me his blessing the day he transferred his shares to you. Once Amara files the paperwork, it's legal."

Her heart was full. Jeremiah's loyalty to Ace and his legacy never faltered. The constant way he loved the Devereaux patriarch was only one of the many reasons she adored him.

"I'm not sure what you mean, Jeremiah. Why would you want to change your name to mine?"

"The only thing I can associate Benton with is pain. I didn't experience joy until Ace gave me a family. Is it so strange I'd want to carry his name after all we've been through?"

She quietly shook her head.

"Before I met you, there was only one way I could change my name, but since I fell under your spell, there's another avenue available to me."

He reached inside of his pocket again, but this time, there was a small square velvet box in the palm of his hand.

"I can file those papers in your hand, or I can put this ring on your finger and take your name when we get married."

He opened the box and she could feel her heart stretching to near bursting when she laid eyes on the ring. Looking at the pear-shaped black diamond, which was a larger replica of the bracelet he'd given her before the Legacy Ball, made her tremble with the force of her love for him.

She blinked away the tears threatening to ruin her perfectly applied makeup. "Jeremiah, I didn't hear a question in there. Is there something you want to ask me?"

"I sure do." His eyes shimmered with the same unshed tears as he pulled the ring from its cushion. "Jordan Dylan Devereaux III, will you make me the happiest man alive and agree to marry me and give me our family's name?"

She didn't remember saying yes, or him sliding the ring on her finger. All she knew was she'd turned into a puddle of happy tears on the floor with him as she collapsed into his waiting arms.

"Don't worry. I got you, baby."

And in the deepest part of her soul, she knew he always would.

* * * * *

Get 3 FREE REWARDS!

We'll send you 2 FREE Books plus a FREE Mystery Gift.

FREE Value Over **$20**

Both the **Romance** and **Suspense** collections feature compelling novels written by many of today's bestselling authors.

YES! Please send me 2 FREE novels from the Essential Romance or Essential Suspense Collection and my FREE gift (gift is worth about $10 retail). After receiving them, if I don't wish to receive any more books, I can return the shipping statement marked "cancel." If I don't cancel, I will receive 4 brand-new novels every month and be billed just $7.49 each in the U.S. or $7.74 each in Canada. That's a savings of at least 17% off the cover price. It's quite a bargain! Shipping and handling is just 50¢ per book in the U.S. and $1.25 per book in Canada.* I understand that accepting the 2 free books and gift places me under no obligation to buy anything. I can always return a shipment and cancel at any time by calling the number below. The free books and gift are mine to keep no matter what I decide.

Choose one: ☐ **Essential Romance** (194/394 BPA GRNM) ☐ **Essential Suspense** (191/391 BPA GRNM) ☐ **Or Try Both!** (194/394 & 191/391 BPA GRQZ)

Name (please print)

Address   Apt. #

City   State/Province   Zip/Postal Code

Email: Please check this box ☐ if you would like to receive newsletters and promotional emails from Harlequin Enterprises ULC and its affiliates. You can unsubscribe anytime

Mail to the **Harlequin Reader Service:**
IN U.S.A.: P.O. Box 1341, Buffalo, NY 14240-8531
IN CANADA: P.O. Box 603, Fort Erie, Ontario L2A 5X3

Want to try 2 free books from another series! Call **1-800-873-8635** or visit **www.ReaderService.com**.

---

*Terms and prices subject to change without notice. Prices do not include sales taxes, which will be charged (if applicable) based on your state or country of residence. Canadian residents will be charged applicable taxes. Offer not valid in Quebec. This offer is limited to one order per household. Books received may not be as shown. Not valid for current subscribers to the Essential Romance or Essential Suspense Collection. All orders subject to approval. Credit or debit balances in a customer's account(s) may be offset by any other outstanding balance owed by or to the customer. Please allow 4 to 6 weeks for delivery. Offer available while quantities last.

Your Privacy—Your information is being collected by Harlequin Enterprises ULC, operating as Harlequin Reader Service. For a complete summary of the information we collect, how we use this information and to whom it is disclosed, please visit our privacy notice located at corporate.harlequin.com/privacy-notice. From time to time we may also exchange your personal information with reputable third parties. If you wish to opt out of this sharing of your personal information, please visit readerservice.com/consumerschoice or call 1-800-873-8635. **Notice to California Residents**—Under California law, you have specific rights to control and access your data. For more information on these rights and how to exercise them, visit corporate.harlequin.com/california-privacy.

STRS23